That's Not
a Thing

A Novel

Jacqueline Friedland

Published by SparkPress, a BookSparks imprint,
A division of SparkPoint Studio, LLC
Phoenix, Arizona, USA, 85007
www.gosparkpress.com

Published 2020
Printed in the United States of America
ISBN: 978-1-68463-030-1 (pbk)
ISBN: 978-1-68463-031-8 (e-bk)

Library of Congress Control Number: 2019915488

Book design by Stacey Aaronson

To my mother
with love

Chapter One
January 2017

I am working my way through a spicy entrée called *renegade scampini*, savoring the hypnotic combination of unusual flavors, completely unaware that my life is about to implode. As I take in this swanky restaurant in TriBeCa, an upscale venue full of beautiful people and thousand-dollar shoes, I want to be above the hype, to be unfazed by the billowing satin sheets draping the walls, the way they dance beneath the incongruous industrial ceiling fans. The nearly haphazard combination of materials decorating the space—sleek glass and decadent fabrics offset by distressed wood and conspicuous, bulging light bulbs—creates something unexpectedly sassy and chic. I have been attempting to adopt an imperturbable attitude in my recently affianced state, as though I have graduated from the excitability of my youth, but I must concede that this place is impressive.

"You can't—I mean really *cannot*—have the wedding in Jersey," Lana is complaining. Always trying to prove herself an authentic city girl, she's reluctant to go anywhere that requires traversing a bridge or tunnel.

"But my mom . . . " I start, between bites of my pasta,

a concoction of angel hair, shrimp, and a creamy, herb-infused avocado sauce that's wickedly delicious. Then Lana cuts me off.

"You know I love my aunt Karen," she lobs at me as she pushes broccoli rabe around in concentric circles on her plate, "but who are you going to trust on this—a suburban woman who's had the same hairstyle since the Reagan administration, or a young Manhattanite who works at a fashion magazine? Wouldn't that mean I know what's *in fashion*?" She raises her blond eyebrows at me in challenge.

As I struggle with which part of her statement to contradict first, I feel Aaron's hand travel to my thigh under the table, squeezing lightly in a show of support, reminding me to be patient in my response. I reach underneath the white tablecloth and squeeze back, grateful that at least one person at the table understands my priorities for this wedding. Lana and Reese are treating us to this exorbitantly overpriced meal in order to celebrate my recent engagement to Aaron. The coveted reservation for four at this hot spot originally belonged to Lana's boss, the accessories editor of *Mode à la Mode*, a haughty fashion magazine that showcases items mere mortals could never afford. When the editor was called away to a last-minute meeting in London, Lana, her dedicated and ambitious assistant, landed first dibs on the booking.

I had expected another dark, cramped Manhattan nook where we would be forced to maneuver between tightly packed tables and shout at each other to be heard. Instead, we are settled in a wide, airy space with whimsical, fresh decor. There is white everywhere; a white patina covering the exposed-brick walls, white tablecloths, the aforementioned flowy white fabric suspended from the surprisingly high ceilings, and a long white bar lining the entire left side of the restaurant. The bar top is one long plank of repurposed wood, now bleached to match its surroundings, and it's stunning in its simplicity. The only splash of color comes from an oversize arrangement of twigs placed near one end of the bar, yellow buds sprouting forth from them in triumph.

I've already explained to Lana that I am not concerned with cachet in regard to the wedding. My objective is to create a meaningful ceremony without too much fuss, something that will allow Aaron and me to celebrate our future without getting caught up in the tragedies of the past. As I open my mouth to argue, I suddenly feel so stodgy in my navy pencil skirt and tan silk blouse—items I purchased with the specific purpose of appearing more conservative and mature. Maybe something about the ambience in this restaurant is loosening me up, but I begin thinking that perhaps Lana is right. Maybe we should have the ceremony in the city, keep it small and elite, utilize an unlikely venue.

As my thoughts careen in various directions, I keep quiet for too long, and Aaron picks up my slack, answering for me. "We're pretty set on using the synagogue in South Orange," he tells Lana with a casual shrug, holding his ground with the gentle authority that is his hallmark. He isn't particular about where the wedding should take place, but he is defending what I have been claiming to want.

My eyes roam up, back to the enormous steel blades of the room's two ceiling fans, which is when I have the idea that maybe we could do it here, at this restaurant, never mind the ridiculous name of the place. Thunder Chicken on Greenwich. It's a good thing they added that last bit with the street name—as though there are so many other Thunder Chickens out there from which it must differentiate itself.

"There's a woman at the temple," Aaron is elaborating, "she handles the catering, and she'll take care of all the prep work. We won't have to deal with any of the nitty-gritty."

"Meredith!" Lana nearly shouts at me. "How can you delegate your wedding planning to a woman you barely know?" She looks like she wants to burst out from her seat and shake me.

"What about doing it here?" I blurt, surprised that I am seriously entertaining the idea.

"Here?" Aaron and Lana both ask at once, looking at me and then at each other.

Reese finally looks up from his iPhone. He's been typing away on it for the last ten minutes, dealing with some sort of catastrophe at the investment bank where he works.

"That's a cool idea, Mer," he offers, before returning his attention to the device in his hands.

I look at Aaron to gauge his reaction and see his dark brown eyes traveling around the restaurant as if he's seeing the space for the first time, considering what I've suggested.

"I like it," he ventures. "It's different, quirky. Definitely more convenient for most of our friends than having them schlep out to Jersey. But it's whatever you want, Mer." He lifts his hand, signaling to a scantily clad, redheaded waitress who is hovering near our table.

"What can I get you?" She glides over, standing too close to Aaron as she eyes him from head to toe, probably admiring his expansive chest and thick, dark hair. People always say that Aaron looks like a younger, broader version of Ben Affleck, but Aaron is built so athletically that I've never been able to see the resemblance. After one quick glance at him, you can guess that he was once a football player. In addition to the typical bulk of a linebacker, he has eyes that are bright and alert in the way of an athlete who is always one step ahead of the other team's play. But it was other details about Aaron that first drew me to him two years ago, when he approached me in the elevator of my office building. His brown eyebrows are velvety and expressive. His lips are naturally upturned at the corners, even in his resting state, as if he knows the punch line to a salty joke and he's just mulling it over again.

"Do you guys do private events?" Aaron asks her, and I melt a little, seeing him so eager to explore any plan I've hatched.

"Private events?" she asks, stepping even closer to him and moving her silver pen to her mouth in a seductive gesture. It's almost as though she thinks he's asking for a lap dance—and come to think of it, "private events" does sound kind of suggestive.

"Like weddings," I interject pointedly, marking my territory.

"Because they are *engaged*," Lana adds, motioning from Aaron back to me with her fork.

"Oh." She purses her lips around the pen she's been mouthing—too tightly, as if she's trying to suck a hamburger through a straw. "I don't know." She glances from

Lana to me. "We've only been open a couple of months, so no one's done that yet. I can ask the owner what he thinks," she offers tepidly.

"Yes," Lana responds. "Go do that, and then come tell us what he says." Lana is as bossy as ever, but the waitress seems unfazed.

After the woman flutters off, Reese finally puts his phone into his pants pocket. "Sorry about that," he apologizes again. "I thought finishing my first year as an analyst meant I'd be able to dial it back a little at work, but apparently I'm still one of the little people." He unbuttons the cuffs of his dress shirt and begins rolling up one sleeve, then the other.

"Not to me, you're not," Lana turns toward him on the banquette, her round blue eyes full of adoration.

"Uh-huh," he answers. His eyes dart to his watch before he finally digs into the crispy duck dish that has been languishing on his plate.

I feel a stab of sympathy for Lana. Reese still treats her like an inconvenience, an interruption, instead of the love of his life. They have been dating since high school, and Lana is desperate to get engaged. Reese, on the other hand, seems prepared for several more years of urban independence and boondoggling before he will be ready to settle down.

When the waitress reappears a few minutes later, she drops a slender hand on Aaron's shoulder and turns her back to me as she stands between our chairs. Is she kidding? We told her not two minutes ago that the apparent object of her affection is engaged.

"Hi," she says again, all throaty-like. "I asked him, but he said he'll come talk to you guys himself. He'll be out in a minute." She looks down at Aaron's plate. "How's the chicken? Everything good?"

Aaron glances at his plate, the roasted chicken thigh that he's been working on mostly finished, and then looks back up at her. "It's thunder-ful."

The blank expression on the waitress's face makes clear that she has failed to comprehend his statement as a joke about the name of the restaurant.

"Okay, good," she finally answers before swaggering away.

The rest of us last only a few seconds before we burst out laughing.

"Oh, man," Reese snorts, "you did not just say that. You've only been engaged a month, and your game is already slipping big-time."

"I don't need game." Aaron laughs. "I've got what I want." He puts his thick arm around me and pulls me closer to his side. "*Who* I want," he corrects himself, kissing me quickly on the side of my head. "Thunder Chicken," he says again, smiling and shaking his head at the name.

As I wiggle back into the center of my chair, I see a man in chef's garb making his way through the restaurant. One customer after another stops him, most likely to compliment the food—which is, admittedly, outrageously tasty. Truly thunder-ful. I wonder if the chef and the owner are one and the same.

The man in white turns toward our table, and I freeze. One glimpse of his face, and it's as though I have suddenly been thrown to the ground, pummeled. Memories reach out to squeeze my heart, crushing me all over again.

He doesn't notice me, doesn't see me, as he glances toward our table but gets distracted by someone else nearby. I know him. Knew him. At one point in my life, I knew him better than anyone. This is his restaurant. Of course it is, I realize now; everything about this sleek room—the offbeat food pairings, the nonsensical humor of the menu—starts to fit into a certain picture, falling into place as Wesley's vision. It's the restaurant I didn't know he had, hadn't known if he would ever manage to create. But here I am, sitting in a chair in what is obviously his establishment, and I can't be here, cannot. My eyes shoot to Aaron for help, but he is focused on his food, still laughing about the absurdity of his own behavior a moment ago. And anyway, I can't tell him, can't talk about Wesley to him. That's the deal we have, what we settled on when we first started dating and I was still so raw from the blame Wesley had placed on me. But as I see him again now, all the air is knocked out of me.

My eyes shoot back to the bowl of pasta in front of me and I duck my head, hoping irrationally that there's some way I can hide. I think about running to the bathroom, remaining unseen, and then smuggling myself out from the restaurant after Aaron finishes talking with him. But Wesley might recognize Reese, I remind myself, and he will definitely know Lana. He'll remember her from all the times he gave her dating advice and helped with her math homework when she was a teenager.

I wonder if I can grab Lana and get both of us into the restroom without him seeing, but he's too close to the table now. I dig my fork into my pasta and twirl noodles, trying to appear nonchalant while I struggle to think what I should say when he reaches us. I will have to admit I know him. But will I have to tell Wesley I'm engaged again?

And now he's standing at our table.

"Hi," he addresses us collectively. "I heard you folks had a question."

The sound of his voice sends shock waves through my veins, as it always has. I look up, reluctantly dragging my eyes out of my pasta. As our gazes collide, his green eyes sharp as ever, I see him swallow in surprise.

His features are more chiseled now; his bones seem to have matured and refined themselves in the years since we last saw each other. If anything, he's grown even more handsome, weathered and masculine. I can't tear my gaze away as I drink him in, not realizing until this moment how desperately I have missed him.

He and I stare at each other for too long. Lana and Reese are shocked into silence. The only one oblivious is Aaron, my sweet Aaron. I can't fathom what I am supposed to do at this moment, how I am supposed to handle the fact that standing before me is the man who still haunts my dreams after all these years. He is the first man I ever loved, the first one I agreed to marry. He is also someone I can never be with again, no matter how often I think about him, no matter how much I still miss him.

Not when he will always blame me for killing his parents.

Chapter Two
January 2008

D *on't be a cockblocker.*

Those were the words I was reading when I met Wesley for the first time. Scribbled in bright yellow marker on the dry-erase board outside my dorm room, Daphne's message had effectively made me homeless for the night, yet again. It was only the fifth night of second semester, and it seemed like my roommate was aiming to screw her way through all of Carman Hall before spring break. I'd spotted the guy from the previous evening a few minutes earlier, clowning around on the library steps with his hockey buddies, so I tried to guess which member of Columbia University's student body had drawn today's golden ticket.

Our friend Bina was definitely going to launch into another tirade when I showed up at her suite, asking to use the ratty sofa in her common area one more time. Recently, Bina had declared that accepting physical attention from the opposite sex without first establishing an intimate emotional connection was one more way in which women on campus were demeaning themselves. Put more simply, she was convinced that hooking up with random guys was bad for female empowerment. She had begun quoting Doris Lessing and other feminists at every opportunity.

I hadn't bothered to point out that only a couple of months earlier, Bina had used many of the same quotes to support the opposite position—that women must be permitted to pursue sexual gratification without critique from others. It seemed to me that she was just decrying Daphne's behavior based on the teachings of the week rather than engaging in the kind of open-minded exploration she purported to espouse, but she had the couch, so I would probably just nod along with whatever doctrines she spewed tonight.

Daphne was my best friend—had been since elementary school, actually—and I was trying to be considerate of her approach to coping with her last boyfriend's sudden defection. If rolling around in the sheets with a vast array of preppy frat boys would prevent her from succumbing to post-breakup depression, who was I to stand in her way? Still, I was craving my own space and wished Daphne had thought to venture out to her new friend's room tonight, instead of bringing the guy to ours. I stared back at those words on the whiteboard and wondered whether it would count as cockblocking if I just snuck in for a few seconds to grab my fleece pajama pants and maybe my toothbrush. Since when had "cockblocking" even become a word, anyway?

"Second night in a row, isn't it?"

I looked up to see a guy I didn't recognize walking toward me from the other end of the dusky hallway. He was tall and muscular, wearing clothes that were covered in paint. As he approached me, I took in his square jaw and full lips, his short, honey-brown hair that flipped up slightly in the front, and I bristled. He was so good-looking that I guess I just expected him to be a prick. His light green eyes were nearly translucent, and somehow, I felt as though he could see right through me.

"I'm Wesley." He stuck out his hand as he reached me.

I looked down at his large palm, splatters of green and white paint littered across fingers that were outstretched and waiting to meet mine.

"I'm sorry—is there a reason you should have anything to do with this situation?" I don't know what possessed me to go straight-up bitch on him, but it's what I did. Maybe I already knew then how easily he would burrow himself into the deepest recesses of my heart. Maybe I just wanted to protect myself.

"Whoa, don't shoot." He held up his hands in surrender and took a step back. "I was just trying to commiserate a little, be friendly. My freshman roommate used to barricade me all the time. It sucks not getting to use your own space." He shrugged, like everything in life was obvious to him, like things came easy.

"If you're not a freshman, why are you skulking around Carman Hall like a creep?" I could feel my spine straightening, preparing for battle even as I continued to wonder why I was being so antagonistic. "And why are you covered in paint, anyway?"

"Jeez, take it easy," he chuckled, and I got the distinct impression that he found my agitation amusing—endearing, even. "I'm your new RA. Wesley Latner." He started to reach out his hand again, but then seemed to think the better of it and curled his fingers into a fist at his side.

"New RA? What happened to Keith, or Craig, whatever his name was?"

"Kevvvin," Wesley answered, dragging out the word like he was trying to prod my memory about the other guy's name, "transferred to some school in California, so this position opened up and I skated off the waiting list."

I realized then that I ought to be a little more cordial if this male pinup was supposed to be the resident advisor for my dorm, especially since it seemed like I might soon need permission to sleep on the withered brown carpet of the hallway floor. There was only so long that I could expect to freeload off Bina and her suitemates. I blinked hard a couple of times and tried to start over.

"Sorry." I tilted my head to the side in a gesture of surrender. "Meredith," I offered, along with my hand. "It's been a long day, and I really didn't feel like sleeping on a couch tonight. I'm not usually such an ass-wipe."

He reached out to shake, and his warm hand felt callused and rough as it met my own. "Apology accepted." He was smirking. I looked down at our hands, wondering if he was holding on for a beat too long, as he added, "I'm actually already aware that you're not usually an ass-wipe."

"You are?" I glanced back up, wary now.

He shrugged again. "I've seen you around, at the soup kitchen on 116th Street. You seem to be a fan favorite up there."

I felt my eyes narrow. "Since when have you been at the soup kitchen? I don't recall meeting." It was a small place, and I would have remembered him.

"I've been working construction next door. I get a pretty decent view of the sidewalk servers when I'm up on the scaffolding. It's hard to miss that pink streak in your hair, even from the rooftop."

I tucked a piece of blond hair behind my ear, pushing at it like I was driving away everything my pink stripe represented. There was no reason to bring my mother's illness into this conversation. I looked him over again from ears to ankles, taking in the worn jeans, the paint splatters covering his heavy gray Henley, the weathered Timberland boots. "So, I don't get it—are you a college student or a construction worker?"

"Both." He smiled with apparent pride. "This was just a job I was working with a friend." He gestured toward himself, indicating his current painty mess.

A muffled cheer sounded from a room down the hall, likely guys watching sports or getting overly excited about a video game. He glanced over his shoulder, where the hall was still empty, and then asked, "So, is there somewhere you were planning to go for the night?"

"Yeah, no worries. I've got it covered. It was nice meeting you." I lifted my silver backpack from where I had dropped it on the floor before reading Daphne's note, and I started to move around him so I could make my way to Bina's.

"Boyfriend's?" He leaned against the cinder block wall and crossed his arms across his broad chest, as if to watch me go. As I slung my bag over my shoulder, I noticed the bulge of his forearms, sinewy and dusted with golden-brown hair where the sleeves of his shirt were pushed to the elbows.

"No, Nosy," I quipped, as a corner of my lip lifted, and I realized that I was flirting in spite of myself. "Dif-ficult as it may be for you to believe, we females are actually capable of solving problems without male in-tervention. So, uh, see ya." I raised two fingers in a half wave and started down the hallway.

I had made it nearly to the stairwell when Wesley called out after me, "So, does that mean there is no boyfriend?"

I kept on walking but couldn't stop myself from re-sponding, even as I marched farther away. "No boyfriend," I called back without turning, glad that he couldn't see the smile still playing at my lips.

After I veered into the stairwell and started up the steps to Bina's floor, I heard Wesley jogging after me. "Wait," he said, "hold up."

I paused on the second step and turned to see that I was now eye-level with him where he waited on the land-ing. I heard the fire door open on the floor below, then female laughter and fast steps advancing toward us. Twin towheaded girls whom I recognized from around campus appeared, chasing each other up the stairs, one of them holding a box of donut holes. Wesley and I nodded at them as they raced past us and continued up another flight.

He waited for the sounds of their boots to recede before he turned back to me and continued.

"Come with me."

"Come with you where?" Was it against the rules for me to sleep in another student's suite? If I couldn't con-coct a way to talk myself out of trouble, this jackass might be writing me up all semester long.

"Come for the night, on an adventure," he clarified. He raised his eyebrows a couple of times, as if to add to his intrigue, and it was disarmingly cute, even with the faint scent of turpentine he was emitting.

"What are you talking about? It's already one o'clock in the morning."

"It is?" He glanced at his wristwatch. "That's perfect." He smiled cryptically and motioned for me to come back down the stairs. "Come on, it'll be fun. You can't go back to your room anyway, and if you have to know the truth, I've been wanting to hang out with you since the first time I saw you ladling soup on 116th. Come on, don't rob a guy of his opportunity to woo the girl."

"What are you talking about? Woo." I laughed out loud. "You're totally crazy. I just met you ten seconds ago, and what about sleep? I have class in the morning."

"So what?" he pushed, glancing at his watch a second time. "So, you'll be tired tomorrow. You can take a nap in the afternoon, when your room is finally unoccupied. Please?" He reached out his hand and gave me an exaggerated version of puppy-dog eyes that just made him look ridiculous.

I laughed again and felt myself tumbling toward his energy. "Isn't there some sort of rule against RAs wooing members of their flock?" I asked, thinking out loud.

"Probably." Wesley grinned as he shoved his hands into his pockets. "But are you really going to let some handbook stand in the way of one of the most thrilling nights of your life?"

"Wow. That's a pretty bold promise." I looked him over again, wondering if I should surrender to his suggestion. I thought of everything going on with my mom and reasoned that I really could use an opportunity to blow off some steam. I had been a model student since I'd arrived at Columbia, careful to prevent myself from adding to my parents' list of worries, and, truthfully, I was feeling ready to succumb to a little recklessness, to abandon my usual fastidiousness. My eyes darted to the ceiling above me as I thought of Bina's room on the next floor, and then I looked back at Wesley. My essay on Georges Braque was already complete, even though it wasn't due for two more days, and I didn't have any exams scheduled for the rest of the week. It wasn't like I was going to get a good night's sleep on that lumpy velour couch anyway. I pictured the Spanish lit class I was supposed to sit through in the morning, the one I was taking simply to fulfill the school's language requirement, and I knew I'd probably zone out whether I got nine hours or stayed up the entire night.

I chewed on my bottom lip as I began to accept that I was about to make a daring decision. Daphne would never believe I'd done something so out of character.

"Can I drop my books in your room before we go?"

"Well, hallelujah." He grabbed my hand and pulled me back from the stairs.

As my feet hit the landing, I was struck again by how tall he was. I was average height at five foot four, but he definitely had nine or ten inches on me.

"Will we be subject to more paint disasters on our adventure? Because this happens to be one of my favorite sweaters"—I motioned to the cropped purple V-neck that he obviously couldn't see beneath my down parka— "and I refuse to get all Jackson Pollocked like you."

"Give me this." He lifted my loaded backpack off my shoulder and started down the hallway.

᠆

WHEN WE REACHED Wesley's room, the one that had formerly belonged to Keith or Kevin, he dug into his pocket for the key. Holding up a finger, he told me, "Give me one minute. Do not leave."

I didn't answer while I considered him, and he bent down so his face was right in front of mine. A Star of David necklace toppled out from his shirt as he leaned forward, and I had the fleeting thought that my mom would be pleased. I smelled the mint on his breath, and something pleasant and soapy beneath the turpentine.

He looked me straight in the eye and repeated himself. "Do not."

"Okay, wow." I took a step back. "I said I would do this . . . this . . . whatever this insanity is going to be, so I will. You don't have to get all up in my face. But let's move it—it's not nice to make a lady wait." I kicked a little at his leg.

Before I had time to seriously second-guess my decision, Wesley was back in the hallway in a clean pair of jeans and a long-sleeved black T-shirt that showcased many of the muscles his other shirt had been hiding. He was holding an olive-green, military-looking jacket. As he turned back toward his door to lock up, I studied him from behind, wondering whether he was too attractive for me, if I should cut and run before disaster stuck. But when he turned around, I looked into those pale green eyes of his and saw him regarding me with such enthusiasm, such energy, that I just wanted to bask in his intensity a little longer.

Even so, I pushed for more information about where we were going, a little nervous about following a virtual stranger to an unknown location. I didn't want to become another news story about a college girl who made a fatally misguided decision, and I said as much to him. He promised that we would stay in public places for the duration of our evening and then reached into his pocket.

"Here," he said, as he handed me his wallet and his cell phone. "You hold on to the important stuff. Like collateral. Now I'm at your mercy."

In retrospect, I don't know why that was enough for me, but I suppose I was simply looking for any reason to follow him—which is exactly what I did after shoving his belongings into my coat pocket.

A SHORT SUBWAY ride and a couple of snowy city blocks later, we were walking into a store on Amsterdam Avenue called Insomnia Cookies.

"This is our adventure?" I looked at him sideways. "We're having milk and cookies?" I'm not sure where I thought we were going—maybe a dance club or tourist site, or even some old speakeasy. Chocolate-chunk snickerdoodles, I was not expecting.

"Hey, Wes." The older woman behind the counter pulled off her hairnet and started untying her apron as she glanced up at the digital clock on the wall, which read 1:26 a.m. The air in the place smelled so sweet that I was instantly hungry. "I'm beat," she said. "Mind if I toss you the last four minutes of my shift?" Her eyes slid toward me, and she added pleasantly, "I see you brought reinforcements anyhow."

He looked from the round-cheeked woman back to me and announced, "Ingrid, Meredith. Meredith, Ingrid. Sure, get out of here. Tell Abby she owes me for the extra four minutes she gets to spend in your company tonight."

"Nice to meet you," I said as Ingrid grabbed a black parka off a hook and began slipping her arm into one of the sleeves. It was difficult to keep my eyes from straying to the display case in front of her, where all sorts of baked delectableness were pleading to be savored. A quick glimpse was sufficient for me to take in an assortment of treats, including M&M cookies, bulging cookie sandwiches, hubcap-size cookie cakes, and dark, gooey brownies.

"You too." She zipped her coat and looked back at me. "Don't let him make too much of a mess in my kitchen tonight." She gave Wesley a friendly slap on the arm and beelined for the door.

"You're the cookie chef?" I asked. How many odd jobs did this guy have?

"C'mon." He pulled me behind the counter and put his own jacket where Ingrid's had been hanging a moment before. "Give me your coat." He waited with his hand out. As I sidled out of the puffy jacket, his eyes coasted quickly over my body and he added, "You're right, it is a nice sweater. Let's get you an apron."

"I'm cooking? Trust me, you do not want me messing with anything in there. I'm like the dream killer of baby cookies and brownies everywhere."

He rolled his eyes at me and pushed against the shiny swing door that led to the back kitchen. I followed behind him, intrigued by the evening's turn of events, lulled nearly equally by the physical appearance of my companion and the overwhelming scent of sugar. We walked into a room that looked like any bakery kitchen I might have pictured in my head—commercial-grade appliances, fluorescent lighting, hoods and vents, complex mixing machines, stainless steel for days. He tossed me a powder-blue apron like the one that Ingrid had been wearing, slipped another one over his own head, and quickly washed his hands at a sink in the corner.

"C'mon," he said, "I'll teach you." He started pulling containers out from steel cabinets and lining them up neatly on the counter: flour, sugar, chocolate chunks.

"Wait, seriously? We're really cooking?"

"Baking." He paused in his calculated actions to correct me and then added, "If you'd prefer to watch and learn, I suppose that's okay, too."

Before I could formulate a response, Wesley had arranged multiple metal bowls on the counter and was pouring out various dry ingredients with surprising speed. He opened a refrigerator under the countertop, removed two cartons of eggs, and began cracking one after another into an empty bowl.

"This," he informed me, gesturing toward the bowl of eggs, "will soon be transformed into our famous deluxe s'mores cookies. Since you've made clear your preference to remain uninvolved in the creation of this hallowed masterpiece, how about you play DJ?" He motioned with his head toward a small computer screen embedded in the wall.

"Wait, what if someone comes in to buy cookies? No one's up front."

"There's a bell." He grabbed for a bag of mini-marshmallows on the shelf beside him. "Also, there's not much traffic in here on Tuesday nights. We'll get a few walk-ins, but most of the orders are for delivery, placed through the website. The delivery guy comes and goes. That's his gig. Mine is the baking."

I walked over to the computerized screen and started pressing buttons, trying to figure out the interface. I found the tab for playlists and saw that there were several different lists, each titled with a person's name. Ingrid's name appeared at the top. I continued scrolling until I found the tab labeled "Wes" and tapped it with my fingertip. Music started playing through speakers clipped to the back wall, and I recognized some old-school Guns N' Roses song.

"For real?" I looked over at him and shook my head in disappointment. "1980s heavy metal? My hopes for you were so much higher."

"You can keep scrolling. My tastes are eclectic," he said, as he continued moving around the kitchen.

"Aha!" I declared as my eyes finally landed on a song I could enjoy. I pressed play, and Dusty Springfield's "Son of a Preacher Man" began to float out from the speakers.

A few years earlier, when my dad still seemed to enjoy my company, he'd introduced me to this song on one of our Sunday-morning drives and it had instantly become one of my favorites. Hearing the notes again now, on this random, surreal, electric night I was having, it did something to me, made me suddenly audacious.

"Wesley . . ." I played with his name, rolling it around on my tongue as I considered it aloud. I started swaying along with the music, grooving my way around the room, briefly examining various knobs and levers that I passed. "Wesley . . ." I repeated, feeling the air slide across my tongue as I drew out the word. I kept dancing around the counters, picking up a wooden spoon as an undetermined prop along the way. Maybe the apron made him less threatening, or maybe I was getting high on dextrose fumes, but suddenly I felt much more comfortable being me.

"Where'd you come from, Wesley Latner? Where's home?" I asked over the music as I danced toward him, holding the wooden spoon out to him like it was a microphone and I was a television reporter.

He played along, leaning forward to speak into the mic. "New York, born and raised," he answered, a quick nod of his head proving his local pride. "Not the city, though," he conceded, as he turned and absently attached the bowl he was holding to an electric mixer. "A stuffy suburb about an hour north."

He switched on the mixer, the sound drowning out too much of the song. I marched back to the touchscreen and raised the volume to the max. Between the mixer and the music, it was now too loud to hear much else, so we both stopped talking. I kept on grooving to the music, my movements growing progressively more outlandish with each step. All the while, Wesley was pouring and measuring ingredients like he'd done it a thousand times before. Eventually, he flipped a switch, silencing the mixer. He crossed his arms against his chest and stopped with the food prep, just watching me as I continued to sashay around the room.

I bopped around the large rectangular island, swinging the wooden spoon like I was an orchestra conductor, shimmying my shoulders to the left for a few beats, then to the right, a faux-diva expression on my face. My movements were definitely more goofy than sexy. As the song neared its end, I was still dancing my way closer to where Wesley was standing. I realized I'd better quit it, or he might see this as a botched seduction attempt by me, which was not what I was intending. I stopped, mid-bop, while I was only a foot away from him, suddenly at a loss. The last notes of the song faded into the ether, and the room was instantly too quiet.

I looked up at him, ready to make some sort of joke, but the way he was staring back down at me stunned me into silence, pushing the breath out of me. His crystalline green eyes were darker now, and he studied me with an inscrutable expression. Suddenly my whole body was hot, alert.

"What?" I finally asked.

"You," he answered.

Chapter Three
January 2017

*L*ana is the first one to break the silence.

"Well, Wesley Latner, as I live and breathe." She stands to give him an airy kiss hello, composed and pretentious all at once.

"Quintessential Lana," Aaron comments, his voice laced with fond amusement, "knowing everyone who's anyone."

Lana looks from Wesley back to Aaron, clearly unsure how to answer. It's one of the few times in my life I've seen my cousin speechless, and Aaron doesn't miss the peculiarity of the moment. He glances over at my face, which must be as white as the sheets draping the walls. Or totally green. Really, who can say?

"What . . . ?" he asks, his eyes narrowing slightly as he looks from me to Lana to Wesley, then back at me again. "Is this . . . Wait, is this *your* Wesley?"

He asks like Wesley isn't there, like I'm the only one who can hear him.

My Wesley. I nod. I can feel Wesley everywhere as he waits, now mute, at the head of our table. Feelings I haven't experienced in years. An internal tilting, a shifting of my inner equilibrium. I'm on fire again, in a way that is exquisite torture, unlike anything I have ever felt toward Aaron. And then I have the horrible thought that maybe I cannot move forward with Aaron. Not when simply seeing Wesley in his chef's attire, hearing his familiar voice, evokes this visceral, debilitating physical response inside me.

"I had no idea this was your restaurant," Lana picks up with false perkiness again, trying to quash the intense awkwardness of this moment—an impossible feat, given the circumstances, but kudos to her for trying. Even she must realize that there is no reason to ask about hosting my wedding here, now that a more absurd idea couldn't possibly exist.

"Hi, Wes," I finally contribute to the conversation. I stand and walk behind Aaron's chair to offer my ex-fiancé a stilted kiss hello. As my cheek grazes his in formality, I feel my knees nearly give out, and I am grateful to have the chair beside me—Aaron's chair—for support. Wesley still smells the same. Like olive oil and forests, clean and spicy. Forbidden.

I want to topple over from the pain, the relief, of seeing him again.

"I didn't know this was your place. It's great." I manage to eke out these sentences and follow them up with another. "I'm happy for you."

"Thanks," he answers, surprise still evident on his face. "It's nice to see you." He studies me a moment longer before his eyes dart to Aaron and he clears his throat. "So, what was the question? Something about hosting a party?" He glances back at Lana and Reese.

"Oh, never mind about it." Lana waves her hand dismissively and forces out a laugh. "We were really impressed with the food and kind of just wanted to meet the chef. Anything to make my coworkers jealous tomorrow, right?"

"Still the same Lana as always." Wesley smiles down at her indulgently, and I want to bang my head against the table in shame for wishing that smile was directed at me. "Well, consider yourself on the permanent guest list, then. Any time you want a res, just tell them you're on my list."

"Amazing. Thank you!" Lana looks really excited for a nanosecond, and then disappointment flashes across her face, likely because she has realized it would be completely traitorous for her to frequent this establishment on any sort of regular basis.

"Okay, well, I'd better get back to it then. Enjoy the rest of your meal." Wesley's eyes travel briefly over each of us before he turns and heads back toward the kitchen, stopping and chatting with other guests along the way.

He has left behind a silent table, none of us sure what to say. I finally turn toward Aaron, meeting his eyes reluctantly. He is chewing lightly on his bottom lip, the same way he does when he mulls over medical notes.

I decide it is my responsibility to get the conversation flowing again. "So . . . that was unexpected."

"And definitely not awkward at all." Aaron laughs halfheartedly and reaches for his water.

"So much for my TriBeCa wedding idea." I shrug as I wonder how I ended up in this situation, engaged to a handsome young neonatologist and panicking about whether I'm still hung up on someone else.

Even though I know, on a rational level, that Wesley

and I have no future, would it be too selfish, flat-out wrong, to marry Aaron when I still react so strongly to the presence of another man—a man whom I may have once loved a little bit more than I do my current fiancé?

But as my mind races in about sixteen different directions at once, I wonder if I might be mistaken. What if I am misinterpreting my shock as some sort of yearning that it isn't?

As I take a frantic bite of my *scampini*, I imagine Wesley cooking this dish, his hands all over my food, and everything tastes different than before. I'm acutely aware of the juices seeping out from the slick pieces of shrimp inside my mouth, the fibers of flesh coming undone against my tongue, and it's suddenly too much, way too much. I cough abruptly, blocking the food, pushing it away from my throat, like I am trying to keep it from entering me, from reaching my insides, possessing me all over again. I grab for my ice water, taking several large gulps as I try to wash away the taste of Wesley, swallowing once, twice, coughing again.

I'm doing a poor job of masking my discomfort, and Aaron signals our waitress for the check. Nobody mentions dessert. I think fleetingly of Wesley's crème brûlée and nearly shudder. Yes, it's definitely time to go.

"Don't forget, this meal is on us." Reese reaches into his back pocket for his wallet as the waitress returns with the little leather folio in her hand.

"It's really not necessary, you guys," Aaron argues as he produces his own wallet. "We obviously appreciate the gesture, but let us split it, at least. The prices here aren't exactly gentle."

"Here you go," the waitress nearly sings as she hands

Aaron the folder. "Your meal was comped, but there's some information inside about special events—you know, wine tastings and prix fixe nights—if you want."

"Well, that was nice of him." Lana looks at me with her eyes wide. After the way Wesley and I left things three years ago, I think Lana and I would both be less surprised if he had kicked us out of the restaurant rather than treating us to a free meal.

"For sure." Reese nods as he starts to stand. "But now we have to buy you an actual engagement present." He laughs lightly as he stuffs some bills into the folder to tip the waitress.

"Oh, please." Lana swats him as she slides to the end of the bench and rises as well. "As if I wasn't going to buy them an actual gift. She's practically my sister." Lana grabs me and gives me a tight squeeze, an exaggerated show of affection.

I am so gutted from seeing Wesley that I just want to lean into her, allow her to do the work of keeping me upright. Her skinny arms are strong from all that time she spends at Equinox or whatever flashy gym she likes these days, and I have the thought that maybe she is stronger than I am in every way. At least she knows her own mind. I can't break down, though, not here, in front of Aaron. And certainly not where Wesley might still see me.

I paste a smile on my face and wrap my arm through Aaron's as we head toward the coat check. He looks down at me and heaves me closer to him as we walk, as though he knows I could use the extra support right now, as though he will always hold me up.

◯

DURING THE CAB ride back to my apartment, Aaron and I are both silent. He knows that getting over Wesley is one of the most challenging hurdles I have overcome in life—although, if my reaction at the restaurant is any indication, it would seem I really haven't gotten over him at all. There is clearly still much work to be done by way of getting over.

"So, that was a surprise," he finally says.

I just nod, as Aaron has told me several times throughout the two years we've been together that he doesn't need to know every last detail about my past. I've already given him the broad strokes of how Wesley and I had to break our engagement due to irreconcilable differences, that he blamed me for things that couldn't logically be considered my fault, but I've always spared him the specifics. He said it would save us both; me from having to relive the pain, and him from having to brood about how close I once was with another man. He insists that he prefers to remain willfully ignorant, that he'd rather think of himself as the only fiancé, not the second fiancé.

"Do you want to talk about it?" he asks, fixing me with his dark, sloping eyes. He sounds guarded, like he's bracing himself for something.

I lay my head on his shoulder, noting that I'm wiped out from the enormity of it all, devastated by the newly niggling prospect that I might not belong with Aaron after all.

"Nah. There's not much to say. I guess he's back from England." I lift my head to look up at Aaron; his jaw is set, like he's prepared to listen if I want to continue, like he can withstand whatever details might be forthcoming. "It's fine," I say, putting my head back down on him. "It was just a surprise. Thanks for helping me keep my cool."

"No problem," he answers, as he angles his own head to rest it against mine. We lean into each other like that, and I am overcome by a rush of warmth and love, which is instantly followed by alarm. Just because I had an extreme reaction to Wesley doesn't mean I can't be with Aaron, does it? The fact that I once loved Wesley so intensely doesn't mean that my love for Aaron isn't also real.

"So, tell me about your day, then, with Moe," Aaron says, clearly making a peace offering. "What was he like?"

Moe is the Burmese immigrant my law firm is representing pro bono. Harrison, Whittaker & Shine, where I have been working since I graduated from law school, allows junior lawyers to represent nonpaying clients every now and then as a sort of training exercise. The firm's partners like to boast that their lawyers complete a certain number of pro bono hours annually. What the senior attorneys don't advertise when they are recruiting all those bright-eyed law students year after year is that pro bono cases are permitted only to the extent that they do not impinge on the firm's ability to assist the large corporations, the clients who actually pay the firm's bills. So taking on a pro bono case means committing to additional hours in the office, rather than replacing one kind of case with another.

Even so, I was energized when I was assigned to assist Moe Hre with his application for political asylum in the United States. I immediately delved in and spent weeks sorting through Moe's paperwork, so many pages written in English and Burmese, documenting his alleged political and religious persecution in Burma. Today, we finally had our first in-person meeting.

"His English was pretty terrible." I nod as I take Aaron's hand in my own and slip our joined hands inside his coat pocket to keep them warm. "Thank goodness for the interpreter. It's kind of baffling." I think back to the two-hour meeting. "He was very different from what I had pictured. Even the way he was dressed. I don't know . . ." I glance at the ceiling of the cab, noticing that there are little glow-in-the-dark star stickers affixed to it. "He looked like anyone else, like he could have been one of your mother's teaching assistants, or an intern at the hospital. I guess it was closed-minded of me to expect political persecution to somehow show on his face."

"But what about the case?" Aaron asks, as he readjusts our hands so that our connected palms now rest on his lap inside the coat. "Now that you've talked to him, do you think you'll be able to get his status adjusted so he can stay in the country?"

I think about what Moe recounted earlier today as he sat with me and my supervising associate, Rose Conway, in one of our firm's many antiseptic conference rooms. He told us about how the Myanmar military ransacked his home and set fire to parts of his village, about how he walked for weeks until he reached the Thai border. He lived in a primitive camp in Thailand until he secured false documents and fled the region altogether. Although certain portions of his testimony were still too vague, like how he actually got himself out of Thailand, the stories he shared about women and girls from his village being raped and groups of men being locked inside huts that were burned to the ground were almost too terrifying to comprehend.

Thinking again about the extreme challenges Moe has faced, I feel familiar guilt about my career choice—selling out as I have, going corporate instead of pursuing a position in public-interest law. I sweated my way through law school because I wanted the skills to help people, but after all the fallout with Wesley, I shifted my focus to finding the job that paid the most generously. My priority has become ensuring permanent self-sufficiency, even if the work in which I engage means nothing to me. Representing Moe Hre in connection with his application for political asylum is the one bit of substantive merit I can see in my otherwise dismal legal career.

"I wonder if I should go back to Community Kitchen, start helping out there again," I muse, not answering Aaron's question. "It was like being delivered from darkness today when I was with Moe, finally doing something that mattered. I mean, the antitrust case is great for racking up billable hours, but I can't say I'm at all passionate about whether one chewing-tobacco company behaved unfairly toward another. As far as I'm concerned, they should both declare bankruptcy and save all their unfortunate customers from nasty breath and probable mouth cancer."

"Why don't you quit, then?" Aaron asks me, not for the first time. "You could go work for the ACLU or the ADL, or any of the other nonprofits out there."

"My salary—"

"Who cares about your salary? If you don't feel fulfilled by how you're spending your days, what good is the money?"

I know he is trying to be supportive, offering to pick up the slack until I find something more gratifying, but for some reason I chafe at his apparent need to manage this situation, to commandeer every predicament he encounters.

"Look, we can't all be heroes like you, okay?" I snap. "Just because I'm not saving infants from neurological defects all day, it doesn't mean my work is meaningless."

"Whoa. Okay." We pass under the glow of a traffic light, and the green hue travels over his face for a moment as he looks down at me. "I know your work is meaningful, and complicated, and I'm sure it matters a great deal to some people, but it doesn't seem to matter to *you*. I only want you to be satisfied, so if you are, stick with it. I'm just saying, you could break your lease and move in with me early, let me support us both until you figure out what job you want to take. But if that doesn't appeal to you, then you should do what you want. Keep the current job but go back to the soup kitchen, like you said." He shrugs as if he has no stake in the outcome, as if my six-figure salary is irrelevant to him, and then turns away to look out the window.

His support of my choices is nothing new. It's one of the many qualities I love about him. As I watch him working his lip again while he stares out the window, I feel contrite. One glance at Wesley and I have begun to treat Aaron like he is disposable, which he is not. He is the man who brought me back from oblivion when I thought I might never be happy again; he is my sunrise on a brand-new day, every day.

"You know what appeals to me?" I say, more gently. "*You* appeal to me." He doesn't turn back toward me, so I kiss his shoulder through his wool coat, feeling the coarse fabric scratch my lips.

Chapter Four
January 2008

I woke up to the sound of staccato knocking outside my dorm room. Straining toward my digital clock was a useless reflex, as the device was entirely obscured by the clutter on the nightstand, a stack of DVDs, Daphne's polka-dotted cosmetics case, and two plastic snow globes of the New York City skyline. I picked up my phone from where it was charging on the floor and saw that it was 3:37 p.m. If I hadn't stayed out with Wesley until six in the morning, I would have already been awake for hours, probably making flashcards about early-twentieth-century cubists for Art History.

I hauled myself out of my warm bed, squinting into the afternoon light that was pouring through the room's two large windows. The knocking was probably some guy looking for Daphne, whose bed sat unmade, like an open invitation, on the other side of the room. What a relief it had been, when I'd slipped back into our room early this morning, to see her alone in that bed.

The person knocking could also have been Bina or Gretchen coming to check up on me and find out why I hadn't been present in either of the classes we had together today. It was atypical for me to blow off class, and I appreciated that a friend might think to wonder why I'd gone AWOL. I wasn't prepared to explain my night with Wesley to anyone yet, however, as I hadn't even had a moment to process it myself. So, as I stumbled across the floor, I started preparing health-related excuses, fake-coughing into my fist with gusto as I yanked open the door with my other hand.

"Finally!" Wesley raised his arms in triumph.

"Wesley!" My hand flew to my chest in an involuntary gesture of surprise, and I realized two facts simultaneously. First, Wesley's sculpted features had not been a figment of my imagination and were, if anything, only heightened in the light of day. Second, I was currently standing in front of him in nothing but a tiny tank and barely-there boy shorts.

His thoughts seemed to be on the same trajectory as mine. He made no effort at subtlety as his eyes traveled down my body inch by inch, perusing at their leisure. They lingered on my chest before sliding back up to meet my gaze.

"I was about to apologize for disturbing your long slumber, but"—the corners of his full lips lifted—"it seems that the element of surprise has worked in my favor. I like your outfit."

I crossed my arms over my chest and tried to ignore the heat in my face. I knew my cheeks were turning pink, and I wished I had some sort of switch to shut off the blushing. It's an occupational hazard of sporting such a fair complexion, the tendency to turn colors at the slightest provocation. I could only imagine that in the present situation, my cheeks must be a darker red than

Tabasco. This was curious, too, since I was reasonably comfortable with my body, never one to shy away from changing clothes in crowded locker rooms. But the way Wesley was looking at me, his green eyes alight with hunger, made me feel particularly exposed.

"What are you doing here?" I asked, trying to sound calm, like his checking me out in my near-naked state wasn't making me self-conscious. I crossed my arms more tightly against my chest, praying that my nipples weren't sending out messages all their own from beneath my top. I wanted to run a hand through my hair, to make sure it was behaving at least somewhat reasonably, but this was now a triage situation, and covering my braless breasts seemed a higher priority. Wesley turned slightly, and I noticed my silver backpack slung over his broad shoulder.

"We forgot about this last night. This morning. Whatever." He slid the bag off his arm and arranged the strap over the knob of the door so the bag was now hanging between us. "We also forgot"—he paused as he reached into the pocket of his faded jeans for his cell phone—"to program in your number."

He held out his phone to me, but I was not about to remove my arms from my chest and expose myself further, so I just started rattling off the digits.

"Hang on!" He laughed as he pulled the phone back toward himself.

Voices started floating toward us, other students walking through the hallway, getting closer to my room. Wesley shifted, squaring his shoulders so that he somehow suddenly filled the entire door frame, and I realized he was intentionally using his size to keep my scantily clad figure hidden from anyone else's view. He kept his eyes locked on mine as the voices passed, and then looked back at his phone.

"Try again?" he asked. "But slow it down so I can get it right. You're slightly distracting in your pajamas, you know, or lack thereof." He looked me up and down again, and I could feel his eyes sweeping over me as surely as a smooth touch, exploring my every line and curve.

I swallowed hard and repeated the number for him. I waited for him to type it in, then asked, "Can I get back in bed now?" As much as I enjoyed the repartee, I was at too great a disadvantage in my present state. If he wanted to continue this conversation, it would have to happen after I'd had a chance to brush my hair and put on a push-up bra. Maybe even a cute sweater on top of it, if I was lucky.

"Sure. I'll call you." He raised a hand in farewell, his eyes flashing with something akin to victory as he looked down at his phone and turned to walk away.

As soon as I climbed back into my single bed and pulled up the covers, my phone started vibrating. I lifted it from the nightstand and saw a number I didn't recognize. My first thought was that something might have happened with my mother.

"Hello?" It came out as a demand as I answered the phone.

"So, what's your schedule later?"

I recognized that voice.

"Wesley?"

"Yeah?"

"Why are you calling me?" I laughed out loud. "You just left my room."

"Right," he answered, his voice sounding even deeper over the phone. "And I said I would call you."

"I didn't know you meant you were calling me right this second! Didn't I say I was going back to sleep?"

"No. You said you were going back to bed. Big difference. You could be doing any number of things in bed. I could list some of them for you, if you'd like. Even talk you through a few of them." I could hear the smile in his voice, and I couldn't help grinning back into the phone.

"How about if I just go back to sleep and you call me another time? Maybe when you're feeling a little more PG-13." I was too giddy from his attention to be tired anymore, but I wasn't about to admit it.

"Nah, I'm good to talk now. I'm not really a patient person."

"Yeah, I'm beginning to see that. Okay, then, what's doing?" I pulled my plaid comforter more tightly around me and burrowed into my pillow, holding the phone against my other ear.

"I have class until seven. Can I take you out for enormous pizza afterward?"

"Koronet?" I tried to remember if I had mentioned to him how much I loved the gargantuan slices at that place. "Wait, I can't. I'm on duty at Community Kitchen until nine."

"I thought they always close up by seven. Now, you know it's not right to open your door for me in your skivvies and then make up excuses to avoid spending time with me. Cruel, really, is what it is." I could hear the confidence in his tone, like he knew I wasn't deliberately putting him off, and I wondered if should make this a little more difficult for him. But the fact was, this conversation felt so effortless that I didn't want to behave like anyone other than myself.

"No, we do stop serving at seven." I thought of the sign posted at the side door of the church, listing the soup kitchen's hours in bold print, but I gave him a hard time anyway. "Pretty sketchy that you've been keeping tabs on my hours, don't you think?"

"Just doing my due diligence," he parried, and I stifled a grin.

"I stick around after closing to clean up and prepare sandwiches for the next day. But I need to do some work tonight. You know, seeing as how I completely blew off my classes today, thanks to my RA, who's apparently a crappy influence. Never mind the tastiness of his cookies." We were both silent for a beat, and then I had a thought. "You could come with me to the library, if you want . . ."

I figured he'd probably shoot down that idea, but I couldn't let this guy completely derail me, no matter how much I admired the definition of his jaw. Even though I was only in my first year of college, I already knew I would be applying to law school in a few years, and I was committed to making grades that would create opportunities for me.

"Okay, sure," he said. "I could do that. Meet me outside Butler at nine thirty."

"Really?" I caught myself and tried to cover my surprise. "You got it, Cookie Monster. See you there."

After ending the call, I rested my head back on the pillow and noticed I was still smiling to myself. Not even a minute passed before the phone, which I was still holding in my hand, started vibrating again.

"Are you kidding me? I'm seriously trying to go back to sleep!" I answered, laughing.

"Meredith?"

"Oh, shit, Mom." I sat up in bed, the covers falling away from me. "Sorry! I thought you were someone else."

"Why are you sleeping in the middle of the afternoon?" she asked, and I could hear the concern lacing her watered-down voice. The depth of endurance required for the aggressive chemo she was undergoing left her with energy for little else. She had only another few weeks before the treatments would be finished, but from where I sat, it seemed like the chemo was more of a danger to her than the breast cancer.

"Would you buy it if I said I was just trying to shore up my immune system and it has absolutely nothing to do with my staying out too late last night?" I offered, trying to keep things light. My mom's health was steadily chipping away at her emotional state, and I'd made it my personal mission to keep her spirits up. The antidepressants she was taking didn't seem to be working, so I cracked jokes with her like it was my job.

"I'm glad to hear you're finally letting loose a little," she answered on a puff of air. "You don't have to be perfect every single second. It won't change my fate one way or the other."

I closed my eyes and willed myself not to snap at her for making another casual reference to her dismal prognosis. She might as well have been tearing my skin clean off my body for the agony I felt every time she talked like she was going to die.

"Anyway," she continued when I stayed silent, and I could hear a rattling in her voice that had me immediately refocused.

"What is it?" I asked, my heart already quickening.

"I need another surgery."

"What? Why?" I demanded. I heard keys in the door and looked up to see Daphne coming in with a pile of books and a container of takeout food. I noticed that her normally curly red hair was blown straight, and I held up a finger letting her know I needed a minute before I could engage with her. I mouthed the word *mom*, and she nodded as she took off her faux-fur coat and starting riffling through the papers on her desk.

"It shouldn't be a big deal," my mother said. "They're just going to remove the port from my chest. I shouldn't even have called it a surgery. It's just that with the infection around it, it's a little more involved than a simple procedure. I'm only telling you so you don't feel out of the loop. I promised you could trust me to tell you the truth about my condition, so I'm just letting you know."

"When?" I asked, trying to stay calm.

"I'm going in Friday morning. You don't need to be there. Go to your classes. Your father will be with me the whole time."

"We'll see," I answered, not bothering to remind her that I didn't have classes on Fridays this semester. "How are you going to finish the chemo without having the port for the medicine?"

"Stop worrying." She was trying to soothe me, but all I heard was the way her voice stalled, like her words were becoming air as the life slipped out of her more each day. "It's only a few more weeks, so they can use a simple IV line until I finish treatment."

She paused, and I waited for her to say more.

"I'm getting tired, too," she finally added, "thinking about you in bed. I'll call you tomorrow."

We said our good-byes and I took a deep breath, trying to contain the rush of feelings that came every time I said good-bye to my mother these days. The fear that it might be a final farewell was always there.

After a moment, I looked over at Daphne, who was sitting cross-legged on her bed, facing me, the takeout container balanced on her lap and a spoonful of quinoa en route to her mouth.

"Everything okay with your mom?" she asked, staring at me hard.

"I don't know," I groaned. "It's all so tangled and confusing. I never know what's a big deal and what's not. But I don't want to get into it now." It was easier for me to function when I could compartmentalize.

Daphne considered me for a moment, and I could tell she was trying to decide whether to push the topic or drop it like I'd asked. She pursed her pink lips into a little tulip, was silent for a moment, and then switched gears. "Okay, time to spill." she commanded, clearly aware that I had not spent the night in Bina's room.

"Can we not talk about spilling while you're holding that power bowl or whatever it is in the middle of your unmade bed? You're going to get little quinoa pellets all up in your business the next time you bring a guy back here, which"—I paused to look at the time on my phone —"should occur in only six or seven more hours." For as long as I'd known Daphne, we had been poking fun at each other with glee.

She rolled her eyes at me as I continued, "You should at least warn the next dude. Quinoa in the ass-crack has got to be a bitch."

She picked up a furry pink pillow from her bed and hurled it at me, missing me by several feet.

"Nice try changing the subject, twat-wad. I bumped into Bina while she was getting her java at the Commons. We had a little chat about vegetarian eco-feminism, and then she mentioned she hadn't seen you since Science and Tech yesterday. I'll tell you mine if you tell me yours . . ." She waggled her eyebrows and took another spoonful of her health bowl, sucking on the spoon for effect.

"Nasty." I shook my head. "No deal. I love you like a sister and all that, but really, I don't need to hear about last night's fuckboy, okay?"

"Fine, then let me put it this way—unless you scoop me on your night, I will tell you every last detail of mine. Starting with what he sucked on first." She narrowed her eyes at me in challenge.

Rather than subject myself to her vile play-by-play, I caved. Especially since I was feeling pretty charged about Wesley.

"Okay, fine. I was with the RA. He works at a dessert place on Amsterdam. I watched him bake for a few hours, and then he took me to an all-night diner for breakfast. It was all very tame—wholesome, even."

Daphne's lip curled slightly, and she looked at me as if I had peed in her quinoa. "You spent all those hours with skinny Keith and his face-full of acne?" She recoiled a little as she considered the thought and then added, "You're too pretty for your own good. It's making you stupid." She pointed her spoon at me in accusation.

I laughed. "Not Keith. There's a new guy," I explained, trying to sound relaxed. "He's meeting me at the library tonight." I felt myself tingling just thinking about him, but then I had a sobering thought. "I just . . . I don't know if I should be starting something right now. You know, with everything going on with my mom."

"Toss my pillow back so I can chuck it at you again." Daphne's phone started ringing from inside her bag, but she ignored it. "You have been busting your ass since you got here, and you're allowed to have some playtime—not in spite of your mom's illness, but because of it. She would not want you putting your life on hold for her like this. She wants to see you living, finding joy, making the most of the time God gave you, you know?"

I felt my eyes stinging as she talked. I knew she was right. She had been my best friend since second grade, when she'd shown up at Hillside Elementary wearing the same sneakers as me and then announced the address of her new house, which was three doors down from my own. She knew my mom almost as well as I did, and I was pretty certain that my mother would wholeheartedly agree with what Daphne had just said. More than anything, my mom wanted to see me content, to know that I would end up settled, with or without her. I wiped at my eyes before any tears spilled out, wondering how I could trust my emotions when I was in a constant state of fear, carrying perpetual preemptive grief.

"Stop second-guessing yourself," Daphne ordered as she rose from the bed. She tossed the remainder of her food into the trash bin and walked to my closet. "And let's figure out what you're going to wear." Standing with her back to me, she flipped through the hangers. "Now, what here says 'soup kitchen–to–library date'? We may have to layer." She pulled out a teal lace-up peasant sweater that I loved, but then shook her head and returned it to its spot. "Too complicated with the laces. We need something that he can peel right off you."

"Stop making me out to be such a tramp." I said, laughing. "If I like the guy, aren't I supposed to make him wait for it?" That was the general philosophy I followed, a *Rules* girl at heart and all, but I'd have been lying if I said I didn't like the intention I saw in his eyes when he scoped me out earlier, that I didn't want him to turn his thoughts into action. I licked my lips, a little ashamed at myself for how quickly I was able to push away the thoughts about my mother.

For tonight, at least, I was going to try to be carefree. I climbed out from under my covers and joined Daphne at the closet so I could help find the right outfit to bring Wesley to his knees.

Chapter Five
January 2008

*T*he January night air was unforgiving, biting at my
face as I hoofed it across campus, nearly ten minutes late to meet Wesley at the library. I had made the
mistake of calling my father on my way back from Community Kitchen, and we'd gotten into another intense
debate about the ugliness of my parents' situation.
Mainly, we were arguing about my dad's insistence on
spearheading my mom's cancer care, despite their impending divorce.

A mere six days before my mom discovered she had
cancer, my parents had announced to Noble and me that
they were planning to split up. To say that I'd been
blindsided would be a colossal understatement. I'd always
thought we had the perfect life—the Altmans of Livingston, with our model family tucked safely away in a
big suburban colonial.

My brother, Noble, hadn't been as devastated by the
news, probably because he was older and already married, already settled into a new life down in Atlanta.
What I realized from my parents' decision was that all
those years of shared weeknight dinners, family treks to

the Jersey shore, and boisterous Jewish holiday celebrations, they had all been a mirage, a farce that my parents had perpetrated on me, trying to maintain the lie until I left for college. They had apparently been waiting all these years for me to vacate the premises so they could get on with some other, more desirable version of their lives.

I barely had time for a few savage outbursts about the injustice of it all before my mother's routine mammogram showed that we had a more dire problem. I may have been angry at my mom about the divorce, all the years of fake family bliss, but I certainly didn't want her to *die*. Even if everything else had been pretend, the connection I had to my mother was real.

My father insisted on sticking around for the duration of the illness, and he immediately began directing my mom's treatment. I couldn't imagine what that was like for her, letting him spoon-feed her chicken broth or carry her back to bed after she vomited, knowing all the while that their relationship was already over. I offered to defer college so I could take care of her, but when I did, my dad went ballistic. He spewed all this bullshit about how I was supposed to live my life, become independent of the two of them. Maybe that was true, but really, all I could think about during my first semester was whether I was missing the last days I might ever spend with my mother.

The blowout with my father tonight started when I told him I wanted to take Mom to her procedure on Friday. He kept saying I should focus on my studies, continue doing my work, and it sent me into a rage. I had been earning straight A's since middle school. I'd graduated second in my class from an enormous high school in Jersey, and I had yet to meet a class I couldn't master. That is not to say I was a genius, but I was a hard-as-shit worker. For my father to try to ban me from my mother's care on the theory that it might negatively impact my grades was bull-crap, and we both knew it. So either it was as simple as it sounded, and my father actually just did not want me around, or my mother's condition was even worse than they were letting on and he was trying to keep me in the dark. I finally decided I would just show up on Friday, whether he wanted me there or not.

As I reached Butler, I saw groups of students congregating near the doors, huddled together beneath the building's stately, cream-colored columns. I adjusted my backpack on my shoulder and scanned the small clusters of undergrads until I finally spotted Wesley. He was surrounded by several athletic-looking guys I didn't recognize, all of whom seemed to be talking at the same time, creating a boisterous but opaque kind of chatter. Wesley saw me approaching and separated himself from the others, handing off a crumpled paper bag to someone in the bunch as he walked away.

"Thanks, Latner!" one of the guys called after him. The others in the group all started grabbing for whatever was in the bag, like a pack of wolves competing in the dark. Wesley just walked on, approaching me as if I was the only person standing outside the library on that frigid night.

"Hey." He slowed his pace as reached me. "Ready to let your inner nerd out?" I could barely see his face with the golden light of the library coming from behind him in the dark night, but I could hear the playful smirk in his voice.

"I hate to ruin your image of me, Sailor, but my nerd is totally out all the time. Nerd pride." I pounded on my chest twice with my fist. I figured Wesley ought to know what kind of lady he was dealing with here. So many times throughout my years of school, my mother had reminded me not to rush, not to give my work "a lick and a promise." Eventually, I'd internalized the message and gone all-out nerd on my own.

"Well, then we better not waste another second. Come on." He started walking into the library, and I followed. "You good to set up on the fourth floor, somewhere food's allowed?" He looked back at me. "I brought goodies." He held up another paper bag, like the one he'd handed off to his friends, and I caught a whiff of something criminally sweet.

As we swiped our IDs to enter the library, I wondered how I was going to focus on my schoolwork with this dazzling representative of the male species sharing a table with me. I had tried to make the responsible choice by suggesting a library date, but I would probably have to redo any assignment I attempted to complete while we were together. Still, I was thinking the extra study time would be worth it if it meant I got to drink in Wesley's broad shoulders and sculpted profile for a while, not to mention whatever sweet treats he was toting.

We chose a nearly empty room on the fourth floor. There were two girls quietly discussing some sort of 3-D architectural model at the table closest to the entrance, so we maneuvered to the back of the room, and I started unloading my textbooks. No reason not to at least pretend I would be getting work done. Wesley picked up the first book I laid on the table and barked out a laugh.

"Science and Technology Studies? For real? I wouldn't have pegged you as the type."

I bristled at his words, thinking perhaps he hadn't shown his true colors during our adventure the night before, that maybe he was actually just another sexist schmuck. As a woman interested in the sciences, I encountered more assholes than I would have expected, so my guard was always up.

"Why, because I'm blond?" I snipped. "Or too cute to have a brain?"

"None of the above," he answered, as I rooted for him to disabuse me of my negative suspicion. "First of all"— he grinned as he pulled out a chair and dropped into the seat—"you're a lot more than cute." Matching dimples appeared like parentheses on his cheeks, and I wondered why I hadn't focused on their hypnotic effect sooner. "And second of all, no, it's just that you were so adamant last night about your inability to bake, and seeing as how baking is just simple science, I guess I assumed you weren't a science person."

"Baking is *not* simple," I retorted, relieved that he hadn't been thinking girls were too dim-witted for science. I opened my laptop and plugged the cord into the outlet on the table.

"Sure it is." He smiled again as he pulled a cardboard container out of the paper bag he'd brought. The scent of sugar and chocolate filled my airways, pulling me toward whatever was inside that mystery box. "See, to make these churros," he began as he opened the box, "I just engineered a series of calculated chemical reactions between water, sugar, some flour, and oil." He shrugged and lifted one of the pastries out of the container. As he passed it to me, bits of granulated sugar fell like confetti onto the table between us.

Faithless as I was that scientists should automatically be capable bakers, I accepted the churro, which I was surprised to feel was still warm. Stickiness seeped onto my fingers as I studied the pastry's perfectly symmetrical piping lines. "I'm sorry, you just expertly whipped up some churros in your spare time? I call bullshit. This is a far cry from baking simple cookies." I took a bite and was delighted to discover that the churro was filled with a rich hazelnut chocolate, which I was sure now lingered in an unflattering display on my lips.

Wesley reached back into the bag and handed me a napkin. "No, I work at a Spanish restaurant on the Upper West Side. Not usually on Wednesdays, but they needed fill-in help for an hour tonight. Thought you might like to sample the merchandise."

"So, you're saying that in addition to the cookie place and the construction stuff, you also work at a restaurant? How many jobs do you have? Are you even really a college student?"

"Only the jobs you listed. Except you forgot the RA gig. I'm very efficient with my time." He shrugged. "Also, I need the hours in commercial kitchens to get into CIA next year."

"CIA? Like, international spies CIA?" I was starting to think this guy was really full of it, but that didn't stop me from taking another bite of the sugary churro.

"CIA is the Culinary Institute of America." He reached into his backpack and dug around for a moment before pulling out a rumpled pamphlet. "Located in picturesque upstate New York." He passed the little brochure over to me. "I need more back-of-the-house experience for admission."

"Wow." I savored yet another bite of the oozing confection and then wiped the paper napkin across my chin. Wesley was studying me intently, like my reaction to what he'd said was of critical importance.

"Wow," I repeated myself. "I wouldn't have pegged you as the type."

Now it was Wesley who sounded defensive. "Why, because a Columbia grad is meant to work at an investment bank or a corporate law firm? I'm failing to fulfill my destiny?"

"No." I laughed. "Because you're too cute to have a brain. No need to have such useful skills inside that pretty head of yours." I polished off the churro and wiped my hands together with a flourish.

This time, Wesley laughed. "Oh, I have skills," he said suggestively. "Trust me, I have skills."

He kept his eyes focused on me, and I felt my cheeks warming up, crimson on the rise. I stared back, feeling as though precious little oxygen was reaching my brain. He leaned across the table, bringing his face closer to mine. I was struck by the intensity of his eyes, the way the green of the iris appeared to be outlined in black, the pupils surrounded by a green so light it was almost yellow. I leaned forward too, thinking that he was about to kiss me and wondering why I was willing to let that happen when we had only begun our evening, when we were in a public place, when I had full-on chocolate-churro breath.

He reached his hand toward my face, and I made no effort to pull away. But then he was wiping at my cheek, gently yet with purpose.

"Sorry, a few crumbs went rogue," he explained as he flicked a grain of crystallized sugar off me.

I exhaled a shaky breath and leaned away, wiping at the same spot he had just touched, checking to ensure there were no lingering particles, trying to soak up a little extra of his touch.

"Sorry to bust your chops." He settled back into his seat and tossed the CIA pamphlet back into his backpack. "People give me a hard time, my parents especially, so I'm kind of uptight about it."

"Why?" I was surprised that anyone would knock the amazing talent he so clearly possessed. "Everyone's jealous that you're a ninja in the kitchen?"

"Hardly." He let out a huff of air, and for the first time since I'd met him, I saw the corners of his mouth turn down. "It's only my parents who get to me. I'm not living up to their fantasy. You know, graduate from an Ivy, proceed to Wall Street, marry a nice Jewish girl, and spend the rest of my life at a boring job, selling my soul to earn more money than my father before me."

"That sounds pretty terrible. Except the part about the nice Jewish girl," I joked, batting my eyelashes at him. "Also, you've totally got that whole Ivy League part locked in, so at least there's that."

"I guess." He leaned back in his chair, tipping it onto its two hind legs. "It's just frustrating that they don't respect it, that they keep trying to bribe me into looking at law school or business school."

"Bribe you?"

"Yup." Wesley righted the chair, reached back into his bag, and retrieved a plastic water bottle. He held it out in offer; I shook my head, and he took a sip himself before continuing. "They're happy to pay for grad school, provided it's *not* culinary school. I'm not playing their game, though. I'm just going to pay for it myself."

The fact that he had so many jobs now made sense. "I think it's pretty commendable that you're working hard to pursue your passion. If you love it, you'll be great at it, and eventually your parents will realize they were wrong."

"Maybe." He shrugged. He was about to say something else, but my phone started chirping from my coat pocket on the chair beside me. I hurried to silence it so I wouldn't get busted for noise by one of the Butler librarians.

"Do you need to get that?" Wesley asked.

My dad's number still flashed on the screen. "Nah, it's fine." Whatever additional point my father was now hoping to argue with me, I was done for the day. I put the phone down on the table and grabbed my Science and Technology textbook back from Wesley's side of the table.

"Now, are we studying or what?" I pointed my pencil at him. "I told you, I'm not going to let you turn me into a slacker."

My phone vibrated on the table, and I saw a text from my father. I clicked on it and stood up in a panic as I read.

Dad: Heading to Sloan K w mom. Not sure what's wrong. Meet us there.

"Shit. I have to go." I started stuffing my books into my bag.

"What? Why?" Wesley asked, concern taking over his features as he pushed out his chair to stand, too.

I glanced back down at my phone as I reached for my

coat. I didn't like telling people about my mother's condition. I didn't enjoy the pitying looks, the furrowed eyebrows and awkward platitudes. Also, I was superstitious about it, like if I mentioned it less, it was somehow less real, less certain. Even so, I had to explain my abrupt departure somehow, and there was no time to come up with something creative.

"It's my mom. She's sick. I have to meet my father at the hospital."

"Okay, let's go," he said, packing his own bag. "I'll get us a cab."

"No, just me. I've got this on my own, but thanks."

Wesley narrowed his eyes at me, ready to argue, but I wasn't having it. "Seriously, I'm good," I told him, as I zipped up my coat. As sorry as I was to cut our date short, I was hardly prepared to drag my flirty new crush out for a hot night cruising the oncology ward. "I don't even know what's wrong, and honestly, you'll just be a distraction that I don't need right now. I just need to be with my family." I spoke quickly, with determination.

"Okay, I get it." He nodded slightly as he threw his bag over his shoulder. "But at least let me put you in a cab." He took my hand and started pulling me toward the elevator.

I'd like to say I was so focused on my mother that the heat of his hand against mine didn't send shivers through my body, that I didn't want to melt into him.

As we hurried toward the elevator, I realized there was some relief to having another person in my corner, that this extra bit of support mattered. I was tired of fighting my father, of putting on a brave face for my mom, of chasing after my brother.

⟲

NEARLY AN HOUR later, I was waiting in a fabric-covered chair in the hospital lobby, wondering how much longer it would be before my mother and father arrived from New Jersey. I sat under the harsh fluorescent lighting, pondering how I could at once be totally freaking out and also bored stiff. As I watched people coming and going, I was surprised by how many of the visitors at the hospital looked happy, like they were checking in for restaurant reservations instead of asking the receptionist where their half-dead friends and family members could be found.

My phone vibrated, and I looked down to see a new message.

Wesley: Update me when you know something?

I wondered if he really wanted to hear back or was just being polite. Before I could make up my mind, my dad rushed into the lobby through the automatic glass doors.

"Mer!" He huffed my name in exasperation as he approached me, his weathered features scrunched with tension. "God, I've been running circles around this hospital looking for you. Why didn't you think to go up to Mom's ward?" There was a bite to his words, like I was just one more hassle.

"Jesus, Dad. Text much?" I held up my phone. "You could have found me right away."

He stared back at me, silent, waiting for me to fall in line. When I didn't back down, didn't apologize for copping the attitude he deserved, he turned away and started walking toward the stairwell in the center of the lobby.

"Come on," he grumbled over his shoulder. "I'll take you to her. We came in a different entrance."

He was speed-walking back toward wherever my mother was, and I found myself wishing that the urgency was out of concern for his wife rather than his own pressing desire to get out of the hospital, out of the marriage, out of the family. Did I mention he was planning to move to LA after my mom recovered? It was as though he couldn't get far enough away from us.

When we reached my mother's room, she was already settled in a bed with wires protruding from her arm and a faraway look on her pasty face. Her headscarf was askew, and I could see blue veins running through the side of her bald scalp. She looked so small and frail in the bed. She looked like a dying woman, really, and I had to swallow quickly to prevent the tears that were stirring behind my eyes from spilling forth. A nurse was crouched over her, fiddling with a catheter bag that rested on the floor.

My mother appeared to be sleeping with her eyes open, but as I walked into the room, she spoke. "Honey," she rasped in a near whisper.

I wanted to surrender to my despair and start bawling, but I forced myself to keep it together. She was struggling enough as it was. I didn't need to make things worse by breaking down in front of her, letting her worry about me even more than she already was. I forced myself to put on my shallow face, not to acknowledge what I was really feeling, not to let my brain go there. I would act lighthearted and oblivious, because that was the role I so often played in my family, and it would be easier for my mother to view me that way. I wouldn't show how devastated I was for both of us, for everything we had lost already and everything else we stood to lose.

"Come," she said, and I saw her fingers twitch against the bedsheet. I knew she was trying to reach out for me and didn't even have the energy to lift her arm.

"Sweetie." The nurse caught my attention as she put her large ebony hand on my shoulder. "I'm sorry, but you'll have to wait in the hall. Your mom's getting a transfusion. She's going to be much better in a couple of hours—you'll see. Fresh blood is an amazing thing, like blowing up a balloon." She put a little pressure on my shoulder, pushing me toward the door. "The sooner we get started, though . . ."

I nodded and held up a finger, signaling that I just needed one second. I went to my mom and gave her cheek a quick kiss, forcing a whimsical smile onto my face despite the waxiness of her skin, its coolness against my lips.

"See you in a few, Mom." I tried to sound breezy as I walked out into the hallway, where I then paced in front of the closed door until a blond-haired desk nurse looked up and raised her eyebrows at me.

NEARLY TWO HOURS later, one of the nurses finally came to the lounge to get my father, who had been busily typing on a tablet for the entire time we'd been waiting.

"She's all finished," the older woman said. It was the same one who had gently booted me out of the room earlier. "Come, sweetie." She turned to me with an encouraging smile. "I'm sure you'll be pleased to see how much better she looks already."

It turned out that the nurse was right. As I followed them into my mother's room, I saw that she was sitting up in bed and her skin tone had returned to its former hue. She hardly had a healthy glow illuminating her features, but she didn't look like a rotted onion anymore, either.

"Wow, I wish I could get one of those every day," she joked, her eyes crinkling slightly. I could see she was still weak, but she at least had the energy to pretend otherwise.

The doctor told my dad they were going to keep Mom overnight for fluids, but the expectation was that she would go home in the morning.

"Can I stay?" I looked over at the pleather recliner in the corner of the room. "I have all my books, and I can finish my work here."

My parents exchanged some sort of a look with each other, and then my father was telling me no, that the hospital would only let one visitor stay through the night, and it was going to be him.

"Please, Mom." I turned back toward my mother.

"Your father's right. It should be him. Otherwise, he'll just have to drive back here in the morning to get me. You go ahead."

I didn't want to exhaust her further by arguing. "Fine," I huffed, "but make him call me if anything changes." I gave her a pointed look before picking up my bag.

She nodded slowly, and I bent down to kiss her goodbye, promising that I would be back the next day if they didn't send her home first thing.

As I walked out of the hospital, the late-night chill assaulted me anew. I tried to redirect my brain, to force my thoughts away from my mother's illness and all the frightening possibilities. For now, I could go back to my cheery campus existence and pretend that life was all about keg parties and basketball games.

After I settled into a cab, I pulled out my phone and saw several missed texts. My friend Gretchen wanted me to meet her at Murph's, the dive bar we all loved so much, mainly because the bouncers there so rarely carded. Bina wanted me to read over her art history essay. Leslie from down the hall wanted to borrow my copy of *Don Quixote*. As I continued scrolling through messages, I saw that I also had another text from Wesley, from almost an hour earlier.

Wesley: Any news?

If he was asking a second time, I figured he genuinely wanted to know. I quickly tapped out a response.

Me: Everything ok for now. Heading back to campus.

It was only a few seconds before my phone vibrated again.

Wesley: Knock when you get back? Your room is ocupado again. Might as well come fill me in in person.

I hesitated for a second, hoping I wasn't agreeing to a booty call. Not that I wouldn't have enjoyed yielding to the temptation, but I wasn't quite sure it was time to give it up to him yet. You know, Rules and all.

Me: Ok, but no funny business.

Wesley: Funny business? Have we traveled back in
time to 1950? Lucy, you got some 'splaining to do!!!

I laughed out loud at his oddball response and the
cabby glanced back at me in the rearview mirror.

Me: Whatever, freak show. Fine. See you in 20.

I tossed the phone into the outer pocket of my knap-
sack and leaned my head back against the plastic seat of
the cab. I had twenty minutes to shake off the cancer
blues and turn myself back into the lively college coed
everyone seemed to think I should be.

Chapter Six
January 2017

I wake up sweating, feeling smothered.

"Move over," I mumble, pushing at Aaron, marveling again that the leg of an adult human can function so effectively as both a space heater and an anvil. As I wonder absently how many inches long his leg must be, trying to subtract an estimate of his torso length from his total height of six feet, three inches, I push at him again, prodding him to start his day. "You have to go," I half whisper as I nudge him.

"Clive asked me to switch. I'm not on today." He resettles himself in the bed, rolling onto his back and taking his leg of steel along with him. The comforter follows his movements, gliding off me as well. I feel sweet relief from the stifling warmth, but it lasts only an instant before the change in temperature becomes too drastic and I'm now suddenly too chilled. I swivel onto my side and he pulls me up against his body, my back flush to his heated chest, as he arranges the duvet over both of us and nuzzles his stubbly chin into my neck.

Even though I'm frustrated by the extreme temperatures to which I keep falling prey in this bed, I do love nestling into Aaron's bulk. I feel locked against him—secure, protected, and perfectly arranged.

I break contact just so I can push the covers away, first with my hands and then with my feet, but then I burrow back into his body, getting as close as I can and trying to savor the feel of him, to interpret it as a welcome offering rather than oppression. Normally, I don't have to flap around in bed like this just to enjoy the sensation of Aaron's arms around me, the way his muscular arm lazes across my rib cage. My thoughts flash to Wesley, and I realize that our run-in last night has intruded on my morning, that Wesley is the reason I am suddenly aggravated by Aaron's embrace. A swell of anger rushes through me, and yet I can't stop myself from replaying the events of the prior evening in my mind, romanticizing them as I go.

Instead of remembering all the nastiness of our breakup, the hurtful accusations and excruciating unraveling of us, I keep picturing Wesley's eyes, greener and sharper than I had remembered. And his food. My God, flavors so sensual and ethereal, each dish was like a love affair, the exquisite combinations so astonishing that they became illicit, lawless. But that was always the very nature of Wesley—exquisite, thrilling. I think of fireworks, explosions so fierce in their beauty, exhilarating and dazzling, but necessarily fleeting, a phenomenon not meant to last but all the more beautiful because of its ephemeral nature. Maybe that was what I had with Wesley, something that was never meant to last. If only I could recategorize him in my brain, label my time with him as an intense experience that was meant to be remembered, learned from, even, but never revisited. As I snuggle into Aaron, I close my eyes and notice with relief that my body does feel right next to his, as though I have landed where I belong.

Less than a minute later, my alarm is buzzing, harsh and grating. I swat at the clock on my mirrored nightstand.

"Well, you may not have to get out of bed, deadbeat, but I have some very greedy tobacco executives who are depending on me for their next windfall, so I'd better hit the shower." I roll away from Aaron and make my way toward the bathroom.

As I wait for the shower to warm up, I look around my little bathroom with the black-and-white penny tiles on the floor and the fluffy white mat. The oval rug is too long for the three-foot space it occupies, part of it curving up against the wall. As usual, the space is a mess, too small for all the cosmetics and personal hygiene products I am always experimenting with, because surely that next eye cream is going to make all the difference. I notice how many of the items mixed in with my hodgepodge of paints and lotions belong to Aaron. His Braun electric toothbrush is too wide to fit in the built-in toothbrush holder, so it's propped up in a corner by the sink. My eyes drift over the glass bottle of shaving oil he recently purchased from the vintage apothecary shop down the block, then his Right Guard, some stray collar stays, and a stethoscope that definitely doesn't belong in the restroom. My prewar apartment is adorable, and it's conveniently located near lots of hip restaurants and funky shops on the Upper West Side, but I understand why Aaron is pushing for me to move in with him into his much larger, airier loft in Gramercy.

I pull off the T-shirt I slept in and catch a glimpse of myself in the medicine cabinet mirror. I wonder if my body still looks the same as it did when I was with Wesley, whether he would still be drawn to all its different parts, so fascinated by idiosyncrasies like the deep curve in my lower back or the small scar on my left knee. I turn sideways to evaluate my reflection. My stomach is still relatively flat, thanks to my penchant for hot yoga and all that time I spend in warrior pose. I lift one of my breasts, letting its weight settle into my hand, and I struggle to remember whether Wesley had been as interested in my midsize bust as he had been in the firmness of my ass. I turn my back to the mirror, twisting to see my reflection over my shoulder, wondering if I would still pass muster, but then I think of the sweet doctor snoozing in my bed at the moment, and I want to smack myself for my disloyal thoughts.

It would be the height of foolishness to waste what I have with Aaron just because I can't stop thinking about my ex-fiancé, picturing how he looked in his chef's uniform last night and wondering what he would make of my naked body. I was so sure I had changed, that I was no longer the girl Wesley knew, but now I am second-guessing myself. If I get my head back in the game with Aaron, perhaps I can force Wesley out of my mind, shove him away, toss him into a drawer like an old travel souvenir, where he will simply collect dust and cease to matter. I don't want to relinquish Aaron, to surrender him as another casualty of my mistakes.

I conjure up Aaron's suggestion about moving in together, sifting it around again, chewing through the possibilities. Maybe his idea has legs, footing that I didn't appreciate at first. Considering the situation on a practical level, I could save a boatload of money on rent if I gave up this apartment, and I'd have much more space for my profusion of beauty products in Aaron's bathroom, with its double sinks and long vanity. Cohabiting, sharing closet space and electric bills, maybe it would bring us close enough to plug the holes in my heart, the unsealed edges where a pest could still burrow its way inside. If I can do that, figure out a way to quell my reaction to Wesley, to exterminate these lingering thoughts, then maybe I can keep my new fiancé. I step into the shower and let the hot water nearly scald my back as I try to forget the smell of hazelnut churros.

IT'S SUNNY OUTSIDE, but frigid in a way that makes my eyes water. I walk to the corner subway station, pulling my wool peacoat more tightly around my body and weaving past a group of schoolchildren who are being poorly shepherded by a frazzled young woman. I am focused on Moe's case, already devising strategies to evade antitrust-related tasks this morning so that I can redirect my efforts toward asylum research. It's true what Aaron said, that I initially hoped to find employment at a place like Legal Aid or a similar nonprofit. But I really do enjoy earning the salary that a heartless, impersonal corporate firm can provide. Not that I care so much about being able to afford luxuries, but it's comforting to know that I will always be able to take care of myself, even if I have sudden, extreme expenses, like bills for cancer treatment. It would be poor planning not to account for my genetic predisposition.

Perhaps if I found more charity work outside the office, I might feel a modicum of relief about the soulless nature of my usual work. I think again of the soup kitchen where I spent so much time in college, where I actually connected with some of the people I served. I remember one specific prepubescent girl who came to the church every week with her mom and baby brother, though now the child's name escapes me. I used to show her my *People* magazines. We'd look through the pictures together while her mom nursed her baby brother. The family ended up moving down South—Raleigh, if I remember correctly—where there was an aunt who'd agreed to take them in. I wonder if I should go back to the soup kitchen, get to know some other little girls, do a better job of remembering their names. Despite the oppressive number of hours I work per week, I think I could secrete some time on Sundays to get up to that church. In fact, I decide, I will try to go this coming Sunday.

When I finally reach my stop, I climb the crowded steps of the subway station, emerging on Fifty-first and Lex with a renewed sense of optimism. I don't have to be a one-dimensional corporate attorney. I can still find ways to make myself proud without having to quit my lucrative job. I ride the high of my new outlook as I glide through the marble lobby of my office building and slip into a nearly full elevator just before the doors close.

I arrive on the twenty-seventh floor feeling reinvigorated. Not even the presence of my office mate, Nicola, already seated at her desk next to the window, is going to get me down. As a lowly second-year associate, I have been relegated to the smaller desk, closer to the door. Also, Nicola hates me.

"You're here early," I say brightly as I glance at my cell phone to make sure I'm not actually late.

"I'm cutting out early for my flight to Miami tonight," she tells me without looking away from her computer screen, "so I thought I'd bill some time this morning." Nicola did tell me that she was going down to Florida to celebrate her sister's recent divorce with some sort of reverse bachelorette party. I kind of thought she was kidding, but I guess not. She glances over her shoulder at me and gives me a quick visual once-over, likely disappointed in what she sees, whether the inexpensive clothing I'm wearing or my hasty grooming for the day, and then she turns back to her screen.

I drop my leather tote on the floor and hang my coat on the back of the door, thinking to at least review Moe's I-589 form before I return to my billable work. Nearly seven months have passed since Moe arrived in the United States. He stumbled through a meeting with an immigration officer at JFK and, despite his limited English, managed to convince the officer that he had the requisite "credible fear" of persecution in his country of origin to warrant initiating asylum proceedings in the United States. The clock has been ticking since that date, and we have only five months remaining until he must file his full application for Asylum and Withholding of Removal with the immigration court. I'm anxious about treading too close to the deadline, as I've read about mistakes with issues as simple as court docketing that have cost applicants their refugee status.

Something about my meeting with Moe has been troubling me since he left the office, but I can't put my finger on it. As I open the Redweld folder containing my case notes and power up my computer, I hear a knock behind me. I turn to see Alexandra Pervez, the senior associate on the chewing tobacco case, standing in the hallway with a rolling cart full of manila folders beside her.

"Hey, Mer."

I'm not sure why she thinks we're buddies or when we got on a nickname basis with each other. Our interactions are generally limited to whatever orders she spews in my direction and the embarrassingly deferential nods I offer in response. I try to affix a polite smile to my face while I wait to see what she wants.

"Great news," she starts. "Defendants 'found'"—she makes air quotes around the word—"an entire file cabinet of documents that they failed to turn over. There was some water damage or something, so the pages couldn't be scanned in digitally. I'll send these down to the conference room on eight, and you can get the review team back together to go through them. Okeydoke?"

Her tone would imply that she is inviting me to meet for muffins and manicures, not sentencing me to more hours of document review. I thought I was finished flipping through the thousands of pages of accounting drivel and random office notes that were provided to our firm by the other side in connection with this tedious case. In a perfect world, someone on our team would find the crucial straw in the wind, the scribbled message that directed the defendant's employees to break a slew of antitrust laws in the name of beating out the other corporation. The chances of that discovery are slim, at best, and in the meantime, five young attorneys are being condemned to so many more hours of torture, with only the occasional paper cut to break up the monotony.

"Okay, you got it," I tell her with a fake smile, because it's not like I have a choice.

After she leaves, Nicola snorts from behind me. "Back to the dungeon, huh?"

I don't answer as I push myself out of my chair and head to the little pantry down the hall. I pop a single-serve coffee pod into the machine and tilt my head to the side, trying to crack my neck. So much for working on Moe's application today. The tension in my shoulders refuses to unlace as I think about the country conditions report and expert statements I still need to finalize before we can submit the paperwork to the court. I had been hoping to learn more about Mae La, the overcrowded refugee camp in Thailand where Moe lived before he traveled to Bangkok, the city where he boarded his first flight.

As I pass the open door of my office on the way to the elevator, I can hear Nicola singing that old Will Smith song "Miami," and I feel a powerful urge to throw something at her. While she's enjoying mango margaritas in front of some art deco hotel tomorrow, I will definitely be back at the office, taking care of the asylum work that I won't be able to do today. I remind myself that Nicola is single and seems to have a very narrow social life. She puts in many more hours than I do, so I shouldn't begrudge her the limited time off. Even so, I feel pissy about the number of weekend hours I'm going to spend working. I suppose I should have known better than to expect pro bono work at Harrison, Whitaker & Shine to mean anything other than extra time and additional complications. Look at me, living the dream.

◯

WHEN SUNDAY ROLLS around, I'm feeling less catty, appeased by the progress I've made assembling supporting documentation for Moe—which, in light of the recent upheaval in US immigration law, is hardly a small feat. I've also compiled a list of additional questions to ask him at our next meeting, which I hope will fill in the remaining holes and leave us in great shape to move forward with his application. Aaron is on call at the hospital all weekend, so I decide to take the day for myself and head up to Crossroads Church, the building that houses Community Kitchen. As I ride the subway uptown from my apartment, I'm flooded with memories of the many hours I spent at the soup kitchen during college.

When I started volunteering at Community Kitchen long ago as a freshman, I thought it would be a short-term project, a splash of good karma to help me out while my mother was battling her breast cancer. I quickly grew attached to the entire concept, though—the program's mission, the interactions I had with the people, the relief I found in helping others. There were several children who showed up each week with their mothers or fathers, and some elderly folks, but mostly they were able-bodied people who just couldn't catch a break. I had been surprised that many of them were not actually homeless, just people who had fallen below the poverty line for one reason or another. Though they could afford rent, or even clothes for their children, they often didn't have enough money remaining for food. Then, of course, there were the mentally ill, the addicts, the runaways—so many people who simply couldn't make it on their own—

and Community Kitchen helped them all, no judgment, just beef stew and apple juice. I was proud of myself for being a part of that back in college, and, thinking about it now, I am sorry to have given it up.

When I finished college, I told myself that I would stay connected to the soup kitchen, that I'd at least visit, maybe go help out from time to time, but then, of course, life got busy and I never did. Today will mark the first time I've returned to Crossroads Church since the week before I graduated.

When I emerge from the depths of the subway at 116th Street, I can see from a block away that a lot has changed at Community Kitchen. For starters, it's only 10:00 a.m., two hours before lunch starts at CK, and there is already a line of people halfway down the block. I hope that means that lunch service begins earlier than I remember, and not that the number of poverty-stricken individuals in the area has increased so dramatically since my graduation.

I make my way to the side of the building and head into the church through the entrance marked for staff only.

Before I'm even through the door, I hear Katie Sue's familiar voice. "No, no, no!" she's yelling at someone. "The heat isn't high enough. Oh, thank goodness," she says, as she seems to notice me coming into the kitchen. "More hands. Wait, Meredith?"

I feel a grin spread across my face as she recognizes me.

"Meredith Altman? Well, I'll be!" She hurries over and grabs me in a bear hug. As she wraps her fleshy arms around me, swallowing me almost entirely with the soft

folds of her chest and belly, I catch the scent of Camp-
bell's bean-and-bacon soup, the first course of nearly
every meal served at Community Kitchen. I am immediately transported back in time nearly ten years, to when
I first started helping here. With a start, I remember the
idealistic girl I was, so full of hope and potential. I'm horrified that I haven't been back, that I forsook this charity
work and, by extension, that I renounced that old part of
myself.

Katie Sue pulls back from me and takes my hands,
her warm fingers enveloping mine as she looks me over
from head to toe.

"It is damn good to see you, girl," she says as she
grants me a smile full of nostalgia. "You here because of
Wes?"

"Wes? What do you mean?"

"Didn't you see that line outside? They're here for
the training program, Wesley came up with it. You didn't
know? You guys aren't still . . . ?" She makes some sort of
gesture with her hand, I guess trying to indicate a couple. Or maybe she's asking if we're even in touch.

"Nah." I try to sound nonchalant. "We ended up going our separate ways."

"Oh!" She loops her arm through mine and pulls me
toward the swinging door to the church gymnasium.
"Well, you've got to see what he's done," she tells me as
she abandons whatever task set her on a tirade a few
moments ago. "It'll make you about burst with pride." She
walks me out of the gym and down the linoleum-floored
hall toward the church's Sunday school classrooms. "Take
a look," she tells me, motioning to a closed door.

I peer through the small plexiglass window in the

door and there's Wesley, pacing back and forth at the front of a classroom, lecturing to a group of about fifteen adults who all stare back at him from the child-size desks. The audience is wide-eyed, rapt.

"What's he doing?" I whisper, looking back at Katie Sue. Her stringy blond hair is pulled back in a low ponytail, just like I remember it.

She takes my arm again and leads me back toward the kitchen, commandeering me in that affectionately pushy way of hers.

"It's called the Culinary Touchstones Training Program," she says while we walk. "He started it here a month ago. He's teaching basic financial and cooking skills, life skills, and the like. It's a fifteen-week program, and when they finish, the students are qualified to be prep cooks for restaurants. Job training. He's donating his time."

"That's amazing," I say.

"Sure is." She nods enthusiastically, her ponytail dancing across her back. "He's also been bringing leftover food from his restaurant on Sundays—Firebird, or whatever his place is called. That's why you got the big line outside. The earliest folks get true restaurant fare, while the stragglers get stuck with soup and macaroni."

"Does he stay to serve after the class?" I ask, hoping he does, hoping he doesn't.

"Of course," she answers, exuberant as always. "But why did I let you distract me, you little thing? We're tight on time as it is!" She starts pulling me back into the kitchen. Before I have time to stress about my impending run-in with Wesley, she has me so overloaded with ladles and trays that I'm momentarily sidetracked.

It amazes me how quickly I can get back into the

routine here, carrying large aluminum trays of carbohydrates from the warmer to the long table out front, setting up Sterno cans like I was just doing it last week. Before I know it, Katie Sue is calling out the five-minute warning, and those of us who are here to serve are retying our aprons and taking our posts behind the long buffet tables at the back of the gym.

There is an extra serving table on the side of the gym today, where I'm told the restaurant food will be provided. I specifically avoided that table when I chose my current post at the green beans. I pick up the enormous aluminum serving spoon and start moving the greens around in their deep tray, halfheartedly trying to bolster their appearance, stirring the melted margarine to keep it from congealing around the edges of the pan.

The back door of the gym opens, and the adults I saw sitting in Wesley's class make their way inside, lining up first at the table full of Thunder Chicken's food. I gear up to see Wesley, but the door closes before he appears.

We begin serving the meal, and I'm on edge the whole time, waiting for him to walk in, wondering whether he will be glad to see me. As the minutes pass and he doesn't appear, I tell myself that he must have left after teaching his class, though I'm also hoping that he is still here, helping in the kitchen or maybe working with a struggling student. I find myself searching, alternately wistful and panicky. I'm terrified that I will have to face him before my shift is over, but I'm equally frightened that he has already left, that I've missed a chance to see him.

When I finally ladle out my last helping of green beans and carry my empty tray toward the kitchen, I push open the swinging door, bracing myself for whatever I will find on the other side. When I enter, I find only Katie Sue and three other volunteers washing dishes. Wesley must have left after all.

I notice the disappointment I feel, and I want to kick myself in the face, if that were a thing I could physically accomplish. It has been only a few days since I promised myself I wasn't going to care about him anymore. It's definitely for the best that I didn't spend the last two hours standing next to him, serving lunch. I think of Aaron, who is probably performing some life-changing surgery on a small child at this very moment, and I have a sharp stab of regret. Aaron is my future, and I need to get steady on that train. I suppose if Wesley is back in New York, I should expect to run into him from time to time, especially if I plan to keep coming back to the soup kitchen. I can't let my entire being flounder each time his name comes up. In fact, maybe seeing him more regularly will help me to get some closure, finally really move on. That's the faulty logic I have grabbed on to when I say good-bye to Katie Sue and promise I will be back the following week.

Chapter Seven

January 2008

7 wasn't sure what I was hoping for as I returned to the dorm, heading toward Wesley's room and wondering whether my hair smelled like hospital disinfectant. I had never really been serious with anyone, unless you counted my high school boyfriend, Rudi Kramer, but that relationship had fizzled in a hazy dust of platonic disinterest long before we approached any physical milestones. I wasn't a prude; I just hadn't yet been presented with any prospects that I found particularly tempting. I most certainly was not going to hand over my V-card to a guy I had only just met. Which was why, I reminded myself, I was not going to jump into bed with Wesley as soon as he made a move. *Was Not.* Still, maybe having Wesley to focus on, a guy so hot he made my eyeballs sweat, was just what I needed to stay sane, a harmless diversion. My mother would not have begrudged me that —she so was adamant that her illness shouldn't detract from my college experience. She would sooner text Daphne to meet me in the hallway with a box of Trojans than try to curb my frenzied hormones.

I trudged up the stairs with my overstuffed backpack

weighing me down, a reminder of all the incomplete coursework I would have to finish the next day. The heat of the building was at least a welcome respite after being out in the icy night. When I reached my hall, I found a group of girls sitting on the floor, cramming for some exam. They had to rearrange themselves in order to let me pass. I stepped over their flannel-pajamaed legs and the long box of jelly beans they were all picking at, the kind where each flavor had its own compartment. I loved this part of college life, the way we were in our own time zone, where 2:00 a.m. was a completely reasonable hour to be awake and socializing. It was hard to believe that less than a year earlier, I had been waking up at six in the morning to get myself out the door in time for high school classes. In my college life, 6:00 a.m. wasn't even the morning yet. Really, it was still yesterday.

I passed my own room on the way to Wesley's and noted the big red *X* Daphne had drawn on the whiteboard. She had also added small *x*'s and *o*'s at the bottom of the board—a little show of appreciation toward me, I guess, a shout-out. Other freshmen might have been annoyed at their roommate for constantly monopolizing the room, but I'd had the space to myself almost every night of first semester while she was dating Todd the ass-hat, so maybe it was fair that she got some nights to herself, too. I considered myself lucky to be boarding with my lifelong best friend, even if it meant that I was sometimes without a room at all.

When I reached Wesley's quarters at the other end of the hall, his door was open. I heard him talking to someone as I stepped closer and raised my hand to knock on the doorframe. He was sitting up on his single bed, resting his back against the wall. In a casual gray hoodie and black sweats, he looked like he was modeling loungewear. He noticed me before I knocked and jumped off the bed.

"Hey. Come in!" He pulled me into the room and started closing the door behind me. "We were waiting for you."

I stepped past the front portion of the room, where a wall had partially obstructed my view of the interior, and saw that we were not alone. On the bed opposite Wesley's sat a girl, a very attractive girl, who was also clad in sweats. The bed she occupied was devoid of sheets or comforters. I supposed Wesley had this double room all to himself and the college hadn't bothered to remove the extra bed. A stack of neon poster board and a haphazard pile of glue sticks and other shiny art supplies lay on the bed next to her.

I looked to Wesley for guidance on the situation I had just stepped into. I certainly didn't want to be a third wheel if I had misunderstood his intentions toward me. My mind flashed back to the way he had looked at me in my revealing sleepwear the day before, devouring me, and I wondered if that was how he looked at this girl, too. I tried to keep calm, telling myself that Wesley had no obligations toward me, that he hadn't made any promises he wasn't keeping. No harm, no foul, and all.

"Meredith, this is Lulu."

And she had a stripper name, too.

"Lucy," the girl said, rolling her eyes in Wesley's direction. "Only my family calls me Lulu, and I've been trying for years to make them stop. Unsuccessfully, obviously." Her lip curled in a dainty snarl at Wesley.

"Family?" I asked. I thought Wesley had told me he was an only child, but this girl did resemble him quite a bit, now that I looked more closely at her. She had the same square jaw and strong cheekbones, the same honey-brown hair. Though she had slanted eyes that were a nondescript brown, a far cry from Wesley's startling, translucent green.

"My cousin," Wesley explained. "Lu came over to help me with these decorations I have to make, but we decided to wait for you. As much as you may be a science scholar, I know for sure you're an art connoisseur, too."

"You do?" We had never discussed my fascination with art.

"Sure." He started pulling off my coat by the sleeve. I let my backpack drop to the floor with a thud and then slipped out of the jacket obediently.

"You told me you take art history," he explained, "and you have that artsy pink stripe in your hair."

I narrowed my eyes at him, unimpressed by his deductive reasoning. He had to know the pink stripe was about my mom, and one art history class did not an "art person" make.

"Okay, fine, I'm full of shit." He draped my jacket on the back of his wooden desk chair. "I just thought you might be kind enough to help, especially since I myself hate art. I'm the dream killer of baby glitter and construction paper everywhere," he joked, referencing my comment about my shoddy baking skills from the previous night. He picked up a few pieces of poster board and laid them on the gray linoleum tiles between the beds. "I was supposed to make decorations for the dorm during break, but I decided no one cares about the hallway decor. The SRA came by today and told me I was not at liberty to veto my assignment, to put our conversation nicely. I have two days to get it done."

"SRA? You and the acronyms," I complained from where I was leaning against his desk. "First the CIA; now this."

"Senior resident advisor. Karen Bromley. I'm sure you've met her."

I nodded, thinking about the extremely perky RA who was always stopping by our room, trying to persuade us to join hokey dorm-wide games in the student lounge. There was one race through the hallways with an egg on a spoon that Daphne had gotten excited about. Beyond that, we had mostly evaded that overly cheerful go-getter from the fifth floor. Karen Bromley was just the type who would lament the lack of jaunty posters adorning the halls.

"Lu came to my rescue," Wesley continued, "but we've spent precious little time creating motivational artwork and most of the last hour hashing out all the reasons why her ex-boyfriend sucks."

"The biggest reason being," Lucy piped in, "that he doesn't want to be my boyfriend anymore." She picked up a pair of art scissors and made a repetitive stabbing motion in the air, reminiscent of the movie *Psycho*.

"Anyway," Wesley said pointedly, as he gave his cousin the side-eye, "now it's poster time."

Lucy hopped off the bed and started arranging a few containers of glitter according to color on the floor next to the poster board. She put down two jars of sparkling silver flakes, a blue and a white, then a pearlescent-looking glitter glue.

"So, Wesley was thinking of doing some sort of winter wonderland theme," Lucy explained to me as she continued flitting around the room, grabbing at paintbrushes and filling a cup with water. "That was Karen what's-her-face's suggestion, but I explained to your friend here that if he does a winter theme, he's just going to have to redo the artwork when spring comes around—you know, to remain seasonably appropriate. Then it'll be all green and pink glitter and, like, Easter bunnies or something. So, I was thinking . . ." She paused to place her hands on her hips and survey the supplies all over again, but a knock on the door interrupted her brainstorming.

Wesley opened the door and stood motionless for a moment before turning to look at Lucy. When she nodded at him, he made a resigned gesture with his hand and stepped back from the door, admitting the visitor. In walked a guy with light, shaggy surfer hair and skin so tanned that he had obviously spent winter break in some sort of tropical location. As he focused his attention on Lucy, I noticed that his red puffer jacket was much too large for his lanky frame.

"Can we talk?" he asked her in a voice that sounded raw, strained.

Lucy's eyes darted to Wesley and then back to the guy, who was clearly the lousy ex-boyfriend, soon-to-be boyfriend again, maybe.

"Uh, yeah. Yeah." She quickly grabbed her Ugg boots and coat before turning to Wesley. "He can walk me back to my building. Let me know if you don't finish the posters, and I'll come back tomorrow." She looked at both of us as she said it, and then she and the repentant boyfriend were gone. And Wesley and I were alone.

"So, what do you think?" He turned to me as the door closed behind Lucy. "Are you game for a little poster magic?"

"Are you for real, trying to put me to work for the second night in a row?" I crossed my arms against my chest in defiance.

"Always. And, if you recall, you refused to cooperate with the baking, so here's a chance to redeem yourself." He smirked. "What do you think we can do with silver and blue that will be sufficiently seasonless? I had been thinking snowflakes and, you know, winter frost when I bought the supplies, but now we need something that says 'January to May.'" He opened his arms wide in a gesture of expansiveness, and I stifled a giggle. "Something that can live happily on the Carman walls until my tenure is complete." He was trying to be sarcastic, but the glow behind his light eyes told me that he was secretly enjoying this project. He crouched down next to the poster and started shaking a jar of blue paint.

I pushed off from the desk, eyeing the copious supplies on the bed where Lucy had been sitting. In addition to the glitter and paint, Wesley had also stockpiled many other crafts supplies, significantly more than necessary for the job with which he'd been tasked. I saw packages of popsicle sticks, cotton pom-poms, pipe cleaners, paintbrushes, and a bag of feathers.

"Googly eyes?" I asked, grabbing a little bag of the jiggly circles. "Judging from the quantity of supplies here, I think you're more into this project than you're letting on. Perhaps even a craft savant." I exchanged the googly eyes for a bag of ice-blue sequins. "I mean, sequins?" I held out the packet in accusation.

"Nope." He twisted the cap off the paint bottle. "Pass me a brush. I just channeled my one summer as a day-camp counselor. I dated the arts-and-crafts counselor that year."

"Uh-huh . . ." I looked at him dubiously as he shifted onto his knees and started painting something on the poster. Instead of studying the blue streaks he was making as he leaned across the paper, I found myself watching his form, the fluidity of his movement.

"Toss me the white. I've had a stroke of genius." I pulled my eyes away from his body to find the proper jar among the art arsenal. As I handed it over, he glanced up at me, and I could see some sort of trepidation in his eyes.

"So, do you want to talk about your mom?" He looked back at the poster and kept painting, his brush moving rhythmically across the poster board as he waited for my response.

"Not really." I plunked myself down perpendicularly on the bare mattress and shifted backward until my shoulders were resting against the wall.

"But she's okay for now?" His eyes were focused on the strange shape he was creating. For a second I thought maybe he was making a chef's hat, but then the shape curved in the wrong direction.

"Yeah, for now," I answered. I worried I was being rude, playing it too close to the vest after his multiple attempts to show support throughout the night. But in the hour since I'd left Sloan Kettering, I had been actively struggling to keep images of my mother's withered body from flashing through my mind, freeze-frame style. Re-hashing everything for Wesley wouldn't help. I tried to think of what else I could say to show I did appreciate the concern, but then the image on his poster started to take shape beneath his brush.

"A cruise ship?" I asked, too harshly, as Wesley had unknowingly alighted on a personal trigger point. "You can't make posters full of cruise ships." I would not live the remainder of my freshman year surrounded by images of cruises and daily reminders of what had happened the last time my family traveled together.

"Why not?" He stopped mid-stroke, sounding genuinely confused. "School colors, right? Blue oceans, white ships. And traveling's not a theme that's tied to any particular season."

"Why can't you use cruise ships as the dorm motif?" I repeated, trying to rein in my emotions, unwilling to reveal the true reason I was so averse to the concept. "Let me count the ways. First of all, it's classist. Not everyone at this school can afford exotic vacations. It's elitist and the antithesis of Columbia's message. Second of all, cruises are just plain cheesy."

"Not if you go on the right cruise ship."

"See? There you go again. Uppity."

"Uppity?" He laughed. "Real people use that word?"

"Says the man who used the word *woo* yesterday," I countered.

"Okay, smarty-pants, what is Columbia's grand message, anyway?" He leaned away from the poster, resting back on his heels, paintbrush in midair.

"Isn't it your responsibility as an RA at this fine institution to be aware of that information on your own?" I jumped off the bed and took the brush from his hand. "Honestly, I'm saving you from yourself here. I mean, you'd be better off doing something juvenile like Smurfs. Still the school colors, right? Or one of those cartoon ducks, Donald or Daffy—people might at least enjoy seeing those vestiges of their youth."

"If you're so in touch with the vibe of the student body, then why don't you come up with a slogan instead, a catchy tagline that makes the hall more welcoming all semester long, just like Karen the SRA wants? Maybe we can work from there."

"I don't know," I retorted defensively, as I looked down at his half-painted ship. Nasty thoughts about my father's philandering lurked just beneath my composed exterior, pushing my internal temperature closer to boiling with every second that I considered the image beneath me. "But I do know it shouldn't be some god-awful quote from the *Love Boat* theme song." I flung the paintbrush upward for emphasis and accidentally sent several white droplets splattering onto Wesley's face. "Oh, shit. Sorry!" I turned around to look for paper towels or a rag. If he was such a crafts whiz, he should have cleanup supplies, too, right? I started toward the box of tissues on the nightstand, but then, suddenly, I felt a powder or something landing on me, particles falling everywhere.

"Oh, no, you didn't!" I spun around, crazed. "You dumped glitter on me? Are you kidding me? That shit's going to stay with me for weeks. Are you insane? You're dead meat." I turned back toward the extra bed, where several large salt-shaker containers of silver glitter sat, and I raced toward them.

"No, no, no!" Wesley lunged toward me in some type of ninja wrestling move. He wrapped his arms around my hips as the top third of my body flopped down on the bare mattress and the rest of me landed on the floor. "No, you don't!" he declared, holding me in place.

I was no match for his strength, but he was clearly trying to avoid hurting me, and I used his gentleness to my advantage. I wriggled upward in his hold until my fingers stretched just far enough to reach one container of glitter. I started twisting off the top as he let go of my legs and tried to wrench the bottle away from me. I held fast to my bounty, though, shielding the bottle underneath me and flipping off the cap before he could stop me. I twisted around to where he was crouched over me, pulled out the collar of his sweatshirt, and dumped the entire container's worth of glitter inside.

"What?" He actually yelped. "You really just did that? Oh, you're in for it now." I was kind of still pinned under him against the bed, and he started reaching behind me for more supplies. I wiggled as best as I could, but he was so much bigger than me that my efforts were useless. He restrained me with his body while he fiddled to open something. I couldn't imagine what crafty torture it might be, and I kept trying to squirm out from under him before he took his revenge. Suddenly, I felt him pushing something against my forehead.

"What? What did you do?" I was laughing and wriggling and clueless.

Wesley was laughing too, as he pulled back his hand and shouted, "Boo-yah! You've been marked." He held out his hand and showed me what he was holding: a small, square stamper that he had pushed against my forehead.

"You marked me? With what? It better not be a raunchy picture!"

He looked at my forehead with a bit of surprise, appearing almost stricken for a second, and then erupted in a fit of laughter again. "No!" He climbed off me as he surrendered to his guffaws, loudly and with glee. I held my hand against my forehead, but I felt only glitter and a bit of residual wetness from the ink. "No!" He wheezed out the word through his laughs as he said it again, doubling over to rest his hands on his thighs like he couldn't catch his breath.

I shot off the bed and ran to the little rectangular mirror in the corner of the room. I looked at my refection: glitter all over my face, my hair, my ears, and a big blue letter in the middle of my forehead.

"*M?*" I whirled around to face Wesley. "Like, for *Meredith*? Why is that so funny?" I demanded, as I wiped some sparkling flakes away from my eye.

"Um, *M* for . . . *mishap*, or *mistake*? Or *my bad*? I did it so wrong." He laughed at himself. "Total fail. I meant to mark you with a *W* for *Wesley*. Ha. *M* for *mangled manhandling; missed maneuver.*" He was still laughing as I rubbed at the ink, trying to determine how difficult it would be to remove from my face.

"It's not so funny, you know," I griped at him. "I have a friggin' letter in the middle of my face. How about *M* as in *mad*? Or, if you still prefer the letter *W*, I can stand on my head and say *what*, as in *what the fuck*?"

Wesley just laughed harder at my outrage, and I felt my lips twitching despite myself.

"This ink better be washable. I can't walk around with a letter on my forehead, whatever it's for. Can you just . . . can we just find something to get it off, please?"

"Sure," he answered, clamping his lips together, clearly trying to stifle remaining laughter. "Just let me deal with this for a sec." He pulled off his sweatshirt, revealing a fitted white T-shirt underneath. He pulled at the T-shirt a few times, shaking it out, and a shower of glitter fell out from the bottom. Seeing the fruits of my resistance did make me feel a little better. He was definitely going to be finding glitter in all his nooks and crannies for days to follow.

He tossed the sweatshirt onto the bare mattress and then went to the cabinet at the back of the room, where he pulled out a gray washcloth and a large pump full of hand sanitizer.

I became momentarily distracted by the Purell. "That's an awfully large bottle of hand sanitizer. Are you a germophobe?"

"Not even a little," he answered, as he pumped some sanitizer onto the washcloth. "With all the cooking, I've gotten a little compulsive about keeping my hands clean. Plenty dirty everywhere else, though." His cheeks were still flushed from all the laughing. He walked over to me and raised the washcloth to wipe at the letter.

"I can do it," I said, reaching for the cloth.

"I've got it," he answered, pulling his hand back and looking down at me. "But I'm reluctant to get rid of that cute little letter, now that I've thought it through. The *M* kind of works for me." He paused as he stepped a little closer. "*M* as in *mine*." He looked down at me, and suddenly it was as if all the oxygen had vanished from the room and left only a charged energy in its place. "There's only one problem," he said as he moved a strand of my hair off my cheek and pushed it behind my ear.

"What's that?" I looked up at him as the room beyond him began to blur.

"How can I call you mine before I've even kissed you?"

And then his lips were on mine. His face had kind of crashed into me before easing up, like it had come in for a landing where it belonged. I could feel the heat of his full lips against my own, pushing. Then I was opening my mouth, and his tongue was gliding over my bottom lip, into my mouth. As I closed my eyes and breathed him in, I was vaguely aware of glitter falling all around us, as if we were figurines inside our very own snow globe. Wesley overwhelmed my senses as he cupped the back of my head with one hand and used his body to push me backward until I was up against the wall. I could feel the length of him against me, could smell his soap or shampoo, something clean and spicy. As his tongue darted into my mouth over and over, I was glad of the wall behind me to help support me, since my legs didn't seem to be working properly.

He moaned into my mouth, and the gravelly noise thrummed through my entire body. Suddenly, I was too hot; it was too much. I pushed against his chest, and he pulled away from me, surprised.

"What? Are you okay?" His words were breathy.

"Yeah, no. I just . . ." I didn't even know what to say. "It was just more than I expected. The whole thing of it. You just . . ." I stalled, confused by my own reaction.

Wesley waited, one of his hands still resting against the wall beside my head.

"I guess you scare me," I said.

Wesley's eyes opened wide, and he took a big step back from me, as he seemed to struggle for a response.

"No, not like that," I huffed. "Not like I'm afraid for

my safety. This just feels really intense, and I'm not sure if I should be doing intense."

He started to nod slowly, like he was trying to digest what I'd said, to process it. "So, you're scared because it's too good?" he asked, shoving his hands into the pockets of his sweats.

"Yeah, I guess. There's just a lot going on in my life right now, and I'm not sure I have the capacity to handle whatever this is becoming."

"Why sell yourself short before you've even tried? Why not see if I can prove you have greater capacities than you've ever realized?"

I picked up the washcloth from where he had dropped it on the floor while his hands had been all over me. I didn't respond as I turned toward the mirror to start wiping at my forehead and thinking over what he had said. Did I want to do this? I hadn't expected to shut him down, but the size of the feelings he evoked in me were more than I had bargained for. Still, maybe it would be nice to have another person to support me while I dealt with all my family concerns.

"How about," he continued from behind me, "if *M* is for *maybe*? Or you could go back into headstand mode and say *W* is for *why not* . . ." He waited for my response.

The hand sanitizer was working wonders on the ink on my forehead, and I quickly finished wiping off the remnants of the letter. The glitter, on the other hand, looked like it was going to be a long-term project to remove. I wasn't sure how to answer Wesley. I could already tell that if it ever came down to it, removing a guy like him from my soul would turn into a long-term project, too.

Chapter Eight
January 2017

*W*hen Aaron walks into my apartment on Sunday night following his thirty-six-hour shift at the hospital, I decide to tell him that I'm ready to move in together.

"You are?" he asks as he takes off his wool jacket and hangs it on the bright pink coat tree that he and I bought at a SoHo street fair last year. He is justifiably surprised after the extreme resistance I put forth mere days ago. I'm obviously not going to tell him that my new enthusiasm has anything to do with a concerted desire to marginalize Wesley, to make my relationship with Aaron stronger than ever before.

"I called the management company already, and they said I can break my lease with twenty-one days' notice." I'm nearly gloating as I flop down on the couch and sit cross-legged, waiting for him to join me. I am decidedly satisfied with my take-charge approach to solidifying our relationship.

"I'm not sure it's a great idea." His response surprises me. "Hang on."

He disappears into my tiny kitchen, and I hear bottles clinking in the fridge. A moment later, he rematerial-izes with two open bottles of IPA in his hand and makes his way to the coffee table, where he sits down on the wooden surface, facing me.

"A few days ago, you were adamantly opposed." He hands me one of the beers, takes a long sip of his, and continues. "Don't get me wrong, I'd love to share my place with you, but not if a part of you still thinks it's too soon." He takes my free hand and runs his thumb against the glittering princess-cut diamond in my engagement ring. "We have a long future ahead of us, so there's no need to rush."

Yes, there *is* a need to rush. But I can't say that. I can't say that I'm afraid that if I have too much space, I will be thinking about Wesley during all the moments when I should be thinking of Aaron.

"I want to. I don't want you to have to schlep to my apartment after your long shifts downtown anymore. I love the idea of seeing you more. I've given it a lot of thought, and I know what I'm saying, and, quite frankly, I'm getting totally seduced by the thought of your bigger bathroom. I mean, that tub alone . . ." I raise my eyebrows.

Aaron studies me, his dark eyes searching my own, making sure I mean it. He knows I can be impulsive, and I appreciate him for pushing, for verifying that I've thought this through. He leans forward, resting his fore-arms on his knees, as he lets the beer bottle dangle next to his leg. He's taller than Wesley, and broader, naturally muscular, built like the linebacker he once was. I realize that I'm comparing him to Wesley again, like I used to do when we first met, and I give myself a mental demerit for bad behavior. I have to do better. I will.

"How was the soup kitchen?" he asks, changing the subject.

"Ugh." I stand and go to the kitchen to fetch a bowl of grapes, even though I'm not hungry.

"What? I know you used to love that place," he calls from his post on the coffee table. "Is it so different?"

"No, there were just, well . . ." I hear the hiss of the refrigerator seal snapping back into place as I walk back toward the couch, "It was unexpected, but Wesley was there."

"Wesley Latner? *The* Wesley?"

"He started some sort of job training program up there a couple of months ago. We didn't actually see each other, but it seems he is going to be a presence at Community Kitchen for the foreseeable future." I drop onto the denim sofa, leaning back as I prop my feet on Aaron's wide lap.

"You're right—unexpected." Aaron takes another long sip of his beer, and I watch his Adam's apple rise and fall as he swallows. "Must be uncomfortable." He rubs a hand across the back of his neck, like he's the one who's uneasy. "But you can't let him take something from you that you were excited about. It's been a long time, and the awkwardness will dissipate eventually." He's silent for a moment, running his thumb over his bottom lip, and I can tell he has more to say. "Want me to go with you next week?"

"For real?" I ask, totally unsure how to respond.

He shrugs. "I'm not on call. I'm not opposed to spending my Sunday engaged in a charitable endeavor. Especially if you wear tight pants." He grabs one of my feet and squeezes, his hand cold from the beer bottle.

"Sure," I answer, trying to keep my voice from sounding weak. "That would be great." And definitely not awkward. Not awkward at all.

THE NEXT MORNING at work, I'm the first one to set up shop in the conference room. I'm hoping our document review team can get through the remaining boxes by midafternoon, and then I can return to Moe's case file. Aaron couldn't sleep last night, despite having spent one and a half diurnal cycles at the hospital. Sometimes it takes several additional hours before his post-surgery adrenaline rush dwindles sufficiently to allow for solid sleep, so he stayed up, collecting articles for me. I now have a stack of reports on the different escape routes from Myanmar and the cramped conditions in Thai refugee camps. I want to read through these materials today, and I'm also hoping to review the information that the country conditions expert sent about the Burmese militia.

I head back to the seat I occupied on Friday, where a pile of papers eighteen inches high sits on the conference table awaiting me. I start flipping through the muddled collection of documents, which the defendant clearly randomized intentionally. Instead of one organized pile of accounting files, for example, what I have here is a receipt for a networking lunch, followed by two pages of marketing materials, followed by a single page out of the employee handbook, followed by a low-level employee's nearly illegible handwritten driving directions, followed by one page of a tax return. As I turn each useless page, irritated by the defendant's blatant tactics to obfuscate information, I place the reviewed pages facedown, starting another pile next to the first.

My cell phone vibrates from where it's sitting on the table beside my two piles of paper. It's Lana, texting about the bridesmaids' dresses. She's petrified that I'm going to choose a dress for my bridal attendants in a color tone that's too deep for her complexion, or worse, something with an empire waist, which she says makes everyone look slightly pregnant.

I type out a quick response.

Me: Epiphany. Everyone picks her own dress.
Thinking it should just be some shade of silver/gray.
Thoughts?

This is going to be a wedding that leaves everyone content. I won't have the drama this time around. The conference room suddenly feels especially chilly as I think about the importance of keeping this version of my life from spiraling out of control like the last draft did. I will not be a prima donna about this wedding, and I will make sure nobody gets hurt.

My phone buzzes again, and I glance at Lana's response:

Lana: OMG obsessed w u!!!!!!

I smile, imagining her squeal of delight. Lana will surely launch into some intense, multipronged dress hunt now that I've given her personal authority, but that's the kind of mission she loves, so no harm there. I've always had a soft spot for Lana, ever since we were kids and she persuaded me to become blood sisters. I shudder now, thinking about all the germs that must have passed between our grubby hands that summer afternoon in my backyard. But Lana is absolutely pulling her weight as both my bridal attendant and my friend. I don't have a maid of honor this time. Shara, Noble's wife, has become so devout in her observance of Judaism over the last few years that she would be uncomfortable with many of the mainstream wedding activities, like raunchy bachelorette parties. Even so, I didn't want to hurt her feelings by asking Lana in her place. So, instead, I've asked no one. Lana gets it, and she has taken it upon herself to perform as the acting maid of honor anyway.

I flip the next page in my pile and find a shelving schematic that appears to be a diagram for how the chewing tobacco will be laid out in a 7-Eleven store. I pause to study it, as the crux of our client's claim is that the defendant unfairly commandeered all the most desirable shelving space at the relevant retail locations. The page looks pretty standard—unfortunately, not any sort of smoking gun—so I add it to my growing pile and flip to the next page.

Liam McIntire walks in, followed by Darren Pool. These two guys have become my closest friends at the firm, in light of the many hours we've been forced to sit in the conference room together, enduring endless eyestrain and mind-numbing documents.

"I'm trying Atkins again," Liam announces without preamble as he takes his seat opposite me at the glass conference table.

"Cutting out scotch?" Darren asks as he adjusts his Clark Kent glasses and then grabs a full box of documents for himself from the stack against the back wall. All we seem to talk about in this room is alcohol and diets.

If we get into any deeper conversations, it's hard to focus on the documents in front of us, but without the small talk, the dreary routine of this discovery project can be crushing.

"I'm trying to avoid the paunch." Liam rubs his belly, which is admittedly rounder than it was when I first met him a few months back, after our different law firms merged. "All these weddings, the cocktail hours—what's a man to do? At least Meredith has the good grace to wait until next winter to have her wedding. I should be in tip-top shape by then."

Yeah, you and me both, Liam, I think. He's got eleven months to drop some pounds. I've got eleven months to drop some baggage. Baggage named Wesley.

Liam and Darren banter back and forth, trading lighthearted insults about each other's waistlines. As I continue flipping pages, I find another schematic for shelving like the one I saw moments ago, but this one is covered in handwritten notes. I pause to read them over, and they seem pretty innocuous, listing which subgroups of tobacco products the sales rep wants shelved in that particular store. But the note scribbled across the bottom stops me. "Continue with category management plan to eliminate competitive products," it says. "Control facings and positions to make our placement larger and force out competition."

I think I've found our smoking gun, and I realize, with a horrifying thud, that I don't really care, at all. This is what I slaved away for in college? Making sure I could get into an elite law school, to secure a job at a top firm, to find a piece of paper that shows one cancer-causing company treating another cancer-causing company unfairly?

"Eureka," I say, as I stand with the document in my hand, failing to muster the enthusiasm I was going for. I hear Aaron's voice in my head telling me that I should look for a different job, and I actually begin to wonder if he is right. I can still be an independent woman on a lower salary, especially considering how well I've been saving since I started at the firm two years ago.

Liam and Darren are both out of their seats, reading over my shoulder, and my mind is still running wild. I remember how I once thought about working at the Anti-Defamation League or some other nonprofit, like a shelter for battered women or a foster-care facility. If I could get through these documents a little more quickly, I could get back to my asylum case, and then maybe I could even take a little time to research alternate employment.

"Okay, you two," I say as I notice they are fist-bumping in a show of joy about this document I've discovered. Clearly, this job is bringing them more satisfaction than it is me. "We still have all those boxes." I realize I'm whining. "I can't spend more weeks in here, so let's keep going."

Five hours later, I finally turn over the last page in my pile of papers. The two first-year associates who are supposed to be reviewing along with us never showed, and I'm wondering how they managed to weasel their way out of joining today's tedious soiree. Even so, between the three of us in the conference room, we have found another eleven documents that show a clear pattern of antitrust law violations and patently prohibited behavior by the defendant. I'm disgusted that the other party thought to delay providing these documents for discovery, perhaps hoping we would lose our patience reviewing everything and never seek their production. This whole sphere of legal practice feels foul to me, and I want out.

I've never been so envious of Aaron's job as a pediatric surgeon. While I further the questionable intentions of faceless corporations, he gets to mend the brains of helpless infants.

As if my thoughts have conjured him, my phone rings. "Hey," I answer, leaning back in my chair and surveying the many piles of documents on the table that now need to be returned to file boxes.

"Want to head out to Jersey tonight for a couple of hours?" he asks. "I got your mom those supplements, and we could take your parents to dinner at Herby's."

Even though my mom has been cancer free for more than eight years, Aaron knows she worries excessively about a recurrence. He helps her find all these holistic remedies that may or may not have a positive impact on her physical health, but they won't hurt her, and they certainly help her emotionally.

"Sure," I answer, already tensing up at the thought of dinner with my parents. I love them dearly, but we've never really gotten past all the garbage from when I was in college, when they were going to get divorced but didn't, when my mom almost died but didn't, when I almost married Wesley but didn't. It's like all we can think of when we're together is the collective trauma we endured. The only time I manage to be relaxed around them is when Aaron is with us, talking loudly and running interference. He manages to keep everything lighthearted and positive. He has made a sustained effort to drive my parents and me back to a better place, and the truth is, I think it's working. It's just slow going.

"Great. I'll call and let them know. Text me when you know your timing, and I'll pick you up."

After we hang up, I feel all warm inside, the way I so often do around Aaron, like I've just finished a steaming bowl of wonton soup. Instead of focusing on the nasty bits of my career, the ashy taste they leave in my mouth, I am filled with gratitude for my fiancé, and then with a nagging guilt about all the time I've spent recently thinking of Wesley. It will be useful, I tell myself again, to get myself back to the soup kitchen regularly and determine that Wesley is not the white knight I've made him out to be. There is more to life than the vibrancy and passion of the relationship I had with him, and I'm just going to keep telling myself that until I start believing it. I know better than to squander a man like Aaron on useless nostalgia. Don't I?

A FEW HOURS later, Aaron, my mom, my dad, and I are sitting at a round, cloth-covered table at Herby's, my parents' favorite neighborhood Italian spot. Even if Aaron and I weren't present, my parents, who are in their late fifties, would bring down the average age of the patrons here by about twenty years, but they love the old-fashioned ambience for some reason I can't understand, and Aaron loves the gnocchi, so here we are.

"How's that preemie with coarctation of the aorta?" my mom asks Aaron. Ever since recovering from her cancer, she has become somewhat obsessed with medicine. She knows all about these random conditions that have nothing to do with anything that has ever happened in her own life. Accordingly, she often goes all fangirl on Aaron, lapping up details of the surgeries he has performed. He's more tolerant than I would be and tends to put up with her questions until he can redirect the conversation.

"One of the cutest babies I've ever treated," Aaron answers as the waiter shows up with my penne à la vodka—so fattening, but impossible to resist at this establishment. "His mom is Samoan and his dad is half black, half Swedish. Man, does that combination make for a cute kid." He refills my wineglass from the bottle of chianti on our table.

"But what about the angioplasty? Did it take?"

"He seems to be doing fine now," Aaron says. I can tell he's being deliberately vague.

"Leave him be, Karen," my dad directs her as he takes the little toothpick full of olives from his martini glass and places it on her bread plate. "You know he's not allowed to divulge the details."

"Thanks," she says as she picks up the skewered olives. She sucks one off the toothpick before adding blithely, "Yeah, yeah, but you can't blame a girl for trying."

I hate it when my mom and dad start with this breezy banter. I still haven't managed to get past my father's shittiness before my mom's illness. Maybe if they had clued me in to what was actually going on in their relationship, I wouldn't have spent a year hating my dad for apparent abandonment of my mother during her time of need. What in fact happened was that my mom's illness made my father realize how important she was to him. The cancer apparently saved their marriage. They reconciled almost immediately after my mother's diagnosis, but they made the asinine decision not to tell me. They thought it would be too difficult for me if my mom didn't make it, knowing how much I had lost. So, instead of telling me that my father's interest in the woman he'd met during our cruise vacation had evaporated, or that my mother had pardoned my dad's philandering, they allowed me to remain submerged in anger. They let me seize on my fury toward my father as some sort of lifeline, like it might keep me going during my mom's treatment. Practically speaking, I've forgiven him, or them, but the intense anger and betrayal I felt for so many months is hard to forget. Looking at them, all cutesy with each other now, so many years later, still has me feeling all twitchy.

"So, I got a call from Mary at the catering company," my mom starts, changing the subject. "She said she has a band and florist all lined up and that she's sure we'll be delighted with both of them."

"That's a relief," I say, speaking into my penne as I push it around with my fork. My mind has gone off in another direction and, against my better judgment, I ask, "Did Aaron tell you who we ran into last week?"

"No, but maybe if you called us half as often as your handsome fiancé does, you could have told us yourself." My mom looks at Aaron and adds, "You wouldn't know it from the way she behaves now, but she used to call me every day, often multiple times a day." She relays this tidbit for the billionth time as she pushes her tortoiseshell glasses up on her nose.

"Mom." It's a command. I've told her over and again that I work long hours and my life no longer allows for random phone calls where we do little more than catalog our activities for the day and listen to each other breathe. And, like I said, a lot has gone down over the past few years, and sometimes talking to my mother requires me to rehash too many painful memories.

"Okay, sorry," she relents as she reaches her manicured fingers toward the next olive on the toothpick.

"Who'd you run into?" My dad tries to get us back on track.

Aaron takes over, responding before me. "Remember I told you Lana and Reese were taking us out for our engagement?"

"Yeah." My mom nods at him, her high cheekbones more pronounced as she sucks on the olive in her mouth. I'm now anticipating the many potential pitfalls of this conversation and wishing I could withdraw my last question. I shouldn't have brought it up in the first place.

"Turns out the swanky hot spot they took us to is owned and operated by none other than Meredith's ex. It's a lucky thing I'm a confident guy, because that man cooks some damn good food."

The penne in my stomach turns to rotting clay. I drag my eyes away from Aaron and reluctantly meet my mother's gaze. All the color has drained from her face.

"He's back?" she asks.

"He's back," I respond, trying to keep it light in front of Aaron. "I'm glad for him," I say casually. "It's nice to see someone achieve their dream, especially when I spend my own days slaving away for cash instead of ideals." I'm hoping this statement will get us off the topic of Wesley. My parents love to discuss career goals with me. Since we can no longer talk about my academic pursuits, my professional trajectory is the next best thing.

"I don't understand why you don't apply for a clerkship with a judge," my mom says, taking the bait and rehashing a conversation we've had a million times.

"I told you, it won't solve anything. It's a great job, but it's only a one-year appointment, and at the end of that year I'll be right back to wondering what to do with myself. It's fine. I'm good at the firm. The pay is right, and the pro bono case is exciting and worthwhile. If I do a good job, I can get more pro bono work. It's all good."

"I think Meredith should go into public interest law," Aaron tells them. "I keep saying it, and she keeps ignoring me." He winks at me, and I know he's just playing.

Even so, I, too, am a bait-taker. "Well, I just don't think it's fair that I have to take a pay cut if I want to do something more meaningful." I realize I'm pointing my fork at him and put it back in my bowl as I continue. "You get to do critical work, life-changing work, and then laugh all the way to the bank." Turning toward my dad, whose dark eyes are fixated on his tuna steak, I say, "You guys should have told me to go to med school." I make a mock mean face just for effect.

"You're a germophobe." My dad.

"And you hate blood." My mom.

"And biology." My dad.

"And needles." My mom.

"Whatever." And just like that, I'm a teenager again. Aaron's presence has somehow worked its usual magic, and I'm relating to my parents like I used to, like we didn't have an acute period of harrowing events a few years ago that drove a wedge between us all.

I look over at Aaron with appreciative eyes. The smattering of freckles across his nose gives him a boyish appearance that makes him seem free-minded, nonchalant. But I'm certain he knows exactly what he's doing. He didn't waltz into Dartmouth on football skills alone. That man has a hustler's brain; he's always thinking. And right now, he is using his sweet grin and strategically placed comments to help bring my parents and me back together.

The conversation turns to the pros and cons of different career choices and what each of us dreamed of being when we were young children (professional break-dancer, veterinarian, airline pilot). It's jaunty and pleasant, but I can feel my mom's eyes on me all through the meal, and I know what she's thinking. She wants to talk about Wesley, see how his return has affected me, ask why I didn't mention it to her sooner. Mainly, I think she wants to know if I'm all right. Or maybe she wants to know if Wesley's homecoming is going to cost her the soon-to-be son-in-law to whom she's so attached.

Chapter Nine
December 2012

*A*s I waited for Wesley at the café on Eighth Street, scribbling notes in the margins of my criminal procedure textbook, I felt relieved to be three-quarters of the way finished with my fall semester finals. The second year of law school had been less daunting than that awful first year, when I had been sure I would fail out, but I was still neurotic about my grades, and my nerves were accordingly frayed. Even so, I had it better than Wesley, who had lost nearly all the money he'd saved for culinary school thanks to some questionable investments and the recession of 2008. He was working as a line cook in a swanky restaurant in Gramercy Park now, saving a new pile of cash and accumulating more back-of-the-house hours.

I picked up my mocha latte and watched my engagement ring sparkle in the winter light. The massive yellow diamond had belonged to Wesley's great-grandmother Florence, and his parents had insisted that we use it. Truth be told, I wasn't much into the yellow, teardrop-shaped stone, but I knew it was valuable, both emotionally and financially, so I tried to enjoy it in the spirit in which it had been intended.

The door opened and I felt a burst of cold air as

Wesley walked in, pulling his knit wool cap off his head. His cheeks were pink from the frigid air outside, and snow had dusted the shoulders of his dark gray peacoat.

"Hey, weasel," he said, as he gave me a perfunctory kiss on the cheek. "It's mad cold out there." He took off his coat and draped it on the back of a chair. "I'm going to grab a hot chocolate. I can't believe we're going to have a wedding when it's so cold out. We should have hopped on a plane to St. Barts or something. Hell, even Vegas would've beaten this."

"Are you really going to start now? After everything?" I asked, gearing up for yet another battle about the wedding. Wesley had more or less been on my side as we'd brokered the details with our families. We'd chosen a date in early January so I would be between semesters in law school, and also because winter was the only time of year during which my Orthodox Jewish brother and sister-in-law would be able to attend. Noble and Shara didn't drive on Shabbat, but once the sun set on Saturday evenings, they were free to use technology again. The early sunsets in January meant they would be able to attend a party that started at 7:00 p.m. In the warmer months of longer light, that would never have been a possibility.

Wesley's parents had resisted the idea of a winter wedding, arguing about potential snowstorms and road closures. They ultimately revealed that their reluctance stemmed from a desire to host the affair in their backyard, which wouldn't be possible during the winter. Of course, my parents couldn't abide the idea of the groom's parents' hosting their daughter's wedding, regardless of the season. They traded comments that only provoked both families further. Wesley's parents had even threatened not to attend at one point. Somehow, Wesley had worn them down, and eventually, we had all agreed on a January date. Except now Wesley was bringing it up again.

"No, I'm not saying that," he replied, as he took his wallet out of his messenger bag. "I'm just cold. Your parents have been through so much over the past few years, it's understandable that they might still behave irrationally sometimes, almost like they have a little PTSD." He shrugged, like he was talking about strangers.

"PTSD?" I blanched at his flip attitude. "Since when was this about my parents being irrational? I thought you agreed that the wedding should be in the winter." I didn't bother to hide my irritation as my mind starting spinning with logistical questions, running scenarios about new dates and other options, but then I thought of the scalding disputes we had all suffered through already, and I prepared to dig in my heels.

"No." He shook his head, as though he had never taken a side. "I just agreed that the constant arguing was tiresome."

I opened my mouth, ready to lay into him for this disavowal, but Wesley held up a finger to pause the conversation and walked off to place an order with the barista. I rolled my eyes, annoyed at him for hightailing it out of this discussion as soon as it became adversarial. Even so, when he returned to the table a couple of minutes later, a steaming mug of hot chocolate nestled between his hands, I decided to take a page out of his book and dodge the conflict. The wedding plans were already set, continuing to bicker wouldn't achieve anything.

"Have you heard from your parents? Did they land

yet?" I asked, changing the subject, as Wesley licked at the whipped cream topping his drink.

"Nah," he answered, plunking down into the seat opposite me. "I guess the whole point was to get away from everything—de-stress from all the tension of the wedding planning, the arguing. I'm going to give them their space so they can get forget about the travesty of having to participate in a kosher wedding."

And there was that. Wesley's parents had insisted on splitting the cost of the wedding with my parents as a condition of relenting about the date. It was a lovely gesture—until the bills started coming in and everyone began fighting about how to allocate the wedding dollars. Serving kosher food cost too much, the Latners complained, but they seemed to think my mother was cheaping out by hiring a ten-piece band instead of sixteen. Sixteen! Weren't we going to hire valet parking attendants, they wanted to know. What about a person to staff the coat room? My mother wanted orchids in the centerpieces; Wesley's wanted tiered candles. Our parents did finally reach compromises on the myriad decisions, but apparently all the squabbling was just too much. Wesley's parents had decided they needed to take an extravagant vacation in order to put the stress behind them and rest up for the big day.

"Oh, here." Wesley seemed to have remembered something, as he started fishing through his pocket. "I saw it on my way to work this morning and thought you absolutely needed to have it." He pulled out a brown paper bag, inside of which was a petite bundle of brown paper that looked to be folded around a very small, egg-shaped item. As he unwrapped the item, it materialized as a necklace with a tiny snow globe charm hanging from it.

"Wesley!" I gushed, feeling my cheeks flush with pleasure at his persistence in spoiling me. "You should not be spending your hard-earned money on me when you still have so much to save up," I admonished him, even as I reached for the necklace.

It was cool against my hand, still chilled from the air outside. As I peered more closely at the charm, I saw mini plastic figures inside, a tiny bride and groom kissing in the middle of the snowy world.

"It's kind of garbage," Wesley hedged, "but with your collection and all . . ." He shrugged sheepishly, as if he was now embarrassed by the romantic gesture.

"I will always feel like I'm living inside my own personal snow globe with you—nothing but the two of us in the world, inside a bubble of perfection," I told him.

I didn't think much at the moment about how the coating of the bubble I envisioned was made of glass, so easily broken.

IT WAS ONLY three hours later when Wesley got a call from the airline. We were snuggling on the denim couch in my compact studio apartment, watching the *21 Jump Street* movie, which we had already seen in the theater earlier that year. Wesley's cell rang, and he didn't even answer the first time.

"Don't they know I'm hanging with my girl?" He wrapped his arm more tightly around me as he silenced his cell with his other hand.

When the phone started vibrating again a minute later, I paused the movie. "You should see who wants to talk to you so badly. It's fine."

He took the phone from his pocket and shrugged at it, like he didn't recognize the number.

"This is Wesley," he said into the phone as he lifted the bottle of wine that was on the coffee table and started refilling our glasses. I took the opportunity to prance to the kitchen for the box of red velvet cupcakes Wesley had made the week before, which I had stashed in my freezer. I was thinking that the cold temperature should have made those cupcakes easier to resist, muted their flavor, when I heard glass shatter.

I dashed back out of the kitchen and saw Wesley standing on the blond parquet floors in the center of a pool of red wine and broken glass, seemingly frozen, the phone to his ear and his face gone gray.

I stared at him, afraid.

"Okay," he said into the phone, in a voice I hardly recognized. "Okay."

He touched a button to end the call and then stared at the device in his hand while I waited and my dread mounted.

After a few seconds, he sank back onto the couch behind him, an expression of utter confusion taking hold of his features.

"What?" I finally asked in a near whisper. "What happened?"

"The plane crashed." He spoke like he didn't understand his own words. "Into the water. They're dead."

"What? Wait, what? Oh my God!"

He dropped his head into his hands and I stood there, mute, not knowing what to do.

When he finally raised his eyes to look back up at me, they were filled with hate.

Chapter Ten
December 2012

*A*t the funeral three days later, we had still barely spoken, even though I had been by his side the entire time. Wesley seemed to be channeling his grief into a take-charge approach. His first phone call had been to the family attorney, as he sought to determine how his mother and father wanted their affairs settled. Suddenly, the corporate executive inside him, the part of himself that he had always resisted, had emerged in full force. From funeral arrangements to the distribution of testamentary funds, he was fixated on discharging his obligations as the surviving son with flying colors, as though he was paying tribute to his parents by becoming the type of man they had always wanted him to be.

Wesley was an only child, and his two aunts and one uncle were much older, leaving him basically family-less as he dealt with this situation on his own. There was only me, and, for reasons I couldn't understand, Wesley could barely look at me.

As we drove back from the cemetery to his parents' house in Irvington, I wondered how he was going to get through the whole week of shiva. Friends and relatives were going to be visiting the family home for seven full days following the funeral in order to pay their respects. I had packed Wesley a bag of clothes from his apartment to use for the week at his parents', and my mother had jumped in to help out with the food, ordering platters of bagels and lox, cookies, and mini egg rolls to serve during the endless rotation of company that was about to begin.

I wasn't sure how long to wait to bring up the wedding. Obviously, we weren't going to be having a three-hundred-person celebration in three weeks. I wondered if we should just do one of those justice-of-the-peace ceremonies and get it done or wait until Wesley wasn't so consumed by his grief. As I looked over at him in the limo that was carrying us back to the house from the funeral, the wedding seemed like the furthest thing from his mind. In fact, it seemed he could barely stomach sitting in the same car as me.

"My mom is waiting back at the house," I told him delicately, looking at the text she had just sent me. "Some of your dad's business people are already there, she said."

"Yup," he answered, looking out the window, the muscles of his jaw working while he stared at the bare trees along the road, possibly seeing nothing at all.

Maybe I should have been more patient. Not maybe. I definitely should have been more patient. Still, as I picked at the plastic label of an unopened tissue box resting between us, I couldn't stop myself from asking, "Is there something I should be doing that I'm not? I just feel like this is more than grief, like you're angry at me . . ."

"Jesus, Meredith. Not everything is about *you*, okay?" he snapped.

"Wow, okay. Sorry." I forced myself not to get defensive. Wesley should have a free pass for just about anything right now.

Suddenly, his eyes shot to mine. It was the first time since hearing the news about his parents that he seemed to actually be looking at me, seeing me.

"Fine," he nearly shouted, his face abruptly flushed. "You want to know what it is? It was your mother who was supposed to die! Not mine! Your family that was supposed to fall apart! Not fucking mine!"

I jerked back as if he'd slapped me. Whoa. Maybe not a free pass for that, though.

"Hold on," I said gently, like I was trying to calm a spooked horse. "None of this was supposed to happen—that's true."

"No shit, this wasn't supposed to happen," he spat back.

I tried to think how to respond, but he kept going.

"And maybe, just maybe, Meredith, if you and your perfect parents hadn't been so high maintenance, so fucking stuck up about our stupid wedding, then my parents wouldn't have gone on that trip, wouldn't have needed to de-stress from the strain that you Altmans put on them with all your fucking demands. Did you think about that? Did you ever fucking think at all?"

I looked back at Wesley, stunned. I didn't know this man. I didn't know what to say or how to react. So I was silent.

The car was pulling up in front of his parents' semi-circular driveway before I had a chance to respond.

"Look," he said, a little more gently, but not contrite, "I just can't do this right now. I need some space. I can't keep looking at you and thinking about all the things that should have been different. Can you just go? That's what I need right now, for you to just give me some breathing room. Okay?"

Maybe I should have argued, refused to leave his side during that time, but I couldn't fathom how he could possibly be blaming those deaths on me, or on my parents. I didn't want to be around a man who would act out at me like that, not even when he had such extreme grief as an excuse. So, instead, I did what he asked. I left.

Chapter Eleven
February 2017

*I*t's a frosty gray morning as Aaron and I walk up Broadway toward Community Kitchen, and I find myself babbling, filling him in on all the minute details of my college life. I point out the little copy center where I used to buy printer paper on the cheap, then the place where Daphne and I ate lunch together nearly every day for the first month of freshman year, then the bodega where Bina and I shared hangover-curing tuna melts on Sunday mornings.

"Not mornings," I correct myself. "It was probably well into the afternoon by the time we meandered out of our dorm."

"Tuna melts for a hangover?" Aaron glances at me sideways as we cross 115th Street. "Kinda nasty, no?"

"Don't knock it till you try it." I laugh, trying too hard to keep everything casual and light. I don't want him to know how nervous I am, how fixated I've been on the idea of running into Wesley.

I made a supreme effort this morning to seem as blasé about this winter Sunday as I would be about any other. I forced myself to leave my hair alone, letting the blond strands fall haphazardly in waves around my shoulders instead of straightening them with a curling iron like I would for a night out. I threw on a solid navy long-sleeved shirt over a basic pair of skinny jeans. My makeup is subtle, only pale eye shadow and light pink gloss. It just so happens that the jeans are my favorite, best ass-hugging pair, and I know that Wesley always loved my hair wavy, but I'm not going to dwell on those facts right now.

"It's right up there," I say, pointing toward the church, where, again, a line of people is beginning to snake around the side of the building.

"You weren't kidding about this being a hot ticket." Aaron surveys the diverse crowd, people of all shapes and sizes waiting in puffer jackets and sweatshirts alongside the wrought-iron fence that encircles the old brick building. His eyes linger on a group of children dashing about, zigzagging around adults who stand restlessly, seemingly unaware of the obstacle course their impatient limbs provide. While the older people bide their time, various shades of boredom and expectation coloring their faces, the children bob and weave as though they are at a playground.

"We go this way." I grab for Aaron's hand, and his eyes slide away from the children. We walk in the opposite direction, toward a fireproof metal door that leads to the kitchen. When we step into the warm air, the scent of tomato sauce and beans immediately greets us, Katie Sue seems surprised to see me again, as though my visit last week had been a one-off that I was unlikely to repeat. I introduce Aaron, who seems suddenly to be all Katie Sue can see.

"Look at you"—she pokes at my ribs in a gesture of pride—"engaged to a handsome doctor," though she pronounces it "doctah" and I'm unsure whether she's making a joke or if Aaron has her so flustered that she's forgotten to mind her Queens accent. She rests a hand on his arm, and I swear she wants to squeeze his bicep. "You sure know how to pick 'em."

She says this lightly, but my eyes dart to Aaron's, worried he will be offended by the reference, by the fact that Katie Sue has lumped him into some amorphous group with the other fiancé I once had.

Aaron's focus is elsewhere, though, his eyes roving around the kitchen, moving from the two older women in back who are silently chopping vegetables to the heavy-set man stirring a vat of dark liquid on the stove.

"So, what's my job, Katie Sue? Where am I most useful?" he asks just as a wiry Asian man walks into the kitchen from the gymnasium.

"Garth could use some help with setup," she answers, gesturing toward the slender man who's just appeared. I met Garth last week and learned only after serving soggy vegetables alongside him for two hours that he's the new priest at this parish. "Garth, show this strapping young man what to do out there," Katie Sue directs.

A flush creeps subtly onto Aaron's cheeks as he seems to finally notice Katie Sue's fawning. He sends me a look of helpless surprise before following Garth back out the door.

I pull a worn apron off the hook by the swinging door and slip it over my head, reaching behind myself to tie the straps.

"Women are going to try to steal that one from you."

Katie Sue motions with her head in the direction Aaron walked, smiling proudly, as she carries a covered aluminum tray toward the oven.

"Yeah, he's a keeper." I try to sound nonchalant even as I glance toward the door, wondering when Wesley might walk in, if he is even here this week.

"Wesley is teaching his class down the hall again today," she tells me, as though I've spoken my thoughts aloud. She removes three bags of celery stalks from a cardboard box on the counter and pushes them in my direction. "You two have a chance to catch up last week?" She asks the question lightly, but there's nothing light about the twisty, convoluted path Wesley and I have followed. Katie Sue always seemed to know what was going on in my head even before I met Wesley, when I was first dealing with my mom's illness and all that detritus. She could see things that other people never detected.

"Nah," I answer, moving over to the industrial sink to hose down the celery, pulling the stalks apart and letting the water rinse off lingering soil. "He took off pretty quickly last week. It's fine, though. It's been a while."

"He's got some stuff going on these days," she says. "You guys should talk." She picks up a large coffee urn and lumbers with it out toward the gymnasium, leaving me to wonder what her comments mean.

AN HOUR AND forty-five minutes later, the food is prepped and the leftovers from Wesley's restaurant are again waiting on the table on the other side of the room. I pull Aaron from where he has been listening to another volunteer, an older woman named Marlene, as she complains about her nursing job at Montefiore. He is giving her suggestions about how to stand up to the doctors who she seems to believe are taking advantage of her.

"What about the nurses taking advantage of kind young doctors?" I whisper as I pull him away to help me staff the lasagna station. I explain on the way over about how we aren't supposed to give anyone seconds until everyone in the line has had their first serving.

"Except kids, right?" he asks.

I shake my head, remembering the first time I had to internalize that bit of soup kitchen procedure. Telling a malnourished six-year-old that she can't have a second slice of bread feels almost impossible when you yourself have grown up with the luxury of a perpetually full belly.

Aaron starts to say something, but Katie Sue announces that she is opening the doors. Within seconds, Aaron and I are both busy ladling out green beans and lasagna, engaging in small talk with women and men of varying ages and nationalities as they make their way down the line.

A few minutes into the food service, I catch a certain movement by the door at the far side of the gym and I know he's here. I glance up casually, somehow certain that I will see Wesley entering the room. When my eyes find him, the first thing I notice is that he is wearing a gray Henley shirt, and I am hit by a mystifying wave of gratitude. He still favors Henleys—something is still the same. He is carrying a black bag that looks almost like it contains a machine gun, but I know it's a carrying case for his knives. Maybe he had been teaching knife skills in class today. As he walks farther into the gym, his eyes scan the room, as though he is looking for something. For someone. My eyes dart to Aaron, who is slicing additional rows of the enormous lasagna, and then back to Wesley. His head finally turns, and his eyes settle on me. A current of electricity passes between us, undeniable, even across the length of the gym. My breath catches, and he is all I can see as he stops walking and just looks back at me.

"Okay, hand me that spatula," Aaron says, reaching out for it.

The spell is broken. I pass Aaron the tool, and when I look back at Wesley, he, too, is looking at Aaron. His eyes shift back to me, and he tips his chin up in a light greeting before making his way toward the kitchen.

For the remainder of the meal, I stand beside Aaron, serving beans and glancing at the kitchen door, waiting to see Wesley emerge. The minutes pass, but he doesn't come back out. As the final trays are emptied, Katie Sue directs us to start cleaning up, and I determine that Wesley must have left again, just like last week. I try to squelch the disappointment I feel as I remind myself that if I want to continue coming to this soup kitchen, I need to get used to this, to simply seeing Wesley in passing. Maybe we'll talk one day, and maybe we won't. I have to learn not to care.

The other volunteers are collecting the large aluminum trays that had held the food, and I follow their lead. A few patrons still linger at the long rectangular tables in the gym, savoring their meals, putting off their return to the cold winter air outside. As we finish clearing, Garth and Aaron begin folding down the table legs and carrying the tables to the storeroom at the back of the gym.

I walk my large platters into the kitchen, using my

elbow to push open the swinging door. I scan the kitchen for Wesley in spite of myself and find myself disappointed yet again. Marlene the nurse and another woman are at the large sink basins, hosing down the greasy trays, and I make my way toward them with my stack.

The door to the street opens, and then Wesley is there, carrying a cardboard box. He doesn't notice me as he makes his way toward the back of the kitchen and puts his box down next to a hulking turkey breast. He doesn't hear my heart pounding in my chest. Judging by the bags of bread protruding from the box he was carrying, I deduce that he is going to be making sandwiches. He doesn't look up as he puts on latex gloves and begins slicing the turkey breast, so I take the opportunity to study his profile.

For the most part, he looks the same, just older. A little thinner than he was a few years ago, I think. His golden hair is still cut close to his head, flipped up at the front just enough to make you wonder if there's gel holding it in place. I see that he still wears his grandfather's gold necklace with the Jewish star. It dangles loosely from his neck as he leans over the turkey, slicing mechanically, over and over.

He must feel my eyes on him because he looks up and our gazes connect again. I see no option but to walk over.

"Hey," I say as I approach.

"Hey," he responds, putting his knife down on the counter. He opens and closes the fist that was holding it, wincing just a little as he does. I can't tell whether it's the hand or my presence that's causing him pain.

"Katie Sue told me about the program you started. It sounds amazing. Really great." Now I want to wince, annoyed by how stilted I sound, how awkward I'm making this.

"Yeah, thanks," he says, reticent as he regards me.

"And the restaurant," I add, trying to be upbeat. "I'm so happy everything worked out for you."

"Not everything," he says, looking down at me. He moves his hand off the counter, and for a split second I think he's reaching out for me, but he just starts clenching and unclenching his fist again, like it's stiff and he's doing some sort of exercise.

"Hey." Aaron's voice is strong as he approaches from behind me. I didn't even hear the door to the kitchen open, and I'd be lying if I said I don't feel like I've been busted. Aaron wraps an arm around my waist possessively, and I resist the urge to shrug him off, to step closer to Wesley.

"You remember Wesley from the restaurant, right?" I ask Aaron, amazed that I am able to sound so calm, gracious, even.

"Of course," Aaron says. He starts reaching out to shake hands but then notices Wesley's rubber gloves and puts his hand back on me. "Mer told me about the workplace-readiness program. It sounds really terrific."

"Thanks," Wesley says. "It's been good." His eyes rove over Aaron, and I can see he's sizing him up—the oversize muscles, the chiseled jaw. I feel proud for a moment to let Wesley see the man who has chosen me, chosen to stay with me—an athlete, a doctor. But then I feel petty, ashamed to have reduced my current fiancé to bullet points.

"I'll let you guys catch up," Aaron says. "Katie Sue seems to have sixteen more tasks for me out there." He squeezes my arm lightly as he gives Wesley a little nod and turns back toward the gym.

"Katie Sue said you have a lot going on. She seemed to think you might want to tell me about it . . ." I remember what she said earlier and hope I haven't overstepped.

A look of anger flashes across Wesley's face, but it's gone so quickly, I'm not sure I read it right.

"Or not," I add. "I was just taking my cues from her, but you . . . whatever." I don't know how to interact with this quiet, subdued version of Wesley. I know him as boisterous and energetic. This guy just seems watchful and sad, the way he was after his parents died and for the last few days of our relationship. I wonder if he's been like this the whole time we've been apart. It hurts my heart to even consider that possibility. All this time, I've pictured Wesley shining his light in other places, on other ideas, other women. Never have I considered the possibility that he hasn't been shining his light at all.

"No, I do. It's just"—he looks around the kitchen, like he doesn't want anyone else to hear—"there's been a lot of pity lately, which I don't need, so don't go there when I tell you, okay?"

"O . . . kay . . ." I say it slowly, wondering what direction we are headed in.

"No, I know how you get, but this isn't your problem to solve, okay?"

"Okay," I say again, "but what is it? You're making me nervous." Although now that he's actually talking to me, I feel like I'm finding solid ground.

"I have ALS." He glances around the kitchen, as if to confirm that no one else has heard, and then looks back down at me.

I feel myself blinking rapidly in confusion. "You . . . Wait, you what?"

"I was diagnosed a few months ago. I only just told Katie Sue recently, so I guess she's still processing." His voice contains mild dismay, but he sounds only casually annoyed, too relaxed for what I think he's trying to tell me.

"ALS? You don't mean . . . not like Lou Gehrig's disease?" I look at him from head to toe, now feeling free to study him openly. I regard him as if he can't possibly be correct in what he's declared.

"Yeah, no, exactly like Lou Gehrig's disease." He picks up the knife and starts slicing turkey again, like there's nothing more to discuss.

I don't know a ton about the disease, but I've seen that movie about Stephen Hawking, and there is definitely, definitely more to say.

"But you can live a long time with that now, right?"

I see a fondness creep into Wesley's features for the first time since before we broke up. The hard green shell is cracked, and there's a warmth in the lines beside his eyes.

"You're thinking of the Stephen Hawking movie."

And now I remember that I wanted to see that movie when it first came out, just a month or two before Wesley and I fell apart. We never actually made it, and I watched it on my own months later. I don't answer as I continue trying to process what he's telling me.

"It's started progressing for me already. I am not the next Stephen Hawking," he tells me gently, as though it's going to be roughest for me. And maybe he's right. Maybe it is. Maybe, even though I've been planning to marry

Aaron, I always thought the future might hold something for Wesley and me at some point. And even after this blow, here I am, wondering if somehow it still can.

"So, what are you saying?" I ask, not caring that I'm starting to sound a little angry, accusatory. "Are you telling me that you're dying?"

"Yeah, pretty much." He says it so matter-of-factly that I feel like I've been slapped.

"I don't understand," I argue. "How? Aren't you too young?"

He shrugs and puts the knife down on the counter, clenching his fist again.

"Is that what's going on with your hand?" I ask as I watch him. "It hurts?"

"No." He shakes his head. "No pain. Just weak."

"So, what is the prognosis? How long do you have?" I ask, trying to speak more gently as I think about his restaurant, which is still brand-new, and his whole life, which he's only just brought back to New York.

"No one knows. Average is two to five years. Maybe longer since I'm young to be diagnosed. Maybe shorter because I've been ignoring symptoms for years."

Years. My brain is working overtime. Did I see signs? I have a flash, a memory from the morning of his parents' funeral, how he fumbled over and over again while buttoning his shirt. I thought it was grief at the time. Maybe it was.

I step forward to hug him but stop myself when I remember we are basically strangers now. I wonder if he is still the man I knew at all.

"I'm so sorry, Wes," I say, nearly whispering, as a harsh pressure builds behind my eyes.

"I know," he says, his words buttery, like he still cares about me. "Looks like you dodged a bullet, though, huh?" He laughs lightly.

"Hard to say." I shrug, trying to match his tone. "How's your life insurance policy?"

The corner of his lip ticks up, and I'm suddenly struck by a grief so fierce it's as though I've been buried by the emotion, by my yearning for him and for what I thought we were going to have. I want to throw myself at him, to attach myself to him like a leech and suck up every last moment he has before this awful disease takes him. I have a vision of myself as his Florence Nightingale, sacrificing everything to care for him in his final days.

His shoulders dip, as though he, too, is sorry, and I know in that moment that he wishes things had been different. For both of us.

The kitchen door swings open, and Garth and Aaron enter behind us, laughing, joking about coffee rinds, for some reason. I step back from Wesley and grab my coat from where I left it, lying on a pile of boxes in the corner.

"I guess we should get going," I say to the room, my eyes darting to Wesley. I pick up Aaron's coat, too.

"Thanks," Aaron says as he walks over and takes his coat from my hands. He looks over at Wesley. "Nice to see you, man," he says affably, never the type to be petty.

"You, too," Wesley answers, looking at me, and I have the sense that he's the only one in the room who can see me at all.

Chapter Twelve
January 2013

*T*he day after the funeral, I walked cautiously through the front door of Wesley's parents' house. Obviously, his outburst the day before had been the result of his grief, and I understood that I needed to be strong for him, to forgive any awful accusations or unwarranted vitriol that he threw my way. Daphne had tried to talk me down as I'd cried the previous night about the loathing that had swelled over the edge of Wesley's every harsh word. With her support and a few choice words from my mother about the importance of showing up for people, I'd eventually convinced myself that my presence would be a comfort to him. So I went back, even though he had asked me to stay away.

When I arrived just after lunchtime, the stately colonial home was still brimming with company. This was only day two of the seven-day shiva. I wandered inside, noticing the exorbitant amount of food displayed on the dining room table—cookies and bagels, large combinations of fruit speared on kebabs, stabbed into foam bases to look like floral bouquets—as if mass quantities of artfully arranged comestibles could somehow alleviate heartache. People were speaking in hushed voices, picking at linzer cookies and wiping teary eyes. Most of these people were unfamiliar to me, work associates of Wesley's parents, neighborhood friends and acquaintances from long ago who had come by to pay their respects. There were a few distant relatives whom I vaguely recognized. An older woman whom I couldn't place stopped me and went in for a hug.

"Oh, dear," she said as she squeezed me, enveloping me in the thick, flowery scent she wore. "I'm so sorry, sweetie. They would have been excellent in-laws."

"Thank you," I responded in a hushed voice, feeling my own sorrow surfacing, my disappointment at the loss of two people I had thought would become my family. Wesley had always been quick to point out their flaws, but I had found a comfort in the idea of two extra parents for myself, both of them predictable, reliable people. Until now.

I inhaled a sharp breath and held it, a technique I had learned during college for tamping down unwanted emotions, and I scanned the room for Wesley. I finally caught sight of him, sitting on one of those low shiva chairs, a foreshortened leather seat that hovered just a few inches above the floor. His legs were folded awkwardly in front of the little chair, and he was deep in conversation with a man who looked to be about the same age as his father. His *deceased* father, I reminded myself with a shudder.

For the first time since he'd heard the news, Wesley actually looked alert, like he was invested in whatever they were discussing. As I approached and he caught sight of me, he suddenly sat up straighter and his eyes flashed with purpose. He said something quietly to the man beside him and then rose to meet me, walking to where I stood.

"Come with me," he said, starting toward the wide

stairwell in the center of the house. I followed, relieved that he seemed to be welcoming me back into the fold.

We went into his childhood bedroom, the winter sunshine sharp as it pushed through the windows, the luminosity at odds with the cold air in the room. As he closed the door and turned toward me, I saw the set of his jaw, the vein pulsing in his neck, and I realized I had read him all wrong.

"Everyone was asking where you were yesterday." A reprimand, accusatory.

"You told me to leave. I did what you asked." I immediately regretted my defensive tone, knowing I had struck the wrong chord. I couldn't find my footing with this angry, sallow version of Wesley.

"Well, maybe I don't know what the fuck I want right now. Did you think of that?" He pounded his fist twice against the wooden footboard of his old sleigh bed, like he was still busy parsing his thoughts.

"Well, I'm back now," I said, walking toward him, reaching for his hand before he started using any real force on his childhood furniture.

I felt him relax a little at the physical contact, like he remembered who he was, or who *we* were. He pulled me closer and kissed the top of my head. "That was my uncle Marty I was talking to," he told me.

I nodded, reluctant to break the calm by saying something that might set him off again. I leaned into the smooth simplicity of his white dress shirt, the scent of his deodorant strong and reassuring. We were quiet for a moment—taking each other in, I thought.

Wesley finally broke the silence. "I'm going to stay with him for . . . I'm not sure how long. A while."

"Who?"

"Marty," he said again, stepping away from me, the air suddenly cool again, biting. I wondered if anyone had turned the heat on upstairs, if he had slept in this cold air the night before, alone.

"Your uncle Marty? As in your mom's brother Marty? England Marty? What do you mean?"

"Well, it's not like we're still getting married in three weeks. I can't go dance and celebrate at a party right after I put my parents in the ground. Especially not when it was our fucking wedding plans that put them there. Jesus!" His hands shot up to his head, his fists clenching as though he wanted to rip his hair from the roots.

"Wes." I sank down into the black leather chair by his desk. I spoke slowly, hoping to calm him, to help him realize he wasn't making sense. "I know we have to move the wedding, but why are you going to England? What does one have to do with the other?"

Wesley just stared back at me, his expression strange and harsh.

"Look," I continued into the silence, repeating myself, "I know the wedding plans have to change or whatever, but why are you going on a trip to England? How does that move anything forward?"

He rubbed his hands over his face as I began to shiver in the cold room. "It's like I already said," he finally answered, sounding less impassioned now. "I just need some time to deal with everything. I know in my head that this wasn't your fault, that you and your family didn't kill my parents, but every time I'm in the room with you, all I feel is rage and blame seeping out of me. I need to get away from you to get past it. I need you to let me go." He stepped toward me, stroked my hair. "I'm going to leave as soon as shiva ends."

He didn't say how long he was planning to stay away, whether it would be two weeks or two months. All I knew was that everything I said seemed to be making him angrier, so I swallowed a sob and held back my words. I tried not to think of all the plans we had made— the glittering wedding, the honeymoon in Vermont, the twinkle lights and chiffon that were supposed to drape the ceiling of the event space, the sparkly life I had thought I was about to begin with this man who was suddenly a stranger. I stared at the striped comforter on Wesley's old bed, finding no comfort at all. I heard him let out a deep sigh, and a moment later he turned and left the room.

FIVE DAYS LATER, he was gone. He called from the airport to say good-bye. He said he would be in touch in a few days, once he was settled at his uncle's. I cried myself to sleep every night that first week, and the week after that.

On what was supposed to be our wedding day, I finally got an email from him. His uncle had a connection at some elite cooking school near Southampton. He was going to take some classes there. His uncle would pay. It was a genuine opportunity for him to study under this particular British chef. And it was better than coming home and seeing me, which was the same, he said, as staring his parents' death in the face.

This isn't what your parents would want, I wrote him back. *Please come back. Let me help you heal. Please.*

I wrote him every day after that. Pathetic, long,

pleading emails. Some were heartfelt petitions for for-
giveness, while others were simply journal-style recaps
of what I had done that day. One feeble attempt after
another, trying to remind him who I was, why he had
loved me.

He never wrote back. I tried calling, but it seemed
like his cell phone wasn't working on the other side of
the Atlantic. I knew I could probably look up his uncle,
Marty Scheiner, maybe find a phone number, but it was
clear Wesley didn't want to speak to me. So what could I
do? I gave him time.

After a month went by and I hadn't heard from him
again, I began to question whether he would ever come
home. My mother visited me at my little studio apartment and tried to lull me out for meals that I couldn't
eat. When we reached the three-month mark after his
departure, I finally slid my engagement ring off my finger
and put it back into its green velvet box. Because of all
the weight I had lost, it was constantly slipping off anyway. I gave it to my mother and asked her to hold on to
it in case Wesley ever wanted it back, in case he ever
returned and asked to put it back on my finger.

Three months turned into six. When six months
stretched into a year, I finally realized that we were truly
over, that he was never coming back, that maybe we
were never meant to be.

Chapter Thirteen
February 2017

*A*s Aaron and I emerge from the thick yellow lighting of the church kitchen and back into the crowd
of people milling about on Broadway, I gulp in the crisp
winter air as though I had been suffocating inside the
building. He starts walking in the direction of the subway
and I follow numbly, still trying to digest the information
Wesley told me moments ago.

"Want to go wait in line at Barney Greengrass?"
Aaron asks, mentioning my favorite bagel shop uptown.
He looks at his watch and adds, "It's so late, there's prob-
ably not even a line anymore."

He turns his head to look at me and abruptly stops
walking. "What is it? What happened?"

I have the urge to sit down in the middle of the dusty
sidewalk, to let the passersby just maneuver around me. I
cannot handle the weight of what I have been told.

"Wesley's dying." And then I do begin to sink, but
Aaron catches me and pulls me up.

"Whoa, whoa, whoa." He has me in both of his
hands. I can feel the confusion that must be etched on
my face. He puts one arm around my shoulders, the other

around my waist, and steers me over to a side street toward the steps of the closest brownstone.

"Sit." He lowers himself beside me and takes my hand. He looks at me, waiting for me to speak, but all I can do is shake my head. I don't want to start crying for Wesley in front of Aaron, but if I speak any words, I won't be able to hold back the tears. I just shake my head a second time.

Aaron leans forward, resting his elbows on his knees. "Look, I know I said I didn't want to know about your first fiancé, that we should keep the subject off-limits, but that was before he reappeared in your life. It was different when he was living in a foreign country. But it seems like you're going to be seeing him at the soup kitchen, and wherever else now, and obviously something is upsetting you. What good am I if I can't be here for you to unload on? Can you tell me what's going on?" He knocks his knee lightly into mine, and I just want to rest my head in his lap, close out everything but his nearness.

"He has ALS."

"Oh." Silence. "Well, shit."

"Yeah." I look down at my black leather boots, noticing that one of them has a new gray scuff mark on the outer edge.

"How long has it been since he was diagnosed?"

"I don't know."

"How are his symptoms?"

"I don't know."

"Where is he being treated?"

"Jesus, Aaron, I don't know!" I stand as I snap at him. "I didn't think to give him the third degree, okay?"

"You're right, you're right," he says, standing too. "I

know it's got to be a lot to process. I'm sorry." He reaches out to put his arm around me and I shrug him off, now not wanting his touch, not wanting to feel anything at all.

He stares at me for a hard moment.

"We can go," I say, pulling myself back together and stepping down from the concrete steps. "Let's just go."

TWO HOURS LATER, I'm alone in my apartment. I'm supposed to be packing boxes for the move to Aaron's loft, but instead I'm frozen in front of Google, learning all sorts of information about ALS. Horrible information. Each sentence I read is more distressing than the last.

The life expectancy after diagnosis can often be as little as two years, or sometimes even a shorter span of time. The brain stops sending messages to the muscles. Progression of the disease varies and can move slowly in some, way too rapidly in others. Unused, the muscles began to twitch, to weaken and atrophy. Eventually, the brain loses the ability to control voluntary movement. Gradually, people lose their ability to speak, eat, move. Breathe.

In my mind's eye, Wesley has always, always been a fireball, filled with more light and movement than anyone I've known. And now all of that energy and verve is going to seep out of him, muscle by muscle, twitch by twitch, day by day. It's too hard to bear, thinking of him fading like that. Like someone dismantling the Eiffel Tower, pulling the iron apart spoke by spoke.

I remember how he said I dodged a bullet earlier today. I suppose. I get to marry Aaron, who is the picture of health, with his football player's physique and many

salutary habits, his penchant for kale smoothies and avocado toast. If Wesley and I had married as planned, if his
parents had never died, I'd be well on my way to widow-
hood by now. I don't feel like I dodged a bullet, though. I
feel robbed of the opportunity to care for Wesley during
this time, robbed of the chance to be with him during his
last good years, or months. Or weeks.

I read and read everything I can find online, as if I'm
somehow going to find a cure for Wesley, or a cure for
the aching strain I feel in my heart.

Aaron sends me a text from the hospital, where he is
working the night shift. He wants to know how I'm doing, how the packing is going. I stand and look at my
apartment, where I haven't packed a single box. I type
out a quick response saying I've been procrastinating, but
then quickly delete it. I don't want to give him the impression that I'm not excited about moving in with him,
because I am, even though at this very moment I feel excited about exactly nothing. Aaron's not the type to get
self-conscious from a flippant text. Still, given my reaction to Wesley's illness earlier today, I feel I ought to
tread lightly, so I respond:

> Me: Moving slowly. Could have used that bagel earlier
> today, I think. Now carb-deprived and lethargic.

I put a little heart emoji at the end so he knows
we're all good, and then I head into the kitchen, where I
start pulling plates from the cabinet and wrapping them
one by one in the bone-colored packing paper the moving company delivered with the boxes yesterday. I fold
and flip and fold again, hoping that my ministrations
will be sufficient to protect the ceramic dishes as they

travel downtown in the back of the moving truck. I find myself progressing too quickly through the recycled packing paper, using too many sheets per dish, and I berate myself for having declined the moving company's packing service, where the professionals come in and pack up your kitchen or other areas. The additional charge would have been negligible compared with the cost of the move itself, but I figured I could wrap breakables just as easily as anyone else and that I might as well save the money. I place the wrapped plates into a brown cardboard box, one after another, thinking all the while that they will most likely end up shattered, useless shards of memory.

I'VE BEEN DISTRACTED at work all week. We finished clawing our way through a few final boxes of documents for the chewing tobacco case on Monday night, and since then, I've had almost three full days to work on Moe's I-589 and supporting documentation. I think I'm just flying under the radar and none of the senior attorneys have realized I'm not currently busting my butt on some corporate, billable case. As I study up on Moe's history and dig for additional historical or political details that will bolster his application, I am struck by the staggering amount of information I myself have learned from working on this case. As much as I was a diligent student throughout my schooling, I never learned anything about the tension between Buddhists and Muslims in Myanmar. In fact, I was never taught anything about Myanmar at all. I can still spout all sorts of trivia about the Magna Carta or King George III, but when it comes to actual current events in countries that do not have a clear impact on the United States, I am more ignorant than I care to admit.

Only from working on this case have I learned that Myanmar is also called Burma, that the countries those labels denote are one and the same, except that the different terms are politically loaded, so people had better choose carefully which one they use. I was also previously unaware that there is a place in the world where Buddhists behave violently. It's antithetical to everything I thought I knew about Buddhism. The more I learn about Moe's past, the better I understand the fear and torment he has suffered at the hands of his country's military, though the militants would claim that Myanmar is not his country, that his ethnic status as a Rohingya deprives him of any of the rights of citizenship. Regardless of the citizenship question, the violence and destruction that have been foisted relentlessly upon his people take my breath away again and again. Coming to the United States was his last hope, and it's on me to make sure he receives permission to stay here. No pressure or anything.

This morning, I spoke on the phone with a country conditions expert who will be emailing me a report that I can attach to the I-589 to support Moe's story. I also have those articles that Aaron found for me, many of which I'm planning to photocopy and affix to the application as additional supporting material.

I hear a knock on the open door of my office and look up from my computer screen to see Ian standing in the doorway, coat in hand.

"Hey. I was just going to head down to Wolfgang's for a steak lunch. Join?"

"Haven't given up on Atkins yet, I see." His brief but

ardent enthusiasm for each new fad he adopts makes me smile. "My best friend is in town from LA, and I'm about to meet her at The Smith. Pretty sure they have steak there, too, if you want to come."

"Nah." He smirks as he shakes his head slightly and shrugs into his wool coat. "I know better than to intrude on a reunion with one of your college girls. As much as I might like to hear you reminisce about the trouble you caused on some wild spring breaks or whatever else you crazy coeds did, I'll leave you to it." He puts his hand out for a fist bump, which I return, before he goes on his way.

From the desk behind me, I hear Nicola scoff. "Is that serious?" she demands, and I turn to see an expression of utter outrage on her round face.

"What?" Nicola is always annoyed. I don't have the patience to massage her indignation today.

"That was, like, total and complete sexual harassment, sexualizing the behavior of college girls like that. You could get him fired."

"No, he's just joking." Sure, if a seventy-year-old partner said the same thing to me, it would be inappropriate, but Ian and I have a long-standing and comfortable friendship and we can rib each other without concern. I stand and start collecting my things so I can go meet Daphne.

"It's completely unacceptable conduct," Nicola continues to complain, her lip curling up so far that it becomes indistinguishable from her nose.

I don't answer as I retrieve my phone and the backup battery that it's been plugged into all morning.

"You should think really seriously about how you're going to handle it," Nicola drones on. There is a timbre to her voice that I don't like, an undercurrent that sounds an awful lot like a threat. I have no idea whether her menace would be directed at me or at Ian, but I just want to get out of here, to see Daphne and finally have an honest conversation with someone.

"Okay, yeah," I say over my shoulder as I head out. "I'll do that."

Man, I hate this place.

AS DAPHNE AND I sit at lunch, dipping handcrafted potato chips into Roquefort fondue, savoring the fat grams that we'll both regret later, she fills me in on what's been happening with her job search out in LA. She's finishing up a PhD program in psychology at UCLA and trying to determine what she will do after she receives her degree in May. Hardly a week goes by that we don't speak or text at least once or twice, but Daphne moves in her own orbit, and sometimes it's a struggle to keep up. She's also going through fertility treatments because she and her husband, Ethan, have been trying to make a baby for two years, with no luck.

"It sucks balls," she says, popping another chip into her mouth, "getting shot up with this hormone that you know is going to fuck with your head, and then you have to go home and have sex on demand. My kid better be one cute motherfucker after all the shit we are going through to get her."

"Or him," I point out.

"Or him," she repeats, her copper curls dancing around her face. "I hear baby boys pee all over the place, though. My friend Joni's son pissed straight into her eye like five times in the first week of his life. Yeesh. Fingers crossed for a girl if that shit's for real."

I laugh then, my first happy laugh since I learned about Wesley's diagnosis. I take solace in Daphne's wide-open face, her nearly translucent alabaster skin. Daphne has always been able to dilute my moments of gloom, to drag me out from under whatever is assailing me. Ever since we were kids complaining about who knows what —our parents, the mean girls in the grade above, my pushy older brother—she could always light me back up with her absurd behavior and her oversize emotions.

"Okay, now you." She has pulled the straw out from her glass of mineral water and is pointing it at me. "What's the latest with your hot hunk of doctor meat?"

"It's been a weird week," I say. My eyes scan the other tables at the restaurant. I'm not looking for anyone in particular among the sea of faces, the groups of twos and threes lunching at small, square tables, bodies settled into trendy bistro chairs. I'm just preparing myself, stalling for a few more seconds, because once I open the levee, I'm not sure what emotions will come surging out.

"Tell me," she says, suddenly focused. My hesitation has betrayed me, alerted her that I've got something real, something bulky, on my mind. Our waiter appears and deftly pushes our platter of chips and fondue to the side before placing matching chopped salads on the table in front of us.

"I saw Wesley again, at the soup kitchen," I confess as soon as the waiter turns away.

She flinches slightly. Blinks. "Wait, hold up. What?" She puts up a hand as if to push away what I've said, or at least to block herself from the fallout. She never forgave Wesley for the way he disappeared, or for how she had to nurse me through my broken heart. She almost moved back from California to take care of me at one point, and I know she's still more than a little pissed off. She made that perfectly clear when I called her after I bumped into him at Thunder Chicken. She spent a good twenty minutes lecturing me about not letting Wesley's presence in the States have any impact on my relationship with Aaron, on the new life that I've worked so hard to build.

I tell her all about the work training program that Wesley started at Community Kitchen, and she seems genuinely intrigued, as if the socially conscious nature of the program has allowed her to forget all about who's behind its creation.

"Well, a pocket full of aces to him," she says. "Maybe he's trying to reclaim some good karma after the world of pain he caused you a few years ago."

"Or he's trying to do something of merit with his life before he dies," I say seriously. "He just found out he has ALS."

She pauses, her fork halfway to her mouth, and then lowers it. "What do you mean, ALS?"

"You know." I try to keep my voice from breaking. "Lou Gehrig's disease. Like Stephen Hawking . . ." I can't find additional words.

"Shit," she says, just like Aaron did.

Oh, crap—Aaron. He was conducting an experimental surgery on a preemie with sagittal craniosynostosis today. He and his team spent so many days preparing to help this child, and I just realized that I forgot to call and wish him luck this morning—I've been too preoccupied thinking about Wesley. I glance at my watch. Aaron said it would be a ten-hour surgery. There's no point in calling now.

"But there's no cure for that," Daphne says about Wesley, like I might not have already been all over the Internet, learning about the disease.

"Yeah."

"Shit, Mer," she says again. "That's just . . . My God. And he doesn't even have family around to take care of him at the end."

Wesley always hated being an only child.

"That's got to be some kind of serious torment." She looks at me searchingly. "I mean for you. To see him after so long and then find out that he's got this fatal disease."

I recognize her psych training pushing to get through, but she knows I don't want to be shrinked. I went through enough hours of that when my mom was sick.

"So, what are you going to do?" she asks.

"What do you mean, what am I going to do? What *can* I do?" Our waiter walks by with dishes for another table, and the smell of garlic overwhelms me. "He's not my guy anymore. I think I have to just stand back and let it happen, right? I can't be all about Wesley when I'm supposed to marry Aaron at the end of the year. Aaron's a patient guy, but he has his limits."

"Aaron *is* a patient guy," she repeats, "but I know you, and you will never forgive yourself if you don't try to help Wesley in some way, or just hang out with him a little before he gets too sick to be with people. You should think hard on this because it's not like you'll be able to change your mind later." She pauses. "And there's a limit to how jealous Aaron can get over it since he knows Wesley won't be around forever. The 'dying man' exemption or whatever."

I flinch at her words, at the thought that Wesley's time is limited, but I know she's right.

"You're not thinking of going to him, are you? Giving up on Aaron, risking everything to nurse Wesley through his dying days?"

Only now that she's put the thought into words do I realize that yes, that is exactly what I've been thinking about. Would a few more months with Wesley be worth sacrificing the many promises of my future? I wonder what exactly I owe Wesley and what I owe myself.

"Well, you better not. You have too much to lose. You know I've got no love lost for Wesley after the way he treated you. Even so," she continues, "I know you, Miss Meredith, and you will not be comfortable with yourself if you don't reach out to him in some way. I'm still not sure he deserves your time and effort, but there's something between all and nothing, isn't there?"

And that's the conversation that leads me immediately back to Google when I return to my office after lunch, and straight onto the website for Thunder Chicken. Nicola has disappeared somewhere, and I take advantage of the privacy her absence is affording me. I dial the number for the restaurant, and when the perky receptionist picks up, I ask to speak with Wesley.

The woman seems surprised by the request, as though I've asked to step behind the curtain and see the Grand Wizard.

"Oh. Okay." She pauses. "I'll see if Chef is available. And who shall I say is calling?"

"Just tell him it's Meredith. He'll know."

"I can do no such thing. I will need your last name, Meredith."

Really? This is the world that Wesley has chosen for himself? I would have imagined him as being above all this fanfare, the pomposity. But I suppose if a person wants to succeed in the restaurant world in this city, the city of all cities, he's got to sell out a little.

The woman places me on hold, and after a brief moment of being assailed by the new-agey music piping through the phone, I hear the rasp of Wesley's voice. "Meredith?"

"Yeah, hi."

"Hi."

He waits for whatever I'm going to say, but I falter.

"Is everything okay?" he asks, filling the silence.

"Yeah, I just was . . . I just wanted to follow up on our conversation from the other day."

"Yeah, I kind of figured I'd be hearing from you. Listen, give me your number and I'll call you when I get out of here. It should be a little after ten tonight. That okay?"

"Sure. Okay." I rattle off my cell number, wondering whether I am getting the brush-off or if he is actually going to call me back. After we hang up, I start brainstorming excuses about why I won't be able to see Aaron tonight for a movie date, as we planned. If Wesley does actually return my call, I want to be available to speak to him without Aaron nearby when the call comes in.

I decide to tell Aaron that I am bringing some work home with me tonight, that I am overloaded with unfinished asylum business, and that we should just postpone the movie until tomorrow. I usually avoid bringing work home. In fact, my main goal each day at the office is to finish enough work during business hours to ensure that my evenings are my own. Even so, Aaron knows how invested I am in Moe's case for refugee status, so if I make my conflict about that, I am pretty sure he'll buy what I'm selling.

I check my watch and calculate that, based on Aaron's estimates, this morning's surgery should still be far from complete. I send him a quick email, which I figure he will see as soon as he checks his phone following surgery. I tap out the news that I need to move our plans to tomorrow evening, my heart pounding its misgivings as I add the false excuse that I will be too busy working my way through certain issues on the asylum case.

Two minutes later, my phone rings, Aaron's number on the screen.

"Hey," I say as I bring the phone cautiously to my ear. "You're finished already?" I wonder if I somehow tipped my hand, alerted him to my fraudulent behavior, my questionable intentions.

"In and out in less than an hour, and everything went off without a hitch, like it was no sweat." I can hear the enthusiasm in his voice, his joy at a job well done, a baby's life improved.

"I thought this was supposed to be a long one," I say.

"Nope. It was endoscopic. That's what made the whole thing so amazing—minimally invasive," he prods. "Remember?"

But I don't remember. Not even a little. Maybe this wasn't even the experimental surgery, except it's way too late for me to ask. I wonder how I've allowed myself to tune him out, to lose myself so completely to the distraction of Wesley's condition.

"Did you see my email?" I want to take it back, my subterfuge, my disloyalty.

"I have an idea," he answers easily. "Meet me for a quick dinner near your office so I get to see your face today, and then I'll drive you home to do your work."

"But then you just have to drive all the way back downtown," I protest, feeling even worse as he continues to be kind, chivalrous.

Nicola walks back into the office with three large folders and dumps them loudly on her desk.

"No worries," he says. "I want to see you, and I can use the drive uptown to call my folks, maybe talk through the pros and cons of buying that house."

Aaron's parents recently decided they want to sell their home on Long Island and move to the Berkshires, where they had a summer home when he was a kid. If they don't buy the country house, their other idea is to relocate to Manhattan, and that is Aaron's preference. He likes getting to spend time with them, doesn't feel suffocated by their presence like I so often do near my own parents.

"Okay, fine," I say, thinking that I could actually use a little time with Aaron to remind myself why he is important me. A couple of months ago, he was my whole world, and now two run-ins with Wesley have made me loosen my grip on everything I thought I wanted. I cannot allow myself to undermine the life I am building just because I'm upset about Wesley's health.

"Come get me at seven," I suggest. "I'll make us a reservation at the Thai place."

After I hang up, I close my eyes, like I'm trying to disengage my brain, prevent it from running all the possible scenarios in my head about the mess that I am creating. I let out a breath and turn back to the country conditions report I was working on for Moe's case. It occurs to me as I'm rereading the report that I don't know enough yet about Moe's personal family history. There might be more details that could help his case. I'm thinking that we should set up another in-person meeting before I file the I-589 so I can review the details with him, confirm I have everything right, and make sure I haven't left out anything that could help him. I reach for the folder that has his phone number written on the outside just as my office phone rings, an in-house number flashing on the screen.

"This is Meredith," I say, as Nicola huffs into the brief she's been paging through, likely annoyed by the continued nuisance I am making of myself by existing in her space.

"Hey. It's Ilana," says the administrative assistant to Ellen Short, one of the firm's senior partners. "Ellen asked me to call. She has a copy of the Dole brief almost ready, and she wanted you to cite check it."

"The Dole case?" I ask, and Nicola glances at me, now interested. "I'm not on that case." I don't add that cite checking is a job for first-years, or even paralegals.

"She knows, but Noah and Arnie are both at depositions today and she said she wants someone competent to do it. It's a big case, Meredith." The woman tells me this like I should feel pleased, puffed up, even, that I've been selected to do the grunt work on this case. "I'm emailing over the document now."

I hang up with Ilana on a sigh. Canceling the movie with Aaron seems to have been the right call, as I'm not going to have a moment for the pro bono case before the end of the day anyway. Having time to do work at home tonight will actually be a plus. That said, I don't feel any less guilty. In my heart, I still know I am doing something contemptible. It's low and staggeringly reckless, but I am charging onward toward Wesley just the same.

Chapter Fourteen
March 2017

*I*t's 10:12 p.m., and Wesley hasn't called yet. I try to stop looking at my phone every five seconds, to focus more on the stack of articles about Myanmar that I finally, finally have an opportunity to review. The instructions for the I-598 form include a lengthy list of documentation that an applicant is permitted to submit, in addition to a country conditions report, to bolster his petition, from affidavits of witnesses to photos, periodicals, and medical or psychological reports. I begin highlighting and underlining, jotting down notes as thoughts occur to me, but my eyes keep straying disobediently back toward the phone, which is pointedly silent beside my laptop. I guess it makes sense that Wesley still doesn't want me in his life. If he made that decision when were so close to getting married, why would he change his position now, when we are basically strangers? Any thoughts I entertained about his attitude toward me having evolved with time were clearly delusional.

When Aaron and I were out for dinner earlier, each disentangling noodles from plates full of pad Thai, I tried to curb the preoccupation, the sense of urgency, that has become a constant since I learned of Wesley's illness. I patted myself on the back for noticing how handsome

154 *Jacqueline Friedland*

Aaron looked in his white button-down with the sleeves rolled to his elbows. He told me more about the endoscopic procedure he performed earlier today, about how the baby will barely have a scar, how the child's skull had expanded almost immediately, and how his head is now round rather than elongated and deformed like it was yesterday and all the days before. I'm fairly certain that Aaron could tell I was distracted, not acting quite like myself. Now that I've woken up to the thought, I realize he's got to know something is going on in my head, and I imagine he's going to connect the dots to Wesley in short order. If he hasn't already.

Aaron told me he was going to hit the sheets early tonight and not pass up this opportunity to recoup the sleep that he misses so frequently. As I picture his large frame sprawled across his bed, without me, I pick up my phone and wonder if I should just power down the whole thing for the night. I can't make myself do it, though. I have fallen right into the same pattern, ending up back in that place that I crawled out of years ago. Here I sit, staring at my phone, waiting to hear from Wesley, who isn't calling.

Except that now the phone suddenly rings in my hand, showing a number I've not seen before. I let it ring a second time before I answer so I don't pick up sounding desperate, definitely not like I've been holding the phone, waiting for him to call.

"Hello?"

"Hey, it's Wesley. I'm just leaving the restaurant." If that's supposed to be an apology for calling later than he said he would, I guess it will do.

"Thanks for calling," I start, leaning back in my swivel

chair and hating how stilted I sound. "I just wanted to touch base, to see . . . I don't know," I stumble. "You kind of dropped a bomb at the soup kitchen the other day, and I just wanted to talk a little more . . . if you don't mind."

"No, I know," he says, sounding ever so slightly out of breath, like he's walking as we talk. "I'm glad we're getting to talk. I've missed having you as a sounding board."

At his words, I feel as if a million tiny rock doves have been released from my heart at once and are now flying forth in celebration. Knowing he's missed me relieves me of a pressure I didn't realize I still felt. It also pisses me off.

"Yeah, well." I stop, reminding myself that I didn't call to fight about the way he abandoned me years ago.

Apparently, he still wants to discuss it, though.

"Look, there is so much to say about what went down before the wedding. Let's not go there. It was a really shitty time for me, and I've been working my way out of it ever since, digging and clawing my way back, and now there's this."

I notice he doesn't even say "the disease" or its name. I also notice that he doesn't apologize for anything that happened between us.

"So we're calling a truce to focus on the health stuff. Okay, I can deal with that," I say, looking toward the lone window in my apartment, out into the dark of the Manhattan night.

"Of course, you can," he says, his voice suddenly lighter. "You're Meredith Altman, savior of widows, orphans, and now dying men." Wesley always took note of my desire to help the downtrodden, commended me for it. "Speaking of which, what's your job now?"

"Ugh, don't get me started," I say, picking up the Harrison, Whittaker ID card that's sitting on my desk and running my fingers idly over the grainy picture of myself on the front.

"Did you go corporate?" I can hear the incredulity in his voice. "You did, didn't you? You sold out to the man?" He says it like he's just teasing, but I know better—he's disappointed in me.

"For now," I hedge, and then change the subject back to his situation. "Can you tell me a little more about your prognosis?"

"What are you doing right now?"

My eyes wander over the ID card still in my hand, the papers strewn about the dilapidated wooden desk that I've had for nearly a decade.

"Um, just finishing up a little work. Nothing. Why?"

"Meet me for a drink? Just to catch up a little. Your beefy fiancé won't mind, right? Not when I'm a dying man and all."

I look down at the sweats I'm wearing and the ratty T-shirt, which, embarrassingly, is actually one of Wesley's that I've saved. I've worn it so many times that I don't even think of it as his anymore, despite the fact that the name of his high school baseball team, the Irvington Bulldogs, is plastered across the front. Before I can stop myself, I begin contemplating how to turn his suggestion into a reality. I put my hand up to my hair, which still feels smooth, acceptably neat. I decide that if I change quickly, throw on some real clothes, a little mascara and gloss, I can be solidly presentable in time to meet him somewhere.

"Um, sure," I say, thinking that yes, actually, Aaron

probably would mind—he would probably mind a lot—
but maybe I don't have to mention that.

"The piano bar on Seventy-sixth Street?"

It's a place we used to go every now and then, and
it's also so utterly uncool, full of lonely senior citizens, I
don't have to worry about bumping into anyone we know.

"Perfect. I can be there in twenty minutes."

We hang up, and I'm suddenly running around the
apartment like I'm on fast-forward. I throw on a pair of
skinny jeans—ripped ones, so it looks like I'm keeping
things casual, not trying too hard. Never mind that it's a
great pair of ass-lifting pants and definitely a strategic
decision in an eat-your-heart-out kind of way. I pick out
a long-sleeved, V-neck sweater to go with them. Conservative, but it shows off my collarbone, an attribute of
which Wesley was always particularly fond.

As I race about, brushing my hair again, picking out a
pair of small crystal earrings just to brighten up my face,
I try to decide whether to tell Aaron about this develop-
ment. Ever. I want to be honest, to treat him and our
relationship with the respect they deserve, the respect
he has earned. But I'm not sure how I can explain the
fact that I blew off my date with him tonight using the
excuse of too much work yet somehow had time to get
out with Wesley. At least I know Aaron is already sleeping, so I can wait until the morning to figure out what to
share with him. I add a little blush, a spritz of perfume, a
booster of deodorant under my arms. I throw my keys
into my purse, pick up my phone, and head out.

Ten minutes later, I'm walking down the steps toward
the entrance of the piano bar, which is half a flight below
street level. It's dark inside, full of rank cigar smoke and

red velvet lounges that look they've been around since long before the Bee Gees made things like velvet cool. As my eyes adjust to the dim red lighting, I see Wesley waiting at the bar, wearing jeans and a dark leather jacket, chatting with the bartender. I take the stool next to him, placing my small bag on the counter and giving the lanky bartender a polite smile.

Wesley turns toward me, and I expect his green eyes to light up, the way they always used to. Instead he is subdued, his face unreadable, like the other day at the soup kitchen.

"Hey, what can I get you to drink?" he asks.

"Whatever you're having," I answer, eyeing his clear, fizzy beverage.

"That's a club soda. Alcohol messes with my meds." He swallows conspicuously once, and then again, and I wonder if it's because of the awkwardness of the situation or if it's a symptom of the disease.

"Oh. In that case"—I look toward the bartender, who's waiting to fetch something for me—"a vodka soda with two limes, please." I definitely want a drink to deal with this conversation. I adjust myself on the stool, turning toward him. "So, fill me in."

He regards me silently for a moment, as if he's choosing his words carefully. "I'm dying," he says. Flip. Irreverent, as he shrugs.

"Stop it," I admonish him, resisting the urge to swat at him and fiddling with the strap of my purse instead.

"Well, I am. The upside is that I already have a buyer lined up for the restaurant, at a definite profit." He watches me while he talks and I wonder what he's noticing, what has changed about me.

"You're selling it already?"

"Yup." His tone is clipped as he takes a sip of his drink and then places the glass back on the bar, clenching and unclenching his fist the way I saw him doing in the kitchen the other day. "But I'm going to keep running it while I can, even under the new ownership." He sees me looking at his hand and holds it up, showing me his palm. "That's how I knew something was wrong." He takes his other thumb and pushes it deep into the first hand, massaging. "I'd been getting muscle cramps here for a long time. I'm not even sure how long ago they started. I always thought it was from the chopping, like an athletic injury but for chefs. But then it started happening in my other hand, too, my left, which I never use for chopping. So then I figured it for some sort of arthritis, which I finally went to check out. There are medicines that could have slowed everything down, if I hadn't been such a shitbag idiot. I waited too long."

"But I thought there's no cure."

"There's not, but by the time I finally got diagnosed there was already a lot of damage, which maybe I could have staved off. I might have gotten a few more good years." He pauses and looks up at the ceiling in obvious frustration. "My fucking life." He shakes his head.

When I'm quiet, he keeps talking. "I was back at the doctor today. He's estimating at least another couple of months before I have to stop working."

"Is it just your hands?" I ask, afraid of the answer.

He shakes his head no and reaches to sip his drink, like he doesn't want to tell me the other things going wrong with his body.

After another beat, he seems to perk up. "So," he

says, his tone lighter—purposeful, even—"tell me about your fiancé." There's another unusual swallow, and I can see now that it's definitely a symptom.

"Because that wouldn't be awkward at all," I counter with a half-smile.

"No, seriously. I want to know where you're going to end up, you know? Nothing's playing out like I thought. I won't get to find out later, so . . ." He shrugs again, like he has accepted everything more than I have.

I resist the urge to cry and figure I can provide some basic information. "His name is Aaron. He's a neonatologist. He went to Dartmouth. I don't know. He's a good guy. A really, really good guy."

"Does he know you're out with me?"

I look down at the bar as I answer, "Well, no, but he was already sleeping. He works nights a lot and took advantage of his chance to go to bed early tonight." The part of me that never stopped belonging to Wesley wonders why Aaron even needs to know, why it's any of his business what goes on between Wesley and me, but the adult in me knows better. "I'll tell him tomorrow. There's no reason this needs to be a secret."

"That's good," he says, studying my face. "You belong with the kind of guy who saves babies for a living."

"Where are you living? How long have you been back?" I ask, suddenly desperate for information about the life he's had without me.

"I've been back about ten months. The whole restaurant thing happened really fast. I took it over from John Irwin when it was already halfway finished."

"The guy you worked with at Depot Café?"

"Yeah, he got hired by a hot new chain in Seattle. Sold

out for the cash, but it created an opportunity for me."

"Where do you live?" I ask again.

"I've been staying at my parents' house. In Irvington."

"Oh." I try to swallow my shock that he still owns the home, which I was sure he'd sold off right after his parents' death. "And you commute to TriBeCa? Isn't it kind of rough going back there?" I'm not sure it's clear that I was asking about the emotional implications, versus the commute, but then I think maybe it's better if I keep it light anyway, stay focused on the travel time.

"Yeah." He reaches for the straw in his glass, fumbles for a moment, and then gets his fingers around it. "I was planning to get an apartment downtown, some swanky renovated loft or something. But I didn't get around to it, and then . . ." Another shrug.

I picture him out in his parents' old house in the woodsy suburbs of Westchester, so isolated and alone. I remember with a sudden flash how cold his bedroom was the last time I was there.

"Do you have people out there who you see? Anyone?"

"I'm not dating anyone, if that's what you're asking."

It wasn't, actually. I was trying to determine who will take care of him when he can't take care of himself.

"I was thinking about your treatment." I offer a sheepish smile. "Wouldn't it be better for you to be in the city? You could probably get into work more easily, and you have more people who could help take care of you." He looks at me defensively, and I add hastily, "If you need it." I'm glad I didn't say "when."

Suddenly, I have an idea. "You should take my apartment! I'm moving out in a week and a half. The building is letting me break the lease, but I'm sure they haven't found anyone to take it yet."

"Where are you going?" he asks.

"Gramercy Park," I mumble, a little embarrassed, since the old me always swore I could only be happy living on the Upper West Side or way downtown.

Wesley barks out a laugh. "I never thought I'd see the day. Wow. I guess it goes with the whole corporate-law-firm theme. Moving on up." He gives a little head shake.

"I'm serious. You should take my apartment."

"Thanks, but no," he says. "I'm good at the old house for now."

We stare at each other for a moment in silence.

"You look good," he says, his eyes sweeping over me. "I'm glad things are working out for you."

"You still haven't answered me, really. Do you have people to help you when things get bad?"

"I'm cool. It's all good." He reaches into his back pocket for his wallet. I wonder if his movements are slower than they used to be or if he is moving slowly on purpose, prolonging our time together.

"I'll walk you back to your building."

I look up at him, unsure whether that's okay. A late-night stroll together feels like it would cross a line that I didn't know I had drawn. At the same time, I've always been anxious about being on the streets alone late at night, and he knows it.

"C'mon, it's fine. Aaron wouldn't want me sending you home alone. No funny business, I promise."

Just like that, he jolts my mind to that night all those years ago when we first met, and he enticed me back to his room. It was so long ago, but in some ways, it was everything. I think he knows it, that he's triggered the memory intentionally. I relent.

As we meander up Columbus toward Seventy-ninth Street, I wonder how many more times I will get to see him before the end. As if he's read my mind, he starts speaking. "I have three more weeks left until I finish with this session of my program at the soup kitchen on Sundays. Will I see you there?"

"For sure," I answer, nodding, as I gaze blankly up the avenue.

"I'm glad we're back in touch," he says quietly as we turn onto Seventy-ninth Street.

I glance over at him and see that his expression has changed—it's more focused, intense. We reach the door of my building and slow to an awkward stop.

"Me too," I respond as I turn to face him, drinking in the way he's looking at me. It's like he can't look anywhere besides my face, like I'm still the most important person in the world to him. I feel the heat rising in my chest, like he and I are having a moment, and it's wrong. So wrong. I don't want to be that person—the cheater, the liar. As much as I want to wrap myself around him like a hundred-year-old vine, I won't. I lean in and give him a lightning-fast peck on the cheek, chaste as can be.

"I've got to go," I say, part apology, part command. I turn and dart into the building, leaving him to stare after me as I run away from a million possibilities.

Chapter Fifteen
March 2017

I'm riding up the escalator into the main lobby of the Kips Bay movie theater when I notice that my hands are sweating. Since when have I become someone who perspires from nerves? Maybe since I lied to my fiancé about where I spent my last evening, that's when.

Aaron is waiting at the top of the escalator, tickets in one hand and an extra-large soda in the other. As I near him, I rub my palms against my thighs, a gesture that could easily signify warming myself from the cold evening air and doesn't necessarily implicate me as the no-good, low-down, rotten liar that I am.

Aaron spent another hectic day at the hospital, two emergency surgeries complicating his usual Tuesday office visits. I, too, had a busier day than expected, having received multiple calls to discuss the Dole brief that I'm now involved in up to my earlobes. The chaos of the day means that we have communicated in only a couple of short texts since I saw Wesley last night. With partners like Ellen Short nitpicking about every word, I barely made it out of the office in time for this 9:00 p.m. movie. When I began law school, I never anticipated the hours I would spend agonizing over commas.

We quickly hustle into the dark theater, where previews are already rolling. As the movie starts and Hugh

Jackman's bearded face fills the screen, Aaron reaches for my fingers and places our joined hands on his lap. A new surge of guilt sweeps through me, alerting me that I most definitely have to tell him about the drink with Wesley last night. The man sitting beside me is going to be my husband, and I don't want to build our future on a base of dishonesty. I have to come clean, take my lumps. Well, maybe not 100 percent clean, but I can lay out the facts, state what actually happened. I don't have to get into all the internal dialogue I've been through. It wouldn't benefit anyone for me to open that can of dog food.

When the movie ends, we walk to the dive bar across the street, arguing amicably about where the movie should fall in our ever-shifting ranking of superhero films. The smell of stale popcorn fills my nose as we enter the bar and make our way to a booth in the back. We each order beers, and we decide to split a plate of wings. That really means I will eat one wing and Aaron will gradually devour all the rest while repeatedly trying to convince me to have another. The yeasty beer will be enough for me as a late-night snack, filling me up like homemade bread.

"So, I have to confess something, and you're not going to like it," I say after the waitress puts our overly full glasses on the table.

"Okay," Aaron says as he arranges his cell phone and pager on the table, his tone light as a cloud, as though nothing I say could actually upset him.

"After you went to bed last night, Wesley called me." I push the words out in a rush. "I had been asking him a lot of questions about his diagnosis, and he asked me to meet him for a drink to discuss it."

Now Aaron's eyes are on me, his expression taut. "And?"

"And I met him at the piano bar on Seventy-sixth for one drink."

Aaron continues to watch my face, waiting for me to say more. The TV behind him is showing some sort of martial arts match; the kicking and punching onscreen draws a whoop from a guy at a table behind us.

"I didn't feel like I could say no." I don't add that I didn't *want* to say no.

"And then?" he asks, his tone clipped.

"And then he walked me back to the front door of my building and I went home."

He's silent while he digests this. "And that's it?" he asks after a moment, his dark eyes searching my face.

"And that's it." I obviously don't mention the heated moment when I was pretty sure Wesley was thinking about kissing me. I certainly don't mention that I maybe wanted it, too. Just for a second.

"Okay." He shifts his gaze away from me, glances around the crowded room.

"Okay?" I ask. "You're not mad?"

"I'm not mad," he says, looking back at me, though his tone suggests otherwise. "You did what you felt you had to do in the situation, and I appreciate that you're telling me. I guess there's not much more to say." He doesn't ask about Wesley's health or what he told me about his prognosis. I guess as a doctor, Aaron has a pretty solid understanding of where Wesley is heading. He probably figures that even if Wesley's return to New York does present a genuine obstacle in our relationship, it's a hindrance that won't be present long, and there's no point in causing a ruckus over this short-term blip.

"Want to play darts?" He looks over at the dartboard on the back wall near our table. Despite our many visits to this place, we've never used the dartboard before.

"Um, okay." I search his face, which is closed off, less readable than I am accustomed to. As we stand and move toward the back of the bar, I decide to follow his lead and drop the Wesley conversation.

He pulls three red darts from the board and holds them out to me. "You first."

I take one and do my best imitation of what I can remember from movies, chucking it toward the board with a flourish-y flick of my wrist. It hits the outer edge of the board and then sputters to the floor in disgrace.

"Try again," Aaron encourages me. His shoulders are beginning to relax as he stands to the side, watching. His hands are deep in his jean pockets, and I get the sense that he's talking himself out of being angry with me.

I throw another and it connects with the board. It's on the outer rim of the bullseye, but I'm a little proud that I made purchase at all.

"You're getting it," he says, motioning with his head that I should throw the third dart.

I decide to put a little muscle behind this one. I begin to launch it forward, but I lose my grip milliseconds before I meant to let go, and that changes the dart's trajectory entirely. It veers off course and nearly hits one of the waitresses on the side of her head. Thankfully, even my strongest throw isn't that impressive, and it doesn't quite connect with the young woman before it plummets to the floor.

I'm relieved that my notoriously poor aim hasn't caused any damage, except that as the waitress flinches and looks to see what almost hit her, or perhaps who's thrown it, she collides with another patron and her tray full of beer glasses topples, falling to the floor with a loud crash. Worse yet, the middle-aged man she has bumped into appears to be a total wackadoo, and he starts screaming at her as though she'd been gunning for him intentionally.

"What the fuck is wrong with you?" the man shouts as he looks down at his shirt and back at her. "Can't you watch where the fuck you're going, you stupid-ass bitch?" He pulls on the arm of his button-down shirt, emphasizing the beer that has spilled on him.

"It was all my fault. I'm so sorry," I say, running over, bending to pick up some of the glasses. "I should have known I would be terrible at darts. Please," I say, looking up at the skinny man, who is nearly snarling at the waitress, "it wasn't her fault." I put the glasses on a high-top table next to him and grab some napkins from the dispenser on it.

I hold them out to him, but the balding man regards the brown paper napkins as though I'm offering him rancid meat. He swats my hand away with significantly more force than is necessary, and I stumble a step to the side.

"What's your problem, buddy?" the waitress yells at the guy just as I feel Aaron, who had been hanging back, appear behind me.

"Hey, hey, hey," Aaron says. "There's no call for any of this. No one meant for any of this to happen. It's just a little beer, man. You've never gotten some beer on your shirt before?"

"It's not just a little beer!" the man shouts back. "This bitch just ruined my shirt! And now she's all smug, like it's not her fault, because your little woman is trying to take the blame." He's gesticulating wildly toward the waitress, but then he stills, his eyes roving over Aaron, clearly cataloging his intimidating size. I can't say whether it's Aaron's six feet and three inches of height, his 230 pounds of muscle, or even his enormous hands, which, I happen to know, measure more than nine inches, but suddenly this brittle guy seems to be reconsidering his behavior.

"Yeah," he says, taking a step back and reaching for a camel coat on the wall hook, "I guess you're right. I was just leaving anyway. This shit's not worth this shit."

My eyes dart away from the fuming man back to Aaron, and I see Aaron trying to contain his smirk at the guy's flustered grammatical mess.

"Yeah, okay, that's probably true," Aaron says somberly.

As the guy makes his way out of the bar, Aaron turns back to the waitress and me, assessing us quickly with his eyes. "You guys okay?" he asks.

"Oh my God, I'm so sorry I brought that down on you," I say to the petite waitress, who nods back at me while her eyes are fixed on Aaron. If this were a cartoon, she would have little red hearts coming out of her eyes at the moment. I can't say I blame her. That little bit of peaceful conflict resolution that he just did was definitely kind of dreamy.

"No problem," she says lightly. "Let me get you guys a couple of drinks on the house."

"For real? But I just sent a dart at your head and set

all that craziness in motion. I should be buying *you* a drink."

She pulls her eyes away from Aaron and smiles at me. I notice that she has a tongue ring as she starts talking again.

"No, it's fine. That was a whole lot of hoopla, and you guys helped us come out on the right side of it. Consider your next round comped." She takes the napkins that I had returned to the table beside us and wipes at her apron skirt as she turns and heads toward the bar.

Aaron guides me back to our table with his hand resting on my lower back. The contact sends a little shiver up my spine, and I'm thankful for it, relieved to know that I do truly have a genuine attraction to him. Whatever else may be complicating my life, my feelings for him are legit.

"Man," he says, as we settle back into our seats, "who knew you'd be such a nightmare at darts? Don't you think you should have mentioned it, like maybe that's something you ought to share with a guy who has to spend the rest of his life with you?" He kicks me lightly under the table and I feel my cheeks warming with at the way he's looking at me. I guess we are trying to move past our earlier conversation.

"Whatever. It's a stupid game, throwing pointy stuff around in public places." I kick him back, less lightly, with just enough force to turn the sexual tension up a notch.

The waitress brings our wings and two more beers. We relax into our drinks and chat about other things. He tells me a little about the conditions of the babies he treated today, and I ask for an update on his parents' house-hunting plans. He informs me that they've changed their minds and have decided to stay put on Long Island.

As Aaron is wiping the buffalo sauce off his hands, sliding the napkin over each finger, one at a time, he glances toward the door of the bar. "Stay at my place tonight?"

We are always negotiating about which apartment we'll sleep at after we have a night out together, but this time he sounds tentative, like the question is not about which apartment we'll be sleeping at but about whether we'll be spending the night together at all.

"Done," I answer breezily, but I suddenly feel a pressure in my stomach, a dismay that only thickens as I realize that my clandestine behavior with Wesley may have changed everything between us. Although I fessed up and told Aaron about my night with my ex, it may have already been too late. Even if Aaron still trusts me to be honest with him, which is now debatable, it seems as if I have managed to weaken his trust in *us*.

As he looks at me in relief, the set of his jaw softening almost imperceptibly, I resolve to fix this, to show Aaron that my loyalty still lies with him. By declaring it to myself, I hope to make it true.

AS SOON AS we are inside his apartment, he's all over me. He knocks the door closed with his foot and pushes me up against it, molding his lips to mine before he even turns on the lights. I can taste beer on his warm tongue, and urgency. He hoists me up without pulling away, and I wrap my legs around his waist, enjoying the heft of his wide body flush against my own. He keeps one hand underneath my butt to support me and the other one in my

hair, bringing my mouth even closer to his, as if he's trying to devour me.

There is a flavor to Aaron's actions that's different
from his usual gentle, almost careful pace with me. He is
always conscious of his size and treats me as though he's
afraid to hurt me. Except tonight, his movements are
fierce, territorial, and I know now without a doubt that
the happenings with Wesley are bothering him more
than he has let on. As he continues to kiss me like he
simply can't get enough, like he wants to inhale my entire being, his hands roam quickly from one part of me to
another. I'm finding his hunger hypnotic, addicting.

I slide my hands underneath his shirt, up over his
rigid oblique muscles, trying to pull us even closer.
Without pausing, he carries me over toward the couch
and begins undoing the button of my jeans before he's
even set me down on the cushions. The clothes prove too
complicated to lose without our pulling apart for at least
a moment, but after a flash of fabrics and tangled sleeves,
we're back at it with as much fervor as a moment before.

He climbs on top of me, and I relish the weight of
him, like I always do. I chew on his ear as he groans,
deep and loud, an announcement of his intentions, of his
latent ferocity. I'm in a stupor of lust, lost in the wild
motions, the roughness that he usually keeps contained.
He pushes against me, every thrust a pronouncement, a
demand, and I surrender to the pull, lost against him.

When we finally finish, a grand finale accompanied
by Aaron's primal roar, we are a sweaty tangle of arms
and legs, our clothes in disarray throughout the room.
The lights from buildings across the street provide the
only illumination as I lie beneath Aaron and wonder ab-

sently how my shirt managed to land all the way over by the kitchen entry.

Aaron leans up on an elbow, cool air reaching my sweaty torso as he pulls back enough to see my face.

"Hi," he says.

"I love you," I answer.

He kisses me gently on the forehead and then disappears into the bathroom for a moment. While he's gone, I open the storage ottoman that doubles as a coffee table and pull out a cozy fleece blanket. I settle back onto the couch, draping the blanket over myself for warmth. I'm sure my hair is a disaster at the moment, but I feel so satiated, gelatinous, and spent that I just curl up back where I was.

Aaron reappears, sipping from a paper cup of water. "Scooch," he says as he reaches me and lowers himself back onto the couch. "Want?"

I shake my head as he holds out the water, and I move farther onto the wide leather sofa, turning my back toward him so he can wrap himself around me, which he does now with ease.

We lie silently for a few minutes as he plays with pieces of my hair.

"I don't like it," he finally says quietly, "the reappearance of Wesley in your life. The way he's getting under your skin."

"I know," I start cautiously. "I don't want to do anything that makes you uncomfortable, but it's so hard to turn my back on him when he has this condition, you know?"

I can hear the neediness in my voice, the desire for Aaron to validate everything I've said.

"But why does it have to be you?" His voice is steady, calm. "Doesn't he have people to take care of him?"

"Not really," I answer on a sigh. "I mean, you know his parents are gone, and he has no siblings. His aunt and uncle live in England."

When Aaron doesn't say anything, I keep talking. "He used to have a cousin, Lulu, who he was really close to, but the last I heard, she had moved to Nepal or something. With a guy."

"Well, what about friends? Doesn't he have any friends who could help?"

"I don't think so," I say, as I shake my head against the couch cushion. "At least when we were together, he was always working so much, hustling to make money for school. He had plenty of friendly acquaintances but never enough time to be particularly close with anyone. I'd guess that with all the work of the restaurant and his having been back in New York only a matter of months, his social situation is probably pretty much the same. As far as personal connections go, he's always been sort of a man with no country."

"Except for you."

"Except for me."

We are both quiet as we digest these words, and the silence begins to stretch between us. Finally, he says the last thing I am expecting.

"Well, then you have to make it your business to be there for him. I'll help."

Chapter Sixteen
March 2017

I'm just getting to work when Lana calls.

"Hey," I answer, dropping into my desk chair. Nicola isn't here yet to roll her eyes at me for engaging in non-work-related chitchat.

"Are your parents hosting Mother's Day again this year?" Lana asks, without preamble.

"I guess so." Mother's Day is still a couple of months away, and I can't say I've given it much thought. "Why?"

"I'm not inviting Reese."

"Okay." I still don't know where we're going with this. I hear voices in the hallway as other attorneys and admins arrive. I push at the glass door of my office with my patent leather–covered toe; the frosted door swings closed while I wait for Lana to explain what she means.

"I've had it. I think it's time he starts getting left out of the family affairs that he enjoys so much, so he can see what life might be like without me."

"Lana, what are you talking about?" I laugh out loud. "Why does Reese care whether he comes to my parents' Mother's Day barbecue?"

"Oh my God, for real?" she demands, her voice rising

a couple of octaves. "It's like the highlight of his year every year, the whole down-and-dirty barbecue thing. *Dope*, actually, is how I remember him describing it to his dad last year. The Altmans are so *dope*." Her voice is laced with ridicule as she draws out the last word. She pauses for a second, and I can hear her sipping on something, which I imagine is her daily nonfat vanilla iced latte. "Also, he's obsessed with your dad's blue cheese sliders."

My dad isn't much in the kitchen, but he does grill like a champ. Between the backyard smoker he added to his arsenal a few years ago and the next-door neighbor's deep fryer, I think it's fair to say that our annual Mother's Day get-together actually *is* pretty dope.

"So, what's the plan? He misses out on his Jeff special and then he decides he can't live without the Altman Mother's Day barbecue, which translates into not being able to live without you? Cue proposal?" I can't say I'm impressed by the plan here.

"No, dumbass," she quips. "I was thinking that I could tell him he's not invited, which is the first blow, and then spend the whole afternoon with one of Aaron's cousins or some hot doctor friend that you can tell him to bring. I'll post a whole bunch of pics on social media for Reese to see after the fact, and maybe that will get him thinking."

"Okay, I have problems with this plan on so many levels, the first of which is that you should not need to make your man jealous in order for him to realize how much you mean to him."

My mind flashes to the mind-blowing sex Aaron and I had last night, and I wonder if I'm actually right about that.

"Secondly, if this is how you're feeling now—today,

or last month, or last year—why are you waiting until Mother's Day to take action?"

She sighs so heavily into the phone that I wonder if she has to grasp it tighter so it won't blow away. As I wait for her to respond, I reach for the mouse on my desk and wiggle it to bring my computer screen to life.

"I just need a little more time," she says, as if she's pleading with me, "before I start making waves. I've kind of given myself until May, and if it seems like he's still not ready to get serious, I'm going to rock the boat. But I don't want to start the rocking until I'm ready to deal with the consequences. I know how to push Reese, and I'm just worried that I might end up pushing him in the other direction."

"Okay, fine. I guess that makes sense. A little." I open my email, tensing as I wait to see if I have any messages from attorneys that are going to ruin my day. Nothing jumps out at me from within the list of bolded, unread messages, just some firm-wide announcements and possible spam. "I can't imagine that the barbecue is anything other than on, but I'll double-check and keep you posted."

"Awesome," she says, and I can hear that subtle shift in her voice that tells me she's turning her focus to something else, maybe readying to get back to whatever work she has sitting on her Lucite desk.

"Hey, Lan," I say, trying to hold on to her attention for one more minute, "you're one of the most fabulous people I know. You're breathtaking and exciting and full of fun. If Reese can't see that or can't appreciate you in the way you want, another guy will. You need to know that." I don't tell her how lucky she is to know her mind, to at least be able to understand her own emotions.

"Thanks, man. I know," she says, with too much resignation in her voice. "I just really wanted it to be Reese."

I TAKE ADVANTAGE of the lack of tyrannical emails in
my inbox and devote my morning to Moe's asylum case.
In only a few more hours, Moe will be returning to our
office for our next client meeting, possibly the final
meeting before we have to file his papers, and I'm trying
to create an efficient agenda. The firm allows me to devote only so many hours and resources to this case, but
there are still numerous questions I need answered. I
have a passing worry that I might face negative consequences when the partners, or whoever it is that reviews
my time charts, notice how many of my ten-minute
billing increments I have allocated to this case. Even so,
this man's whole future is at stake and I can't give anything less than 100 percent.

I pull up the Human Rights Watch report, the document I used as my first jumping-off point to learn about
Myanmar when I began working on this case. I read it
over again and find the information still useful but a bit
broad, too generalized, sort of like the stories I've been
hearing from Moe himself. I'm having a hard time actually
putting myself into Moe's narrative, following the
chronology from point A to point B. After another Google
search, I find several videos about resettled Burmese
people who are now living productively in the United
States. Many of them have settled in Southport, Indiana,
which is where Moe says he plans to go once his immigration status is settled. I click on one link after another,
reading articles and stories about displaced Christians,

tortured Muslims. I see the same statistics over and over, and my eye keeps catching on the fact that 1.2 million Muslims continue to endure human rights abuses in Myanmar. I wonder how it's fair that such a small percentage of these people escape to safety. I wonder what happened in the cosmic universe that allowed for Moe to get out while so many others were murdered or trapped in his very same village.

Against my will, my thoughts jump back to ALS. I don't remember the statistics I saw about the prevalence of the disease, what percentage of the population it affects, but I again wonder about fate and what made Wesley fall into the category of the damned.

Before I know it, a couple of hours of online searching have passed and the honest truth is that I feel no more well versed in the workings of Burmese society than I did when I walked into the office this morning. I've consumed an overwhelming amount of information, and it's difficult to separate truth from propaganda. For example, I discovered something called the 969 Movement, which one website says is a violent initiative meant to limit the spread of Islam, and which another site describes as a peaceful attempt to preserve Buddhist culture. I'm not familiar with the organizations behind either website, and there's no way for me to decide which information to believe. Instead, I ignore the question for the time being and stand up from my chair to seek out Rose Conway, the senior associate who is technically supervising me on this case. Although I'm doing all the work, she joins me for the meetings with Moe, and when the time comes to present our case before the immigration judge, she will sit first chair.

I find Rose in her office and fill her in on the work I've managed to complete, as well as the holes that still need addressing. We have ample data about Moe's home district, the political climate of the region as a whole, and the day on which the Myanmar military plundered his village, but we are still missing adequate details about how those attacks affected Moe personally. Beyond the obvious devastation that a military attack would precipitate, we need to populate Moe's application with personalized details to bolster our claims: names of lost loved ones, specific actions of enemies that have led to a continued fear for his safety in his home country. We also need more background on the time he spent in the refugee camp in Thailand. I want to know why he avoided speaking about that period when we last met.

Rose nods while I talk but doesn't jot down any notes. Instead, she fishes for a pair of eyeglasses that she finally pulls from her purse. Along with her dark hair pulled into a low ponytail, and a long pearl necklace hanging over her pink sweater set, the wire-rimmed spectacles are the final touch, completing her costume as an up-and-coming superstar attorney.

We head down the hall to the conference room where we will be meeting with Moe. It's noticeably chilly, the air-conditioning blasting forth in the odd display of corporate bluster that turns our office into an icebox, even during the winter months. It's as though there's an unspoken understanding that whichever firm can afford to keep its rooms the coldest must somehow be filled with the smartest, most desirable attorneys.

Rose's assistant has taken care of stocking the room with platters of pinwheel sandwiches, cookies, and petite bottles of soda. There's enough food for a party, even though there will be only four of us here once Moe arrives with the interpreter. I wonder how it must look to him, all this excess, after having grown up in one of the world's least developed countries. His life was so different from the average American's that he had to be shown how to flush a Western toilet after he arrived in the States.

I hear the ding of the elevator and look through the all-glass wall of the conference room to see Moe emerging from the opening doors, along with another young man who is probably the interpreter. Though it's not the same interpreter who was with him last time. Rose walks out to the reception desk, and I follow behind her to greet them.

"Good afternoon," the man with Moe says. "I am Arnie, the translator."

"Excellent." Rose speaks first, showing herself to be the one in charge. She reaches out to shake Arnie's hand. "I'll try not to keep you too long."

Arnie is older than Moe, probably in his mid-thirties. He's taller, too, somewhere around five foot eight, as opposed to Moe's mere five feet, four inches of stature. They have the same caramel-colored complexion, but Moe is the handsomer of the two, with his sparkling brown eyes and wide-open smile. I notice for the first time that his teeth are in surprisingly good shape, though I wish he would lose the silver hoop in his left ear.

"It is . . . good . . . seeing . . . you." Moe ekes out the greeting word by word, as he nods at Rose and me. She and I exchange an openly impressed glance, silent kudos to the bit of progress Moe seems to be making with his English.

We sit down at the conference table, Arnie and Moe on one side, Rose and I on the other. I have the irrelevant thought that we're in the perfect position to begin a rousing card game as Rose charges straight to business. She begins asking Moe for elaboration on his prior statements, one after the other. He tells us again how his village was inhabited by Rohingya people like him, a Muslim group that has been persecuted in Myanmar for decades. He explains that the Tatmadaw, which are the Burmese armed forces, have been targeting the Rohingya people for ethnic cleansing.

I hold up a finger indicating that Moe should pause in his story, and I turn to Rose. Her dark eyebrows are rising in what appears to be impatience. "This is the same information he's already told us. We need more information about how these conditions affected him personally. Can you try to steer him in that direction?"

Rose sighs as she turns back toward Moe and Arnie, rewording her question. "What happened to you, Moe, in your home, that made you decide to leave?"

Arnie repeats the question in Burmese, and Moe's eyes shift from Rose to me and then back to Arnie before he responds in Burmese. "They arrested my uncle, but with no reason," Arnie speaks as though he is Moe, his eyes on Rose. "They took him away." Moe is finally telling us something new. "My mother, she told me to go, to escape before they came back for me. I did not want to go, because then my mother and my sister would be unprotected. The secret police, they are known to commit terrible violence on the village girls or sell them. So I would not go away."

He stops then, as though that is the whole story.

"What happened next?" I press. Rose shoots me a look like I've spoken out of turn, as though only she can ask the questions.

Moe eyes scan the room as he answers the translated question, looking everywhere except at us.

"My cousin told me the Tatmadaw were coming back, that they were at the other end of the village, making more arrests, that they had my name and they were coming for me. So then I did run." He swallows. "I don't know now, about my mother."

I remember my musings from earlier, about Moe being one of the lucky ones, but as I watch his face tighten, I begin to rethink the word *lucky*.

"What about your sister?" I ask, and I feel Rose tense up in the leather chair beside me, her anger at me for commandeering the conversation escalating.

Arnie repeats the query in Burmese and Moe swallows hard, like the question has surprised him. The interpreter says something else, in his own words, and Moe shakes his head, his jaw clenched.

"What is it?" I ask as Rose's phone pings with a message from its spot beside her notepad on the table. I glance her way as her eyes dart to the screen.

"You know what?" Rose interrupts, pushing back from the table. "They need me downstairs for a few minutes. You seem like you've got this." She flings the words in my direction, her tone acidic.

I am too focused on the question of Moe's sister to care whether Rose is miffed that I've somehow encroached on her authority.

"Thanks for your help," she adds to Arnie as she whisks up her papers and marches back toward the elevator.

"Your sister," I say again as soon as the glass door swings shut, my eyes focused on Moe.

He shakes his head no, and I'm surprised he understood.

"Please," I say directly to Moe, but then I glance quickly at Arnie, wondering if he can help convince Moe to reveal the information. "The more we know about what happened to you, the better we can argue your case. Evidence about your other family members is important to your application."

As Arnie repeats my words, Moe lets out a heavy breath of air, his eyes shifting from Arnie to me, then back to Arnie, and finally to his hands. He pulls absently on a loose thread hanging from his chambray shirt before speaking again, quietly.

"I found her," Arnie translates, "in Mae La, in Thailand. I didn't think I would see her again, but then she was there, standing in the center of the small market, just beside the mangoes, on my fifth morning in the camp. She had a wound healing down the side of her face, a scar coming, but besides that, I thought she was all right. All she knew of our mother was that the military men had taken her somewhere. We couldn't go back for her, so we started making plans to go somewhere else together—Australia, America."

He looks up at me, and I nod encouragingly.

"She was not all right, though."

Though I can't understand his words directly, I can hear that Moe's voice is laced with anger now.

"She had been made pregnant by the Tatmadaw."

Moe pauses to clear his throat, turning his gaze out the window in an effort to compose himself. While I wait, I realize that he hasn't mentioned his sister's age. Finally, he continues.

"When I found people to get us the documents," Arnie translates, "so that we could go out from the country, through Bangkok, she was so near the time when the baby would come. I said we should wait to go until after the baby came, but she refused to travel with the child. She thought it was safer for them both just to stay at Mae La. Safer for me also, if they didn't hold me back, she said. She refused, refused," he repeats.

Moe looks at me and pauses for a moment to wipe his eyes.

"And I left anyway. I left her behind."

We are all silent as we absorb the enormity of Moe's words.

"How did you make the choice?" I ask, my curiosity genuine, not simply a desire to fill in blank spaces on the I-589.

He purses his lips, thinking for a moment. When he finally speaks, Arnie nods before translating:

"I decided that she would not want me to give up my future for her."

Although Moe makes this declaration as though the decision had been a simple one, I can see virulent emotions simmering just below the surface. As I watch the vein pulsing in his forehead, I wonder what I would have done in his place. My lawyer's mind notes that Moe's application will, in fact, be significantly stronger with this new information about his uncle's arrest, his mother's disappearance, and his sister's sexual assault, all of which will establish that the alleged pattern of mistreatment by the military directly affected his family. Shame on me for not having discovered this information sooner, as the offenses committed against his family go toward proving the legitimacy of the threat of harm he perceived toward himself. It will help if Moe has any proof of these events —papers regarding his uncle's arrest, or even a photograph of his sister with a bulging belly. I worry that if I ask, I'm going to find myself holding a photo of twelve- or thirteen-year-old girl.

I open my laptop to stall for a moment, and I see an email waiting from Peri Holz, the administrative assistant I share with a few other junior lawyers. I click the message and read, *Emergency Kinderwohl meeting in twenty minutes.*

I quickly tap back a reply: *Thanks. Pls let them know I'll be a few min late bc I'm with another client.*

Screw them and their chewing tobacco. I'm not leaving this meeting before it's good and finished. Maybe there's a part of me that wants to poke the hornets' nest, provoke the higher-ups into firing me. But when I think about how pissed Alexandra, the supervising associate, will be that I didn't come running to the meeting, I flinch. Okay, so maybe I should start wrapping up this conversation.

I ask about a photo, but Moe has nothing of the sort. Rose reappears and sits back in the chair she had vacated, without saying a word, as if she is waiting for me to fill her in. Moe's reference to his future has reminded me that we still need more information about his plans, about how he is going to become a contributing member of American society if his application is granted. I remind Rose about this line of questions, and she asks Arnie.

"The IRC got me a position in a Chinese restaurant

uptown. I wash the dishes and sweep the floors. I hope soon they are going to give me more hours of working time."

I wonder if I should try to get Moe into the class Wesley is running at the soup kitchen, help him learn skills that could translate into more hours of work for him somewhere. But then I remember that Wesley is almost finished with the course. If he's not teaching another semester of the life skills class, he must know that his health is about to start deteriorating more rapidly. I swallow the lump that has suddenly risen in my throat and turn my attention back to Moe. "We're going to do everything we can," I say, looking directly at him, as though we don't need Arnie's help in order to communicate, "to make sure you get the future your sister wanted for you."

Chapter Seventeen
May 2017

I wake up to bright sunshine streaming in through Aaron's weak excuse for blackout shades and feel strong arms wrapping themselves around my middle. It's been more than five weeks since I moved in, but I still haven't finished unpacking my boxes. I tell myself that it's some sort of new procrastination trait I've developed and not a metaphorical act symbolizing a reluctance to commit. I'm trying my level best not to let any of my lingering feelings for Wesley jeopardize my future with Aaron. While I must admit to myself that I haven't completely ejected Wesley from my thoughts since I saw him last, I have made a concerted effort to avoid him, which is also an effort to protect my relationship with Aaron.

Although now, as I lie in bed with my eyes open, staring at the six closed moving boxes piled on top of each other against the opposite wall of the bedroom, I wonder if I should just check to see how Wesley is doing. When Aaron asked me nearly two months ago, the day after our argument on the topic, what I was going to do to help Wesley, I told him that I didn't think the disease had progressed all that far yet, that I could wait until

Wesley really needed physical assistance before I stepped in. Neither of us has brought it up since. I have also stopped going to the soup kitchen, having finally realized that my plan to desensitize myself to Wesley by spending increased time in his orbit was just a weak rationalization on my part.

It's Saturday, and Aaron is starting a shift at the hospital in a few hours. I decide to get up and make us brunch before he heads to the gym. Better yet—I pull out the stack of takeout menus above the fridge in his kitchen, pick up my phone, and order us some crêpes and omelets from the French-Greek gastro-diner down the street.

The food arrives twenty minutes later, and I marvel at the speed at which things can happen in this great city I've lived in for the last decade. I tiptoe back into the bedroom and then ask myself why I'm creeping, since I'm planning to wake Aaron anyway. I sit on the side of the bed and take a moment to admire the expanse of his naked back. I feel a primal surge of lust thinking about the vast amount of space this one human manages to occupy, and an equal sense of contentment as I run my hand over his bare shoulders.

"Good morning, Dr. Rapp," I say too loudly, knowing the noise will jar him into consciousness.

He turns over relatively quickly and fixes me with one of his irresistible grins, all teeth and just the littlest hint of a single dimple. "Ooh, are we role-playing? Are you finally going to be my nurse?"

"Shut up." I punch him playfully in the thigh, or what I think is his thigh, beneath the white sheet. "I ordered Nutella crêpes and spinach omelets. Come." I give a little yank on his hand. He ambles out of the bed, pulling on a pair of drawstring jersey pants that greatly flatter his abs, and then follows me to the living room.

As we sit on the couch and each unwrap the foil from our crêpes in our standard "dessert first" brunch move, I breathe in the smell of chocolate spread and decide that today I am going to wear my big-girl panties.

"So, I think I'm going to visit Wesley today," I announce, proud of myself for declaring my intentions in advance of my actions.

Aaron glances over at me and then looks back to his crêpe. "Okay."

"I thought I'd go down to the restaurant this afternoon, just see how he's doing."

"Okay," he says again.

I turn my body on the sofa to face him and take his chin in my hand, turning his head toward me. He raises his eyebrows at me and keeps chewing. For all I can tell, he looks genuinely calm.

"I'm going to take what you say at face value," I tell him, "so if you've got a problem with this, say so. Otherwise, I won't know it bothers you."

"It does bother me," he says, and I wonder what to say, "but I think it's the right thing to do, and you need to do it."

We stare at each other in silence for a moment, each evaluating the other's position.

"Okay," I finally say.

"Okay," he says, and turns back to his food.

"But," I say, and I wait for him to look back over at me before I continue speaking, "you are my priority, and I don't want to do anything you're aren't okay with, so

you have to speak up. If you see something, say something."

"Okay."

"You're my priority," I repeat, willing it to be true.

THREE HOURS LATER, I am standing on Greenwich
Avenue, wondering if I should be here, staring at the
painted door of Thunder Chicken. I think back to that
moment outside my building several weeks ago, when I
felt like Wes was going to kiss me, when I almost let that
happen, and I know that I am playing with fire. But then
I remember the way Wesley and I used to be, the magic
that seemed to swirl around us like a vortex every time
we looked at each other, and I push open the door of the
restaurant with an involuntary burst of excitement.

A willowy hostess awaits at a podium just past the
vestibule. "Good afternoon," she greets me with some
sort of Eastern European accent that I can't place and
not even a hint of a smile. "You have a reservation?"

I didn't expect the restaurant to be so full at
lunchtime, but every last table appears to be occupied,
and another group of people is walking in the door behind me. I hadn't meant to come at such a busy time, and
I second-guess myself. But then I see the hostess looking
behind me at the next group, getting ready to dismiss me,
and that gets my goat.

"I'm not here to eat," I tell her. "I'm looking for Wesley
Latner."

The young woman's eyes snap back toward me as she
looks me over now from head to toe, taking in my casual
white T-shirt, black leggings, and white platform sneakers.

Clearly, in my informal garb, I am not from the health department. Maybe she thinks I'm some sort of stalker who's pining after Wesley and tracking him back to his restaurant. Which, actually, is precisely what's going on.

"Chef is very busy with the brunches. It is about what?"

"Oh. I'm just . . ." I look back at the room full of diners, bustling servers, and laughing patrons, a group of fashionable people all clearly in the know about clothing, eateries, and everything else that makes someone *someone* in this high-stakes city. "I'll come back another time." I pull my phone out of my purse and glance down at the screen as I turn to leave in a lame attempt at looking busy and important while I go.

As I scoot past the two couples that have been waiting behind me, I hear someone call my name and turn to see Wesley coming toward me. I'm struck, as always, by the draw I feel toward the vivid emerald of his eyes, his thick lips, but then I notice his awkward gait and I look down to see that he's using not one, but two canes, as he hobbles toward me. His jaw is clenched as he approaches, and I can tell that he is expending great effort to make it appear as if this hurried walking is not enormously difficult. I hustle back past the other patrons who are still waiting for the hostess so that he can stop the charade.

"Hi," I say as I lean in to give him an awkward kiss on the cheek. He leans forward on his canes, and our cheeks connect for a split second before I step back.

"Sorry," I say in a rush, "I was coming to check in on you, but I didn't realize you guys would be so busy. I don't know why I assumed you did primarily a dinner business."

"No worries," he says as the hostess passes by, four

slate menus in her hand, leading two couples around us. She dips her high cheekbones down in a nod toward Wesley, who nods back absently.

"They don't really need me," he says, his eyes back on me. "I've handed over the reins and have only been coming in to oversee my replacements. For better or for worse, it seems I've found two very capable guys, and I've effectively made myself obsolete."

"Oh, well, then do you want to sit and catch up for a minute?" It's more forward than I usually am, more forward than I expected to be today, but I don't want Wesley to remain standing on my account. I glance around quickly, wondering where we can even sit down, as even the seats at the bar are full.

"Sure," he says, sounding relieved, perhaps even pleased. "There's an office in the back."

He turns toward the interior of the restaurant, and I start following him just as the hostess passes us again, returning to her post. I raise my eyebrows at her as I set off behind him, as if to say, *Suck it, bitch.* It reminds me of all the times over the years when other women would hit on Wesley. He was either completely oblivious or totally uninterested in them, but it always left me with a little ego boost, and I can feel myself getting high off those same self-congratulatory fumes right now.

Except as I turn back and follow Wesley, I see the way he's walking and the joy seeps straight out of me. He seems to be putting nearly all of his weight on the canes as he limps along. One leg is clearly much weaker than the other, but both are apparently in bad shape. I feel tears springing to my eyes as I watch the awkward up-and-down movement. His whole body seems to rise up, shimmy a little, and sink back down between each step. He's like an ill-equipped sailboat making its way doggedly over dangerously large waves, one after another. I bite down hard in attempt to keep the tears at bay, and I try to distract myself by letting my eyes wander the restaurant. Nobody is paying us much attention. The couples and groups are all engrossed in their meals, their mimosas, one another.

We finally reach a door at the back of the restaurant that reads EMPLOYEES ONLY. I follow him into a dark hallway where there appears to be a couple of offices and a bathroom. He stops at the first office, a dimly lit room with a glass desk at its center. Two deep black chairs face the desk, and a black sofa sits against one wall. Even though I know it's sunny outside, it has suddenly become nighttime in this dark space. I look for a light switch as Wesley leans his canes against the side of the desk. He lowers himself with a thump into the chair behind the desk and sighs with relief.

"Please, sit." He motions toward the two empty chairs across from him.

"Want me to get the lights?" I ask, finding the weird purple glow from the funky wall sconces a little too nightclub-ish for this reunion.

Wesley lets out a loud, exasperated breath. "I didn't even . . ." He starts over. "Sorry. Yeah. They're there." He points toward a panel in the corner.

I hit a couple of switches and the room lights up, plunging us back into a corporate scene—swanky corporate, but still greatly improved over the strip-club vibe that the dark violet lighting had been creating a moment ago. I lower myself into one of the leather chairs opposite him, keeping my back straight despite the way the seat's plush middle is calling me to sink deeper.

"I like what you've done with the place," I say, for lack of a better opener. I glance around at the bachelor pad style of the room—the stark, grid-like metallic shelving covering one wall, a Captain America shield displayed proudly on one of the higher shelves. There are a couple of black-and-white prints on the wall that look like updated versions of Keith Haring art, just trippier. Next to the sofa sits a tall silver halogen lamp that curves at several odd, robotic angles. It's all very modern and rigid, and not at all how I would have pictured Wesley decorating. "All you're missing is the animal-print rug."

"Oh, this is all Calvin's," he says dismissively as he runs the back of his hand along his forehead, as if he's wiping away sweat. "The guy I sold the restaurant to. We've basically made the transition, but I still come in a few times a week, just to . . ." He looks at the ceiling.

"It's gotten so much worse already?"

"No, I'm okay," he says, sounding a little defensive.

"But the canes." I gesture toward the side of the desk, where one dark cane still rests and the other has fallen to the wood floor.

"Yeah." He sighs. "I have something called foot drop. My muscles can't lift the front of my foot the way they're supposed to."

"I know what it is," I say, thinking back to the many hours I spent researching ALS when I first heard the news. "Both feet?"

"Only the right so far. But the other leg is weak now, too."

"Doesn't this mean it's time for a wheelchair? If you

fall and get hurt, it will only make everything worse."

"No," he says with finality, his lips closing tightly.

I start to argue, wishing someone in his life were doing more to help him. "But—"

He cuts me off. "I can't. I can't be coming into this hip restaurant in some big wheelchair, weaving in and out of the tables. Think about that."

"You're not handicapped accessible?" I ask, surprised that the restaurant wouldn't have been required to make those accommodations for people before opening.

"No, we are, but I'm just saying they won't want me in here like that. I was supposed to be the enterprising super-chef rising to stardom, not some gimp knocking his wheelchair into the table legs."

"Well, then maybe it's time to do something else. Maybe it's time to stop coming in."

"Don't you get it, Mer?" He lifts up, like he's going to stand, but then slumps back into his chair. "This is all I have now. After you, I made this . . . this . . ." He gestures into the room, as if to indicate the restaurant, the cooking. "This is my life. If I stop coming, then that's the end of all of it, of everything."

"It's not all you have. You have me," I say. I'm not sure exactly what I mean, except that I know that I want to be there for him, to help him however I can.

"No, I don't," he answers, the anger in his voice growing. "I have an empty house in Irvington. And while you're off with your new fiancé, living the life you were meant to have with me, I'll be sitting in my dad's old Barcalounger, watching bad TV, and waiting until I get sick enough to move into a hospital so that I don't have to be alone anymore."

"No!" I shout back, devastated by the picture he has painted, devastated by his regrets.

He looks back at me, a mix of challenge and defeat in his eyes as he cocks his head.

"I refuse to accept that," I add, as I stand.

"Okay, Miss Fix-It, what other option do I have?" The tension in the room is billowing, but I thrive on this, the push and pull that I've always had with this beautiful, withering man.

"Well," I stall, looking away from him. I shove my hands onto my hips and roll my eyes back toward myself as I struggle to concoct a plan.

"Yeah," he says when I don't offer more. "Exactly." He absently begins opening and closing his fist again, like he did the last time I saw him. I notice his movements seem slower this time.

"Look," he continues, more calmly, "I don't mean to get belligerent. It's really nice that you came to see how I am. I didn't mean to freak out on you. It's hard to remember that I have to behave politely around you, to maintain a respectful impartiality or whatever. It doesn't feel like we're so far apart, though, like years have passed since we were together."

I know what he means. When I'm standing in front of him, everything is as fresh in my mind as if it happened only days ago. All of it—the beginning, the awful end, everything in between. Except so much is different now. I remind myself that Wesley is no longer my most important person. That title has to belong to Aaron. Aaron, who has invited me into his life, into his heart, his home. As I feel the urge to move toward Wesley, to protect him in any way I can, guilt creeps into my limbs, little pinpricks locking my feet where I stand. But this is what Aaron wants, I remind myself. He wants me to help, to take care of Wes during this time. And then I have the answer.

"It doesn't have to be like that," I say, a new energy taking hold of me. "I know what you should do. What *we* should do."

He sits silently, looking across the desk at me, waiting for me to continue.

"You can move in with us. It's perfect. We have a second bedroom that's empty. You can stay for as long as you want."

"Us?" he asks. "You and your fiancé?"

"It's perfect," I say again. "You'll have all the conveniences of the city, instead of being out in the 'burbs. You won't be alone, so if you need something, you'll have people to help you. And Aaron's a doctor!" I nearly shout, as I realize this added benefit. Never mind that neonatal surgeons don't usually deal in ALS; his medical training could still come in handy.

Wesley regards me silently for a moment and then squints, like he's trying to see me better. "You're joking, right?" His lip ticks up on one side.

"Not even a little." I shake my head.

"Right." His voice is ripe with skepticism. "And this will be just what Dr. Aaron wants, too, right—his fiancée's old flame shacking up with them? Thanks for the suggestion. I know you mean well, but I think you're entirely insane." He gives me a genuine smile, and I melt a little inside.

"Do you at least have a wheelchair lined up?" I ask, relenting. "I know they can take a long time to get, and you should have it ready for when you need it."

He nods. "I do, actually. I'm going straight to motor-ized. The way I see it, if I'm strong enough to use my arms to push a chair, I'm strong enough to balance on my canes. So, basically, no wheelchair until my arms go, too."

"That's so dumb," I tell him, affection taking hold of me, grabbing at my whole body so intensely that I feel like it's even clouding my vision. "Can I at least come back and visit you? Make sure you're doing okay?"

"Of course." He nods up at me, and I feel like we are genuinely connecting for the first time this decade. The relief I feel at penetrating his force field is intense, like I can finally let out a breath I've been holding since he left.

He glances over at his ebony canes, and I quickly duck down to retrieve the one that's fallen to the floor beside of the desk, and then the other.

"And please think about using a chair," I say as he begins to stand, using the armrests of the desk chair for more support than he should. "I don't want our next visit to be in a hospital."

"I like knowing that there will be a next visit," he says as he takes the canes from my hand, his fingers lingering against mine. A shiver of electricity runs through my body, and what I feel from his touch is definitely not guilt.

THAT NIGHT, I'M drizzling balsamic glaze on slices of fresh mozzarella when I hear Aaron's key in the door. The timing of his shift at the hospital prevented us from having dinner together, but I've gotten into the habit of making a small bite to share even when he gets home late. Somehow, eating together in the evening feels inti-mate, homey, like we're a family. I'm trying to get into the spirit of my upcoming role as Mrs. Aaron Rapp, wife of the illustrious Dr. Rapp. I think about all those yoga instructors and motivational speakers who insist that the physical act of smiling can boost your mood, even if you have to force the expression onto your face. I know my feelings for Aaron aren't forced, that I'm not preparing this cheese platter for him in an effort to mimic emotions I don't feel. It's just that after each time I've been with Wesley, I have to dig deeper to locate my attachment to Aaron, and I don't want to lose my way or forget what's important to me.

I walk out from the galley kitchen with the plate of cheese and greet Aaron as he drops his leather messenger bag near the door. He's still wearing his powder-blue scrubs, which is unusual for him. I worry that it was a rough day at the hospital, that a baby died. I feel a flicker of annoyance that I'm going to have to play therapist for the devastated doctor who couldn't save a life today, and then I hate myself for having that thought.

"Why the scrubs?" I ask.

He looks down at his body, as though he's forgotten what he's wearing. "Oh, nothing. A surgery ran late, and I didn't want to waste time changing before I got home to you."

Oh. Right. Well, I just suck.

He walks toward me and grabs a disk of mozzarella off the plate in my hand, pecking me on the cheek with his warm lips before putting the entire piece of cheese into his mouth.

"Hey," I protest. "You're messing up my display. This is meant to be enjoyed with wine. And maybe even a fork. Come, sit."

I place the platter on the wooden coffee table and scamper back to the kitchen for the red wine I opened moments ago.

"Did you see Wesley?" Aaron calls out from the living room.

Well, I guess there won't be any beating around the bush today. "Yeah, hang on." I'm stalling, unsure how much I want to share

But then I walk out of the kitchen and see Aaron with his feet up on the coffee table, the expression on his broad face tolerant, collaborative, even, as he waits for me to answer. As usual, the comfort that I feel in his presence takes hold and I just want to unload, to share my feelings with him, to lean on someone. It's probably unfair of me. It's definitely unfair of me, but I need to talk through my feelings.

"He looks terrible." *Well, not his face*, I think. I place two bulbous wineglasses on the coffee table and sit down next to Aaron, my hip pushing into his. I pour us each a copious amount as I continue. "He's already hobbling around on two canes. I don't understand it. I thought ALS was slow in how it progresses. It's barely been a couple months since I saw him last, and already he's starting to fall apart." I can feel myself looking to Aaron for answers, for some sort of emotional foothold.

He sighs as he leans forward to pick up his wine, as if it genuinely dismays him to hear that Wesley isn't doing well. "ALS is like that. Some people have good luck and the disease moves slowly. For other people, not so much. It's one of those conditions with little rhyme or reason to it."

"Do you think it's his fault for not getting diagnosed

soon enough? Like, maybe getting on medicine sooner might have slowed the progression?" I ask, feeling a little desperate for a direction in which to cast blame.

"Maybe." He shrugs. "There's no way to know." He hands me the other wineglass, then takes another piece of cheese from the platter. We're both quiet as he chews.

I break the silence as I slump back onto the couch. "I just feel so bad." The taste of the wine is bitter against my tongue. "He doesn't have anyone. He's taking Ubers out to his parents' empty house in Westchester every night and then Ubering back into the city when he wants to go to the restaurant. Oh, and he sold it, the restaurant, to someone who may totally ruin its vibe once Wesley's completely out of the picture." He must have made a killing on the sale, so at least he's got some funds.

"It's just about the worst story I've ever heard, and I see a lot of ugly," Aaron says.

I look toward the dark night outside his oversize windows, twinkling city lights framing the view, as I absorb the weight of Aaron's words.

"It's like he's cursed," Aaron continues. "Losing his parents, then you, then his health and his restaurant. I just . . ." He pauses, and I can't guess what he's thinking. "I'm glad you're there for him. It's the right thing to do." I get the sense that he's speaking to himself as much as to me, trying to convince us both.

"I had an idea that maybe is a little too crazy, but I wanted to get your opinion."

He raises his dark eyebrows and nods, waiting.

"I was thinking we should offer to have Wesley stay here with us." My words are coming in a rush. "In the spare bedroom. Obviously, it would only be temporary, until he needs to go into a facility or whatever. But I think it would really improve his quality of life for the time he has left."

Aaron blinks a couple of times and shoots me a good-natured smirk, like he thinks I'm joking around.

"No, seriously." I hold on to his dark eyes with mine, trying to show him that I mean it.

He squints at me for a second and then asks, "Are you insane?"

I don't tell him that Wesley also squinted at me and called me insane.

"No, I've given it a lot of thought, and I really think it makes sense. I hate to say it, but I think the two of you would really get along well, and we are kind of the only people he has. It'd be a real mitzvah," I add, playing on the Jewish phrase for good deeds, the expression Aaron's mother uses so often when she's talking to him. *Invite Dad to a Yankees game; it'd be a real mitzvah. You should call and check on your brother in Colorado; it'd be a real mitzvah. Help me with the dishes; it'd be a real mitzvah.* Now I'm just adding, *Let me shack up with my ex-boyfriend; it'd be a real mitzvah.*

Aaron looks away from me and fixates on the television across from us, which is not currently on. He stares at the dark screen, and I can see him processing my suggestion as clearly as if he were a kid disassembling a Lego project, piece by piece, to see how it works.

"You just want to put him up in the spare bedroom?" he asks, without anger but with palpable curiosity.

I nod, and I can see his next question forming already. "And who's going to take care of him?"

Loud sirens pass beneath the window while I process

Aaron's question. "Well, he doesn't really need anyone yet," I offer. "I mean, he's still living entirely on his own. When he starts to really need help, we can both help him. Until we can't."

"And you think he's going to just come and live with your new fiancé, like he'll think that's an improvement over his current situation?"

"No, he already said he doesn't want to do that, but I thought if you asked him, instead of me, he might go for it."

"Wait, you already suggested this to him?" His head whips toward me. "Without talking to me?"

Shit.

"Well, I thought of it when I went to see him and just kind of blurted it out, but I would never have actually finalized it without getting your blessing. Of course not."

"Jesus, Mer. You can't just invite some guy to come live with us. Your ex-fiancé, the great love of your life, who has been too precious to even discuss with me until recently. You just ask him to come and live in your spare bedroom. Christ, maybe you want me to take the spare room so he can share the bedroom with you. Better yet, maybe I should just get out altogether. Is that what you want?"

"No, Aaron, no!" My voice has risen to match his. "He was a big part of my life, okay? And he's dying. Wanting to help him has nothing to do with my feelings for you. Of course, I don't want to replace you." I argue hard, hoping that I actually believe what I'm saying.

"I don't know, Mer," he says, more quietly, resignation in his voice. "Am I just the consolation prize because the guy you really want is dying?"

"No!" I shout back at him, as if what he has suggested is entirely ridiculous, as if it's never crossed my mind, as if I haven't been wondering the exact same thing myself for months already. "How could you even say that? What I had with Wesley is so long over and done with, and it doesn't begin to compare with what I have with you. Yes, Wesley was a huge part of my life, and I loved him, for sure, but it was an immature love based on excitement and fun, not on a true commitment to be with each other through the hardest days. It was nothing like what we have," I repeat.

"Why?" he asks, challenging me. "What do we have?"

"Now you know you're just fishing for compliments." I'm trying to lighten the mood, but he just stares back at me, waiting. "We have"—I struggle to find the right words—"a deeper sense of sharing, of acceptance of each other's flaws. We have the kind of love that makes the entire world seem like a better place. Like a place where you want other people to feel happy because it's not fair that you should get to be so content while others suffer. We have the kind of love that makes us want to be better people, to do mitzvahs." As I finish speaking, I realize that I mean every word of what I've said, that I've been allowing my passion for Wesley to taint my recent perception of Aaron, but that my college boyfriend kind of can't hold a candle to the guy sitting beside me. The guilt that I've been pushing away suddenly comes at me like a tidal wave, and I feel sick at how disloyal I've been, even if only inside my own head.

I reach out to Aaron and kiss him. He's stiff for a moment, rigid, but then he relents, softening and kissing me back. As our tongues mingle and I breathe in his warm, clean scent, I feel my body react, but I pull back because I have more to say.

"I'm so sorry. Forget it." The words tumble out of me. "Forget I ever suggested that he move in. I just want you to be happy. To be comfortable. It was a stupid suggestion, a dumb idea that I never should have voiced aloud. Just forget it, please."

"No, stop it," he tells me, reaching out to push a strand of wayward hair behind my ear. "It wasn't a dumb suggestion. Unexpected, maybe. A little unconventional of you, for sure. But it's part of what I love about you, your consistent desire to help people, your ability to look beyond the confines of standard behavior. I think we should do it."

"What?" I feel myself blanch. "No, seriously, forget it." Now I don't want it. I don't want Wesley to be in such close proximity to us, clouding my judgment like he has since the day I found him back in New York, blurring my love for Aaron. I regret that I ever mentioned it.

"No," he says, getting more animated, "I can't believe I'm saying this, but I think it's actually starting to make sense to me. It'll be a big help to Wesley if he doesn't have to commute, and my medical skills might be at least somewhat useful. It can delay his need to go into a facility, give him some quality of life, like you said. And then you'll never have regrets. Besides, it's not fair for me to be jealous when I know that the competition is temporary. Sorry," he adds hastily. "But seriously, even if you were to fall for him all over again, it's not like you're going to run off with him, and I know you love me, too. I know you'll remember that in the end, and who am I to say you shouldn't have even more love in your life? I'll talk to him, make it happen."

I'm silent as I try to digest the way our roles have reversed during this conversation.

"Here's a thought," he adds as he picks up his wineglass and takes a hefty sip. "Maybe when things get really bad for Wesley, it'll inspire you to quit your job, take care of him full time until it becomes too complicated."

"What is it with you and my job?" I snap. "This isn't 1950, where your wife is supposed to stay home ironing all day."

"I know that." He laughs lightly. "I just want you to have a job you enjoy, a place you look forward to going, and Harrison, Whittaker is definitely not that."

"So, instead of sitting through depositions and document review, I should nurse my dying ex from dawn to dusk?"

"Look, you're the one who suggested we do this." Aaron holds up his wide hands in surrender, like he's retreating. "Now that you've convinced me, you can't act like I'm all crazy for thinking through some of the logistics of it."

That may be true, except now I think it was a terrible idea. And I don't know how to tell him that we should put the kibosh on the whole thing, that I shouldn't be allowed such unfettered access to Wesley because it will make me dismiss my feelings for Aaron. And then I wonder if I'm being selfish, making everything about me, yet again. Aaron is right. Even if I do fall for Wesley all over again, it's not like we have a future together. And Wesley does need people. A place to stay. People to care whether he's had a meal or fallen down.

"I just want to do what you want to do," I relent. If Aaron is happy, I tell myself, then I will be happy, too.

"Okay, I'm calling him tomorrow, and we'll make this happen. In the meantime, can you please come into the bathroom with me already and help me shower off the hospital?" He finishes the remainder of his wine in one big gulp and pulls me up from my seat before leading me toward the hot, relentless cleansing that I need.

Chapter Eighteen
June 2017

"*T*hat's the last of them," Aaron announces as he pushes Wesley's suitcase against the wall with the others and closes the door behind himself.

Wesley wheels out of the spare bedroom in his manual wheelchair, the one that he finally started using after Aaron went to see him. I'm not sure what Aaron said to convince him about the wheelchair, or about moving in with us, but clearly Wesley finds Aaron more persuasive than he does me.

"The place is great," Wesley tells us both, his eyes still roaming around the airy space, lingering on artwork, photographs. "Thank you so much for convincing me to come here."

We're lucky that Aaron has a loft-style apartment with wide doorways and generally open spaces. It won't provide much by way of privacy for the duration of Wesley's stay, but it will certainly make it easier for him to maneuver in his chair.

"I'll bring your suitcases to your room," I say, grabbing the handle of the black rolling duffel closest to me. I'm not sure why I didn't process sooner how incredibly uncomfortable this situation would be for me.

"Let me give you the grand tour," Aaron says, a little

facetiously. Even though we have a big apartment by New York City standards, it's still a relatively compact space.

"Sure thing," Wesley says as he wheels behind Aaron, following him toward the kitchen. I begin to realize that the only one who feels flustered seems to be me.

I watch them for a second before taking the luggage toward the bedroom. Aaron looks like a walking advertisement for vitamin supplements or one of those horrible nutrient-dense smoothies. He's wearing worn, dark jeans that hug his body and a simple gray T-shirt that showcases his broad back and wide biceps. His dark hair is rich and thick, the little bit of kink in it adding to its boyish charm. As he disappears around the wall to the kitchen, my eyes travel down to Wesley, who is moving slowly in the wheelchair, probably still adjusting to the bulk of it, minding the walls and any obstacles as he rolls. Though he is narrower than Aaron, he still looks too strong to be sitting in a wheelchair. His shoulders are straight, his own arm muscles still relatively toned. Not hulking like Aaron's, and surely smaller than they once were, but he hardly looks a man who is progressing steadily toward death. I wonder for a moment if the weeks of using canes are what have kept his arm muscles robust for longer, and then I turn toward the room that will be Wesley's quarters, rolling the duffel behind me.

After lifting the duffel onto the bed to make it easier for him to reach, I make two more trips for Wesley's other bags. As I drop the last tote onto the thick gray duvet, I wonder if I ought to unpack for him. We really haven't set any parameters on how this arrangement will work, and I don't have a clue how self-sufficient, or how dependent, Wesley is at this point.

I hear the guys making their way toward the bed-
rooms, joking and laughing with each other like the best
of friends. I suppose it shouldn't surprise me. Aaron has
always had a way of connecting with people especially
quickly.

"Hey, Wes," I say as I emerge from the bedroom and
meet them coming toward me in the hallway, "do you
want me to unpack your stuff for you?"

"Nah, that's okay. I can still handle moving some
shirts around. I just use the lower drawers." He offers a
self-deprecating smile.

"Oh, okay; then I'll leave you to it." I head toward my
laptop in the front room, happy to seek distraction on
the Internet.

Aaron follows Wesley into his bedroom, and though I
can no longer hear the words they are saying, the ca-
dence of their voices through the walls tells me that they
are continuing to chat at very friendly pace.

I don't know what I was thinking, suggesting that
Wesley move in with us. I shouldn't be around him. It's
bad. I'm bad. Bad, bad, bad.

And now what? Are we going to all three eat dinner
together every night? Until Wes is so sick that he has to
be spoon-fed by an aide? Speaking of aides, I remember
that I wanted to discuss the issue of professional assistance with Wesley, figure out what kind of help he
needs, when we should hire someone. Lord knows I do
not want to be the one wiping his ass after he uses the
toilet.

I type a search into the computer: *home health aides
for ALS NYC.* One ad after another pops up at the top of
the screen for in-home health care. I scroll down until I

find the first non-sponsored link. I discover a company called Bayada. Its website says that the company has worked with the ALS Association to develop the one and only certified training program for in-home healthcare aides working with ALS patients. I wonder how that can be, that only one organization has a reputable training program for this service. I continue poking around on the website. I click on the link that says *Assistive Care Services.* My heart sinks while I read: *Assistance with communication devices, such as symbol and picture boards, dressing and grooming assistance, safe bathing and toileting.* The list goes on and on, but I can't stomach thinking about all the ways in which Wesley is going to unravel. I hit the BACK button and start reading about the company's other services. When my eyes hit on the word *hospice* at the bottom of the page, I freeze for a moment, trying to internalize that Wesley is actually, truly, imminently dying.

I hear Aaron making his way back toward the front room, and I quickly hit the *X* in the top right corner of the screen, returning to the tab with my emails on it.

"So," he says, as he approaches from behind me and puts his hands down on either side of me on the desk. He kisses the side of my head mildly. "How about if I take you out for Thai food? We can give Wesley a little privacy to settle in, and I can get some date time with my girl?"

"Yeah, that sounds great." Breathing some air outside of this hotbed of awkward sounds just right. "Give me five minutes to change."

WHEN WE SIT down at a quiet table in the Golden Lotus, our favorite neighborhood Thai place, I can tell that Aaron is excited to discuss something. He's practically glowing as he unfolds his cloth napkin and places it on his lap. I hope it's not the Wesley effect. He can do that to people, pump them up, invigorate them with the force of his own internal energy. I can imagine why Aaron would be juiced up after a few hours of basking in Wesley's attention.

"I'm so glad we're doing this," he starts, and I know that, unfortunately, he's referring to the arrangement with Wesley, not the fact that we're eating Thai food together, which is something we do all the time. "I'm not going to lie. It's weird, and I'm not sure whether I'm comforted or annoyed to see that Wes is actually a pretty stand-up guy."

Wes. Aaron is calling him Wes now? What the actual fuck is happening in my life?

"If things were different," he continues, "I could see myself being good friends with the guy."

"Except that he doesn't make good friends—he doesn't do that whole thing." I notice that my voice is snippy, that I'm feeling annoyance and jealousy that I can't quite contain.

"Right. Well." He sounds nonchalant, unaffected by my attitude. "It gave me a crazy idea, this whole day, this whole chapter of our existence . . ." He's interrupted by the waitress who comes over to take our order. "The usual?" he asks me, and when I nod, he rattles off our standard choices: vegetable spring rolls, green papaya salad, chicken pad Thai, and beef satay. A beer for him. A house red wine for me.

"So . . ." he starts again, slowly, after the waitress

walks away, like he's trying not to spook me. "Here's a thought. Just something I was toying with. What do you think about having a baby?"

I lower my eyebrows in a lack of understanding before I answer.

"You know I want kids. We've talked about it a million times." I can't imagine why we are revisiting the topic at this moment.

"No, I mean have a baby now."

"Now?" I ask. I glance over at the round table of older women beside us, smiling women in their seventies, and I wonder if everything is easier for them, if they are finished with all the drama that pervades the younger years. I wonder if you ever grow up enough that the tensions and complexities abate, that you can get through one freaking meal without having to consider the lifelong implications of your every action.

"Yeah, now. Just hear me out. Being around Wesley has made me realize how short life is, how unpredictable. One of the experiences I've been looking forward to the most is getting to be a parent with you. I know it feels like we're just starting out and there will be plenty of time for all that, but what if there's not? Maybe we should be taking our opportunities while they're there for the taking."

"You do know you've gotten the progression wrong, the standard sequence? It's supposed to go marriage first, then kids." I still don't really believe he means this, and my flip response shows him as much.

"I'm not kidding around. It can take couples a really long time to get pregnant, and then, after you wait out the whole pregnancy, babies die. I hate to be morbid, but

I see it all the time, babies that lose their grasp on life within just the first few days, the first few hours, couples who decide to start over. We might be able to have a baby nine or ten months from now, but it could just as easily take us years before we actually become parents. Why should we wait—when we know we love each other, when we know we're in it for the long haul and we have the same end goal?"

As I breathe in the restaurant's pervasive smell of peanut sauce, I digest that Aaron actually means what he is saying, and I wonder at his motivation. Is he trying to mark me, impregnate me with his seed, so to speak, in reaction to having Wesley so nearby?

"I guess what you're suggesting is kind of sweet," I say as I parse through ways of firmly closing the lid on this ludicrous idea, "but I don't think you've really given this thought. The logistics of it all. I mean, what, am I supposed to get a maternity wedding dress?"

"Why not?" He shrugs. "You'll look hot no matter what we do."

"No." I shake my head and then say it again. "No. I'm shutting this down. It's an interesting idea, and I applaud you for your creative thinking, but I've spent too many years avoiding that whole unwed-and-pregnant thing. I'm not going to change my approach now."

This is definitely not something I would ever agree to. I have a quick flash forward to what my poor mother's face would look like as her daughter walked down the aisle with a big bulge under her white wedding dress. It probably wouldn't even be white. They'd make me wear red or something, to mark my shame. I bristle, thinking that Aaron clearly doesn't know me at all if he thinks he could convince me to do something so avant-garde. How can it be that the man I'm meant to marry is so oblivious to who I am?

"Okay, fine," he says. "I know this is not something you would ever normally go for, that you're never the first one to get in line for the unconventional."

Oh.

"But having Wesley move in with us is pretty unconventional, isn't it?" He doesn't wait for an answer. "Just keep it in the back of your mind," he suggests. "Let it simmer."

With that, he changes the subject and starts telling me about the latest political saga at the hospital. Two of his fellow neonatologists, Dr. Pam and Dr. Spencer, as I call them, are always bickering, angling to get the better, more prestigious surgeries in their rat race to be the next department head. If I had to guess, though, my money would be on Aaron getting the spot when it opens. Present impulsive suggestion aside, he is generally the most level-headed doctor in the group, and completely meticulous—not to mention, he's totally brilliant. Every time I voice my opinion that I think he'll be the next chair, he waves my comments away. He's not gunning for it, like his peers. He's happy with the position he has now, content to be doing a job he loves and improving the outcomes for as many infants as he can.

When we walk back into the apartment, it's only a little after 9:00 p.m., but the lights are off and Wesley's door is closed. When Aaron hits the switch to illuminate the hallway, I see a sticky note hanging on Wesley's door.

A loose scrawl reads, "Turned in early. Thanks again for everything."

I'm surprised. Wesley was always a night owl. But things change, I remind myself. His condition must take a lot out of him, and he needs a different kind of rest now. I try not to think about it. I don't want to spend every waking minute being sad about Wesley's fading vitality. Aaron and I head into our room quietly, closing the door behind us.

And then, without any sort of prelude, he's all over me. His hands are in my hair, and he's pushing me up against the wall as his mouth descends on mine. I didn't even have a chance to turn on a lamp or anything. I kiss him back, enjoying the feel of his warm tongue, the faint taste of mint lingering. I know that having Wesley in the apartment has done something to Aaron, made him more aggressive, almost feral, like he can't possess me hard enough. It's like he's intoxicated by me when he starts in like this, and I can't deny that I dig it.

He rips his mouth from mine to step back and lift my blouse over my head. I comply, eager to get back to him. When he pushes me back against the wall again, I bump the bookcase beside me, knocking several books to the floor with a loud thud. I laugh for one second, and then I remember Wesley in the room across the hall, and I freeze.

Aaron feels me stiffen and pulls back, the mild ambient light from the city night casting him in a soft blue glow.

"What? What is it?" He's whispering, which somehow feels exactly appropriate in the moment.

"Wesley."

Aaron glances toward the closed door and then looks back at me.

"He's right across the hall," I explain. "We're making a racket. It's just weird if he hears."

"Don't worry. The door is closed, and he's sleeping. It's fine," he says, lowering his face back toward mine.

I turn away, and Aaron sighs loudly. "Look," he says, "the guy could be living with us for months, or longer. We can't put a moratorium on sex for that whole time."

As with so many other details, I hadn't really thought this part through before Wes moved in. It's true he could be living with us for a long time and spending an increasing amount of time in the apartment or in bed. I guess Aaron has a point.

"Fine, but can we just make an effort to be a little quiet? At least on his first night?"

"You got it," Aaron says, as he rushes my mouth again, now fiddling with the button of my jeans. He pushes my pants toward the floor, and I step out of them without breaking our kiss.

Then he's steering me toward our bed, his hands exploring my body as we go. As the backs of my legs connect with our white down duvet, he pulls away again, this time lifting off his own shirt and tossing it to the floor, then getting to work on his pants. It's too dark to see all the details, but I can still make out the shape of him, and I am arrested, as usual, by the utter perfection of his physique—the width of his shoulders, the angle at which his sides dive toward a V at his waist.

I pull him down on top of me, anxious to feel his warm skin against mine so he can make me forget that my dying ex-fiancé is just across the hall, make me forget that I have any feelings of conflict, that I am anything less than 100 percent loyal to this beautiful man above me.

Aaron climbs on top of me and rearranges us so that my head is on a pillow. And then he is jamming into me with such force that I again wonder whether he is trying to mark me, to prove that I belong to him. The headboard begins banging against the wall. I try to move down on the bed a little to limit this unmistakable sound of sex, which I imagine is reverberating through the entire apartment and perhaps beyond. But Aaron holds me in place, possibly oblivious to my efforts in his current haze or, more probably, totally on purpose, so that Wesley can hear us, so that he knows, in no uncertain terms, that I belong to Aaron, not him. By the sound of it, Aaron is currently fucking my brains out, and, speaking as a participant in the action, I wish I could say that were true, that my brains weren't working overtime inside my head, that I could stop thinking for even a moment, stop focusing on Wesley.

I feel the urge to push Aaron off me, mortified that Wesley could be listening to this, but, in spite of everything, I am also enjoying the feel of Aaron pounding into me. I can feel myself building toward something, and I don't actually want to stop. Even when my head is not in the game, Aaron's efforts seem to overwhelm my body. When I finally find my release, I fight the urge to cry out in pleasure, biting down on Aaron's shoulder instead. That seems to put him over the edge and he, too, reaches his climax, releasing a deep guttural moan —a growl really—that's significantly louder than any of the sex noises he usually makes. If I had any question about Aaron's intention of trying to be heard, the volume of his battle cry has just provided a definitive answer. This sex was as much about putting on a show for Wesley as it would have been if he'd been sitting in the room, watching us.

While I'm totally mortified, I'm also kind of touched that Aaron feels so possessive of me, that I matter enough to make him this jealous.

"Well, I think you definitely made your point there." I push at him gently so I can roll out from under him.

"What point? That we should do that again and make a baby?" He flips onto his back and pulls me toward him so that my head is resting on his chest.

"Yeah, no." I stop, wondering if I should just let it go. He is housing Wesley only out of his love for me. If this loud, exhibitionist banging session was what he needed to feel a little more comfortable with the arrangement, then maybe I should just cut him some slack. It's possible that my judgment is being clouded by a post-orgasmic fog, but I don't want to fight with him.

"I will be very happy to make a baby with you," I tell him as I snuggle a little closer and settle in for sleep, "in, like, two to ten years."

He kisses the top of my head and then reaches to pull the covers over us. It occurs to me that there's a good chance that Wesley will be dead before we ever have a child. I don't know what's harder for me to picture: a world with my child in it, or a world without Wes.

Chapter Nineteen
June 2017

I'm using Aaron's car to drive out to New Jersey, navigating my way through the modest Sunday traffic on the Jersey Turnpike, when I get a call from Lana.

"Hey," I say, as I press the button on the steering wheel to answer. "Hello?" I say it a second time and then a third as I wait for the phone to establish its connection to the hands-free speaker.

"Guess what?" Lana finally says, excitement in her voice.

"What?" I play along as I flip on my turn signal and move right to exit the highway.

"Spencer called and asked me to dinner." Spencer is Aaron's physician friend, the one I asked Aaron to bring to Mother's Day at my parents' because I didn't have the energy to convince Lana that her plans to taunt Reese were naive or ill-advised or shortsighted or all of the above.

"Oh. Wow. Are you going?"

"I don't think so," she says, "even though he is super cute. It was just good that Reese heard the message Spencer left me when I accidentally played my voicemails on speakerphone." I imagine her making air quotes around the word *accidentally.*

"What'd he say?" I ask, worried that Lana is making life too complicated for herself. Not that I am one to speak. Glass houses and all.

"Just that it was great meeting me, that maybe we could grab dinner sometime. The usual stuff."

"No, not Spencer, Reese. What did Reese say when he heard the message?" The June sunshine is blazing unforgivingly against the asphalt, and I rummage through my purse with one hand, double-checking for my sunglasses. Coming up empty, I lower the sun visor, but it provides little improvement, so I snap it back into place again.

"Before or after he started hyperventilating?" Lana asks, laughing. "No, he was totally pissed, wanting to know if that's why he wasn't invited to Mother's Day this year, because I wanted to hang out with Aaron's doctor friend."

"Spencer happens to be a pretty great guy. You might want to give it some thought. I mean, he's sort of aggressive about moving up the food chain at work, from what Aaron tells me, but you can't fault a guy for being motivated, and he's super smart—like, wizard, mastermind smart."

"And super cute," Lana adds.

"Super cute," I agree.

"But he's not Reese," she says, exhaling wistfully into the phone. "And I think this might have been the kick in the ass he needed. I *told* you it was a good idea to boot him from Mother's Day."

"If you say so," I tease.

"So, fill me in on the latest in the apartment. Is it getting any less bizarre?" I can hear her inner journalist angling for the scoop.

"Nope. Not less weird at all," I quip. "Luckily, it's rare that all three of us are there at the same time. Wesley's been spending most of his time at the restaurant, at least during the hours when Aaron and I aren't at work. I think he's going to have to slow down soon, though. I feel like he's deteriorated in even just the three weeks he's been with us."

"Does Noble know about any of this?" she asks, mentioning my brother, but I barely speak to him these days. He and Shara just had their sixth child in ten years, and he doesn't have much time for chitchat with all those little ones running around.

"No, and please don't tell him." My tone is firm. "The last thing I need is a lecture from him. It was bad enough when I had to tell my parents. They only let up on their tirade after I explained what kind of shape Wesley's in already—the canes, the wheelchair."

"It's so sad," Lana says, stating the obvious. "What about a nurse or something? Are you getting someone to help look after him?"

"He's not quite there yet, or at least he says he's not. He interviewed a few people because Aaron convinced him that he should decide who he likes while he's still coming from a position of relative strength."

"So, he and Aaron get along okay?"

"Ugh," I groan. "They're having this weird bromance. I'll get home from work and find them watching sports or going out for meals together when Aaron's not on call. It's like living in a hallucinatory state."

"I'll bet," she responds. "Well, listen, call me when you finish at the synagogue. I need to hear every last detail."

"I'll bet," I repeat back to her.

After parking next to my mom's silver Toyota Camry in the front lot, I make my way past the groups of parents congregating outside, waiting to retrieve their children from Sunday school. I find my mother and Mary, the catering lady, in Mary's office, engrossed in a deep discussion. They are speaking in hushed tones, but, from the few words I catch, I gather that someone in Mary's life is battling cancer and my mom is offering some of her copious advice on the topic.

"Honey!" My mom beams. "Isn't this exciting?" Like Lana, she tends to get fired up about wedding planning. She's also still overcompensating, trying to make everything different, more upbeat, than my first, disastrous engagement experience. Initially, she was walking on eggshells, like she thought any similarity to the last time might break me, but now, ever since she found out Wesley has reentered my life, it's like she's taking wedding steroids, sprinting hard and fast toward the finish line before I let Aaron get away.

"Hi." I look at Mary as I say it and then step farther into the carpeted office to give my mom a quick kiss on the cheek.

As I sit down in the burgundy armchair beside my mother, she dives right in. "We were thinking of finalizing the menu choices, and then we'll talk linens."

"I'm happy to weigh in on the menu, but you guys pick the linens. That is so not my thing." A large arrangement of calla lilies is situated on the corner of Mary's crowded desk, probably left over from some event last night. Their syrupy scent fills the office, and I wonder if I'm the only one who's bothered by it.

"Okay, food first," Mary says, her almond-shaped eyes brightening with enthusiasm as she opens a manila folder on her desk and looks down at the papers inside. "I took the liberty of making suggestions. You tell me what changes you want to make. For the cocktail hour, I was thinking we'd have eight stations around the room and then several types of passed hors d'oeuvres."

She rattles off the different food choices she is envisioning: a carving board, sushi, a fajita station, Peking duck wraps. It all sounds very similar to what I've seen at friends' receptions over the past few years, but much more elaborate than I was expecting for this second attempted wedding of mine. I don't have the wherewithal to argue about it, though. If it's what my mother wants, she can have it, just so long as I end up married to Aaron when everything is said and done.

Mary works her way through the entire affair, including the types of rolls in the bread basket at the sit-down dinner. "After you and Aaron cut the cake, we will also bring out a dessert sampler for each person at their seat. Everything is mini, so it's adorable, a real crowd-pleaser. A little chocolate lava cake, tiny apple streusel, and pint-size donut sticks served in shot glasses with a chocolate dipping-sauce base."

The donut stick shooters actually do sound kind of cute. As I wonder whether a donut stick is the same thing as a churro, I make a note to tell Wesley about them later. Oh my God, Wesley.

"Are we supposed to invite Wesley to the wedding

now?" In my sudden panic, I blurt out the question to my mother before I've had a chance to think it through.

My mom recoils like I've smacked her, her tortoise-shell glasses slipping an inch lower on her nose.

I answer my own question before she has a chance to respond. "Of course we do." I release a frustrated breath. "I mean, he and Aaron have complete man crushes on each other, and he's living with us. It doesn't seem like there's any choice to be made."

"But after the way he left you . . ." my mother says.

Mary's dark eyes dart between us, trying to determine what we're discussing, perhaps assessing whether she should intervene. She probably sees many arguments between brides and their mothers. I imagine that, as a wedding planner, she must have some hardcore dispute-resolution tactics in her arsenal.

"I still haven't digested the fact that he's living with you," my mom continues. "But it's your wedding, your decision. Just please"—she holds up her manicured hands in surrender—"remember that it's your day. You do what is best for *you*. You owe that man nothing."

Mary furrows her brow and looks at me questioningly. When I don't explain, she turns to my mom.

"Her ex," my mom nearly whispers, as if Wesley might be outside the room, listening in.

When the meeting finally ends, after we've discussed table linens, and china patterns, and the bride and groom's grand entrance, and the father-daughter dance, and the anticipated toasts, and the cutting of the cake, I am wiped out. In addition to my ambivalence about each of these party-planning issues, I find it very difficult to decide in June what I will want to do when the wedding actually rolls around in December. I'm remembering all over again why I left the planning to my mother the last time around.

I climb back into Aaron's SUV and follow behind my mom's car until we get to Bibb and Butter, our favorite salad place in town. After we each order our usual Cobb salads—mine without the bacon, hers with extra avocado—we settle into a booth in the crowded restaurant.

Before she starts on her salad, my mother removes a small green notebook from her purse. "Okay," she says, all business as she opens the notebook and flips pages until she gets to a clean sheet. "Now that we've finished the meeting with Mary, the next task is the dress. Let's lay out where we're going first."

"Mommm." I find myself drawing out the word, whining like a child. "You're like a drill sergeant. I don't want it to be like last time. It's supposed to be easier, smaller. I feel like it's spiraling out of control all over again. Eight appetizer stations during the cocktail hour? Really?"

"Look, honey." My mom pinches her thin lips together for a moment, in a way that tells me she can't be swayed from her position. "Just because there will be fewer guests does not mean that we will be throwing a slapdash party. The food will be ample; the decor will be elegant. As you like to say, that is just how I roll." She raises her eyebrows, challenging me, as she removes the plastic top from her salad container.

When I don't respond, she continues.

"You are my only daughter." Her tone is softer. "I just . . . all I want is to see my baby happy. I want that for both of us." Her voice cracks as she finishes, and I immediately feel contrite.

"Jeez, Mom, you don't have to get so emotional about

it." I reach out for her hand across the table and find her skin cool against my own. "If you really feel so strongly, fine, whatever you want, okay? I can put up with a carving station and a little Peking duck."

"Okay," she says, squeezing my hand for a second before we release each other. Her eyes are all watery, like she's fighting back tears. It seems like she wants to say more, but she just lifts her paper napkin from the table and wipes at her eyes instead.

If Aaron were here, he would know just what to say to defuse this situation, to cheer her up and make this no big deal.

"Let's call Aaron and fill him in. He should be finished with the gym by now, and I'm sure he'll be thrilled to hear about the exorbitant amounts of food," I joke.

I dial Aaron on speaker and place the phone on the table between us. When the call goes straight to voicemail, I feel a thud of disappointment, followed by a nagging jealousy. He's probably busy doing something with Wesley yet again—taking him out for a meal, hanging in Gramercy Park. With a sudden lightness, I realize that it's Wesley I'm jealous of, for getting Aaron's attention, and not vice versa.

WHEN I FINALLY walk back into the apartment with two bags of groceries and a pile of mail in my hands, it's nearly 7:00 p.m. and I am ready for a lazy night in sweatpants. I don't know how many dresses I tried on as my mother and I argued over bustles and veils and trains. If we keep it up, we may soon be blacklisted at all the wedding dress boutiques in Jersey. Here's hoping.

I'm glad to have a little time to myself this evening, as Aaron is on call tonight and Wesley has probably long since left for the restaurant in order to get there before the dinner rush.

I toss my keys down on the painted table in the entryway and turn my attention to yesterday's mail, which I grabbed from the mailroom on my way upstairs. As I flip past our electric bill, I hear the crackling sound of wheels rolling over the apartment's hardwood floors.

I look up to see Wesley navigating his chair in my direction.

"Hey. I didn't realize you were here." I drop the mail into the wooden bowl beside my keys.

"Yeah," he says. "I meant to be at the restaurant already." He glances down at the watch on his wrist without moving his arm. "Not sure I'm going to head in at this point."

"Why?" I realize as I ask that I'm worried about his answer. Worried that another part of his body has started failing him, worried that he's depressed, worried that he's going to want to hang out with me while Aaron's not here, worried that I'm going to agree.

"I wasn't feeling great earlier. Better now, but . . ." He shrugs, like I'm supposed to simply intuit whatever he's implying.

"But what?"

"I don't really want to roll in during a busy time in the chair, you know?"

"Oh." I'm quiet for a second. "Watch a movie with me?" I'm surprised at myself for suggesting it, but also not that surprised.

"Yeah. Good. Let me just grab a snack."

He rolls past me toward the kitchen.

"You want anything?" he calls back to me as he reaches the refrigerator.

"No, thanks," I say to the sliver of the back of his head that I can still see.

He pushes himself out of the chair then and stands to his full height. He opens the freezer and stares into it for a second before grabbing a container of Ben & Jerry's. He then sits back in the chair as though he's settling into a La-Z-Boy.

"I don't understand," I say as I bring my bags of groceries into the kitchen and start unpacking them on the granite counter. "You don't need the chair?"

"I'm not paralyzed," he says, turning the chair toward me and opening the drawer beside me to grab two spoons. "Not yet."

I stare back at him.

"I'm just weak. I get tired. But I can still stand and get myself in and out of the chair."

"Right," I answer, as I wonder whether he would be comfortable discussing the many other questions I've been harboring over the past few weeks. I've assumed he's been in and out of the chair in order to perform basic self-care, like bathing and getting into bed. I figure he stands to dress himself, that he doesn't yet need help buttoning his shirts or putting on his socks. I wonder if now is the time to address all this. But I am also a little flustered being alone with him like this—for the first time, I realize, since he moved in with us.

We head back to the living room and I drop myself down on one end of the microsuede sofa, leaving a wide birth in case Wesley wants to get out of his chair again to sit on the soft cushions, but he just pulls the wheel-chair next to where I'm sitting and puts on the brake, settling in.

"What are we watching?" he asks, upbeat, like he's been waiting all week for movie night. He hands me one of the two spoons he brought over and pulls the cover off the chocolate fudge brownie ice cream. I watch as he looks around for where to put the lid. He's eyeing the coffee table, but it's a few feet away, and I can tell by his face that he thinks getting the cap over to it will be an effort. I reach over and take the lid out of his hand, putting it down on the coffee table and picking up the remote in one fluid action. I return to the sofa, tucking one foot beneath myself as I sit back down and turn on the TV.

As I pull up the Netflix menu, I decide that now is as good a time as any to broach one of the topics that has been weighing on my mind.

"So, what about an aide?" I ask the question casually as I click on the button for comedies.

"What about one?" There's a defensiveness in his voice.

"I don't know." I shrug a little, trying to sound light. "I just thought you'd want to line someone up, so that, you know, when you do need it, I don't know . . ." I lose my nerve for a moment. But then I catch sight of the ice cream cover again, streaks of chocolate on the inside, already melting a little against the sweaty cardboard backing, and I find my grit once more. "You're going to need more help. It seems to me that you'd want more choice in the matter, that you'd want to come from a po-sition of strength when you find a person to help you and not wait until you're desperate."

Wesley is looking at the movie menu on the TV, chewing on his lip a little as he thinks. "Yeah, okay," he finally says, and I let out a breath. "I've kind of been thinking about it, too. Not, like, someone to move in here —just a few hours a day or something to start. When it's more than that, I'm moving myself into a home. We're not turning this place into some sort of hippie commune."

I start to smile at the idea of a commune, but I catch myself as I note the serious expression on his face.

"Okay, good. Yeah, I'm glad you've reached that conclusion." I respond like we've negotiated a business deal, but I feel a surge of relief that surprises me. I don't know if it's because he is making responsible choices for himself or because he said he's going to move out before he reaches a catastrophic state. I don't want to think too hard about it.

"Good," I say again. "For a minute there, I thought you were going to be all salty boots about it."

"Salty boots?" He laughs and looks at me sideways, the bright green of his eyes sliding in my direction.

"Yeah. Like, bitchy and resistant."

He's still looking at me like he's suspicious, and now I feel the need to defend myself. "It's a thing," I tell him, like that settles it, and I go back to scrolling through movie titles.

I let the blinking cursor pass over one random film after another. There are so many titles that mean nothing to me, so I keep on scrolling. As I pass by the movie *Chef*, with Jon Favreau, Wesley tells me to wait.

"You've got to be kidding, right?" I laugh. "How many times have you watched this already?"

"I've actually never seen it."

"What?" I can feel my forehead turn into an accordion of wrinkles as my eyebrows shoot up in disbelief.

"What?" He shrugs. "Have you watched every movie ever made about lawyers?"

"Right. Okay, fair point." I click on the movie, and the screen shows that it's loading.

Wesley reaches over and puts his hand on my arm, like he's trying to get me to look at him, which I do. When our eyes meet, the energy in the room shifts abruptly. In a split second, he's gone from being my charity project back to being the man who used to light every flame inside me. I don't know whether it's the raw, elemental look in his eyes, the physical contact, or just having the time alone together, but suddenly he's Wesley all over again. I feel myself unraveling in his presence, my heart rate revving, my breath hitching, and I have the fleeting thought that this man is becoming a verb, that he's Wesley-ing me. I can't manage to look anywhere other than his face, watching his eyes grow darker as he stares back at me.

"I'm really glad that we reconnected," he says quietly.

"Yeah, me too." I croak out the words. It's like an invisible thread is pulling me closer to him. I'm vaguely aware that our movie should have started playing by now, that there must be some problem with the way it's loading.

"I'm glad you have Aaron," he tells me, and I feel myself nodding. "You guys are good together. And I'm glad to know you're going to have a happy ending."

Hot tears spring to my eyes at his words. I think back to all those years when I believed that Wesley was my happy ending, when I had no inkling that his story would end so much sooner than mine. I can sense all my old feelings for him swirling just beneath the surface of my consciousness, fighting to be heard. I wonder if I will ever feel for Aaron emotions with the same ferocity as the ones I'm struggling to ignore when it comes to Wesley. His generous attitude toward my new relationship only makes me adore him all the more. I want to crawl into his lap and embrace him, to burrow my face into his neck and breathe in the scent of him.

And maybe I can. Maybe cheating with a man who's dying doesn't really count as cheating. I just want to feel Wesley against me one last time, one last kiss, like a good-bye. I feel myself leaning toward him, and I can tell from his eyes, from the way he's leaning in toward me, that he wants it, too. I watch his eyes as they dart to my lips, then back to my eyes. That's all I need before I'm leaning over the edge of the couch and attaching my mouth to his.

His tongue is cold, like the chocolate ice cream he was just eating. But it's Wesley, and my knees go weak just the same. I feel him everywhere. It's not like I remember; I can't say if it's better or worse than my memories, just that it's different. Yet I'm falling to pieces just the same, like I'm finally receiving something I have been too long denied, like I am forgiven. His hand is in my hair, pulling me closer to his face. I wonder for a flash whether I will be the last person he ever kisses, and I think probably yes, so I'd better make it great for him. I kiss him like it's not just his last but like it's mine too, giving over to the part of me that will die along with him.

I breathe in the warmth of his skin, the feel of his hands pulling me toward him, and I bask in the glory of his touch. I feel him swallow against me, in that new way he's been doing since the ALS. If anything, I kiss him even harder at that, trying to give him more life, to transfer some of my good health into his body.

The longer we kiss, the more my mind whirls. He's holding my head so tightly against his own, it's like the kissing won't ever be enough, and I'm overwhelmed by the urge to give him more, to take more, more than kisses, more than this moment.

As if he can hear my thoughts, Wesley's free hand moves to my waist, aggressive and wanting. He's pulling at my shirt, sliding his hand underneath the fabric. I await the sensation of his fingers against my bare skin, desperate for his touch. The shirt lifts, and his flesh finally connects with my own. A wave of heat nearly knocks me backward as his hand grabs hold of me, a brief sensation of dizziness adding to my physical mayhem. I need to feel more of him, to be finished with waiting, with obstacles. I pull back from the kiss to yank my T-shirt over my head. I want him to look at me, I want to watch his eyes as he considers me, but it's all secondary to my urgent need for his continued caresses. After a flash of eye contact, my mouth is back on his. As his warm palm travels up my rib cage and finally settles on my breast, I feel an instant of relief, but it's replaced almost immediately by the need for more. I'm like an addict, every touch just whetting my appetite for something bigger, better.

I move my hand to the waistline of his pants and I can feel him, hard and waiting beneath his jeans. I remember reading that ALS doesn't interfere with a man's ability to get an erection, but I'm still surprised by how strong and vibrant he seems beneath my fingers. I can feel the heat coming off him straight through the denim.

Both of Wesley's hands are on me now, pulling me closer, as if he wants me on top of him, to straddle him where he is. I envision myself climbing into his wheelchair, wondering if that can work, whether I'll topple us both, but then I determine that I'd rather help him onto the couch, on top of me. As I try to work out the mechanics of this situation, my thoughts flash to Aaron and what I am about to do, what I'm about to lose. For a blissful, cloudy moment, I wonder if I can have them both, even if it's for only a few months, only a few weeks. I can't tear myself away from Wesley, not now, not with his flesh against mine, his breath inside my mouth. In the fog of my neediness, I decide that it would be worth losing anything to feel his weight above me one more time, to hear him whisper my name in exquisite agony just once more, the way he used to.

And then he groans quietly, and the sound of his voice changes everything. It's different, too different from how it used to be, too different from how it is with Aaron. The spell is broken. Suddenly his tongue feels thick and foreign in my mouth, wet and wrong, and I realize that my memories and fantasy have overtaken my reality. I push back, horrified at myself for letting things go this far.

"Sorry, sorry," I stammer, retrieving my shirt from the floor and scrambling to push it back over my head. "I don't . . . Wow. Sorry."

"Yeah, no." Wesley clears his throat. "We shouldn't have let that happen."

I look away. Those Netflix dots are still turning in circles on the TV screen as the system attempts to load our movie, and I don't know where to look, what to say. I don't understand how I could have allowed this to happen, how I could have confused memories with present feelings so completely. I've risked all the carefully crafted goodness in my current life, exposed all of it to potential explosion. My lack of loyalty, my extreme error, my ability to be so very wrong is appalling.

I wish I could get us back to where we were an hour ago; I wish I could rewind my life. I wipe at my mouth with the back of my hand as he waits for what I'm going to say. And yet, even regretful of my actions, I can't say I felt nothing when his hands were in my hair, his hot breath was against my mouth. I can't get a handle on what the fuck I feel, except that I am completely schizophrenic when it comes to these two men.

"My parents," I finally grunt, changing the subject. "We let them use our Netflix account when they want, but then my mom always leaves it running on too many devices. I should call her, or it won't let us watch." I stand to get my phone.

"Wait," he says. "We have to talk about what just happened."

"We do?" My voice has risen several octaves in my current panic.

"Listen," he starts, swallowing hard. "I'm just going to lay it out there. I can't keep pretending that I don't regret leaving, breaking our engagement when I did. It was never your fault, none of it."

His words release something in me, as if there's a muscle I've been clenching since the day he left for England and now I can finally, finally let go. I wish we could go back to that cold day in his childhood bedroom, that he could wrap his arms around me and forgive me then, when I was breaking apart inside. Not now, when none of it matters anymore, not when I'm going to marry another man, not when Wesley's going to evaporate into another memory.

"And I'm not going to pretend I don't still have a shitton of feelings for you. But I'm also not going to let you fuck up what you've got going with Aaron. I don't want to be that kind of dick. And second, no matter what might still be here"—he motions with his hand between the two of us—"I'm dying. I'm leaving you all over again. And at least this time, I know I won't be leaving you alone. So don't let me fuck you over again. Don't let me, even if I try."

I look back at him, trying to digest what he's said, and he starts back up.

"If I were a better guy, I'd get out of here. I'd stay the fuck away from you and Aaron both. But the fact is, if I only have a short time, I want to spend it near you, looking at you, soaking up every last bit of you that I can."

"I don't know." It's all I can say. The only truth.

"Think about it," Wesley says gently. "If you want me out of here, I'll go. The only thing I know for sure is that there's no point in pursuing this." He gestures back and forth between us again. "Not this time. Not anymore." He turns away from me and gazes off into the ether for a moment before slowly turning his head back toward me and swallowing again. "The best thing is if you would just be happy. Let me be certain that when I leave this time, I won't be destroying you all over again."

Against my will, a sob racks my body and escapes from me. It feels selfish, crying over his losses, and I force myself to quiet down.

"I can't," I tell him, shaking my head. "I can't do this."
I'm not even sure what "this" I am referring to, but I get
up from my seat and retreat to my bedroom. As I close
the door behind me, I hear the movie finally starting up
on the TV.

Chapter Twenty
June 2017

*W*hen I roll into work the next morning with a cup of bitter Starbucks coffee in hand, my head is cloudy, as though I stayed up the whole night partying. As if. What I actually did all night was lie in my bed, alternately crying and staring blindly at the wall. I drifted in and out of a disturbed sleep until Aaron returned home from his hospital shift sometime around 4:00 a.m. It was only after he climbed into our bed and folded his bulky arm around my rib cage that I finally entered a deep sleep. Even so, the three hours of shut-eye that I managed did not take the edge off the extreme emotional tornado swirling through my organs.

I drop my tote bag on the floor next to my desk and burrow into my leather chair. Nicola is already at her desk, but she doesn't say hi or good morning or anything, so neither do I. I don't have it in me to pretend today.

While my computer powers up, I sip my coffee and try to control the barrage of images coursing through my mind. It's as though I have a split screen in my brain, like two different movies are playing on simultaneous loops. The memories of Wesley's lips against mine, the feel of his raspy breath against my face, assail me repeatedly. At the same time, I see Aaron's body wrapped around me in bed, his brawn shielding me from everything except for myself.

Outlook opens with a flash on the screen and I see that I have a new email from Alexandra Pervez, the senior associate on the Kinderwohl tobacco case. She says that Malik Thompson, the partner on the case, wants me to participate in the upcoming depositions. I have a quick spark of excitement at being tapped for this task, like my superiors are finally recognizing my extreme genius. But then I stall, thinking of the enormity of hours and manpower generally required to prepare for depositions like these. I scroll through the email to see how many weeks we will have for prep, and then I notice that the depositions, which will take place in Wisconsin, are slated to occur during the span of one week in late July, a week that directly conflicts with the date of Moe's court appearance.

Without hesitating, I tap out a quick reply to Alexandra, cc'ing Malik Thompson, telling her that I won't be able to participate in the depositions because I am committed to representing an asylum candidate on that date.

Alexandra's response is almost instantaneous: *Not to worry. I staffed another first-year associate on the asylum matter. You're off that case and free to devote your full schedule to Kinderwohl.*

What the what? For a moment, the words on the screen blur before my eyes, and I have to read them again, twice, before I can process what they say.

I frantically type back a response that they can't take me off the case, that I have a connection with the client, that I've devoted months of work to the matter, that I have to do the right thing and see it through. Again, I cc Malik Thompson, hoping he will put this presumptuous senior associate in her place.

Again, I get an immediate reply, this time from Malik: *Done deal. Let it go.*

TWENTY MINUTES LATER, I'm standing in bright morning sunshine on the corner of Fifty-first and Third, dialing Aaron with shaky hands.

"Hello?" I can hear from the heavy, syrupy word that he is only just waking up.

"I can't believe it," I pant into the phone. "I quit! I just quit!"

"Wait, what?" His tone is suddenly alert, and I imagine he's just sat up in bed.

"I quit, as in my job," I repeat, feeling a smile creep onto my lips, pride in my decision. I quickly recount what happened with Moe's case. "I guess everything you've been saying, suddenly I could see it all, too. I hated that fucking job." I turn in a circle on the busy street corner, unsure where I am heading.

"Yeah, you did!" he hoots into the phone like we've just won the lottery. "Where are you?"

"Right outside the office. I'm kind of at a loss." I glance back up at the towering glass building I've just left, its dark windows opaque, foreign. "What do I do?" People rush around me on the pavement, hurrying toward their destinations, grazing past my stationary form as though I am a utility pole, as though I am not there.

"I know exactly what you do." I can hear rustling and movement on his end of the phone. "Get your ass in a cab and meet me at the Four Seasons. We're celebrating. First stop is a boozy brunch. Don't think. Just do it."

"For real?" I say with a smile, even as I pivot and move closer to the street corner, raising my arm to hail a cab that's turning onto Third Avenue. "Okay. See you there." I laugh and end the call. I can't believe what I've done—the impulsiveness, the recklessness. I try to process that I am now unemployed. As I slide into the taxi and tell the driver where I'm going, I wonder whether I haven't just torpedoed my life, if perhaps I'm making one asinine decision after another because I'm on emotional overload.

I push the thought away and lean my head back against the seat, trying to empty my mind. I force myself not to look at any emails on my phone, not to scroll through any social media sites where I might stumble upon acquaintances' professional successes or other information that will make me regret my actions. Instead, I close my eyes and try to keep my thoughts from reeling. I take a deep breath and inhale the faint scent of cigarette smoke, which I assume is emanating off the driver. I wonder if his tobacco use is limited to smoking or whether he perhaps chews the stuff, too. I have another flash of glee that I am finished with the Kinderwohl drudgery, and I tell myself again that I made the right move, that Aaron and I will figure out where I should go from here.

It's a short cab ride, and as I step onto the corner of Madison Avenue, I realize that I'd better start being more frugal, now that I'm unemployed and all. I really could have walked from my office. For the time being, I have to recategorize cab rides as a splurge. I determine that I will immediately begin a job hunt so I can continue to live in the manner to which I've become accustomed, and do so on my own paycheck.

I walk into the airy lobby of the Four Seasons and climb the half staircase up to the Garden restaurant, which I've been to only once before. Aaron and I came here last summer before seeing a magic show in one of the hotel rooms. It was a swanky, intimate affair for small groups of well-heeled adults. There was a speakeasy kind of a vibe to the clandestine nature of the show, the audience all in cocktail attire and the magician holding court. No, not magician—*conjurer* was what he insisted on being called. I remember now how Aaron spent the entirety of the show running his fingers along my inner thigh as we sat in the audience in the darkened hotel room, the exquisite torture of his hand teasing me, making promises. I haven't thought about that night in months, but I remember it now with nostalgia and a sharp stab of pain at what I've risked.

After the maître d' leads me to a table, I settle into a wide beige chair to wait for Aaron, who appears only seconds later in jeans and a dark, fitted T-shirt. He's bounding up the steps of the restaurant, his lips tight, like he's trying to contain a grin, as he searches the room for me. Our eyes meet, and I'm struck by a sudden and intense love for this man. Ever since I discovered Wesley was back in New York, it's like I've just been floundering, out of control, turning my life into a hot, sludgy mess. It's the opposite of what Aaron brings out in me: order, comfort, peace. This extra time with him is just what I need in order to find my footing again.

He makes his way across the restaurant, past the many real trees that are sprouting up through the floor, their branches reaching toward the high ceilings, as if these topiaries do not realize they are inside a building. The closer he gets to me, the more I am able to recognize the feeling coursing through me as relief. He turns sideways to avoid bumping his broad shoulders into a waiter carrying a carafe of hot coffee, and then he's upon me. I stand up to greet him, and he grabs me into a forceful bear hug, lifting me slightly off the ground as his solid arms squeeze extra tight.

"Oof," I grunt just before he releases me.

"I'm so thrilled that you finally did this." He pulls out the chair across from mine and signals a waiter, who hurries over to our table. "Can we please have two Ty Bar toddies?" Aaron asks.

"Right away." The man nods without writing anything on the notepad in his hand and hurries off.

"Ty Bar toddy? What is that?"

"I have no idea. It's some cocktail I saw on their brunch menu when I pulled it up in the cab. I think big news makes me hungry." He smiles as he reaches across the table to take the menu I had been looking at.

"Everything makes you hungry," I snort, basking in his wide-open presence, shoving away thoughts of how I have betrayed this beautiful man, mentally swatting at my already battered conscience.

The drinks appear, and I take a cautious sip. It's some sort of bourbon and maybe apple cider concoction. It feels totally inappropriate to be drinking cocktails like this before the hour has even struck 11:00 a.m. When I say as much to Aaron, he protests.

"C'mon, get into the spirit here. I'm off for the rest of the day, and apparently you are, too."

He holds out his glass, waiting for me to clink mine against his.

"Cheers to that," I say, a little annoyed by the trepidation I can hear in my voice. Our glasses connect, and the amber liquid swirls precariously. I take a big gulp, and the alcohol burns my throat on its way down.

AN HOUR LATER, Aaron and I have worked our way through two Bloody Marys each and half a bottle of prosecco. I assume we will go home and nap off this ridiculous brunch before we can do anything productive with ourselves.

I'm still picking my way through the branzino I ordered, using my fork to flake off bits of the white meat, when Aaron starts to laugh.

"What?" I'm smiling back, wondering what's so funny, wondering if I can really just pretend that nothing ever happened with Wesley, if I can make it as irrelevant as it feels in this moment.

"Who gets branzino for brunch? Fish for breakfast. Who does that?"

"What do you mean?" I laugh back. "People do that. That is something people do." I think I might be slurring my words a little. I can feel the alcohol clouding my brain, and suddenly everything seems funny. "Lox!" I nearly shout as the idea comes to me. "That's fish for breakfast. See, something people do." I'm inordinately satisfied by my genius revelation.

"Okay," he says, nodding, as one side of his mouth lifts in amusement. "You're right. I stand corrected." He lifts his hands in defeat. "Fish for breakfast. Totally a thing."

"And anyway, the Four Seasons wouldn't have fish on the brunch menu if it weren't a thing."

"Okay, Counselor, I get it. You're right. You can rest your case." He's smiling at me with such affection, like he's exactly where he wants to be, and suddenly my own cheeks burn.

I have the overpowering sensation that I must, this minute, come clean to him, unload completely. I know I can talk to him about what's going through my mind, and we will figure things out. I've always been able to talk to him.

"I kissed Wesley."

Time stops as I wait for his response. The haze of alcohol that I've been basking in suddenly clears for a moment, and I realize what I've done. What I did last night. What I did just this minute.

"That's not a funny joke." His smile is gone. He's completely focused on me, on my eyes.

"It's not a joke." I swallow. "It was last night."

He's silent for a moment as he continues to stare at me, hard, unyielding. And then he shoots out of his seat. "That motherfucker!" His chair scrapes against the floor as he stands to his full height, his hands already balled into fists. I grab his forearm, stopping him from the hunt on which he's about to set off.

"No, it was me." He looks at me like I can't possibly know what I'm saying. "Please." I tug on his arm. "Sit back down."

I see our waiter eyeing us, probably wondering if we're going to make a scene. Maybe this already is a scene.

"With tongue?" He's rooted to his spot.

"Just sit, please."

He hesitates for a moment but then slumps back into his chair, deflating. "Fine. Tell me everything, and let's figure out how we're dealing with this."

As he speaks, with such clarity and logic, I realize how much more drunk I am than he is. I shouldn't be surprised. We've had the same amount to drink, and he's a trillion times my size.

"I didn't mean for it to happen," I start.

"Can we skip the clichés," he snaps back, "and just get into the details? I need to know what happened. *Exactly* what happened." His face is taut, like he's struggling not to combust.

"I don't remember exactly," I whine. "He was saying all these nice things about you, about us. We were going to watch a movie, and then I just felt so sad that he's dying. I just wanted to be close to him one last time. It doesn't mean anything about my feelings for you. It has nothing to do with what's between you and me."

"Nothing to do with us?" He sounds genuinely confused for a moment, but his tone turns hot, livid, as he says, "It has everything to do with what's between you and me."

"But he's dying," I argue, trying not to slur my words. "It's not the same as cheating."

"It is precisely the same as cheating." He's whisper-shouting at me now. "You can't be in love with me and want to kiss another guy at the same time. Is that even all you did, just kiss?"

I squint in concentration, trying to figure out how to classify exactly what Wesley and I did. I'm assaulted by memories of Wesley's hands in my hair, my T-shirt flying to the floor, my hand fumbling desperately at the button of his jeans.

"You slept with him?" Aaron demands before I answer, his tone incredulous, shattered.

"No!" I sputter back, surprised by his assumption, even though he's not so far off the mark, considering. "No, no, no!" I add more forcefully. "We didn't! We stopped. Before it went that far. . . ." I taper off.

"Before it went that far." He repeats it as a statement, understanding that whatever occurred was far more than a simple kiss. He doesn't wait for me to elaborate before he lights into me. "How far exactly *did* it go? Kind of weird and fetishy of you, no? Molesting a cripple." He's nearly spitting at me, and I'm surprised by the cruelty of his words.

"It wasn't like that," I argue. "It wasn't a physical thing, really. It was just about the past, and . . . he's dying . . ." As if that answers everything, I pause, waiting for him to understand.

He's silent for a moment, his eyes darting from side to side like he's trying to decide what to believe, or how to wrap his mind around this situation. He takes a deep breath and begins again.

"If you have feelings for him, his disease doesn't make those feelings any less real. And if you have feelings for him, what does that say about your feelings for me?" He leans back in his chair and regards me, taking a deep breath, like he's trying to intercept his fury. "You have one heart. You can't give it to two different guys at once. That is not a thing."

As he says this, I picture myself taking a heart-shaped organ out of my purse and giving part of it to

Aaron and the other part to Wesley. I want to argue that you can, in fact, divide your affection like that, but then I realize that the heart in my mind's eye is already in pieces. Maybe I've started this phase of my life with a heart that's already broken, and that makes it easier to divide, to divvy up.

"Do you want to be with him?" Aaron asks. His tone is almost solicitous, as if he'd like for me to have what I desire.

I look out across the restaurant as I struggle with how to respond. My failure to answer immediately seems to ignite Aaron's anger all over again, and I realize belatedly that the emotional betrayal is infuriating him as much as the physical disloyalty, maybe more.

"I need a minute," Aaron says. He stands and reaches into his back pocket for his wallet. He tosses a wad of cash onto the table and looks back at me. "Why don't you go sleep off the alcohol, and then maybe we can have a real conversation about this?"

I start nodding, as I would, in fact, prefer to be sober to face this discussion.

"Do me a favor, though. Go to Lana's."

He walks out of the restaurant without even saying good-bye, and it's like all the warmth in my limbs has gone with him. I guess he doesn't want me going back to the apartment, where I will see Wesley. I don't really want to see Wesley right now, either. Unless Aaron just doesn't want me living with him anymore. Or with Wesley. My head is beginning to pound with the weight of the confusion I'm feeling. I finish paying the tab and then hail a taxi to Lana's apartment, extravagance and all. I just don't have the wherewithal to get myself through the New York City subway system at the moment.

WHEN I GET to Lana's building, I'm grateful that her doorman knows me and allows me upstairs without even checking the list he keeps on a clipboard behind the desk. The pounding in my head has reached a crescendo, and I just want to lie down.

I keep a spare key to Lana's apartment among the many others hanging from the key ring that my brother and Shara gave me when I graduated from law school. The ring is decorated with two charms that now feel like an affront as I see them against my fingers. The first is a small rectangle engraved with the words "Trust me, I'm a lawyer," which was obviously intended as a joke. The other, which is decorated with small green gemstones, is shaped like the scales of justice. I suppose that charm was meant to inspire me toward fairness and integrity as I moved from one phase of my life to the next. Well, so much for that.

As I turn the key and open the door to the glistening apartment, I am greeted by acute silence—another reminder that I am now utterly alone. I drop my bag on the parquet floor and let the door slam shut behind me. I head straight into Lana's tiny bedroom and lie facedown amid the many gray throw pillows on her pristine sleigh bed, hoping that my makeup won't smudge off on the cream duvet. Turning my head to the side, I notice absently that the room is much more orderly than is the norm for Lana—no clothes strewn about, no rejected outfits decorating the carpet. It seems even Lana is growing up. Everyone is getting their shit together, except for me. I close my eyes to soak in the warmth of the sunlight streaming through the window, but all I feel is the rhythmic thumping in my head.

THE NEXT THING I know, voices wake me out of oblivion. I have clearly been asleep for hours, and I can hear Lana walking into her apartment with company.

"I'm here, Lana," I call out before she has the chance to be startled by me. The bedside clock tells me it's after 5:00 p.m.

"Meredith!" Lana rounds the corner into the main room of the apartment just as I walk out of the bedroom, wiping at my eyes. "Why aren't you at work?" She is flawless in her monochromatic gray romper and a long, beaded necklace.

Everything comes rushing back at once. "Oh my God." I sink down onto the armrest of the tan love seat beside me. "I don't have a job anymore." I drop my head into my hand, and the pounding inside my forehead begins again. "I quit this morning, and Aaron and I are a disaster. I'm sorry. I just needed a place to crash for a few hours today." I lift my eyes again and see that Lana is not alone. Standing behind her is Aaron's colleague, the handsome Dr. Spencer.

"Oh, hey, Spencer," I add, wondering what exactly he's doing here.

"Hey, Meredith. Everything okay?" He's dressed in a crisp blue button-down and slacks, like he's on his way somewhere more fun than the hospital.

I don't want to embarrass Aaron by getting into the

details with one of his colleagues, so I nod and try to compose myself.

"Yeah, yeah, just a crazy day, and I didn't want to bother Aaron while he was resting for his next shift." Spencer obviously knows I'm full of it, since this is completely inconsistent with what came out of my mouth just a few seconds ago.

"I'm going to get out of your hair." I stand and turn in a half circle until I see the spot where I left my tote bag. "Lana, can I just borrow you in the hallway for two seconds? Sorry, Spencer." I glance over at him apologetically and grab Lana's cool hand.

Once we're out in the dimly lit hall, I let loose with everything.

"I kissed Wesley. And now maybe I'm going to end up without either one of them." I can feel the helpless look that has settled on my face, and I know that Lana has no idea what to do with me. This is not our dynamic. She is usually the helpless one and I am the level-headed straight arrow helping her to navigate her complicated life.

"And why is Spencer here?" I add.

"Wow." Lana answers, her blue eyes wide, like she's stunned. Or stumped. We're quiet for a second, staring at each other, perhaps both taking in the enormity of the shit storm in which I have landed.

"Wow," she repeats. "You know what? Let me cancel. Let me tell Spencer we'll go out another time. Give me two minutes." She starts heading into the apartment.

"No, don't." I grab her arm. "Don't give up your night with him. Don't let this be another thing I'm screwing up. I just need some time to think. Go. We'll catch up tomorrow. I'll be wanting details." I motion toward her apartment door, trying to sound upbeat. As much as I would love to have Lana as my sounding board for the night, it's true that what I really need is a way to sift through my thoughts, arrange them into some sort of logical order.

"But—"

"No." My voice is firm. "Please, don't cancel your plans. It'll only make me feel worse."

Her eyes search my face for a moment before she lets out a heavy breath. "Fine. But you are coming to my office tomorrow to meet me for lunch. Promise."

"Promise." I hold out a pinky, and she wraps her own little finger around mine in our age-old deal-sealing move. I give her a quick hug and send her back to whatever night she was meant to have.

When I emerge from her building onto the street, I realize I don't even know which direction to walk. I wonder who would be waiting if I returned to the apartment in Gramercy Park, the home I have been sharing with Aaron and Wesley. For all I know, those two could be attacking each other at this very moment, although I know better than to think Aaron would ever hurt a man in a Wesley's physical condition. More likely they are sitting around commiserating about what a selfish bitch I am. And they wouldn't be wrong, either. I have always, my whole life, struggled against my tendency to focus too much on myself. I consciously work to ensure I think of others, like going out of my way for a sick friend or helping at the soup kitchen. Even choosing my career, I really did mean to find a job where I was engaged in some kind of righteous endeavor. But then I sold out, choosing my own self-interest, cash over caring. Well, until today.

I stagger on the street as I feel another stab of panic about the fact that I have quit my job, that I now have no source of income. But then I remember that I followed my conscience, that I allowed my principles to guide me, and perhaps I should be proud of that. Maybe it's the one smart move I've made this week, this month, this year.

I've been absently walking eastward on Eighty-second Street since I exited Lana's building, taking myself toward East End Avenue, the river, oblivion, but my newfound pride in my professional decision awakens something in me. I decide that I need to go home, to figure out what direction my life is going to take—personally, professionally, everything, everything.

When I return to Gramercy and turn my key in the apartment door, I realize I am holding my breath, nervous about who I am going to find inside. The apartment is dark in the main room, and for one blissful moment, I think that I am home alone, but then I hear music playing from the bedroom area. I recognize "One Tree Hill" by U2, and I know it's Wesley. He's always loved that haunting, whimsical melody. If I had to bet money, I'd say he's got it playing on repeat. As I stand frozen in the dark, listening to the words, Bono singing about a dear friend who died in a tragic motorcycle accident, I'm struck. Suddenly I know exactly what I'm here for, exactly what I need to do.

Chapter Twenty-One
June 2017

I walk quietly down the dark hallway, passing Wesley's closed door and slipping into my bedroom. Flicking the lights on as the door closes behind me, I stare down at the cell phone in my hand. I close my eyes and take a quick breath in, like I'm preparing to jump into a swimming pool, or a lake, or a freezing, swirling abyss, and I dial Aaron's number.

"Hi," he says cautiously when he picks up on the second ring.

I hear some sort of announcements in the background. "Are you at work?" I know he wasn't scheduled to work tonight, despite what I said to Spencer earlier, who probably knew the schedule too.

"Yeah, I crashed in one of the on-call rooms earlier, and then I figured I'd just stick around." His voice sounds thick, wary.

"I was hoping we could talk." I lower myself onto the bed, moving gingerly on the down comforter, as though everything in my world is now fragile.

"Where are you?" he asks, and I hear suspicion in the sudden crispness of his words.

"Home." I ease my feet out of the patent leather ballet flats I chose for work this morning, noticing the red indentations they've left on my insteps.

"Is Wesley there?"

"Yeah, he's in his room. We didn't see each other. I was at Lana's all afternoon. His door is closed, and so's mine. Can you come home?"

"I'm not sure I can be in the same room as you tonight. Or tomorrow. I need some space and time to figure out where we go from here."

"What are you saying? That you're thinking about ending things with me over this?" I balk.

"I don't know," he snaps. "I don't know what I'm saying," he repeats, his voice hard. "What you did was a complete and utter betrayal. I have to figure out how I'm supposed to marry someone I can't trust." He sighs heavily into the phone, like he doesn't want to have said those words, like he's being forced to behave this way. I listen to the rustling sound of his breath and I feel my eyes pooling with tears, my vision blurring at the damage I have caused.

"But I wanted to tell you that I figured it all out. That it's going to be clear-cut going forward."

"What did you figure out?"

I notice the background noise on his end has stilled, and I imagine he's walked somewhere more private at the hospital to have this conversation, maybe an empty exam room. I picture him in his scrubs, a stethoscope draped around his neck, the phone to his ear.

"I'm not going to look for a job yet. I'm going to spend the next few months, or however long, taking care of Wesley." I lie back against the bed, staring up at the white ceiling.

"What the fuck, Meredith? This is supposed to make me feel better?" His voice is rising.

"I realized why I kissed him."

"Kissed?" He repeats, his voice heavy, knowing, like he wants me to get into the dirty details of everything else we did all over again. I can't undo what happened with Wesley, so instead, I move forward with my original point.

"I was trying to find that light, that brilliant sunshine, that I used to feel when I was with him. I realized tonight that the light never came from him. It came from me, when I was happy with myself, and I haven't been happy, not with myself. I've been so fucking miserable."

"You've been miserable?" Now I hear hurt, anger.

"Yes, with my job. With the way I spend my days. With the anger I've held on to for the years since Wesley and I fell apart. I've become someone other than who I am, and I'm ready to change it. I realized tonight that all of my actions have been reactionary, the results of pain that I suffered before I even met you, scars on my soul. And, well, I'm done with it."

"So, what's your plan?" I can't tell if he's warming up or mocking me.

"I'm going to use the next few months or however long to take care of Wesley and find the right job for me. I am going to rediscover the light that used to shine out from me so that I can be worthy of you. All this time, I wondered if I missed Wesley, and I finally realized tonight that I miss who I was when I knew him. I want to be that person for you."

"But I like the person you are now. Liked," he corrects himself, and I feel the blow.

"Please, Aaron. Give me another chance to prove who I am, who I can be."

"Meredith." His tone is flat, distant. "I can't tell you what you need to hear. Not tonight. I need some time to process this. I can't make any promises about where I'm going to come out."

"Are you saying you might not forgive me?" My breath hitches as I wait for his answer.

"I don't know. Maybe."

"What? No, Aaron," I sob into the phone.

"You guys can stay in the apartment. I don't have it in me to kick Wesley out, not in his condition. I will make other arrangements for myself until we figure the rest of this out. *If* we figure it out."

And then the phone goes dead.

I'm not sure how much time passes while I lie on our king-size bed, crying into the duvet, but I finally sit up and wipe my face with the sleeve of my white button-down shirt, which is now riddled with wrinkles and smudges of eyeliner.

I stare at the wet stains on my shirtsleeve, trying to process that it was not even twenty-four hours ago that I woke up and went to work in a freshly pressed shirt, that I had a job, a fiancé. Now, less than a day later, it seems I may have lost it all.

So I do what I always do when all else fails: I pick up the phone again, and I call my mother.

When she hears my soggy voice on the phone, she is immediately concerned, as I knew she would be. I quickly fill her in on everything that's gone down, including the make-out session with Wesley. I would have preferred to leave that part out, but she won't be equipped to help me unless she knows everything. When I finally finish with the grand finale, that Aaron and I might be finished, I hear her sharp intake of breath.

"Oh, honey, no." Her tone is partly sympathetic but also part command, as though she won't accept this behavior from me.

"It's not like I have a choice, Mom," I snip back at her, wondering how I can be so reliant on her and so annoyed with her simultaneously.

"No, sweetie, just hear me out," she argues, her voice kind but firm in the way she's always had when she needs to steer me in the right direction. I almost feel hopeful for a second as I wait to hear what she says next.

"If you love that man, you don't give up without a fight. You remember what happened with your father and me back when I was sick."

Yes, what I remember is how easily she forgave my dad for almost abandoning her. I remember her closing me out of their relationship and keeping secrets from me. I remember my relationship with her hitting a low point that we are still clawing our way back from. I reach for a tissue on the bedside table and blow my nose loudly into the phone. Then I realize that, true to form, I'm thinking all about me, not about her or and my dad—pity party for one over here. Forcing my mind back to their marriage, I don't recall my mom fighting for my dad. I recall her fighting for her life.

"A lot went on between us that you know nothing about," she starts.

"Yeah, no shit," I quip.

"Meredith." A reprimand.

"Sorry. Keep going." If I were less distraught at the

moment, I might marvel at how quickly I revert to a teenage mentality whenever I argue with my mother, but right now I just want her to tell me how to climb out of the shit pudding I'm swimming in.

"You really messed up, sweetheart."

Okay, not helping.

"Frankly, I don't understand why you thought it made sense to have Wesley staying in your apartment with you, anyway. You've always been the one running after wounded animals, never minding the risk to yourself, even when we thought they might have rabies. It's always been one of your best and worst qualities. So, basically, Wesley is your rabid racoon. You've gotten him to the vet, where they might fix his broken leg, but the animal still has rabies."

"Wow, Mom. Thanks for that." I blow my nose again.

"Listen," she starts again. Her voice is quieter now, and I can tell she's about to tell me a secret. "I'm not supposed to say anything. Gladys wanted to wait as long as possible—she said until after the wedding—but I keep telling her it's going to be obvious well before that time."

"What is, Mom? What's obvious?" Every time I say more than two words, I feel like I'm going to start bawling again.

"She's sick," my mom says. "Lymphoma."

"What?" I sit up, immediately sharp. "Aaron's mom has cancer?"

She's silent for a second, letting me process.

"And Aaron doesn't know? Mom, no, that's wrong. She has to tell him."

"No, sweetie. It's not on us to make this decision for

them. And you don't tell him either—you respect her wishes. When she's ready, she will tell him herself. You can't know what it's like to have to tell your child you might be dying. You can't know."

"It's not right, Mom. This isn't right!" I'm shouting now. I am imagining all of the emotions Aaron would be feeling if he knew his mother was keeping this from him, and I have to do something. It doesn't matter that we're fighting, or decomposing, or whatever. This is not okay.

"All I was going to say," she continues in her pointedly calm tone, the tone that is meant to alert me that I've gotten out of control, "is that this is not a good time for you and Aaron to be estranged. I have every confidence that he would come around at some point anyway, but who knows how long that might take, and this is a time when you need to be there for him."

"But he doesn't even know," I argue as I toss my dirty Kleenex toward the small trash can in the corner of the room. It's a feeble misfire, and the tissue sails down at least a foot from the wastebasket.

"Well, once he finds out, he's going to need you to be there for him."

We sit there on the phone together then, neither of us talking, as we digest each other's words and our own. I have a quick memory of Aaron's mother complaining of pain in her abdomen a couple of months ago at the Mother's Day barbecue. Aaron offered to get her an appointment with a gastroenterologist at NYU. She said it was probably nothing.

"Is that what you were talking about with Mary when I came to the synagogue for the wedding planning?" It's dawning on me all at once. I remember the way the caterer and my mom were whispering about someone with cancer.

"Yes," she admits. Caught.

"I'm going to go out and see her tomorrow. Can I do that, at least?"

My mother sighs loudly into the phone. I picture her sitting at the kitchen table in Livingston, twirling the curly cord of the landline telephone around her finger like she did when I was a little kid. Rationally, I'm aware that my parents' house is equipped with only cordless phones and has been that way for well over a decade, but I have a longing for those other days, so many years ago, when my mother could actually fix the messes I made.

"She's going to kill me," my mom finally says, "but if you feel you must, I won't stop you."

After we get off the phone, I stare at the blank wall beside the bed. All I wanted was to help people—Wesley, Moe—but everything turned into such a mess. I haven't really done anything to help either of them, and my own life has burst into shards of disaster. And now, as I lie on the bed, feeling the urge to help Gladys and Aaron, I wonder if I'll only muck things up worse.

My phone vibrates on the bedspread beside me and I pick it up, hoping for a call back from Aaron. It's a text, from Wesley, across the hall:

Wesley: Everything OK?

I guess he heard me crying, or yelling. Or the pain I'm feeling throughout my body is so rank he can just smell it from across the hall.

Me: Yup. Just a standard-issue fight w mom. No biggie.

I'm sure he knows I'm lying, but I can't get into it with him right now. I have to stay focused on Gladys, on Aaron.

I tap on my calendar app to see what time I can visit Gladys in Long Island tomorrow, and then I toss the phone down without looking. No need to check my calendar. It's not like I'm gainfully employed or anything.

As much as I want to crawl under the covers and set time back by six months so I can do everything over, do it better, I think about Gladys and how frightened she must be. And Aaron. He'll be devastated when he learns the news. Especially if she doesn't let him help her. I have failed Aaron so completely in our relationship. I will not fail him on this.

I STEP OFF the Long Island Railroad in Syosset, sweaty from the un-air-conditioned train car. It took me until after eleven this morning to get a hold of Gladys and tell her I wanted to visit, and now, standing on the concrete train platform in the heat of the summer afternoon, I feel myself turning into a puddle of sweat and nerves.

Gladys clearly assumed I would be driving Aaron's car out to the North Shore of Long Island. Otherwise, she would have insisted on picking me up at the train. I didn't want to tell her by phone what happened between us. Nor did I want to concoct a fake story about why I wasn't using the car. So I just let her know when I'd arrive at her house and then hurried off the line.

Now, as I step toward the navy-blue cab in the line outside the corner coffee shop, I wonder what I will say. I wonder if Aaron has spoken to her yet. I wonder how to tell her that I know she's sick. I wonder if the sweat on the back of my thighs is showing through my clothes, leaving noticeable wet marks on my denim shorts.

After the cab pulls down the long driveway to Aaron's parents' house, I find a turquoise sticky note waiting on the front door: "Meredith—come around back."

I climb the stairs at the side of the driveway and open the wrought-iron gate to the backyard. I walk past the deck outside Aaron's parents' bedroom, an addition they built when he was in high school. I continue to the main portion of the deck, where they keep an outdoor table and chairs, the grill. Gladys comes into view now beyond the far end of the deck, lounging under an umbrella in a chair set back from the freeform pool. She's wearing one of those big, floppy hats that make me think of sea creatures like stingrays and jellyfish. I think she might be sleeping, but because of the distance I have yet to cover before I reach her and the large sunglasses hiding her eyes, there's no way to know.

I cross the slate stones that lead from the deck to the brick patio surrounding the pool and continue making my way toward her. My flip-flops snap under my feet, preventing any sort of stealth arrival.

"Meredith!" Gladys sits up as I approach, her copper-colored hair long and loose under the hat and a large smile illuminating her face. "Oh, I was so glad you called. Come, sit." She pulls the adjacent lounger a little bit closer to her. "Let me text Suzette that you're here, and she'll bring out some iced tea for us." She's already tapping away on her phone.

Suzette is the Antiguan housekeeper who's been working for Aaron's family since he was an infant. She's nearly seventy years old, and Gladys adores her. She was hired as a babysitter for Aaron and his younger brother, Cole, but Gladys grew so attached to her over the years that she convinced Suzette to stay long after there were any children to care for.

"Why don't I just go and get it?" I start backing toward the house.

"No, sweetie, it's fine. Suzette and I are practicing our texting with each other. I'm trying to catch her up with the times, you know?" She shrugs prettily, looking younger than her years. Now that her face is tilted up toward me, I can see her cheeks beneath the hat. She has applied too much rouge.

I sit on the long lounge chair next to her, kicking off my flip-flops and crossing my legs into a pretzel in front of myself.

"So, I guess you haven't spoken to Aaron?" I ask, cutting to the chase.

Her face falls as she looks at me.

"He might have broken up with me last night."

"Broken up." She repeats it, as if trying to determine that meaning of the phrase.

I can only nod.

"Oh, honey, that can't be." She straightens like she's about to stand, to run off to go fix this misunderstanding. Her floral cover-up rises along with her, giving me a glimpse of the dark bathing suit she has on underneath. But then her posture slackens again as she settles back into her seat and asks, "Something with Wesley?"

"We kissed." I wince as I add, "And then some."

She swallows but otherwise shows no immediate reaction. I might have preferred for her to flinch or slap me. I'm ready to be punished.

"And?" she asks, cautious, controlled.

"And it gave me closure. Clarity. It erased any doubt about whether my feelings for Wesley should stand in the way of my future with Aaron. There are no feelings for Wesley. Not like that. Not anymore. It took me too long to figure it out, but now I finally understand."

"But Aaron saw?" I can tell she's working to sound neutral.

"No, I told him." I wrinkle my whole face, scrunching it up as I lean backward, bracing for the tirade I deserve.

"Mm-hmm," she says.

Just then, I notice Suzette walking toward us with a tray.

"Merry, merry, bo berry!" she sings as she approaches, her long red sundress trailing behind her.

"Hi, Suzette." I smile up at the willowy woman and feel tears spring to my eyes when our eyes meet.

"Oh, honey, what?" She puts the melamine tray down on a small, circular table and steps closer.

"She and Aaron." Gladys waves her hand dismissively. "Some trouble. He'll get over it." She's surprisingly flip as she reaches for the pitcher beside her and pours me a glass of the reddish plum tea she loves.

Suzette looks from Gladys to me, the dark ponytail at the base of her neck moving from side to side.

"Mama always knows." Suzette shrugs. "You hang on in the meantime." She nods in encouragement and then starts making her way back toward the house.

"That's not why I'm here, though." I turn back toward Gladys and sip the tea. Too sweet for me.

"Oh?" Gladys asks as a slight breeze picks up. She moves her cell phone, placing it like a paperweight on top of the *Wall Street Journal* that is rustling beside her on the lounger.

"I know about the cancer." I let that sit for a beat, before adding, "You have to tell Aaron."

She's silent, and I imagine that she is trying to determine how to respond to me. She hates any sort of confrontation. Like her son, she prefers to remain a people-pleaser.

"Your mother told you?"

"Last night." I nod, noticing that I'm sweating again, despite the breeze. "After I told her about . . . everything."

"Sweetie," she starts slowly, fiddling with one of the tassels on the end of her cover-up, "I appreciate your coming out here, especially when I know you have my son's interests at heart, but I disagree with your position. Wholeheartedly." She lifts the glass of iced tea Suzette left for her, sips thoughtfully, and then places the glass back on the end table before returning to a supine position, as if to say the discussion is closed.

"Gladys."

She doesn't move.

"Gladys."

She turns her head toward me without raising it off the cushion, and I can see her eyebrows rise beneath the glasses. "I understand not wanting to put a damper on the wedding or whatever, but that might all be moot now anyway. What was your plan, just delay chemo all these months until after the wedding? Your condition could get so much worse in that time."

I shudder at the sudden realization that I could have been held responsible for yet another groom's mother dying as some consequence of my wedding plans.

"I'm still deciding whether it's worth having chemo-therapy." She says it without looking at me, her eyes closed as she rests her head against the back of the chaise.

"Wait, what? Why?" I shoot out of my seat.

"The cancer is pretty advanced. The odds aren't good, honey." She opens her eyes briefly before closing them again, and I wonder how she can be so calm. I stand there above her chaise, gaping at her. "As soon as Aaron finds out," she continues, her voice lazy, as if she is contemplating sleep, "he will drive himself crazy, run himself ragged doing everything he can to save me. And when he realizes that he cannot dictate the outcome here, he will feel like a failure. The longer I wait to tell him, the more blame he can put on me, the less on him-self."

"No, Gladys. That's wrong. I had a parent who had cancer. I know what it's like." My voice is rising, but I can't keep my emotions in check as I continue. "You can't shut him out. How would you feel if the tables were turned, if he kept something like this from you?"

She opens her eyes, blinks hard at that question, and brings a manicured hand slowly to her chest.

We stare silently at each other for a moment.

"Okay, Meredith," she says gently. "I hear you. But I'm not ready yet. I'm struggling enough with my own concerns. I just don't have it in me to navigate his vigi-lance, too—not now. Can I say I'll think on it? And in the meantime, let's figure out what you're going to do to convince my son to forgive your indiscretion."

She pats the chair beside her, and I sit down again.

Chapter Twenty-Two
June 2017

*O*n the train back to Penn Station, I tap out a text to Wesley.

> Me: Will you be home tonight? Would like to discuss some stuff.

Hardly an eloquent message, but equal parts direct and vague, just what I was going for. I wait for his response, but after a few seconds pass with nothing, not even the little dots on the screen to indicate he is typing, I open the Internet browser on my phone and start searching public-interest law jobs in New York. Just before we enter the tunnel to Penn Station, where I always lose reception, I get a new text.

> Wesley: Just got to the restaurant. Don't anticipate staying too long. Meet at Rome for dessert.

A second text immediately follows:

> Wesley: Home. Not Rome. Voice texting sucks balls.

I text back a thumbs-up emoji to tell him we're on, and then I wonder if I should ask Lana to come, too. It might help to have a buffer, to make sure he understands that any romantic anything is over, but it might also make an already awkward situation that much more un-comfortable. The train enters the tunnel, and the lights go out. I sit in the darkness, my seat jiggling aggressively from side to side as the train races toward Manhattan, and all I can think of is how much I wish Aaron were sitting beside me.

After the remainder of the train trip, plus two subway rides, when I finally emerge from the subway station back into the late-afternoon sunshine on Seventy-seventh and Lexington, I pull out my phone to call Lana. I pace on the street corner while the phone rings, walking halfway up the block and eyeing the enticing floral arrangements that sit outside the gourmet Butterfield Market. She doesn't pick up, so I leave a quick message, apologizing again for bailing on the lunch plans we made for today and then explaining what I want from her.

I retrace my steps toward the corner, look up at the awning of Lenox Hill Hospital, swallow hard, and walk inside. I make it all of three or four feet when I see the guard stationed at a podium just inside the door. I com-pletely forgot about needing clearance to get upstairs, and I have no viable excuse as to why I am here.

The elderly guard is deep in a heated discussion with a young couple at the moment. They're holding a large bouquet of balloons and arguing over what time visiting hours begin. I take advantage of the guard's distraction and walk right past him with purpose, as though I abso-lutely belong in the building. Maybe he recognizes me from the many times I've walked upstairs with Aaron and figures I belong, or maybe he simply doesn't notice me.

There is an open elevator door straight in front of

me, and I just keep walking until I'm in the elevator. I turn around and gaze into space, avoiding eye contact with the two women in scrubs who stepped onto the elevator behind me. They are too busy complaining about politicians posting on Twitter to be interested in me. Once the elevators doors slide closed, I let out a sigh of relief and press the button for the sixth floor, where I know I will find Aaron at this time of day.

I quickly readjust my clothing, straightening the vertical row of buttons on my sleeveless blouse, tugging on my shorts to make them sit lower and hopefully cover another inch of each thigh. I didn't realize I would be coming to the hospital when I got dressed this morning, and I might have chosen something more conservative if I'd known I'd be bringing my pleas to Aaron's workplace. I rub my hands up and down my arms, trying to stave off goose bumps from the hospital's aggressive air-conditioning.

When the doors open, I hear Aaron's voice before I see him. "Going down?" he asks, as he approaches the doors from the side.

"Up," one of the women in scrubs answers before Aaron's eyes shift and he catches sight of me.

I step off the elevator and he backs away from me across the linoleum tiles, as if I'm carrying something contagious.

"Hi," I say tentatively, hoping he'll be happy that I had the sudden idea to come see him in person.

"What are you doing here?" he asks, his voice more surprised than bitter.

"I thought we could talk."

He pushes back the sleeve of his lab coat and glances

at his watch. "Yeah, uh, okay. C'mon." He turns back toward the double doors that lead to the NICU and starts walking.

I follow silently behind him, the antiseptic scent of hospital cleaners filling my nose. His lab coat is stretched taut across his broad shoulders, the tail lifting slightly behind him as he walks, and I think he looks more like an actor pretending to be a doctor than the actual article. He nods at a couple of orderlies who pass by as we make our way down the bright hallway toward the lounge that I know awaits at the end.

Once we're alone in the small break room, he pushes the door shut and turns to face me. Another member of the hospital staff could walk in here at any moment to grab a cup of coffee or read the paper, but I suppose it's still more private than the hallway.

He motions with his hand that I should sit at the single round table in the room. I pull out a chair, and he walks to the other side of the room. He leans back against the credenza that sits against the windows, his blue scrubs wrinkling as he folds his arms across his chest.

"Won't you sit so we can talk?" My voice sounds plaintive.

"I'd rather keep some distance between us. I can't think rationally if I'm close enough to touch you." He says it almost lovingly, and I begin to hope that all is not lost.

"Maybe that's a good thing? Maybe it means you should give me a second chance?"

He's quiet for a couple of seconds. Only the sound of the coffeemaker humming behind me fills the room, so I stand up and start walking toward him.

"Don't," he says, stopping me in my tracks, making me flinch.

I retreat and flop back into the metal chair.

"If that's why you're here, to ask for a second chance, the answer is no." His tone is firm but somehow not unkind; the lack of vitriol makes its bite that much worse. "We're way beyond that," he continues. "You got a second chance after you went down to Wesley's restaurant and invited him to move into my apartment without discussing it with me. Or maybe your second chance came after you went out for drinks with him months ago without telling me about it, when you canceled a date with me that night and said you were working."

My mouth opens to argue that I did tell him the next day, but he's picking up steam.

"What I know now is that I can't take any more. I can't lie in bed at night, wondering if you'd rather be across the hall. All this time, I was hoping you would prove me wrong. But I can't keep asking myself if I'm only the consolation prize because your first choice is dying."

"No, Aaron!" I stand again as I interrupt, realizing I'm yelling, but not caring. "I had a lot of screwed-up emotions invested in that relationship, unresolved feelings that were all the more intense because they were tied up with my mom's sickness and my parents' almost divorce. Everything was more intense because of the high velocity emotions during that time of my life. And then it all ended so abruptly. My parents' relationship was fixed. Wesley was gone. My engagement was over. Two people were dead. It was confusing to have him come back, okay? I won't lie. I thought I still had feelings for him. But I thought wrong. I was so caught up in nostalgic memories that I forgot all the ways I found him selfish, the ways I had to change my life to fit into his. Being around him these past months, I guess I was on a quest to be forgiven, to know that he didn't really believe that his parents died because of me. Everything else, it was just my own baggage that I had to work out. But I've resolved it all now, and I see what I want, and I know where to find it. The only place I have to look is right in front of me. At you."

Aaron's lips twist at that, hostility taking hold of his features.

"Then why were you searching for answers at the bottom of Wesley's throat? Fishing for truth with your tongue?" He has rediscovered his anger, but I don't let it sway me. I don't back down.

"Look, I came here to tell you that I love you, that I'm not giving up on us. I don't care what I have to do to prove it to you, but I won't give up." My voice cracks, and a quick sob escapes from my throat against my will.

His features relax at that, and he steps toward me. My heart rate picks up, and I wait for him to tell me I'm forgiven. He places his hands on my shoulders and leans down so that his forehead is resting against mine.

"Mer," he says quietly, longingly, and his breath grazes my cheeks, "I can't imagine that I will ever stop loving you. But the more time I have to think"—his lip begins to curl, like he's disgusted—"I just keep picturing his hands all over you, the two of you tangled together, and I can't. I can't be with you. Instead of proving that you've moved on from Wesley, that your feelings for me are as legit as you say, this time with him in the apartment has only shown me the opposite, that I can't trust you." He steps back and lets out a weighty breath. "You've screwed us both, I guess."

He walks toward the coffee carafe that's resting half full on the machine and reaches for a cup. The white Styrofoam nearly disappears inside his large hand. His back is tense as he pours the coffee.

"I really have to get back to work," he says, now all business. "If you could text me a time tomorrow when the apartment will be empty, I'll come by for some things. I'm assuming you'll take care of canceling all the wedding stuff. I know you have experience with that."

He clips past me toward the door without meeting my eyes, and then I am alone.

WHEN I REACH Twenty-first Street a short while later, still swiping at tears with the heel of my hand, I find Lana leaning against the brick exterior of our apartment building.

She straightens when she sees me and tosses her phone into her white leather satchel. "Hey," she says, "I was just on my way up to you, but the doorman said you weren't back yet." She fiddles with the latch on her bag, trying to fasten it, before she finally looks up and notices the tear-stained nature of my face.

"Meredith, what the fuck?"

"Come," I say, taking her by the arm. I glance behind me, wondering whether Wesley is still on his way home or already upstairs, waiting to have the meeting I requested. I nod at the new night doorman as we enter the bright lobby, and instead of walking toward the elevators,

I pull Lana into the little alcove before the mail room. I need somewhere private to fill her in properly, and this little anteroom will have to do.

"I told Aaron that I made out with Wesley," I spout without preamble, rushing to get all the salient details out. "Aaron dumped me and is moving out until Wesley goes into a facility, at which point I will be homeless, too. Oh, and I'm also unemployed."

Lana does a little shake of her head, like she's trying to get water out of her ear. "I'm sorry—what, what, what?"

I then tell her a slightly less abrupt version of the events, adding a few details here and there, my words bursting forth like shrapnel as I try to get her to understand the catastrophic state of my affairs.

"And the reason I called you," I race onward, "is so you can be my wing-woman while I tell Wesley that there is absolutely nothing, nothing, nothing romantic between us, even though Aaron and I aren't a thing anymore."

"Huh." Lana stares at me, her blue eyes narrowing slightly. I can see her processing everything, and I feel a surge of love for her because I know she's trying to figure out the best way to help me. I get a little hopeful, wondering if maybe there's something I haven't thought of, some way to fix this.

"Okay, yeah," she says finally, cocking her head toward the elevators. "Let's go dump Wesley."

"No, it's not like that." I feel a surge of protectiveness for him. "He didn't do anything wrong. Not recently. I still care about him, a lot, just not that way."

"No, I know." She reaches out and gives my upper arm a light squeeze. I stiffen at the touch, too raw to accept any affection. Her hand drops as she continues, "But maybe if we can get him out of the apartment, it might help in your quest to get Aaron back."

"There is no quest. Aaron was über clear; he's not coming back." I cover my mouth with my hand to stifle a sob before it escapes.

We're silent for a moment, the scent of Lana's flowery hair-care products enveloping us both.

"Although maybe it would tell him something," I start thinking aloud. "That even without Aaron, I don't need to be near Wesley. But no, he'd probably just add that to the list of what I've done wrong, actions that make me a bitch. You know, kicking out a dying man just to serve my own ends."

"Okay, yeah, I get it. C'mon, hon." She links her slender arm through mine, and I surrender to her authority, feeling suddenly as though her allegiance is all that's keeping me on my feet, the only fragment of my life allowing me to remain physically upright. "Let's get this over with."

As we round the corner from the alcove back to the main lobby, I see Wesley by the elevators, his shining wheelchair pointed not toward the two elevators but toward the mail room. I don't know how much of our conversation he heard, but the expression on his face tells me it was enough.

I brace myself for whatever hateful words he is about to spew, wondering if there is any way I can possibly make things worse than I have already. When he finally opens his mouth, his tone is kinder than I expected, his words a startling balm.

"We'll fix this," he says. "C'mon, I've got prosecco

cupcakes for you guys." He tilts his chin downward, and I notice the white bakery-type box on his lap.

We're silent as we step onto the elevator, Lana in front while I push Wesley's chair.

"How much did you hear?" I ask.

"I was already thinking about moving into a facility," he answers matter-of-factly, like he's telling me about a business meeting and not his end-of-life palliative care. "I've had a couple of little things in the past couple of weeks, so . . ."

"Things?" I'm trying to get a handle on what he's saying, to get a handle on anything at all.

"Things. That's not the point. The point is that I started looking into aides, home health care workers, you know? But it doesn't feel like the right solution."

The door opens on the eighth floor, and Wesley keeps talking. "There's a place I found, in Massachusetts. It's a one-of-a-kind care facility dedicated to patients with ALS. Everyone gets their own apartment in this one building, and the staff helps the patients maintain normal lives for as long as possible. They have engineers dedicated to making communication devices that suit each individual's different needs. Things like that."

"Communication devices?" Lana interrupts as she walks next to me, the two of us trailing Wesley.

"Yeah, for when we lose our ability to speak." He sounds so calm as he glances back over his shoulder at Lana, like he's teaching her about ALS the same way he used to teach her about trigonometry when she was in high school.

"I saw that place," I say as I step in front of him and use my key to let us into the apartment. "When I was looking around online. It looked amazing but very small. They have room to just take anyone?" I hold the door open as Lana and Wesley file into the apartment.

"Well, it's expensive," Wesley says, as he swivels back toward me. "I don't think that many people can afford it. And I guess that with their particular clientele, they probably have a lot of turnover." He shrugs sheepishly.

"That's not funny." I swipe the box of cupcakes from his lap and huff my way to the couch.

Lana charges onward as though Wesley has been a part of this conversation from the beginning. "So, how are we going to convince Aaron to get over your lapse in judgment?" she asks as she plops down next to me and peers into the cupcake box that I'm opening. Her phone buzzes, and she reaches into her clutch. "Ooh. Spencer." She's pursing her lips at her phone, like she's trying to formulate a response, or maybe just thinking about kissing.

"Seriously?" I demand, suddenly annoyed at her. "You're cheating on Reese for real? We're like Sodom and Gomorrah over here."

"No, I'm not 'cheating on Reese'"—she mimics my tone back to me—"but I do think I may be finished with him. He's never around, and I'm not sure he'd miss me if I moved on. I think I've been so focused on fixing our crappy relationship over the years that I've never paid much attention to whether Reese was even capable of making me happy. We have almost nothing in common at this point, and I'm kind of over him." She looks from me to Wesley and shrugs, as though this is not a topic that has consumed her for the past several years, as though her new epiphany is no big deal.

"Doesn't it take you back though? I used to come to

you two all the time for advice about Reese back in high school." She makes a heaving sound, like she's clearing her throat of a nasty taste. "I don't even think he was making me happy back then, so it definitely makes sense that I should be ending it. I just have to find a time to talk to him. He keeps being too *busy* every time I tell him we need to talk." She pauses for a second, fiddling with the zipper on her clutch. "I'm still talking about myself, aren't I?" Her cheeks turn a bit pink, and she looks as pretty as ever as she reaches for her phone again and starts typing a response to Spencer.

She's trying to make herself invisible now so that I can say whatever needs saying to Wesley. I wish she could do all the talking, that I didn't have to be the one to turn him away.

I turn my eyes reluctantly back to Wesley, knowing I can't procrastinate any longer, but he angles his chair so that he's facing me head-on and starts the conversation for me.

"So, how are we going to convince Aaron that I'm a loser, like Lana said, and that he's your first choice?"

"You're not a loser." I roll my eyes, exasperated.

"What, I can't make jokes now?" He's speaking differently than I'm used to, a little more slowly. The change is subtle, but it seems like it's becoming an effort to form his words.

"Look, Aaron's mom has cancer, and she doesn't want him to know, and I can't tell him, and I can't not tell him. I just feel like in a blink, everything has started going to shit. Shit, shit, shit!"

"Cancer?" Wesley and Lana ask at the same time.

"Lymphoma," I answer. "And she won't let me tell

him. I told her she can't keep it from him, but she doesn't want him feeling guilty when she dies, so she thinks if she keeps it from him, he can blame her instead."

"That's rough," Wesley says.

"Yeah," I answer.

"Well, do you know where she's getting treatment?" Lana asks.

"She hasn't even decided yet whether she wants to get chemo. She said she would think about telling Aaron, but what if she doesn't tell him?"

"It's not your place, especially now," Lana says. "You can't tell."

"I agree." Wesley nods, and I notice that even little movements now look kind of floppy. I wonder if he has suddenly gotten noticeably worse or if I've been so caught up in my own drama that I haven't noticed him deteriorating right in front of my eyes.

"Well, if she asked you not to tell," Lana says, pushing her phone back into her purse, "you can't tell. The best you can do is try to take care of Gladys yourself. Convince her to get the chemo, or radiation, or whatever she needs, and then go with her when she does."

"You know, Lana"—I tilt my head toward her—"for someone who tries to act all shallow and bitchy, you're really pretty insightful."

"I know. You say that all the time."

"I'm going to rest," Wesley says, his words less sharp than they were even a few minutes ago, his energy apparently further depleted from our conversation. I wonder how long it will be before he completely loses the ability to speak. A year? A month? I really still have such a limited understanding of ALS that I have no idea what's coming next for him. He starts wheeling himself toward his room.

"Wait, Wes!" I don't know why I sound panicked—maybe because of dwindling time. He looks in my direction but doesn't turn the chair. "I think it's a good idea," I say, standing. "The facility. It sounds like the best way for you to maintain your quality of life for the longest time. But lonely, no?"

"I'm used to lonely." He says it without rancor, without snark, and shrugs lightly. "Now I just want easy."

My heart aches for what he's losing, for opportunities he's never even had. But I realize, with relief, that it is absolutely not aching for what *we* once had. I know without a doubt that I am over him, that my heart is fixed on Aaron. I push his chair down the hallway and help him into his room. He shoos me away and says he can take care of the rest on his own.

Suddenly, I find myself thinking about Moe and what he said about his sister, that she wouldn't want him to give up his future for her. It occurs to me now that Wesley also wouldn't want me to give up my own future for him, that there are different ways to care about people. I'm only sorry that I wasn't as astute as Moe, that it took me so long to figure out my best path forward. I wonder what else I could have learned from Moe if I'd had the opportunity to spend more time with him. I pull my phone from my pocket and make sure that his hearing date still appears on my calendar. It does, and I add a reminder to the entry so that I will get a notification as the day approaches. Even if I can't be there as his representative, I can still show up and cheer him on from the back of the courtroom.

⟲

AFTER WESLEY GOES to bed and Lana heads out to meet Spencer, I hop on my computer and start googling lymphoma treatment facilities in New York. Lana is right —if I can't tell Aaron about Gladys, at least I can do everything in my power to help her. I click on the link for NYU's Langone hospital and start reading about all its cancer specialists.

After another hour online, I've narrowed down the best options to either NYU or Sloan Kettering. As much as I hate the idea of ever setting foot back inside Sloan, the hospital where my mother was treated, if it's what's best for Gladys, I'm going to have to cross the Rubicon and head back into that glass-covered, memory-filled high-rise. I print out several pages from the computer and turn off the arched desk lamp, resolving to call Gladys in the morning so that I can magically persuade her to start treatment.

Inside the bedroom that was Aaron's, then ours, then mine, but is really still his, I strip off my clothes and leave them in a jumbled mess on the floor. I open the dresser and pull out one of Aaron's old Dartmouth T-shirts. It's gray heather, with a growing tear beneath the neckline. He has staunchly refused my entreaties to convert the shirt into a rag, and as I slip the soft cotton over my head, its fibers barely registering against my skin, I understand his attachment to this heavenly, worn fabric. I lift the front part of the shirt up to my nose, hoping it will smell like him, but all I detect is fresh laundry detergent.

I pick up my phone to text him, thinking to show him

that I'm not easily giving up. But then I remember the Rules and second-guess myself. Rules girls do not beg, not even after they've fucked up. My best course of action is to let him miss me.

As I climb into bed and plug the phone into the charger on the sleek bedside table, it vibrates with a text, and my heart flips when I see Aaron's name. But I'm brought down just as quickly when I read his words.

Aaron: I'm coming by at 11 tomorrow morning for clothes etc. Please don't be home.

For reasons I can't delineate, this text stuns me more than anything he has said so far. He means it. He truly intends for us to be over. As though a curtain has been lifted from my eyes, I suddenly see my new reality with startling, scalding clarity. The weight of understanding is instantly more than I can bear, a pressure on my chest like nothing I've felt before.

This is the second engagement that I have failed at. And this was the one I was meant to keep. I start tallying up the actions that I'll have to complete. I will need to call the venue tomorrow and tell them we're canceling, see if we can get any of our deposit back. I picture the catering woman, Mary, answering my call amidst a calla lily haze in her office, her small, dark eyes judging me, seeing through me even over the phone. And my poor parents . . . As the enormity of what I've done and what I've lost settles over me, the tears start flowing again. I finally type a hasty response to Aaron, surrendering.

Me: OK.

I'm surprised when I get a reply in just a few seconds.

> Aaron: I know this sucks. For me too. But it's how it has to be, and the sooner we both accept that, the easier it will be. Good night.

It's like he can see me in the bed, lying here in his ratty T-shirt, weeping for all that I've lost, for the pain that I know Aaron is feeling, as well.

Well, I won't let him lose his mom, too, at least not without a fight. For once, I am going to do something properly.

Chapter Twenty-Three
June 2017

I'm finishing a second cup of my weak homemade coffee and waiting for the clock to strike 9:00 a.m. so I can call Gladys. She's always been a painfully early riser, up with the sun, as she says, but I'm worried she needs more sleep these days and I'm afraid to disturb her by calling too early.

I hear movement in the hallway and look away from the computer printouts that I've been carrying around to see Wesley rolling toward me in his chair. The sound of his wheelchair against the wood floor makes me think of packing tape being ripped from cardboard, a repetitive tone of reluctance. As I watch him, I notice that like last night, he still looks fatigued, ill. I can't put my finger on exactly what has changed recently, except that I can see extra effort in everything he does.

"Hey. Can I make you some toast?" I ask, glancing at my own piece of multigrain bread untouched on the porcelain saucer beside me.

"No, thanks." He seems at a loss for a moment, his eyes scanning the closed wooden cabinets before they slide back in my direction, a look of defeat about him. We're both silent for a beat, and I don't know what is coming next, but then his cheeks lift a little and he says,

"If you wanted to microwave one of those single-serve oatmeal containers for me, I wouldn't argue."

I hop off the stool and open the cabinet above the stove where we keep all the cereals. It would have been nice, I realize now, if we had thought to move those boxes to a lower spot, even the countertop, where Wesley could reach them without having to push out of his chair. I nudge the kitchen faucet, warming water to add to the container.

"Are you going to the restaurant today?"

"No."

He doesn't elaborate, so I turn to look at him. He's staring out the window at the back of the kitchen.

"What is it? What's happened?" I ask.

"Just all of it," he answers, a blanket of resignation enveloping his voice. "I feel it taking over my body. I'm getting cramps in my back almost every night now, and I can barely even swallow my pills. I'm going to have to start opening them and putting them in applesauce soon. It's just . . ." He sighs. "This is really happening." He looks at me for a moment longer, and I stare back, wondering what's next, wondering when his motorized chair is coming, wondering if there is anything I can do to ease his burdens, wondering if I can ask without upsetting him.

"Anyway," he says, making a clear effort to sound brighter, "remember my cousin Lulu?"

"Of course, I remember Lulu," I say, thinking back to Wesley's first apartment after college, the one-bedroom in Midtown that he shared with her during her first year of medical school. Lulu's doting parents agreed to pay her rent each month, since she was still a student, and they didn't retract the offer when she brought Wesley into the arrangement. He installed one of those temporary walls that we used to see in all our friends' apartments, creating a makeshift second bedroom and securing free housing for himself. Lulu was so wrapped up in med-student life that she was basically never there. Even so, there's no way I would have forgotten her. I fill the oatmeal container up to the designated line inside the container and shut off the water.

"Well, she's in town from Nepal. She's just here for a few hours on a layover to Miami. She's coming to get me in an hour, and I guess we'll go out for coffee or something."

"Aaron is coming by at eleven to get some of his things. He asked me not to be here. I think he said the same of you, but he probably doesn't care as much."

"It's fine. I'll stay gone until noon."

I put the oatmeal in the microwave and press a few buttons. I then take five steps away from the machine, a habit I developed as a kid when my mother convinced me that standing too close to a working microwave could cause sudden death. I almost want to laugh now, thinking of all the ways people try to protect themselves from harm, and then these cruel diseases strike at random, paying no heed to the merits of the person they attack.

"Yeah, I have to go to my office. I'm theoretically working for the next two weeks, even though they won't let me see any privileged material anymore, which means I see nothing and do nothing." The microwave beeps, and I set Wesley's oatmeal down on the small table in the corner, along with a spoon. "I'm just going to show my face for a minute. I guess I'll clear out a few things from my office."

Wesley pulls his chair into the open spot at the table

and picks up the spoon. He looks at me expectantly, like he wonders if I'm going to say more, and it dawns on me that he might not want me to watch him eat.

"In the meantime," I add, "excuse me for a sec while I go call Gladys." I grab my papers and head to the bedroom. I push the door closed behind me as the phone at Aaron's parents' house rings. I don't want Wesley to hear if I start crying.

"Hello?" I hear Gladys's loud voice shouting into the phone, the way she always answers a call, like she is surprised the phone has rung at all.

"Hi, Gladys. I didn't wake you, did I?"

"Meredith? No, of course not." I can hear her snort on the other end, her morning lark's pride apparently offended.

"Listen, we need to talk," I start, lowering myself onto the corner of the bed, feeling small.

"I know why you're calling, sweetie, and let me save you the trouble." Her tone is not unkind.

"You do?"

"Yes, you really got to me yesterday, with your big puppy-dog eyes and your pleas on Aaron's behalf. So, fine, I fold."

"You're going to tell him?" I ask, relief flooding my limbs.

"No, of course not." Gladys is curt. "But I'm going to do the chemo."

"Oh." Well, that's definitely better than nothing. I know that Aaron would want her to do everything to try to beat this, even if the odds are against her.

"Well, good," I say. "Good." I repeat, processing. "Where? When?"

"Easy, Fido." She laughs her big laugh, and I wonder how she can possibly be in such good spirits. "I still don't want you telling Aaron. We're clear, yes?"

"I won't tell him. But I won't stop telling *you* to tell him." I stand again and walk toward the windows, looking down into Gramercy Park, eight flights below. There are a couple of women pushing strollers along the path, a man walking a poodle.

"Whatever. That, I can put up with."

"When is the treatment? Can I come sit with you?"

"Oh, honey, that's sweet. Mitch and I would be delighted for the company, I'm sure. It's at NYU."

I feel a little guilty at the weight of my relief, not because Gladys is getting chemo, but because I don't have to return to Sloan and relive all those memories of my mom being on what I thought was her deathbed, my dad leaving us, etc. etc.

"I expect to start next week," she adds.

A second wave of relief washes over me as I process what she has said. She is going to get treatment, to take care of herself the way Aaron would want her to.

"Send me the time when you know it and I'll meet you guys there, okay?"

My relationship with Aaron may truly be over, but that won't stop me from doing right by his mom, from being there for her when she won't let her son be by her side. I'm doing it for Aaron but also for Gladys—another woman who I thought was going to be my mother-in-law.

I walk out of my room feeling a little lighter. Even if Gladys's odds of survival are not generous, at least she isn't giving up. It reminds me that I shouldn't give up, either.

Wesley is no longer in the kitchen but has moved over to the TV, where he's watching the news, footage of a small brick building on fire, firemen with hoses.

"You're just going to watch TV all morning until Lulu gets here?"

"Yeah, you inspired me with that Jon Favreau movie the other day. I just found another chef movie, with Bradley Cooper."

"You've never seen *Burnt*?" I ask in disbelief. I actually walked out of the theater when I went to see it a few years ago with my law school friend Nikki. The smoldering, complicated chef character reminded me too much of Wesley. "Well, no time like the present." I try to sound upbeat, sorry to see him stuck in front of the TV on a sunny summer day. But at least he will get out for a bit when his cousin arrives. When Aaron will be at the apartment. My stomach sinks at the thought. I wonder if I should leave Aaron a note on the bed or something, but I can't think what I could write that might do anything other than irritate him.

I grab my messenger bag and head for the door, forcing myself out before I concoct a reason to be here when Aaron arrives.

"Off I go to my office, where I'll be busy not working," I call lightly over my shoulder to Wesley.

"Okay. I'll be just as busy not cooking," he calls back with a smile. "See ya," he adds, as he turns back toward the screen, and I feel like he and I have reached a new place. More than a détente. An actual friendship. A shame it will be a finite experience for us both.

○

WORK IS AS slow as I expected. Everyone seems to know that I quit in the midst of a tantrum, and I've become something of a pariah. Partners look at me with hasty disapproval as I pass them in the hallway and younger associates, whom I might formerly have called peers or colleagues, are shunning me, as though they're afraid they might catch whatever social conscience has recently infected me. Either that or they're worried they might tarnish their images by consorting with me. The good news is that, with the exception of Ian and Darren, who I know approve of my decision, there's not a single person from this office whom I will miss following my departure.

I settle in at my desk and use the idle time to search for new jobs online. After looking at websites for the ADL, the EPA, the PLI, the ABA, and even the FBI, I feel completely overwhelmed. I don't have a career dream, some professional goal I've always fantasized about achieving, and I hate myself for that lack of passion. Aaron and Lana and even my brother, the tax attorney–math geek, have all known what they wanted to do with their lives since they were kids. All I wanted back then was to be a unicorn. At this point, there is only one stagnant motivational kernel that I can latch on to—one that I've always felt, but which, sadly, is useless in its current, amorphous state. My goal is simply to spend my days helping people in one way or another. Or to work as a backup dancer in pop music videos. Since I've always been somewhat clumsy and the dancing thing isn't going to pan out, I try to make a more directed plan for how I will find my next job.

I open my desk drawer and pull out one of many blank notepads, the empty sheets of paper emphasizing how little I have achieved in my time at this office. I will do better in my next position, find something where I am more than another cog in the wheel, somewhere I can perhaps become essential.

As I arrange highlighters next to the notepaper, readying to make a chart, some basic method of organizing my thoughts and options, Nicola breezes into the office and snorts when she sees me. "Doing art projects until your two weeks expire?" she snarks.

"Wow, Heather," I respond, referencing the '80s movie in which Winona Rider is the bitchiest of all high school bitches, "nice to see you, too."

"Nicola," she says, confused.

Of course she wouldn't get it.

"Never mind. I'm sure you'll enjoy having your own office once I'm gone."

"I would have, but they're putting a first-year in here after you go," she whines at me as she slumps into her chair, as though she expects me to comfort her.

"Well, look," I start, my instinct to console kicking in in spite of myself, "it can't be any worse than being with me, right?"

"Ha." She looks at my almost fondly, her round cheeks turning slightly pink. "So true. Always carrying on about your pro bono case like that's the only one you ever cared about." She switches into a high-pitched voice that I presume is meant as an imitation of me, "Asylum, asylum, asylum. All I want to work on is asylum."

I have a split second of anger, offense at her taunting, before I have an epiphany. Oh my God. She's a genius! All I want to work on *is* asylum. I want to work on asylum cases all the time.

I tune Nicola out as I turn back to my computer and start searching anew. She makes a few more comments, but when I don't respond, she leaves the office again. I imagine she is returning to a meeting somewhere else in the building, but who knows. I find website after website dedicated to organizations that help refugees seek asylum in the United States. I don't think I should be emailing these places from my computer at Harrison, Whittaker, so I just start printing out information on the different opportunities while my heart races with excitement about the possibilities. More than an hour passes, and I amass a pile of twelve different agencies and organizations that I'm going to pursue.

Liam pops in, his eyeglasses perched crookedly on top of his head, and asks if I want to grab lunch.

"Nah," I tell him. "I'm working on a new project. Check it out," I say, holding up the top sheet from my pile of printouts.

He reads the page for a moment before regarding me with a proud grimace. While I wait for him to respond, I notice that he's looking a little thinner, that the Atkins seems to be making a difference after all.

"Now, this," he says, looking up with avuncular pride on his alabaster face, "*this* makes sense for you. I could see you being really happy at a place like this. Not that we won't miss you here—the sane ones of us, at least."

I smile at him as he leaves and then glance at my desk clock. It's 12:30 p.m. By now, Aaron has probably been to the apartment, gathered what he needed, and left. I want to call him and tell him about my new career goals, the refugee centers I've found—the Refugee and Immigrant Fund's Asylum Support Group, the In-

ternational Rescue Committee, the Center for Human
Rights at Weill Cornell—names that I had seen and
glossed over when I was working on Moe's case because
they weren't completely germane to what I needed at
that moment, but now they seem to be everything.

I may be the ultimate failure in the romance department, but at least I am beginning to feel like there's hope
for getting one aspect of my life back in order.

I hear my phone vibrating and take it out from my
leather tote. My mom. Again. I press IGNORE and toss the
phone back into my bag. I know that once we speak,
we'll have to start calling all the wedding vendors to cancel everything. At least this time around I insisted on
paying all the deposits with my own money, so I haven't
screwed my parents in that regard. Even so, I'm just not
ready yet to begin the excruciating process of dismantling my second romantic future.

Chapter Twenty-Four
June 2017

*T*he room where Gladys is receiving her chemo-
therapy treatment is at the end of a long hallway
swathed in fluorescent light. It's midday, and I know she's
been here with Mitch since early this morning, completing paperwork and some additional testing.

I knock lightly and then push the door open cautiously.

"Hey, sweetie." Gladys's face lights up. She's not lying
in a hospital bed, as I expected, but is sitting in a large
recliner chair, an IV attached to her arm. Her suede
purse is still in her lap, like she might get up and leave at
any minute. Mitch is on the patient exam table beside
her, resting his back against the wall and balancing an
iPad on his lap. Gladys's red hair is in a cute little ponytail at the top of her head that makes her look younger
than she is, and her makeup is as meticulously applied as
ever. I wonder whether this is all a facade, meant to hide
the effects of her symptoms, or if she actually feels as
good as she looks.

"Come, sit." She motions at one of the two chairs
against the wall opposite her seat as Mitch hoists himself

off the exam table. He gives me a quick kiss on the cheek, and I catch the scent of Liquitex paste, the glue he uses for his architectural models. I imagine him at home, worrying about Gladys and tinkering with his mini-replicas of the Freedom Tower or the Ryugyong Hotel into the wee hours of the morning.

"I'm going to grab bagels," he says, looking at me. "An everything with lox and low-fat veggie cream cheese, right?"

His questions hits me like a full-fingered slap. To think we would have been family, that this tall, soft-spoken man who remembers how I take my bagel would have been a second father to me.

"Yup. Thanks." I look away quickly, glancing down at my silver sandals as I force myself to think of Gladys today, not myself. I don't think I'll be able to eat while watching poison pump into her veins, but I obviously can't say as much.

When Mitch leaves, I lower myself into the black plastic chair across from Gladys. "So, how's it been going so far?"

"Fine, now." She scratches a little at her chest, her manicured nails creating red lines across her freckles and age spots.

"Why? What happened?"

"Oh, it was nothing." She blinks twice in rapid succession, and I can tell there is something she's not saying.

"More bad news?" I hold my breath, wondering how her news could get any worse, what that would look like.

"No, really, it was just an allergic reaction to the first bag of medicine. They switched it out, though, and I'm fine now. Mitch noticed I was getting red welts on my face. All I felt was some heat, itching on the chest. It's fine," she repeats.

The way she keeps looking toward her lap says that really, it's not fine, that it was frightening, but she doesn't want to discuss it anymore.

"So, um, I quit my job?" It comes out as a question, and I realize I'm anxious to know her opinion, worried she'll be disappointed in me, that I'm not on the same kind of ascending trajectory as her superstar son.

"I heard." She smiles as though she's proud. She doesn't ask why I haven't mentioned it sooner. "Aaron was really happy for you."

"He told you?"

"Last night." She shifts in her seat, like she didn't mean to bring him into the conversation.

"I think we're really finished, Aaron and I," I say.

She's quiet for a moment as she fiddles with the fringe on her navy purse. "It's hard for him," she says gently. "His world may simply be too cut-and-dried to allow for the shades of gray that you explored. I asked him what exactly he thought was going to happen when you moved your ex into the room across the hall. Of course the situation spun out of his control. There are worse things in life than kisses, than a little ambiguity, but he didn't want to hear it." She sighs. "You've betrayed his trust." She's not argumentative, just remarking.

What *did* he think was going to happen? I suddenly wonder. What possessed Aaron to insist on inviting Wesley into our apartment after I retracted the suggestion? As I pull and stretch the question that Gladys has asked, turning it this way and that, trying to consider what Aaron might have imagined, I suddenly realize that it was a test; the whole crazy living arrangement was engineered by Aaron, and it was a test—a test that I failed. He was already skeptical about my feelings for Wesley back in May, back when he encouraged me to visit Wesley at the restaurant, when he then co-opted my idea about living together. He was giving me an opportunity to prove my commitment to our future, and what I verified instead were my lingering feelings for Wesley. I should have realized that Aaron, a man who always needs to be in control, a man who thinks through his every move, was not relinquishing control of anything by luring Wesley into the apartment. No, he was creating a deliberately constructed experiment, and by jumping into Wesley's lap, I proved his hypothesis. Heartbreak is simply a by-product of the results he obtained. I want to be angry that he set me up, but I'm the one who failed the test.

"I guess I'm going to have to live with this outcome for the rest of my life," I finally answer, as I tilt my head back toward the ceiling and try to prevent too much emotion from slipping forth.

"Oh, honey," she says, and I realize how pathetic I must seem, stalking my ex-fiancé's sick mother and complaining about my failed relationship.

"You'll find someone," she tells me, and I think if she'd been sitting closer to me, she might as well have bumped my chin up with an encouraging nudge of her fist.

The fact that she believes Aaron really isn't coming back causes actual physical pain in a part of my body that I can't pinpoint. I thought I had started moving on to acceptance of my failure, but the disappointment I feel at her words tells me I was still secretly harboring hope. I

attempt to let the truth sink in, to bask in the epic pro-
portions of my errors, as Gladys continues talking.

"It's obvious that young men like you plenty. You'll
have men banging down your door in no time—you'll see.
You're what the teenagers call a 'dick magnet.'"

"Gladys!" I laugh at her uncharacteristic profanity.

"What?" Her cheeks pink up as she shrugs, only a
little sheepish. "My friend Myrna taught me that. Her
daughters, you know." She waves her hand in the air
dismissively. "So, tell me about the job hunt."

I force myself to switch gears, to push my sorrow
into a different mental corridor, like kicking dirty clothing under the bed to deal with at a later time. I start
telling Gladys about the refugee organizations that I've
been contacting, and she asks a flurry of excited questions.

Before I know it, Mitch is back in the room with our
bagels. I hold mine on my lap, wrapped in its white,
waxy paper, as I continue explaining the missions of the
different organizations to Gladys and now Mitch, too.
The smell of fresh lox and toasted bread reaches my nose
and my appetite is back, despite my emotions.

Half a bagel later, the nurse returns, telling Gladys
that she is finished with her treatment for the day and
can head home shortly. As the perky blond woman removes the tubes and needles, I see Gladys's shoulders sag
with relief, and I think about how difficult this day must
have been for her. I wish she would tell Aaron about her
condition already and at least take that one weight off
her shoulders.

"Can I come back?" I ask Gladys. "When you have
your next treatment?"

"Of course, dear." She starts loading various items

into her oversize purse: a small notebook, a paperback book with a plantation home on the cover. "Only"—her eyes catch mine and then quickly shift away—"just check in with me. At some point, I will eventually break the news to my son, and I'm sure it'll be more comfortable for everyone if you two aren't both here at the same time."

I know she doesn't mean harm, but my knees nearly buckle at her words.

"Right." I force myself to sound chipper, airy. "That makes sense. Okay, stay in touch." I give her a quick kiss on the cheek and head out of the room before she can see the tears that are about to spill from my eyes.

A FEW DAYS later, as I walk into to the apartment from a job interview, feeling cautiously optimistic about this one thing, I hear voices coming from Wesley's room. A woman. I can't imagine he has found some new paramour and brought her home, but still, I decide it's best not to bother them. Instead, I make my way toward the chocolate chip cookie dough ice cream that I know is waiting in the freezer. I open a messy drawer to look for the ice cream scooper, the one with the cow-shaped handle that Aaron bought randomly at the mall near my parents' house last year. I run the scoop under some scalding water in hopes of warming it sufficiently to soften the ice cream and ease its removal from the container. I'm about to turn the water off when I hear Wesley and his guest making their way from the bedroom toward the main room of the apartment.

I look up to see a heavyset Asian woman wearing scrubs with little pictures of Homer Simpson all over them. She's carrying a large cardboard box that's wider than she is and tall enough to hide the top half of her body and the bottom of her face.

"He'll be really grateful to have these," she says as she ambles toward the door, Wesley following in his wheelchair.

"Hi," I say, and they both look in my direction, apparently surprised I'm here.

"Hey," Wesley rasps. He clears his throat, a quiet rumble, and continues, "This is Peggy. She's helping me get ready for the move."

"Hi, Peggy." I smile politely, trying not to let it show that I am forlorn about Wesley's impending departure. I hate that he is journeying to a new home in order to more peacefully end his days. I keep thinking of salmon swimming upstream as they prepare to die. That's when I notice Wesley's wheelchair.

"Your new chair came!" I exclaim.

"Yeah, finally," he says. "They delivered it this morning right after you left. Lots of bells and whistles." He makes a nearly imperceptible movement with his hand, and the motorized chair spins in a proud circle.

"No popping wheelies in the house." I laugh and then turn back toward Peggy. "Are you from Bernard Mildred?" I ask, referencing the facility where Wesley is moving.

"Synergy Home Care," she answers with a thick Brooklyn accent, her tone friendly.

I'm not certain, but I believe Synergy is a local home health care agency.

"I called them for help getting ready to move," Wesley adds.

I shoot him a look as if to say he should have asked

me for the help, not hired out the task, but I figure I will wait until Peggy leaves to lay into him.

"He's all packed up now," she tells me, lifting her small leather purse off the doorknob of the coat closet, "except for what he'll need for the next week and a half."

"Week and a half?" I balk. "What do you mean? That's not when you're leaving."

"Yeah, the apartment at Bernard Mildred is ready for me, and I'm feeling like an interloper. I just want to let you get on with your life. You and Aaron both." He shrugs, as if it's no big deal that he's moved his timeline up by two weeks. I'm suddenly short of breath, thinking that I have only a few more days with him and then he'll be gone. I imagine going to visit him, but I have no income at present, and then I will presumably be stuck at a brand-new job for a while, and who knows how quickly he will deteriorate? Lately, I feel as if he's weaker every day.

I have a vision of sitting by his bedside as he dies, and suddenly tears cloud my line of sight for the second time today. I turn toward the ice cream container and start scooping with all my might, channeling my frustration and dismay into my movements instead of my words. Amazingly, the ice cream comes right out, and I realize I never got myself a bowl. I rest the scoop back in the container and turn toward the cabinet as Wesley and Peggy say their good-byes.

"Thanks again," he tells her, and I notice again how different his voice sounds. I wonder what's going on inside his body to cause that change, whether it's a respiratory condition or some deterioration of his vocal chords. For all my Internet research, I'm hardly an expert on the workings of ALS.

"Nice meeting you," she calls in my direction as she walks out the door.

"You too," I squeak back, failing to keep my own voice even.

As the door closes, Wesley turns toward me. "Please don't get all weepy," he says, and there's an edge to his tone.

"What? I'm not." I say, wiping away the wetness beneath my eyes with my forearm and picking up the ice cream scooper in one fluid movement.

"Good," he says, "because I need to make choices that work for me."

"Of course you do," I answer, not sure why it suddenly feels like we're arguing. My mind flashes to that moment four and a half years ago, when his parents died, when he totally shut me out, and I wonder if that is what he is doing again, pushing me away because it's easier than confronting his grief. Well, this time I am not going to engage.

"I guess I should start figuring out where I'm going to go, too." I try to keep my tone casual, mellow, like I didn't notice this uptick in his aggression. If Wesley is moving out, it's time for me to find my own place as well, so I might as well get busy on that. I have a stab of regret that I gave up my old apartment uptown. "I'm going to call around to some brokers. I'll catch you later." I take my bowl of ice cream and head straight to my bedroom. I'm not going to let Wesley attack me to make himself feel better.

I pass an hour alone in the bedroom, alternating between calling brokers and staring at the ceiling. After I hang up with the sixth broker, I lie back on the bed, absorbing the warm sunlight streaming through the window and listening to the quiet of the apartment. I wonder what Wesley is doing, alone in another room, and I begin to regret my behavior. Even though I'm devastated to be losing him, he is the one being forced to confront his own death, and I would do well to remember that I'm supposed to be supporting him. If he needs to vent a little, I should let him. I can try to have thicker skin.

I roll off the bed, grabbing the list of brokers and apartment buildings I've created. I amble into the hallway and see that Wesley's door is open. I figure I will try to apologize for skipping out on our conversation earlier, but when I poke my head in, I pause. Wesley has his wheelchair next to the bed and he's trying to hoist himself out of the chair, onto the mattress. I know he's been doing this on his own for weeks, but this time he looks like he is really struggling, like he might not be able to make it. This chair is much larger than the other one and moving out of it seems more difficult.

"Can I help?" I ask, stepping into the room.

Wesley turns, still half raised from his seat, clearly surprised to see me. "Nah, I've got it," he says lightly.

"It doesn't look like you've got it. Come, just let me—"

"I've got it!" he snaps through gritted teeth. With what looks like Herculean effort, he pushes himself out of the chair and allows himself to collapse onto the bed.

"Jeez. Fine." I can't push down my annoyance, even though I'm trying. "I guess you had it."

I walk back to my room, but now I get it, why he's moving sooner than he originally planned. It has very little to do with availability and much more to do with his continued deterioration. I feel contrite that I don't know how to respond to him better. I hope the people in his new home will give him the kind of support he needs. I wonder who will give me the support that I need.

Chapter Twenty-Five
July 2017

I'm waiting on what may be the slowest line I've ever witnessed at a Starbucks. There are only two people ahead of me, but I've already been standing here for fifteen minutes. I glance at my watch again, stressed that I'm going to be late to see Gladys at her second chemo appointment. I called her earlier this morning, offering to bring coffee with me when I arrived. Now I can't leave without a caramel frap for Mitch and a simple tea for Gladys. I watch the rawboned teenager working behind the counter, and I'm amazed that it's even possible for someone to move so sluggishly. Coupled with the day's indecisive and chatty clientele, this shopping experience is enough to make me contemplate quitting caffeine.

Finally, *finally*, the woman in front of me decides what she wants to order, and it's about to be my turn. I step closer to the counter, and I notice that the petite barista has a purple ring looped through her nose. As I open my mouth to rattle off my order, the girl turns to her coworker and starts complaining about how some appliance behind her was malfunctioning earlier.

The two of them walk over to the machine, some sort of coffee-brewing apparatus, and start pushing various buttons. After brief but apparently ineffective fiddling, the male barista pulls out his phone, declaring that he can find an online version of the instruction manual. I wait a few more moments, checking my own phone, and look up to find the two baristas giggling over whatever they have discovered on the guy's phone. After another minute of being completely ignored, I finally find the nerve to speak up. "Miss, I'm sorry, but I'm in a big hurry. Could I place my order?"

The barista's head whips toward me at warp speed. Suddenly, she has found the ability to move quite quickly, and for a petite little thing, the glint in her eye has turned surprisingly ferocious. She begins to chide me with her teeth clenched tightly together, uttering each word slowly, as though she is on the verge of erupting, "I am in the middle of something."

It's the way my mom used to yell at me when I was maybe five or six years old and simply driving her crazy. Like if she opened her mouth any wider, she would be unable to contain the savagery of her roars.

"You and your Hermès bag don't run the world," the girl continues, stepping closer to me, "and I will help you, only"—she pauses to look me up and down with a sneer—"when I am ready. Bitch."

Her reaction to me is so shocking that I am still trying to catch my breath when a voice speaks up from behind me. "Excuse me!"

I turn to see my former office mate, Nicola, standing in line a couple of people behind me. Great. Two against one. I brace for whatever criticism Nicola is about to throw at me, seeing that this day is clearly just not going my way.

To my surprise, she lays into the barista instead. "That is no way to speak to a customer. Not only is it entirely unprofessional, but it was also completely uncalled for, given the circumstances of the current situation. This line has been moving at a snail's pace—a pace, which I may add, that has not been warranted by the behavior of the patrons in line nor by the complexities of their orders. Which would lead one to conclude that fault lies with you, the barista in charge of the orders, who is slowing the pace of this line and the productivity of everyone waiting herein. Moreover, this particular customer was only alerting you to the fact that she was in a hurry. She did nothing to condemn or insult you, and your reaction was thoroughly unjustified. I think that you owe her a free coffee this morning, wouldn't you all agree?" She turns back toward the gaping customers on the line, a few of whom begin clapping. I know my chin must be on the floor, so surprised am I that Nicola would ever defend me in any way.

The barista doesn't know what has hit her. Her eyes dart to her bleary-eyed coworker and then back to Nicola. "Um, uh, yeah," she stammers, "you're right. Uncalled for. I can do a free coffee." She never even looks in my direction, her focus solely on containing Nicola's wrath. She scribbles something on a cup and then seems ready to serve the customer behind me.

"Wait." I try to use an authoritative tone like Nicola's, and I rattle off the two other drinks I had been waiting to order.

Apparently satisfied that I've been treated properly, Nicola turns from the counter back to me. She's changed something about her hair since I saw her last. The blond color is less white than I'm used to, more golden. The softer look suits her.

"I don't think I even want a coffee now," she tells me

with a sigh. "I've been trying to cut down my caffeine, and maybe this was the tipping point."

"Thanks for having my back there," I offer.

"Well, if there's anything I can't stand for, it's lack of professionalism, right?"

True that, I think. "Still, I appreciated it."

"Well, once you go into public-interest law, you won't even be able to afford things like Starbucks, so I thought I should help make one of your last upscale coffee experiences worth what it costs, at least."

I can't decide whether she's being obnoxious or actually trying to joke with me. Her eyes sweep over me, and she turns back to the barista. "And by the way," she calls toward the girl, "that bag is not Hermès. It doesn't even look like Hermès." She glances back at me like that was the clincher. "Gotta go. Some of us still have a job." She shrugs and heads out, taking a gust of air with her.

I shake my head quickly to clear it from that unexpected experience, reminding myself that people are complicated. Realizing I'm still running late, I grab the cardboard tray full of frothy drinks and hurry out the door to the hospital.

When I finally arrive, the nurse is just finishing attaching Gladys's IV bag to the metal stand beside her recliner chair.

"I'm so sorry I'm late," I announce as I feel myself burst into the brightly lit room with too much force.

"Nonsense." Gladys looks up with a smile as Mitch walks over and takes the Starbucks tray from my hands before kissing me on the cheek. Gladys is wearing a gray zip-up hoodie, and I think this is the first time I've ever seen her in such casual attire.

"It's great you're here," Mitch tells me, reaching for his Frappucino. "They found a structural issue with one of our projects, and I really should head in to the office at some point today. It's a relief knowing Gladys won't be alone."

"Go now," Gladys tells him. "That way, you can be back before she has to leave."

"I can stay the whole time," I tell them. "My schedule's kind of wide open these days."

"Well, if my darling wife could see fit to tell our son about her condition, we wouldn't even be in this predicament. There'd be a whole other person to lean on." He looks at her pointedly, as though they've clearly had more than one discussion about the issue.

"When I can't hide it anymore, I will tell him. Not before." She looks toward me and adds, with forced nonchalance, "Always beating dead horses, this husband of mine."

"Go," I tell Mitch. "We've got this." I smile at Gladys as Mitch nods and begins collecting his things—a newspaper, his briefcase.

After he leaves, I settle in to update Gladys on my job search and the great interview I had yesterday at the Tri-State International Advocacy Group. As I'm talking, I notice that she keeps rubbing her chest, a slight grimace on her lips. "You okay?" I ask.

"Fine, dear. Tell me, what would the hours be like there for you?"

"Strictly nine to five," I answer with a proud nod, acknowledging how different the work schedule would be from the potentially infinite hours that I was required to be available to Harrison, Whittaker & Shine.

As usual, the bitter black coffee that I ordered from Starbucks has gone right through me, and I excuse myself to hurry to the restroom down the hall. I'm drying my hands with a brown paper towel that feels like cardboard, hoping that it at least came from recycled material if it is going to feel this unpleasant, when I hear a commotion in the hallway outside. I step out of the bathroom cautiously, not wanting to obstruct any emergency medical care, and two women in scrubs hurry past me. I hang back in case anyone else will be following, but then I notice that the women are running to Gladys's room. I imagine they've gotten the wrong room—I was only in the restroom for a minute or two, and she was perfectly fine before I left. But then I see an orderly running from the other end of the hallway with a gurney, also heading this way. I hustle back to Gladys's room and see one woman racing to add a medication to Gladys's IV line and another nurse frantically adjusting the recliner that Gladys is in, like she's trying to open it up so Gladys can lie flat. As the dark-haired woman moves to the side, I catch a glimpse of Gladys's face and see that she's unconscious.

"Oh my God!" I shout. "What's happening?"

The dark-haired woman barely glances at me as the man with the gurney pushes past me.

"Let's lift her," she tells the orderly while the other woman in the room starts putting an oxygen mask on Gladys.

"What's wrong with her?" I shout again.

"Ma'am, you need to give us space to work," the orderly tells me, as he shoves me a little to the side.

"Oh my God, is she going to be okay?" I realize that tears are streaming down my face.

Nobody answers as they transfer Gladys to the gurney and reattach the oxygen mask. I stand there, frozen. Finally, one of the women—I don't even know if they're doctors or nurses—turns toward me. "An allergic reaction to the meds. She's in anaphylaxis. We have to get her to a resuscitation room. Someone will get you as soon as she's stable."

With that, they push past me and hurry down the hallway with Gladys between them, the metal wheels of the gurney squeaking out their own alarm. One of the hospital workers shouts something about possible cardiac arrest, and my blood runs cold.

Before I know what I'm doing, I have my cell phone in my hand and I'm calling Aaron. The phone rings three times, and I'm frantic that he's not going to answer.

"Oh, thank God it's you," he says.

"Aaron!" I shout his name.

"Listen, it's Wesley," he says.

"What?" I ask, confused.

"He fell. I'm with him at the hospital. His leg looks to be broken in multiple places, possibly his pelvis, too. They're prepping him for surgery."

"Aaron, listen to me." I feel myself taking charge. "I'm at NYU, at the hospital. Your mom is having a severe allergic reaction. You need to come here, now."

"What? What are you talking about?"

It feels like neither of us can make sense of the other's words.

"I don't know. The doctors have her. She was unconscious, Aaron."

"Oh my God," he says again. "Okay, I'm on my way. But Wesley . . ." He hesitates.

"It's fine." I can't get my words out fast enough. "Just get here. And call your dad from the cab while you're on your way, okay? I'll take care of Wesley."

"Right, okay," he answers, his voice clipped, his tone equal parts worry and confusion.

We hang up, and I start making other calls.

FINALLY, I SEE Aaron exit the elevator and beeline toward the nurses' station. He's in jeans and a T-shirt and looks more like a frat boy than a neurosurgeon at the moment. I get up from my chair in the waiting area and dash over to him. In my frantic state, I really don't know whether it's been fifteen minutes or two hours since I hung up with him. I call his name as I approach, and he looks away from the nurse he was talking to, surprise registering on his face.

"Mer? But what about Wesley?" His voice sounds thick to me, muddled by agitation and alarm. "Why aren't you on your way?"

I want to move closer, to embrace him like I would have a month ago, but everything is different now. I keep my feet planted where they are, my hands to myself. "Don't worry. I took care of it." Before I can explain further, the nurse interrupts us to answer whatever Aaron said before I reached them.

"The doctors are still in with her. Someone will come update you as soon as they can."

"Aaron!" someone shouts.

We turn in unison to see Mitch stepping out of the elevator bank, heading toward us.

"What the hell happened?" He looks at the nurse, who has just risen from behind her station. "How does someone make a mistake like that?" he demands.

"Dad, calm down," Aaron tries. "There was no way for them to know she'd have an allergy to the medication.

What was she even here for in the first place?" He looks from his dad to me and then back to his dad again.

Mitch freezes and then lets out a large sigh, all his venom suddenly replaced by a posture of defeat.

"It was chemo," he answers flatly. "And it *was* a mistake, because it was her second round. We discovered the allergy last time we were here, before this place caused her any major trauma." He shoots a pointed look at the nurse, and the lawyer in me is already thinking about liability and the lawsuit that is waiting to happen—negligent mistakes that were made.

"Chemo?" Aaron repeats.

"Mom has lymphoma," Mitch says gently.

"She . . . lymphoma? Since when? What are you even talking about?" Aaron's neck is getting red, the way it does when he's angry, and I wish I could do something to ease this blow. I move a little closer to him, surrendering to my instincts, and slip my hand through his. He allows it, but I'm not sure he even realizes I've done it.

"She didn't want to tell you," his father explains. "She had her reasons. We argued with her, but it was her decision."

"Who's we? You told Cole and not me?" he spits back.

"No, Meredith and I."

"You knew?" His eyes dart to mine, accusation written across his features.

"Only since we broke up."

He yanks his hand from my grasp and backs away a step. He looks from me to his father and back again.

"Why are you even here?" he demands, his eyes harsh.

I open my mouth to answer and then close it again.

"Meredith has been amazing." Mitch steps in for me

and puts a warm hand on my shoulder. "Whatever your story is as a couple, you should be appreciative of the care and compassion she has shown your mother." He looks back at the nurse, who has been following the whole conversation. "Now, when are we going to get an update?" he asks.

The nurse taps a few times on the screen of a tablet computer and then lifts a manila folder from her desk. "I'll go check," she says, her voice neutral, accommodating, and she turns to walk down the hall.

The three of us watch her go until she turns a corner and disappears from view. Then Aaron turns back toward me, and when I see the emotion settling into his features, I recognize the precise sense of uselessness that Gladys was trying to prevent when she made the decision to keep her cancer a secret. He glances from the waiting room to the nurses' desk and then down the hallway.

"I guess we should go sit?" I ask cautiously, seeing the tension in the way both Aaron and his father are regarding their surroundings.

Mitch puts an arm around Aaron's broad shoulders, as if he's trying to corral him. I wish for a second that Mitch were taller than Aaron instead of two inches shorter—that for once, Aaron could feel contained and protected by someone else.

"Yes, c'mon," Mitch says, as he leads us back toward the orange plastic chairs.

I sit first, and Mitch takes the seat opposite me. Aaron sits down beside him. There is an older couple sitting together at the end of our row and only a smattering of other adults biding their time in the mostly empty waiting area. We're silent for a minute, and then Aaron looks at me.

"You don't need to stay," he says, but not unkindly.

"Stop it," I command, with more assurance than I feel. "I'm staying."

Mitch puts a hand on Aaron's knee, and I can see his fingers squeezing a little. "Well," Mitch says, "we appreciate having you here. And I know Gladys does, too."

After a few more minutes of staring silently at the walls, at our fingers, our shoes, the blond nurse reappears and Aaron shoots to his feet.

"She's stable," the pretty young woman starts, and I see Aaron's entire posture change, relief rising off him like steam. "The doctors are still with her, but you'll be able to go in and see her soon."

The nurse is unable to tell us more than that, so we wait longer. Finally, Mitch and Aaron are given permission to see Gladys. I stay in the waiting room, knowing I don't belong with them during this ameliorative moment meant for family. My thoughts begin to spiral about how I was almost a part of that family, about all that I've lost, but I shove at them, pushing them away so I don't start weeping in the waiting room.

While I wait, I make a few calls to check on Wesley. He is still in surgery. No news yet. I lay my head back against the wall behind me and wonder how I ended up in the middle of this shit storm of catastrophes.

The next thing I know, I'm being awoken by repetitive nudging of my shoulder. I open my eyes to see Aaron standing over me. My eyes are sticky, like I've been asleep for at least an hour, maybe longer. I don't know how I fell asleep when I was so amped from the panic I felt for Gladys earlier, and for Aaron.

Aaron has a look on his face that I can't decipher.

"Is she okay?" I ask through my groggy disorientation, the panic coming back.

He nods, his dark eyes opaque. "For now. They're going to keep her overnight, but . . ." He looks toward the windows and I notice that the lighting has changed outside, that it appears to be late afternoon, nearly evening. "I think you should go see how Wesley is doing."

"No, I—"

"It's okay." He holds up a hand to stop my protests. "I mean, everything here." He motions in the general direction of the room where his mom is. There's a softness that I haven't heard in his voice since before we fell apart. "But just come see my mom before you go."

I follow him down the hallway, past the rooms of many other patients. I catch glimpses of tubes and machines of every stripe, everyone with their own personal mountain to climb. When we cross the entry to Gladys's room, she puts her arms out wide to hug me. "Meredith." she beckons.

I collapse into her embrace and instantaneously erupt into ugly sobs. Seeing her alive, hearing her voice, I realize how frightened I was that we would lose her, that I had somehow failed her.

"I'm okay now." She strokes my hair for a moment, and I begin to collect myself. My tears have already left a wet mark on the shoulder of her hospital gown.

"I'm sorry." I try to laugh through my tears.

"It's fine. I'm fine. I'm *going to be* fine. Just ask your friend here." She jerks her head in Aaron's direction.

Aaron is leaning against the air vent by the window, watching us. He shrugs. "Positive thinking is important," he says, and I'm not sure whether he's addressing Gladys or me. "There are so many studies."

We visit for a few minutes longer, the conversation restrained and stilted as my eyes repeatedly stray toward Aaron. Finally, I begin to excuse myself, thinking I should give them their space after the day they've had.

"I'll walk you out," Aaron says, straightening off the back wall.

I'm surprised when the elevator arrives that he doesn't say good-bye but follows me into the box. I push the button for the ground floor and then we stand, silent and stiff, as nurses and hospital patrons enter and exit on the various floors.

As we emerge into the lobby, I can tell Aaron wants to say something. I stop walking beside the door to the gift shop and turn toward him. "What is it?" I blurt, unable to tolerate the charged silence any longer.

He sighs, like he's not sure he wants to divulge whatever is on his mind. I stand and wait while Aaron looks from me to the bustling hallway beside us and then back to me again.

"Why did you stay?" he finally asks. "Why didn't you go to Wesley?"

I chew on my lip and decide I don't have the energy to play it cool. I'm just going to lay it all out there. "I care about your mom, genuinely. And, you know, you." I offer a matter-of-fact shrug, fully cognizant that I have little left to lose by being frank. "You may be finished with me, but my heart is still yours, and I would do anything to protect you. Which includes protecting the people you love." I'm almost defiant as I admit my feelings, my so-sue-me attitude functioning as a shield.

He nods thoughtfully while I regard him. His hands are stuffed in his pockets, and he studies the floor as though he expects to locate a response to my statements somewhere within the linoleum tiles. I find myself feeling hopeful that something I've said may resonate with him, may produce a change of heart about our relationship. Maybe my loyalty has become apparent to him through my actions today and he might be willing to give me another chance. I take a step closer to him, but when he looks up, his eyes are rigid, impermeable.

"Well, I appreciate it." There's a finality to his voice. "Please let Wesley know I'm thinking of him." He offers me a curt nod before he turns back toward the elevator, toward his family, away from me. I watch him go, sure that he is going to turn around, that he is going to come back, but the elevator doors open and he steps in without glancing in my direction. And then he is gone.

I hold it together until I reach the street, but as soon as I'm outside, I let the tears flow down my face, obscuring my vision while I search for a taxi. I don't know why I let myself get my hopes up, why I thought that Aaron was softening his stance toward me. I curse myself for the umpteenth time, so angry that I let romanticized memories derail my future with Aaron. I picture what he must be doing now at his mother's bedside, holding her hand and telling corny jokes to make her laugh while Mitch looks on from across the room with mild amusement. I should be there, holding Aaron's hand, busting his chops for the bad jokes, lightening the mood. Instead, I'm trudging up First Avenue in the humid evening heat while strangers glance at my tear-stained face and then look away.

I finally snag a cab that's coming down First Avenue, going south, and tell the driver I want to go to Mount Sinai. He points out that I am heading in the wrong direction. As if I didn't already know.

Chapter Twenty-Six
July 2017

I'm sitting in a hospital room for the fifth day in a
row, poking around on my laptop while Wesley naps.
The doctors put a plate in his leg when they reattached
all the pieces of his body that broke apart, that shattered
and splintered when he fell. No one really has a sense yet
how long it will take him to heal, though obviously *healing* is a relative term. If he were a more typical patient,
not already condemned to die, they would be trying to
plan physical therapy, pushing him to start moving and
rotating, but ALS complicates the recovery plan, just like
it complicates everything else in its path.

I'm not entirely privy to the arrangements he has
been making, nor the prognoses he's received from the
three different doctors currently overseeing his care.
Wesley has made clear that he prefers privacy when the
doctors provide updates on his condition, so I hang back
and listen only when he wants to share information,
which is not frequently. Beyond that, I'm just trying to
keep him company, offer him some emotional comfort or
a little entertainment until he can get out of here. Once
they are ready to discharge him, he says he wants to go

directly to that ALS care facility in Massachusetts. I understand his decision—the fall seems to have exacerbated many of his symptoms. He will be safer there with more help, more specialized care. Maybe if he had gone sooner, he never would have been in a position to lift himself out of a motorized chair on his own, never would have fallen and hurt himself so badly in the first place. His cousin Lulu told him yesterday that she is relocating from Nepal to be with him near the Bernard Mildred Center. She long ago ended her relationship with the man she followed to Nepal, and with her impressive résumé, she should have an easy time finding employment elsewhere. It's a relief to know he will have family near him, that he won't be utterly alone up there. From the way his facial muscles seem to relax every time Lulu's name comes up, I get the sense he feels the same way.

I hear a light knock on the door, and I'm surprised to see Nicola, as in, my former office mate, in the doorway. I glance toward Wesley, who is still asleep, and hold a finger to my lips, hoping she won't wake him. Scurrying out of my chair, I set my laptop down in my place and usher Nicola back into the hallway.

"Hi." I nudge her a little farther down the corridor so we aren't right outside his door, and we end up in a petite alcove next to an ice machine and a supply closet. "What are you doing here?" I try not to sound as shocked as I am. Her blond hair is stark and straight as it falls around her face, and I think it's the first time I've ever seen it loose.

"I came to see how Wesley was doing. Ian told me he was still laid up."

"You . . . Why? You know Wesley? Since when?" I'm

instantly running all these crazy scenarios in my head about the different ways they might have met. Her trip to London last summer, an event at his restaurant? Did they put it together, realize they both knew *me*? I've definitely complained to Wesley about her on more than one occasion in recent months. Did he realize it was the very same Nicola whom he already knew?

"Well, I don't—or I didn't—know him, but I came with Ian."

I cock my head to the side, still trying to make sense of what she's telling me.

"The other day," she says. "Before the surgery."

Well, that's a shocker. Ian definitely did not mention that tidbit to me when he gave me the recap on all that had happened with Wesley at Mount Sinai while I was at NYU with Gladys and Aaron.

"I don't understand. Why?" I'm squinting at her, and I don't even attempt to hide my skepticism.

"Look, you got to me, okay?" She starts fishing around in her leather tote bag and pulls out a ChapStick. "You, with all your pro bono work and your ideals." She waves a hand in the air, dismissing something, the ChapStick suspended between two fingers like a chunky cigarette flopping along for the ride. Then she drops the ChapStick back into the abyss of her bag without having used it and pulls the satchel closer to her body. "I heard Ian at the office, talking about how you called him because Wesley had fallen, how he was alone because you couldn't get here, and, I don't know . . ." She sounds exasperated. "So I came, too. I'm just trying to be a little more"—her eyes dart back and forth while she searches for a word—"good." She shrugs and then adds, "Like you."

We're both silent for a couple of seconds, perhaps equally surprised by what she has said to me.

"Look, I just thought, you know, that visiting Wesley after everything he's gone through was the right thing to do. Something you would do. And clearly . . ." She motions toward me with both hands and doesn't finish her statement. I suppose she's trying to indicate that yes, I am indeed visiting Wesley.

"Oh. Well, great." I guess. "I think he'll be happy for the visitor when he wakes up." What else can I say?

"He probably won't remember me. We were only with him a few minutes, and he was in pretty awful shape. We left as soon as Katie Sue got here. Still." She shrugs again, everything about her falling like a whim.

"Wesley remembers everyone. He'll know who you are." I motion that we should walk back toward his room. If not from seeing her before surgery, he'll know her name from all the times I complained to him about my intolerable office mate. I try not to laugh thinking what a kick he will get out of seeing her transformed into Nicola the Beneficent.

"Do you have a new job lined up yet? Are you leaving law?" she asks, her voice hushed as we pass by other hospital rooms, and she actually sounds curious, not snarky.

"I'm still thinking public interest." I don't mention the interview I had last week at the Tri-State International Advocacy Group or the fact that I still haven't heard from them. "I'm trying to see what's out there."

She nods, but I can tell her focus has shifted already. "Can we see if he's awake? I don't have that long." She pulls a phone from the pocket of her blazer and checks the time.

When we return to the room, Wesley is still sleeping, his head turned toward us on the pillow. I think it's best for a man in his condition to get the rest he needs, so I don't disturb him. I look at Nicola and raise my eyebrows, as if to say there's nothing I can do to facilitate her visit. She raises her eyebrows right back at me, and I don't know whether she is mocking me or trying to indicate that she agrees with me, that we're a team. Then she reaches into her cavernous bag again, and this time she extracts a small gold box that looks to be Godiva chocolate. She leans over and whispers in my ear, "Tell him I left these." She hands me the box, which is so small that it must contain only two chocolates, at best, and sashays out of the room. Her spicy perfume lingers after her departure, and I hope that I will again become desensitized to the thick, sweet aroma, like I did day after day in our office.

I resume my post in the green synthetic recliner and wonder what Nicola's angle is here. I might think she was putting the moves on Wesley, but for the fact that he's a condemned man and she knows it. Maybe she really meant what she said, that she's had some sort of epiphany, is trying to be a better person. Well, I hope so.

Opening my computer back up, I nearly jump when I see an email waiting from the Tri-State International Advocacy Group, subject heading: *Your Application.* I glance again at Wesley, nervous to open the message on my own, wanting reinforcements, but he hasn't moved since I've been back in the room. After a few more seconds staring at the screen, I berate myself for my inaction and click the link. Holding my breath, I read:

Dear Ms. Altman,

Thank you for meeting with us last Wednesday. We are delighted to offer you a position as an associate at The Tri-State International Advocacy Group with a starting date of August 7, 2017. Jeanine Hall, head of Human Resources, will contact you to take care of logistics. We look forward to having you onboard.

Best,

Joe Reiser, Chief Legal Counsel

The Tri-State International Advocacy Group

I let out a triumphant yelp as I read the email and then clamp my hand over my mouth, hoping I haven't disturbed Wesley's slumber. I release a breath when I see that his eyes are still closed, and then I read the email two more times, amazed that something positive is actually unfolding for me.

"What happened?"

I look back up to see Wesley staring at me.

"Shit. I woke you."

"Maybe," he rasps with a halfhearted smirk. Recently, everything he does seems only halfhearted. "It's hard to sleep with all the sunlight coming out of that ridiculous grin on your face. What's on that computer?" He swallows hard, twice, and I can tell he wants to say more, that he's adjusting something inside himself. He gets himself back in gear and adds, "You finally start perusing Internet porn?"

"Shut up." If he weren't in such a fragile state, I would have thrown a pillow at him. "No, you perv. I got the job!" I squeak a little in my excitement.

"I knew you would. Congrats, babe."

"Oh, you just missed a visitor. Nicola Shore was here to see you." I reach for the windowsill where I left the chocolates and shake the box for him to see.

"Ha. She's probably here for her fee."

"Fee?"

"Yeah." He stops talking, and I know he's seeking the energy to continue, so I wait. "Before the surgery," he finally continues, "I was only with them for a second, but all she could talk about was how I should make a will with Ian."

"You made a will with Ian?" I force my brain away from the pain of that thought, the constant talk of Wesley's imminent death. Instead, I focus on my competitive streak. "I could have made a will for you. For free, you know."

"Nah." He waves a hand in the air dismissively and then lets it flop back to the bed, as if he's forgotten how to control it. "I did that months ago. Totally done." His eyes close again.

He seems to be drifting off to sleep once more, so I stay quiet, but then he opens his eyes again. "Whatever's left after I pay for my care is going to Community Kitchen. For the job training program to continue."

Before I have time to reflect on his largesse, he changes the subject. "Any word from Aaron?"

I shake my head, knowing that if I try to talk, I might start crying again. I've been in touch with Mitch and Gladys. I know that she's doing all right, that Aaron has insisted on taking over her care. I figure she is in good hands and that I should just let them be.

"But at least I will be gainfully employed again." The brightness in my voice sounds false, even to me.

He nods his head without lifting it off the pillow, and I know he sees right through me. "He's smarter than I am," Wesley assures me. "He'll come around faster than I did."

I try to block out Wesley's words, knowing that false hope is the very worst kind.

AFTER THE CONCLUSION of visiting hours and my subsequent eviction from Wesley's room by the hospital staff, I meander to the subway station, heading back toward my apartment. Well, not *my* apartment—Aaron's apartment. With Wesley planning to move directly to Massachusetts after his release from the hospital, it's incumbent upon me to find a new apartment and give Aaron back his living space. Now that I have a position lined up at the TSIAG, I have a sense of what my new salary will be and what kind of (teeny-tiny) apartment I can afford. I am actually contemplating going to New Jersey and, in the ultimate act of sticking my tail between my legs, living with my parents for a while. I'm sure my mom would be thrilled, and maybe it would be the opportunity we need to really repair our relationship, get back to the place we inhabited together before the cancer, before Wesley, and the plane crash, and the canceled wedding, and the next canceled wedding. I'm exhausted just thinking about all the drama we have attempted to weather together.

I emerge from the subway station, climbing the steps into the dusky summer twilight that is bathing Park Avenue South in an ethereal purple glow. The storefronts and office buildings glimmer as if the lighting has been artificially created, like a movie set. As I make my way toward the loft, I consider stopping at the bodega across from our building to pick up Wonder bread and peanut butter for dinner, but when I round the corner onto Twenty-first Street, I see Aaron's large frame halfway down the block. He is leaning against the apartment building, one foot up and flat against the gray stone wall, reading something on his phone, as though he's waiting for something, for someone. I wonder if he is waiting for me, but then I realize he must want something from the apartment. He's probably trying to figure out how to get up there without seeing me. If he doesn't want to see me, I think I should respect his wishes. I owe him at least that. So I quickly turn around and head back in the direction I just came from. I can get ramen for dinner instead, sit and eat my noodle bowl while Aaron does whatever he needs to do. I wonder if I should text him to let him know he can go up, but I flinch thinking about how he will likely bristle at the unsolicited contact.

I hear a thumping noise approaching, and I move over to the right so that the jogger behind me can pass. But when I turn my head, I see that it's Aaron, not a jogger, who is next to me, slowing. I don't understand why he's come after me when I was so careful not to impose my presence on him.

I stop. He stops.

"Why'd you turn around? I've been waiting for you." He squints, apparently confused, but I feel like I have a premium on confusion at the moment.

"Waiting for me?"

"Yeah, for the past two hours." His eyes sweep over me from head to toe, and I'm sorry I didn't choose to wear something more flattering than my ripped cargo shorts to the hospital today. He takes a step closer to me, crowding my space, stealing my air. His hand goes to my hair, pushing a stray strand behind my ear, and I am surprised by the touch, electrified against my will. I can feel his breath on my cheek as he adds, "Where were you?"

I don't want to tell him that I've been with Wesley. I don't want to see the look of disdain reappear on his face. Especially not now, when he's looking at me with eyes that are decidedly kind—affectionate, even. But I'm not lying to this man, not anymore.

"I was with Wesley. At the hospital." I look up at him, waiting to see irritation, resentment, readying myself for him to step back from me.

He nods, and his expression doesn't change. "Good. I'm glad he's not alone. When he fell last week, I realized what it meant that he called me after he couldn't reach you, that he didn't have anyone else to call."

I'm not sure whether he's telling me that he understands why I have been committed to helping Wesley or if he's saying something else.

"He's starting to have people. He has a cousin. She's going with him to Massachusetts. There's a facility there where he's going right after he gets discharged. I'm getting out of the apartment, too—don't worry," I hasten to add. "I just need another couple of days to pack up."

Aaron nods, quiet, contemplative. A breeze rustles around us, enveloping us, as if we're inside our own private vortex in the middle of the city street. Pedestrians continue to make their way around us, as though they don't even see us, as though the breeze has made us invisible.

"Good," he says quietly, running a hand tenderly over my hair, as if to remember it, as if to say good-bye. The pieces that he tucked behind my ear comes loose again in the warm wind. "If that's what you want."

I nod, unsure what else to say, afraid that telling him it's not what I want, that uttering any words at all, will lead me to cry again. I just shake my head lightly, curl my lips in toward each other.

Then his face changes, brightens. "No, not good. That's not what I came here to say at all." He sounds firm, like I shouldn't need so long to vacate the apartment, like he was here waiting to tell me he wants the return of his space forthwith.

"I can probably . . . I can try to get out by the end of the day tomorrow, but nothing is packed yet." I mentally catalog how much I have in the apartment. It's mainly clothing and personal items, not furniture or other large pieces that would take longer to move.

He shakes his head at me, and I brace for the impact of whatever hurtful words might follow. "I almost lost my nerve," he starts. "For a split second, I thought maybe you were saying you were happier without me."

I open my mouth to ask what he means, but he holds up a hand to silence me.

"Just hear me out for a sec?"

It's a request, not a demand, so I nod.

"All the stuff with my mom—hell, I probably already knew it before. But you chose me." He takes my hand in his, and I let him, as though I have no volition in my arm. His warmth envelops my fingers, my palm, my being, and I want to cry out at the relief of his touch, as he continues, "You had no obligation. I don't know why it took me so many days to act on it, but I knew, as soon as I saw you in the hospital waiting room last week, that I was the one you chose. You stayed with my mother to protect me, even when the other guy needed you too."

As I process what Aaron seems to be saying, the background noise around us begins to dull. I notice absently that the sky has suddenly gotten much darker, that dusk has turned to night.

"I don't understand." I look up at him, my eyes involuntarily traveling to his mouth, then the cleft in his chin, before shifting back to his dark eyes.

"Clearly, you had some unresolved feelings that you needed to explore, and that was shitty." He says it lightly, like an afterthought. "But even after I pushed you away, you kept showing up; you were there, protecting me when I needed it the most." It sounds ludicrous that such an enormous person, someone so successful, so strong, could need protecting from anything, but I finally understand what he is trying to say. He knows that he has my heart, and unless I am completely delusional, which is of course possible, I think that he is forgiving me.

"I'll always protect you," I tell him. "I will also make more mistakes. I don't mean kissing other guys, not like that . . ." I start to stumble, wondering if Aaron is just setting himself up for more disaster by standing anywhere near me. "But it's part of who I am, a mistake-maker," I warn him.

"Would you shut up?"

I can't read his tone, and I panic that I misinterpreted his actions, that we are not moving in the direction I thought. He may have come to complain about my behavior, to say that what I perceived as dedication felt to him closer to harping—stalking, even. But then he's reaching toward the back of my neck, cupping my head, and leaning down to kiss me. Before our lips actually meet, I surprise myself by pulling away.

"What are you doing? What is this supposed to be?" I ask, my every sense seemingly muddled in the present moment, as though I can't understand anything in my world anymore. I want to melt into him, but I am suddenly worried that this isn't for real.

"This is supposed to be me accepting the apology you offered weeks ago, and now you accepting the apology that I am offering today."

His hand is still on the back of my neck, and I feel myself relaxing into his hold, into his words and the tenderness I see in his eyes. His head moves toward mine again, cautiously but with determination. He hesitates at the last second, giving me a chance to pull back, but I don't.

And then we're kissing. His hands are in my hair and his body is surrounding me, right there on the street. I feel like I can't get enough of his warmth, his strength, his promise. As he holds me, the preceding days of anguish begin to slip away, melting onto the sidewalk, trickling into the street, evaporating into the air. I feel as though I've been wrapped in a remedy and I'm drinking up my revival.

Then, much too soon for my liking, Aaron pulls away and looks down at me. The familiar crick in my neck shows up as I attempt to meet his eyes from such a close vantage point, and I relish the recollection, even as a fresh memory is being made. He moves his hand from my neck to the side of my face.

"What do you say we go put our wedding back together?" he asks.

"Umm . . ." I hesitate pointedly, making clear there's something I'm reluctant to tell him.

"What?" His eyes have gone all squinty again.

"I never actually took our wedding apart. I donated it." I scrunch up my face, preparing for the force of his reaction.

"You donated it?" He cocks his head. "What does that mean?"

I nearly groan aloud, reluctant to admit what I did, but, seeing no other option, I confess.

"I heard something on the radio a few months ago about a woman who broke her engagement at the last minute, but the reception was nonrefundable, so she invited 150 homeless people to come enjoy the food and dancing, and then she went on her honeymoon with her mom."

"Don't tell me you donated our wedding to homeless people."

"I called Katie Sue about it, and, well, yeah." I shove my hands into the pockets of my tan shorts as I await his response.

"Wow." He doesn't look pissed, more surprised, like he's just making sense of it all. "So, what, are they busing 150 people out to Long Island? Is it the same date? Can we go?" He sounds excited.

"No, I'm having the food delivered to the soup kitchen. And it was only going to be seventy-five guests, so . . ." I look back at him but can't read his face, so I keep talking, nervously filling the silence. "And the band is going. Yes, it's the same date, and I guess we could go, if you wanted." I feel myself holding my breath, bracing for his anger.

"You are a piece of work, you know that?" He steps toward me again and then backs away a couple of steps, like he's working something out.

My heart sinks and I flinch at his words, distressed to have disappointed him again already, but then he surprises me by hooting into the air, a battle cry. "Yes!" he shouts, answering a question that was only in his own mind, his eyes raised to the sky.

I stare blankly at him, waiting to see if that was as positive an outburst as it sounded or if he will deal me another blow. When he looks back at me, his eyes are bright.

"I fucking love you," he says.

"What?" I feel like someone has spliced together two different movie scenes, like his words and actions have nothing to do with mine.

"So fucking much."

"What?" I repeat.

"Only you."

He steps closer and kisses my forehead, his lips warm and dry. "Only you would take your personal misfortune and turn it into joy for other people. Only you would donate a black-tie wedding to a soup kitchen. It's amazing. I'm, I'm . . . what's the word?" He's overcome with a new energy, something I can describe only as glee, and I feel myself starting to smile, too. He searches his head a moment longer, seeking the right word, and then he exclaims, "Gobsmacked! That's how you make me feel. Gobsmacked."

"So, you're not mad?" I chance.

"No." He leans into me again. "I'm . . . What am I? I'm . . ."

"Gobsmacked," I tell him.

Again he seems to be searching his mental lexicon, and his eyes flash as he says with a shrug, "No." He shakes his head. "Not just that. What I am is yours." He puts both his hands on my shoulders, looking me directly in the eyes. "So, will you have me? Am I too late?"

I feel tears spill over, one from each of my eyes, traveling down my cheeks in tandem, as if they've been choreographed. Aaron's grip loosens as he moves to wipe away one of the droplets, but I push his hand away, swatting at him before he makes contact, not wanting to tidy up this messy situation, not wanting to pretend any of this has been easy or that the journey I've taken has been anything other than excruciating. I throw my arms around his neck, standing on tiptoe to reach all the way around, and bury my head against his chest. I can feel additional tears seeping into his cotton T-shirt, but I am so utterly grateful that he has come back to me, that I am standing so close to him, I can do nothing other than cling to this man who I thought I had lost. It's impossible to let go.

After a quick, stunned moment, he wraps one arm back around me and with the other hand he caresses my hair, letting me cry. I feel him lean down and kiss the top of my head, softly, cautiously.

"So, is that a yes, then? Or . . ." He still sounds tentative, unsure.

I squeeze more tightly for a brief second and then step back. "It's a yes. Of course, it's a yes, you dumbass." I wipe my face myself, taking ownership of my pain and my mistakes.

Aaron's lip ticks up and his eyes contract slightly as he stares down at me. We regard each other for a moment, processing all that we've just covered. Then he takes my hand and tugs gently, guiding me back in the direction of the apartment building.

It is a balm to let him slide his large fingers through mine, to hold on to him for support, to feel the warmth of his skin against mine.

"How about tomorrow?" he asks while we walk, his words emerging with a buoyant quality now, bouncing down onto the sidewalk and then back up to me.

"For what?"

"Our wedding. We can go out to my parents' house, just the two of us, and my parents and yours. We'll ask the rabbi to meet us. Any rabbi who's free. We'll bring bagels."

"Tomorrow? Really?" I don't understand this impulsivity, this urge to rush, which is so out of sync with Aaron's meticulous nature. I wonder if it means he is questioning me, thinking that if we don't lock this in, I might do something else to ruin our chances.

"That way, my mom can see us get married for sure," he tells me, his voice suddenly and conspicuously neutral, and I realize that Gladys's prognosis must really be as dire as she described—none of her signature exaggeration, apparently.

"Yeah, okay." I smile at him, shocked by the events of the last ten minutes, amazed at our ability to be spontaneous, thrilled to be able to give Aaron something he wants.

Aaron nods to Gus, the doorman, as we enter the building. I notice Gus's eyes dart downward, taking in our clasped hands, and I'm fairly certain I see a small smile of approval appear on his lips. I have the sudden urge to pump my fist in the air, to run up to the roof and shout out about my new state of ecstasy.

"Let's do it." I nod, squeezing Aaron's hand to show my enthusiasm.

As the doors close behind us in the elevator, he lifts me into a hug, my feet dangling in the air, several inches above the floor, my toes unmoored, all of me unsure how I will land. I have the sensation that I am on a precipice, a cliff, an embankment of new beginnings. I am exactly where I want to be.

Acknowledgments

People often remark that a writer's life is a solitary one, devoid of sufficient human interaction and camaraderie. I have found the opposite to be true. During the time I spent working on this novel, I enjoyed several chances to connect with fantastic people, writers and nonwriters, who helped make the finished product all that it could be. I'm delighted to have the opportunity to recognize several of them here.

First, I'd like to thank everyone at SparkPress, especially Lauren Wise, Brooke Warner, and Crystal Patriarche, for their guidance and enthusiasm in connection with this project. I'd also like to thank Erica Silverman at Trident Media, whose insights made this story stronger than it ever could have been without her. A heartfelt thank you to Caitlin Hamilton Summie, whose wisdom and kindness I will remember well into the future.

There were a number of medical professionals who were gracious enough to lend their expertise as I worked out the details of characters' ailments. Thank you to Dr. Avi Retter, Dr. Avi Deener, Dr. Ayelet Jonisch, and Dr. Ari Jonisch for taking my questions and providing critical information and perspective. Your understanding of both the physical and emotional aspects of the conditions we discussed was invaluable.

To my friends and beta readers who have stepped up time and again to support me in my efforts as a writer— Amy Blumenfeld, Aliya Sahai, Amy Tunick, Joceyln Burton, Susie Schnall, Robyn Pecarsky, Jenna Myers, Ali

Isaacs, Stacey Wechsler, Nancy Mayerfield, Robin Grossman Polikoff, Courtney Sheinmel, and Reyna Marder Gentin—"thank you" doesn't even cut it.

To my family, you guys are my best and loudest cheerleaders, and I am so thankful for each and every one of you. Special shout-outs go to Seymour, Allison, Samantha, Sheila, and Bob for reading an early draft. Thank you to Samantha and Michael for spreading the hype on the West Coast. Thank you to my sister for reading an even earlier draft and providing legal, political, and grammatical insights, and for introducing me to Koronet pizza. Thank you to my father for the countless hours he spent debating the placement of commas and hyphens and also for not giving me a hard time about the sex scenes. Thank you to my mother for believing in me, for talking through my ideas, and for sometimes just listening to me breathe. Thank you also for providing the kernel that was the inspiration for this novel and then allowing me to twist and bend all the details to suit my story's needs. Thank you to Abe, Asher, Shep, and Nava for getting to know the characters along with me and asking all the right questions. Finally, thank you to Jason for sitting with me at a romantic restaurant in Nantucket and helping me figure it all out.

A Note about ALS

Amyotrophic lateral sclerosis, better known as ALS or Lou Gehrig's disease, affects as many as 30,000 people in the United States and 450,000 worldwide each year. According to the ALS Association, approximately fifteen people in the US are newly diagnosed with the disease each day. There is no known cure.

For more information about ALS or to make a donation toward research and innovation, please visit The ALS Association at www.alsa.org or The ALS Foundation for Life at www.alsfoundation.org.

About the Author

Jacqueline Friedland holds a BA from the University of Pennsylvania and a JD from NYU Law School. She practiced as an attorney in New York before returning to school to receive her MFA from Sarah Lawrence College. She lives in New York with her husband, four children, and two overly pampered dogs.

SELECTED TITLES FROM SPARKPRESS

SparkPress is an independent boutique publisher delivering high-quality, entertaining, and engaging content that enhances readers' lives, with a special focus on female-driven work.
www.gosparkpress.com

And Now There's You: A Novel, Susan S. Etkin. $16.95, 978-1-68463-000-4. Though five years have passed since beautiful design consultant Leila Brandt's husband passed away, she's still grieving his loss. When she meets a terribly sexy and talented—if arrogant—architect, however, sparks fly, and neither of them can deny the chemistry between them.

The Cast: A Novel, Amy Blumenfeld. $16.95, 978-1-943006-72-4. Twenty-five years after a group of ninth graders produces a *Saturday Night Live*-style videotape to cheer up their cancer-stricken friend, they reunite to celebrate her good health—but the happy holiday card facades quickly crumble and give way to an unforgettable three days filled with moral dilemmas and life-altering choices.

Trouble the Water: A Novel, Jacqueline Friedland. $16.95, 978-1-943006-54-0. When a young woman travels from a British factory town to South Carolina in the 1840s, she becomes involved with a vigilante abolitionist and the Underground Railroad while trying to navigate the complexities of Charleston high society and falling in love.

The Balance Project: A Novel, Susie Orman Schnall. $16, 978-1-940716-67-1. With the release of her book on work/life balance, Katherine Whitney has become a media darling and hero to working women everywhere. In reality, her life is starting to fall apart, and her assistant Lucy is the one holding it together. When Katherine does something unthinkable to her, Lucy must decide whether to change Katherine's life forever, or continue being her main champion.

About SparkPress

SparkPress is an independent, hybrid imprint focused on merging the best of the traditional publishing model with new and innovative strategies. We deliver high-quality, entertaining, and engaging content that enhances readers' lives. We are proud to bring to market a list of *New York Times* best-selling, award-winning, and debut authors who represent a wide array of genres, as well as our established, industry-wide reputation for creative, results-driven success in working with authors. SparkPress, a BookSparks imprint, is a division of SparkPoint Studio LLC.

Learn more at GoSparkPress.com